# THE SCAR

# THE SCAR

S ERGEY  D YACHENKO

*and*

M ARINA  D YACHENKO

A TOM DOHERTY ASSOCIATES BOOK  NEW YORK

THE SCAR

English translation copyright © 2012 by Marina and Sergey Dyachenko

Originally published as ШРАМ in 1997 by ACT in Moscow

Copyright © 1997 by Marina and Sergey Dyachenko

A Tor Book
Published by Tom Doherty Associates, LLC
175 Fifth Avenue
New York, NY 10010

www.tor-forge.com

Tor® is a registered trademark of Tom Doherty Associates, LLC.

Library of Congress Cataloging-in-Publication Data

Diachenko, Serhii, 1945–
 [Shram. English]
 The scar / Sergey Dyachenko and Marina Dyachenko. — 1st ed.
    p. cm.
 ISBN 978-0-7653-2993-6
 I. Diachenko, Marina.   II. Title.
 PG3949.14.I15S3313 2012
 891.73'5—dc23

                                            2011025177

First Edition: February 2012

# Acknowledgments

We are grateful to all who contributed to our book publication in the United States.

Special thanks to Robert Gottlieb, chairman of Trident Media Group in New York. He discovered us in the midst of an unlimited pool of Russian literature.

Special thanks to Elinor Huntington for her great translation and to Patrick LoBrutto for his smart editing and belief in our book success.

Sincere compliments to Zamir Gotta, Trident Media Group associate, who has been and still is the advocate for this project.

—Marina and Sergey Dyachenko

# THE SCAR

# PROLOGUE

Where did he come from and where is he going? He wanders the world like the constellations wander the sky. He roams along the dust-laden roads and only his shadow dares to follow in his footsteps.

It is said that he possesses great powers, but they are not of this world.

Even the mages avoid him, for he is not subject to them. Whoever stands in his way, either through the whim of fate or through his own folly, curses the day of that encounter.

His intentions are unknown. The roads serve him like dogs.

The mountain heights and the pebbles of the far sea; the hills, ravines, and fields; the forests and foothills; the plains and shores; the lanes and highways: all hide his secrets.

It is said that he will roam and wander eternally. Take care not to meet him, either in a crowded fair or in a hermit's den—for he is everywhere.

And if one day you should hear the footsteps of the Wanderer at your door . . .

# PART ONE

*Egert*

PART ONE

# 1

The walls of the crowded tavern were shaken from the boom of drunken voices. After solemn mutual toasts, after good-natured but pointed jests, after cheerful scuffles, it was now time to dance on the table. They were dancing with a pair of maidservants who, although as sober as their work required, were flushed and giddy from the glitter of epaulets; from all the gleaming buttons, scabbards, and ribbons; from the passionate glances directed at them; and from their efforts to please the gentlemen of the guards. Glasses and jugs tumbled to the floor. Silver forks twisted into fanciful arabesques, crushed by nimble heels. The maidservants' full skirts fanned through the air like decks of cards in the hands of a gambler, and their happy squeals rang in the ears of the onlookers. The landlady of the tavern, a wise, gaunt old woman who only occasionally stuck her nose out from her refuge in the kitchen, knew that there was nothing to worry about: the guards were rich and generous, and the damages would be recouped with interest, and more important, the popularity of the establishment would increase a thousandfold after this evening.

After dancing, the revelers calmed down, the din of voices quieted just a bit, and the maidservants, panting and adjusting their clothing, refilled the jugs that had escaped being smashed and brought new glasses from the kitchen. Now, having returned to their senses, both girls bashfully lowered their eyelashes, ashamed at how freely they had behaved. At the same time, an ardent, chimerical hope for something vague, something entirely unfeasible smoldered within the soul of each girl, and whenever a dusty boot brushed against one of their tiny feet as if by accident, that hope flared up and imbued their youthful faces and tender necks with color.

The girls were named Ita and Feta, so it was only natural that the befuddled carousers kept confusing their names; moreover, many of the guards could no longer manage their tongues and thus were scarcely able to compliment the girls further. The impassioned glances were fading, and together with them the girlish hopes for something unrealizable were slowly diminishing, when a heavy battle dagger suddenly slammed into the doorjamb right above Ita's head.

The room became quiet immediately, so quiet that the landlady stuck her inflamed purple nose out of her kitchen. The revelers looked around in mute amazement, as if they expected to see the menacing Spirit Lash on the smoke-fouled ceiling. Bewildered, at first Ita just opened her mouth, but then, finally realizing what had happened, she dropped an empty jug on the floor.

In the tense silence, a heavy chair scraped back from one of the tables. Trampling the fragments of the broken jug under his boots, a man unhurriedly approached the girl. The knife sheath on his belt was empty, but soon the sinister weapon was extracted from the doorjamb and slid back into its place. The man took a piece of gold from a fat purse.

"Take it, girl. Would you like to earn more?"

The tavern exploded with shouts and laughter. The gentlemen guards—those who were still in any condition to move—joyfully clapped one another on the shoulders and backs, rejoicing at the bold and fortunate amusement thought up by their comrade.

"That's Egert! Bravo, Egert! A daring brute, upon my word! Well, do it again!"

The owner of the dagger smiled. When he smiled, a dimple appeared on his right cheek near the corner of his mouth.

Ita helplessly clenched her fists, unable to take her eyes off that dimple. "But, Lord Egert, you can't just . . . Lord Egert!"

"What, are you afraid?" Egert, a lieutenant of the regiment, asked smoothly, and Ita broke out in a sweat before the gaze of his clear gray blue eyes.

"But!"

"Stand with your back to the door."

"But, Master Egert, you've all been drinking so heavily!"

"What! Don't you trust me?"

Ita's feathery eyelashes fluttered repeatedly. The spectators crawled onto the tables in order to see better: even the truly drunk ones sobered up for the sake of such a spectacle. The landlady, more than a bit agitated now, stood frozen in the kitchen doorway with a mop held motionless at her side.

Egert turned to the guards. "Knives! Daggers! Whatever you have!"

Within a minute, he was bristling like a porcupine.

"You're drunk, Egert," Dron, another lieutenant, let the words drop as if by accident.

A swarthy young man peeled himself from the crowd of guards. "Really? He hasn't drunk all that much. Why, it'd barely wet a bedbug's knees, the amount he's drunk! How can he be drunk?"

Egert burst out laughing. "True! Feta, wine!"

Feta obeyed: not immediately, but slowly and mechanically, and simply because she would not dare to disobey the request of a customer.

"But, but," stammered Ita, watching as a gurgling waterfall of wine tumbled down Egert's throat.

"Not a word," he spat, wiping his lips. "Stand back, everyone."

"Oh, he is drunk!" The shout came from among the gathering of spectators. "He's going to kill the girl, the idiot!"

A small brawl ensued, but it was soon quieted. Apparently, the heckler had been dealt with.

"I'll give you a coin for each throw," explained a teetering Egert to Ita. "One coin per shot. Stay where you are!"

The girl, who had been slowly trying to withdraw from the oak door, fearfully staggered back to her previous position.

"One, two . . ." Egert took the first throwing knife that came to hand from the mass of weapons. "No, this is so boring. Karver!"

The swarthy youth appeared next to him as if he had been awaiting this summons.

"Candles. Put candles in her hands and one on her head."

"No!" Ita burst into tears. For a moment, the silence was broken only by her distressed sobs.

"How about this?" An extraordinary thought, it seemed, had dawned on Egert. "For each throw, I'll give you a kiss."

Ita slowly raised her tearstained eyes, but the few seconds of procrastination were enough.

"Let me!" Feta pushed her friend out of the way, stood in front of the door, and took the lit candles from the hands of Karver, who was snickering.

The blades clipped the quivering flames ten times, they entered the wood directly over the girl's head another two times, and they passed within a fingerbreadth of her temple yet three more times. Lieutenant Egert Soll kissed the lowly maidservant Feta a total of fifteen times.

Everyone considered it well played except for Ita. She fled to the kitchen to sob. Feta's eyes were lowered, and the skillful hands of the lieutenant rested on her waist. The landlady looked on sorrowfully, yet with understanding. It soon became obvious that Feta was feverish and swooning from passion. Somewhat uneasy, Lord Soll decided to take her to her room; he was not gone for very long, but once he returned, he encountered the rapturous, somewhat envious looks of his comrades.

The night was already well past its peak when the company finally quit the welcoming establishment. Lieutenant Dron spoke to Egert's swaying back. "All the mothers in the district scare their daughters with stories of Lieutenant Soll. You truly are a rascal."

Someone chuckled.

"That merchant Vapa, you know, that rich man who bought the empty house on the embankment? Well, he just brought in a young wife from the provinces, and guess what: He's already been informed by the local gossips that he should fear neither pestilence nor ruin, but a young guard by the name of Soll."

Everyone laughed except for Karver. He frowned at the mention of the merchant's wife, gritted his teeth, and said, "That's what I thought. Someone let it slip in all innocence, and now the merchant doesn't sleep a wink. He guards her." He crossly tossed his head. Obviously, the merchant's wife had long occupied his thoughts, but her jealous husband had managed to disoblige him by his very existence.

Wobbling, Egert stopped, and the blissful vacancy of drunkenness on his face gradually gave way to interest. "Are you lying?"

"If I were lying?" reluctantly responded Karver. The conversation seemed oppressive to him.

The whole company gradually sobered up enough to consider the situation; someone chuckled at the thought of intrigue.

Egert drew his sword from its sheath, his renowned sword of ancient design, and holding its narrow edge close to his face, he solemnly pronounced, "I vow that the merchant shall not protect himself, not from pestilence, not from ruin, and definitely not from—"

His last words were drowned out by an outburst of laughter. Karver's face darkened, and he hunched his head down into his shoulders.

The glorious city of Kavarren was as ancient as it was militaristic. In no other city did there live, side by side, so many renowned descendants of venerable houses; in no other city did there grow such an assortment of family trees. Nowhere else were valor and military skill so highly valued: the only thing Kavarren valued as highly as prowess with a blade and bravery in battle was skill in breeding and training boars, whose fights were the primary entertainment in the city.

Any House in Kavarren could, if necessary, withstand the onslaught of hundreds of troops. The walls of every manor were surpassingly strong and thick, the unassailable, narrow windows cut in these walls loomed darkly, and a multitude of steel spikes protruded here and there on both gates and doors. An entire arsenal, consisting of myriad types of weapons, was carefully deposited in the vault of each house, and above each roof a banner, adorned with fringe, waved proudly. On the exterior side of the gates, each house boasted a coat of arms, one sight of which might put an entire army to flight from fear of the numerous claws and teeth, the fiery eyes and the ferociously grinning jaws therein. The city was surrounded by a fortress wall, and the gates were protected by such forbidding engravings that even Khars, Protector of Warriors, would either lose his head or flee for his life should he choose to attack Kavarren.

But most of all, Kavarren was proud of its elite force, the regiment of guards. As soon as a son was born into one of the esteemed families, his father would immediately strive for the rosy-cheeked babe's enrollment in these glorious military ranks. Not a single holiday passed by without a military parade to show off the prowess of this regiment; on the days without a parade, the streets of this peaceful city were constantly patrolled, the pubs prospered, and although mothers constantly and severely appealed to their daughters to be prudent, duels occurred occasionally. These duels were long discussed by the town gossips with both satisfaction and pleasure.

However, the guards were renowned not only for their debaucheries and adventures. The regiment's history was full of victories during the internecine wars that had broken out entirely too often in the past. The present-day guards, the descendants of the famous warriors of old, frequently displayed their military skill in skirmishes with the wicked, well-armed bands of high-waymen who occasionally flooded the surrounding forests. All the respect-able men of the city spent their youths in the saddle with a weapon in hand.

However, the most terrible event in the history of the city was by no means some war or siege, but the Black Plague, which appeared in Kavarren many decades ago and in the course of three days cut the number of townspeople nearly in two. Walls and fortifications and sharp steel proved powerless against the Plague. The old men of Kavarren, who lived through the Plague in their childhoods, enjoyed recounting the terrible story to their grandsons; however, the young men were quite capable of ignoring all these horrors, possessing that happy talent of youth that allows admonitions heard but a moment ago with their right ears to instantly fly out their left.

Egert Soll was the flesh of the flesh of his native Kavarren; he was a true son and embodiment of its heroism. If he had died suddenly at the age of twenty and a half years, he would have been lauded as the very spirit of Ka-varren; it must be said, however, that in his attractive, blond head there were absolutely no thoughts of death.

If anything, Egert did not believe in death: this from the man who man-aged to kill two men in duels! Both incidents were discussed widely, but inas-much as they were both questions of honor and all the rules of dueling had been strictly adhered to, the townspeople soon began to talk of Egert with respect, rather than with any sort of condemnation. Tales of Egert's other victo-ries, in which his opponents escaped with mere wounds or mutilation, simply served as textbook examples for the city's young boys and adolescents.

However, as time went on, Egert fought fewer and fewer duels, not be-cause his combative vehemence had been exhausted, but because there were fewer volunteers willing to throw themselves on his family sword. Egert was a devoted student of swordplay; the blade became his sole plaything at the age of thirteen when his father ceremoniously presented him with the family heir-loom in lieu of his childhood practice sword.

It is no wonder that Egert had very few to balance out his abundance of friends. Friends met with him in every tavern, friends followed at his heels in packs and involuntarily became the witnesses and participants in his impetu-ous amusements.

A worshipper of all kinds of danger, he recognized the distinctive charm of dancing on the razor's edge. Once, on a dare, he scaled the exterior wall of the fire tower, the highest building in the city, and rang the bell three times, inducing by this action a fair bit of alarm among the townsfolk. Lieutenant Dron, who had entered into this bet with Egert, was required to kiss the first woman he encountered, and that woman turned out to be an old spinster, the aunt of the mayor—oh, what a scandal!

Another time, a guard by the name of Lagan had to pay up; he lost a bet when Egert, in full view of everyone, saddled a hefty, reddish brown bull, which was furious but completely stupefied at such impudence. Clenching a horse bridle in his teeth, Lagan hauled Egert on his shoulders from the city gates to his own house.

But mostly the cost of these larks fell to Karver.

They had been inseparable since childhood. Karver clung to Egert and loved him like a brother. Not especially handsome but not hideous, not especially strong but not a weakling; Karver always lost in comparison with Egert and yet at the same time basked in the reflection of his glory. From an early age, he conscientiously worked for the right to be called the friend of such a prominent young man, enduring at times both humiliations and mockery.

He wanted to be just like Egert; he wanted it so fervently that slowly, imperceptibly even to himself, he began to take on his friend's habits, his mannerisms, his swagger, even his voice. He learned to swim and walk on ropes, and Heaven only knows what that cost him. He learned to laugh aloud at his own spills into muddy puddles; he did not cry when blows, accurately thrown by a young Egert, left bruises on his shoulders and knees. His magnificent friend valued his dedication and loved Karver in his own way; this, however, did not keep him from forgetting about the existence of his friend if he did not see him with his own eyes even for a day. Once, when he was fourteen years old, Karver decided to test his friend: He said he was ill, and did not show his face among his comrades for an entire week. He sat at home, reverently waiting for Egert to remember him, which of course Egert did not: he was distracted by numerous amusements, games, and outings. Egert did not know, of course, that Karver sat silently by his window for all seven days of his voluntary seclusion nor that, despising himself, he once broke out into hot, spiteful, angry tears. Suffering from solitude, Karver vowed he would break with Egert forever, but then he broke down and went to see him, and he was met with such sincere joy that he immediately forgot the insult.

Little changed as they grew up. Timid Karver's love affairs all fell apart, usually when Egert instructed him in the ways of love by leading girls whom

Karver found attractive away from him right under his nose. Karver sighed and forgave, regarding his own humiliation as a sacrifice for friendship.

Egert was wont to require the same daring of those around him as he himself possessed, and he did his best to mock those who fell short of his expectations. He was especially unforgiving to Karver; once in late autumn, when the river Kava, which skirted the town, froze over for the first time, Egert proposed a contest to see who could run over it, from bank to bank, the quickest. All his friends quickly pretended to have important business to attend to, sicknesses and infirmities, but Karver, who showed up as he usually did just to be at hand, received such a contemptuous sneer and such a scathing, vile rebuke that he flushed from his ears to his heels. Within an inch of crying, he consented to Egert's suggestion.

Of course, Egert, who was taller and heavier, easily skimmed across the slick ice to the opposite bank as the fish in the gloomy depths gaped at him in astonishment. Of course, Karver got scared at the crucial moment and froze, intending to go back, and with a cry he dropped into a newly made, gleaming black opening in the ice, magnanimously affording Egert the chance to save him and by that act earn himself yet more laurels.

Interestingly enough, he was sincerely grateful to Egert for dragging him out of the icy water.

Mothers of grown daughters winced at the name of Egert Soll; fathers of adolescent sons put him up as an example for the youths. Cuckolds scowled darkly upon meeting Egert in the street, and yet for all that, they hailed him politely. The mayor forgave him his intrigues and debauches and ignored any complaints lodged against Egert because an event that had occurred during the boar-fighting season still lived in his memory.

Egert's father, like many in Kavarren, raised fighting boars. This was considered a sophisticated and honorable art. The black boars from the House of Soll were exceptionally savage and bloodthirsty; only the dark red, brindled boars from the House of the mayor were able to rival them in competition. There was never a contest but that in the finale these eternal rivals would meet, and the victory in these battles fluctuated between the two Houses, until one fine summer day, the champion of the mayor, a crimson, brindled specimen called Ryk, went wild and charged his way through the tilting yard.

Having gutted his adversary, a black beauty by the name of Khars, the maddened boar dashed into the grandstand. His own brindled comrade, who happened to be in his path and who gave way with his belly completely shredded to pieces, delayed the lunatic boar for a short moment, but the mayor, who by tradition was sitting in the first row, only had time to let out a heart-rending scream and, scooping up his wife, jump to his feet on the velvet-covered stand.

No one knows how this bloody drama might have ended; many of those who came that day to feast their eyes upon the contests, the mayor and his wife among them, may have met the same sad fate as the handsome Khars, for Ryk, nurtured in ferocity from his days as a piglet, had apparently decided that his day had finally come. The wretch was mistaken: this was not his day, but Egert Soll's, who appeared in the middle of the action before the public in the back rows even understood what was happening.

Egert bellowed insults, most offensive to a boar, at Ryk while a blindingly bright piece of fabric, which later turned out to be the wrap that covered the naked shoulders of one of the more extravagant ladies in town, whirled without ceasing in his left hand. Ryk hesitated for all of a second, but this second was sufficient for the fearless Egert, who having jumped within a hairsbreadth of the boar, thrust his dagger, won on a bet, beneath the shoulder blade of the crimson-colored lunatic.

The stunned mayor presented the most generous of all possible gifts to the House of Soll: all the dark-red, brindled boars contained within his enclo-sures were instantly roasted and eaten, though it is true that their meat turned out to be tough and sinewy. Egert sat at the head of the table while his father swallowed tears of affection and pride; now the ebony beauties of the Solls would have no equal in town. The elder Soll felt that his impending old age promised to be peaceful and comfortable, for there was no doubt that his son was the best of all the sons of the city.

Egert's mother was not at that feast. She often kept to her bed and did not enjoy noisy crowds of people. At one time, she had been a strong and healthy woman; she had taken to her bed soon after Egert killed his first opponent in a duel. It sometimes occurred to Egert that his mother avoided him and that she was nearly afraid of him. However, he always managed to drive away such strange or unpleasant thoughts.


One clear, sunny day—actually, it was the first real spring day of the year—an agreeable new acquaintance befell the merchant Vapa, who was strolling along the embankment with his young wife near at hand.

This new acquaintance, who seemed to Vapa such an exceedingly distinguished young man, was, curiously enough, Lord Karver Ott. What was remarkable about this meeting was that the young guard was promenading in the company of his sister, a girl of uncommon proportions with a high, magnificent bust and humbly lowered gray blue eyes.

The girl was named Bertina. As a foursome—Karver alongside Vapa and Bertina next to the beautiful Senia, the young wife of the merchant—they nonchalantly sauntered back and forth along the embankment.

Vapa was astonished and simultaneously moved; it was the first time one of these "cursed aristocrats" had shown him such warm regard. Senia stole a passing glance at Karver's youthful face and then immediately lowered her eyes, as though fearful of what the punishment might be for even a single forbidden glance.

They passed by a group of guards, picturesquely stationed along a parapet. Casting a wary glance at them, Senia discovered that the young men were not chatting away as they usually did. Instead, they all stood with their backs facing the embankment and their hands held to their mouths; from time to time they trembled strangely, as if they were all suddenly stricken by one and the same ailment.

"What's wrong with them?" she wondered to Bertina.

But Bertina merely shook her head sorrowfully and shrugged her shoulders.

Anxiously shifting his gaze from the guards to his sister and then from his sister to Senia, Karver spoke suddenly in a lowered voice. "Ah, believe me, there is such a strong tradition of debauchery in this city! Bertina is an innocent girl; it is so hard to choose friends for her when one is wary of all the pernicious influences. Oh, how good it would be if Bertina could become friends with Mistress Senia."

With these last words, a sigh slipped out of him.

The foursome turned and began to walk on the opposite side of the embankment; the guards on the parapet were now fewer, but those who remained stubbornly watched the river: all but one who was sitting squarely on the cobblestone pavement and having some sort of fit.

"They're drunk, as usual," Karver noted in condemnation. The one who was sitting raised his clouded eyes and then doubled over, unable to control the laughter that pulled at his chest.

———

On the following day, Karver and his sister called upon Vapa. Bertina confessed to Senia that she did not know a thing about embroidering silk.

On the third day, Senia, who was intolerably bored from whiling away her days in solitude, asked her husband to allow her to meet with Bertina more often: this would undoubtedly amuse them both, and furthermore Karver's sister had asked Senia to give her lessons in embroidery.

On the fourth day, Bertina presented herself. She was guarded by her faithful brother, who was unaccountably sullen, and as soon as he had greeted them and deposited his sister, he bowed his apologies and left. The merchant sat down to go over his accounts while Senia led her guest upstairs to her own rooms.

A canary chirped in an ornamental cage. Needles and delicate linen were extracted from a basket. Bertina's fingers, far too stiff and coarse, refused to comply with the task, but the girl seemed to be trying her best.

"Dearest," said Senia thoughtfully in the middle of the lesson, "is it really true that you are completely innocent?"

Bertina pricked herself with a needle and put her finger in her mouth.

"Don't be embarrassed." Senia smiled. "It seems to me that we can be completely open with each other. So are you really, well, you know what I mean?"

Bertina raised her gray eyes to Senia, who saw with amazement that those eyes were unimaginably sorrowful. "Ah, Senia, that is such a sad tale."

"I thought as much!" the wife of Vapa exclaimed. "He seduced you and then dropped you, didn't he?"

Bertina shook her head and again sighed heavily.

The room was silent for a short time and then from the street came the sound of friendly laughter from two dozen young throats.

"The guards," Senia muttered, going to the window. "They are laughing again. What are they always laughing for?"

Bertina let out a sob.

Senia turned away from the window and sat next to her. "I see. Was he, your beloved, was he a guard?"

"If only," whispered Bertina. "The guards are tender and honorable, the guards are faithful and manly, the guards . . ."

Senia pursed her lips incredulously. "I highly doubt the guards are faithful. I think it is more likely that your beloved is called Egert Soll, isn't that so?"

Bertina jumped slightly on the cushions. The room again became quiet.

"Dear one," began Senia in a whisper, "you know you can tell me. Have you ever experienced, well, you know, they say that women can also experience, um, pleasure. Do you understand what I mean?" Senia blushed; such candor made her uneasy.

Bertina again raised her eyes, but this time they were astonished. "But, my dear, you're married!"

"Yes, that's just it!" Senia abruptly stood up, entirely out of humor. Forcing the words out between her teeth, she said, "I am married. So I am."

Her guest slowly set aside her embroidery.

Their conversation went on for about an hour. Bertina talked and talked, but her voice never gave out: on the contrary, it discovered an almost musical quality as she progressed. She closed her eyes and tenderly stroked the back of the chair; she practically cooed at one point. Senia, unable to move, stared at her with widened eyes; she could only breathe and from time to time lick her parched lips.

"And all that really happens?" she asked finally in a shaking, choked-up voice.

Bertina slowly, solemnly nodded.

"And I'll never experience it?" Senia murmured, paralyzed by distress.

Bertina stood up. She took a deep breath as if she were planning to plunge into cold water. She tugged at the front of her dress, and two round, padded sacks fell, one after the other, onto the floor.

Senia's breath caught in her throat, and she could not scream.

The dress slid from Bertina like skin from a snake. Muscular shoulders, a wide chest covered in curly hair, and a stomach with well-defined ridges of muscle were revealed from beneath the dress.

When the dress slipped even lower, Senia covered her eyes with her hands.

"If you scream," whispered the voice of the man who had been Bertina, "your very own husband will . . ."

Senia did not hear the rest; she simply fainted.


Of course, Egert would not take advantage of the helplessness of a languishing woman. Of course, he quickly managed to bring Senia back to consciousness. And of course, their confidential conversation quickly resumed, though it was now of a decidedly different quality.

"You promise?" asked Senia, shaking from head to toe.

"Upon my word as a guard."

"You! You're a guard?"

"How can you ask! I'm Egert Soll!"

"But—"

"Only with your consent."

"But—"

"One word, and I'll go."

"But—"

"Should I go?"

"No!"

On the first floor, the merchant Vapa was frowning angrily; his accounts just would not add up. The two dozen guards standing below the windows of his home got bored and decided to wander off.

The needlework basket had long since tumbled to the floor, spilling colorful tangles of thread. The caged canary was silent, astonished.

"Oh. Glorious Heaven!" gasped Senia, embracing Egert's neck with her arms. He was silent; he no longer had the ability to speak.

The poor little bird was beginning to get frightened. Its cage, which hung over the bed, was swaying, rhythmically and vigorously. An ancient clock emitted a majestic series of chimes, and then it did so yet again, and again.

"Oh! Good Spirits! Glorious Heaven!" Senia did not know to whom else to pray; she was almost ready to burst from trying not to cry out at the top of her lungs.

The merchant Vapa rubbed his hands contentedly: the mistakes had been corrected, and a careless scribe would soon lose his position. And how good it was that Senia had become friends with the sister of Lord Karver! For a whole day she had been neither seen nor heard; she did not fidget in front of him, or pester him, or ask to go out walking. The merchant smirked suddenly, thinking he might even have time to go out and visit his mistress.

He raised himself up, intending to escape the confines of his armchair, but he winced at a pain in his back and remained seated.

Lurching slightly, Egert Soll peered out the window toward the embankment. Naked and enervated, he stood in the window aperture and regarded his comrades with scorn. The merchant Vapa jumped and winced. Cursed guards! What did they have to laugh about so?

A few minutes later, Senia and Bertina came downstairs. It seemed to Vapa that his wife was not herself, as if the lesson in embroidery had exhausted her. Saying good-bye, she looked into Bertina's eyes with special tenderness.

"You'll come again, yes?"

"Without fail," breathed the girl, "I have not yet mastered this . . . stitch, dearest Senia."

The merchant sneered contemptuously. These women are so sentimental.

"I'll cut out the tongue," Egert told his friends in the pub, "of anyone who gossips. Is that clear?"

There was no doubt to anyone that he would do so if the secret of the merchant's wife Senia became gossip in the town. They all remembered their hereditary blades and their family honor, and they held their tongues.

They winked at Karver and shook his hand because it was clear to them that he had played a significant role in this whole affair. The congratulations, it seemed, afforded him little joy; heedless of the reflection of Egert's glory that fell to him, his "brother," Karver first got extremely drunk and then silently slipped away.

Spring broke forth with driving rains; muddy currents coursed through the steep, cobbled alleyways, and the children of cooks and shopkeepers launched wooden shoes with canvas sails attached to them off to sea while the young aristocrats peered at them from high, oriel windows with quiet envy.

One morning, a simple highway coach drove up to the inn the Noble Sword, which was located near the center of Kavarren. The coachman, going against the usual habit of his kind, did not rush to open the door of the coach, but instead sat indifferently on the driver's box; apparently, the passengers were not his masters, but nothing more than renters. The carriage door swung open on its own and a young man, slight and lean, kicked open the running board so he could step down.

Outsiders were not all that rare in Kavarren, and it is possible that the arrival of the coach would have gone unnoticed had not Egert Soll and his friends been whiling away the hours at the Faithful Shield, a tavern opposite the inn.

"Take a look at that one!" said Karver, who was sitting by the window of the tavern.

Two or three heads turned in the direction he was looking; the other gentlemen were far too engrossed in their conversation or their wine.

"I say, check it out!" Karver nudged Egert, who was sitting next to him, in the side.

Egert glanced over. By this time, the young man had already jumped down onto the wet cobblestones and was offering his hand to someone unseen, someone still inside the coach. The youth was dressed all in dark colors, and Egert instantly felt that there was some sort of oddity in the figure of the young stranger, but he was not sure what.

"He's not carrying a sword," said Karver.

Only then did Egert see that the stranger was unarmed, that he was not even wearing any empty baldrics, and that on his thin belt there was no sign of a dagger, not even a kitchen knife. Egert looked at him more intently; the stranger's clothes seemed extremely formal, but if they made up a uniform, it was in no way military.

"He's a student," explained Karver. "Definitely a student."

In the meantime, the student, having conferred with the person who still remained inside the coach, went to pay the coachman, who still did not display a single sign of obeisance; obviously, in addition to not being the coach's owner, the student was not wealthy.

"I suppose," drawled Egert through his teeth, "students, like women, don't wear swords?"

Karver snickered.

Egert smirked disdainfully and was about to turn his back on the window when a girl, leaning on the arm of the student, emerged from the carriage. All sound in the tavern immediately ceased.

Her face was anxious, pale from exhaustion, and doleful from the rain, but even this could not spoil it. It was a perfect face, almost as if it were finely cut from marble; only, whereas a marble statue's white, dead eyes would have stared dully, this girl's dark, tranquil eyes gleamed lustrously without the slightest shade of coyness.

Like her companion, the newly arrived girl was dressed simply. However, her simple traveling dress was unable to hide either her elegant figure or the lightness and suppleness of her movements. The girl jumped down onto the cobblestones next to the youth. He said something, causing the soft lips of his tired companion to quirk in a small smile and her eyes to become even more penetrating and vivid.

"That's beyond belief," murmured Egert.

The driver touched the reins. The two arrivals leapt back to escape from being splattered with the watery mud thrown up by the wheels. Then the young man hauled a large bundle up onto his shoulder, and the visitors entered the premises of the Noble Sword hand in hand. The door, carved with entwined monograms, closed behind them.

In the tavern, everyone started talking at once; for a moment Egert held his peace, unresponsive to the questioning glances of his friends. Then he pulled Karver to the side. "I need to know who they are."

He stood up, prepared, as usual, to do a service for his friend. Egert watched as Karver, hopping over puddles, rushed across the street to the Noble Sword; the carved door slammed shut yet again, and nearly a quarter of an hour passed before Egert's sidekick returned.

"Yes, he's a student. Evidently, they're staying for about a week." Karver fell silent, waiting with satisfaction for his friend's questions.

"And the girl?" Egert nearly spit the words out.

Karver smirked strangely. "She is neither his sister nor his aunt, as I had hoped. She is the fiancée of that boy and, it seems, the wedding is not far off!"

Egert was silent; Karver's report, although not completely unexpected, piqued and almost outraged him.

"It goes against nature," said one of the guards. "A complete misalliance."

They all boisterously agreed.

"Do you know what I've heard?" interjected Karver as if in wonder. "I've heard that all students are castrated so they can't be distracted by earthly pleasures, and so they fully consign themselves to their studies. Was that all a lie?"

"It seems it is a lie," muttered Lieutenant Dron, sounding disappointed. He knocked over his forgotten wineglass.

"If he doesn't carry a sword, he might as well be a eunuch," said Egert quietly. They all turned in his direction. A predatory and insolent sneer stalked over Egert's face. "What use does a eunuch have for a woman, anyway? Especially a woman like that!"

He stood up, and all his friends respectfully made way for him. Having tossed a few gold coins at the innkeeper, enough to pay for the entire company, Lieutenant Egert Soll walked out into the rain.


That very same evening, the young man and his companion were dining on the first floor of the Noble Sword; their meal was quite modest until the innkeeper, grinning widely, came over and placed a wicker basket bristling with bottle necks on the table in front of them.

"Master and mistress, compliments of Lord Soll!"

With these words, and with a meaningful smile, the innkeeper bowed himself away.

Egert, who had made himself comfortable in a far corner of the dining room, saw how the student and the lovely young woman glanced at each other in surprise. After a long deliberation, the cloth covering the basket was whipped away and joyful wonder blossomed on the faces of the pair leaning over the gifts, which was no real surprise, as the viands and wines had been selected with impeccable taste.

However, bewilderment soon replaced joy; after saying something heated to his companion, the student hopped up and ran off after the innkeeper to find out who exactly this generous benefactor, this Lord Soll, was.

Egert drained his mug to the dregs, stood up leisurely, and made his way through the room to the girl, who had been left alone. As he walked, he purposefully avoided looking at her, fearing disenchantment. For what if this beauty, when seen too close, turned out not to be as beautiful?

The dining room was half-empty. A few guests were eating and a well-behaved group of townsfolk were whiling away their time in amiable drunkenness. The Noble Sword had the reputation for being a calm, decorous establishment; the innkeeper carefully guarded against boisterous carousals and brawls. Delaying the moment of meeting the beautiful lady, Egert noticed a new face among the guests. Apparently, this tall, middle-aged traveler had arrived very recently because Egert did not know him by sight.

Having finally come to within a hairsbreadth of his goal, Egert mentally prepared himself to gaze upon the fiancée of the student.

Oh yes, she was magnificent. Her face no longer seemed so tired, and her cheeks, smooth as alabaster, had gained a bit of color. Now that he was close, he could distinguish small, previously unnoticed details, such as a constellation of tiny beauty marks on her long, proud neck and the unusually steep, bold sweep of her eyelashes.

Egert stood and gazed at her. The girl slowly raised her head and, for the first time, Egert met the gaze of her serious, slightly aloof eyes.

"Good day," said Egert, and he sat down in the spot vacated by the student. "Does the lady object to the company of a humble worshipper of beauty?"

The girl did not become confused or frightened; she only seemed somewhat taken aback. "Excuse me, you are?"

"My name is Egert Soll." He stood, gave a short bow, and again sat down.

"Ah." It seemed she was about to smile. "If that is so, then we should thank you."

"Not at all!" Egert seemed dismayed. "It is we, the humble citizens of Kavarren, who should thank you for the honor you have bestowed upon us—" He had to pause and fill his lungs with air to finish the florid phrase. "—bestowed upon us, by favoring us with your presence. How long may we shower you with hospitality?"

The girl smiled, and at that moment, Egert wanted nothing more than for that smile to never leave her face.

"You are very obliging. We will be here for a week, perhaps a bit longer."

With a proprietary gesture, Egert produced the first bottle from the basket and adroitly uncorked it. "Please allow me to fulfill the duties of hospitality and offer you some wine. Do you have any relatives in Kavarren, or perhaps some friends?"

She managed to shake her head no, but just then the student returned and the girl smiled at him, and her smile was so joyful that it completely overshadowed the smile she had just given Egert. Egert noticed this and an unpleasant feeling slid into his soul, a feeling that almost resembled jealousy.

"Dinar, this is the Lord Soll who so generously presented us with all these marvels. Lord Soll, allow me to introduce my fiancé, Dinar."

The student nodded to Egert, but he did not offer his hand, which was lucky because Egert would die before shaking that bony paw, unaccustomed to weapons and stained with what appeared to be darkened spots of ink. Up close, the student seemed even more despicable and awkward, and Egert felt like crying out to Heaven at the grievous wrong of allowing both the student and his wondrous companion to sit at the same table.

However, at the moment, the beauty and Egert were the only ones sitting at the table. As there were only two chairs, the student could only hover nearby.

Paying him not even the slightest bit of attention, Egert again turned to the girl. "Pardon me, but I don't even know your name."

The girl and the discomforted student shared a look, directed at Egert, who was lounging in his chair. The girl answered as if by rote. "My name is Toria."

Egert repeated her name as if he were examining the taste of it. In the meantime, the student had come to his senses and dragged a third chair, which had been lying vacant nearby, to the table.

"You have neither relatives nor friends here." Raising himself up a bit,

Egert bent over Toria's wineglass, and his hand, in a seemingly natural fashion, touched hers. "Or rather, you didn't have any, but now the entire city, I believe, will want to make your acquaintance. Are you simply traveling for pleasure?"

The student, frowning slightly, took a glass from the serving girl and poured himself some wine. Egert smirked with the corners of his lips because the noble beverage hardly filled a third of the student's glass.

"We are traveling," confirmed the girl in a slightly restrained manner, "but not for pleasure. Here in Kavarren, many centuries ago, lived a man who interests us from an academic point of view. He was a mage, an archmage, and we are hoping that he left some sign of himself in the ancient archives, manuscripts, and chronicles."

With every word, she became even more passionate, forgetting her momentary consternation. Some moldy papers were dearer to her, apparently, than her own brothers would be: at the word *archive* her voice trembled with reverence. Egert raised his glass. It was all the same to him what evoked enthusiasm in the woman, just so long as it gave fire to her eyes and flush to her cheeks.

"A toast to travelers who search for manuscripts! But I don't think there ever were any chronicles in Kavarren, and there certainly aren't now."

The student puffed out his lips. Without any expression, he said, "There is an extensive historical library in Kavarren, in the Town Hall. Is this news to you?"

Egert refused to trouble himself by entering into conversation with him. Toria, it would seem, was able to appreciate good wine; her eyes had closed with delight after the very first sip. To afford her more opportunities for pleasure, Egert took the next bottle out of the basket.

"Note this wine; it is the pride of Kavarren's wine cellars, the offspring of southern vineyards, Serenade Muscatel. Would you like to try it?"

As he once again filled her glass, he inhaled the scent that emanated from her. It was the scent of a perfume, of insistent tart herbs and flowers. Then, caressing her warm, twitching hand, he put a tiny slice of rare brisket on her plate. The student sullenly twisted the bottle cork in his long fingers.

"So, what is it about this lucky fellow that interests you even after so many centuries?" asked Egert with an engaging smile. "If only I were in his place."

She willingly proceeded to tell him the long and entirely uninteresting history of the mage, who founded some kind of order and called them an army.

Egert did not understand immediately that she was talking about the Sacred Spirit Lash, to whom some people somewhere, he supposed, really did pay homage.

"Yes, and after he died, his followers claimed he was a god. Historians think that in the end of his life the great mage went mad, and his insanity infected the Order. Can you believe that they're still sitting around waiting for the End of Time?"

Egert listened to Toria, and the girl's words flowed past his ears, but her voice, her sweet, uncommon voice, fascinated him. Her velvet lips opened smoothly, allowing her white teeth to flash through; Egert broke out into a sweat, imagining the kiss these spectacular lips could give.

He wished that the girl would talk forever, but she paused, having glanced in passing at the student. He was sitting with his cockles raised like a wounded bird and was looking at her reproachfully.

"I beg you to continue," said Egert ingratiatingly. "I find this extremely interesting. So this Order of Lash still exists?" The student glared eloquently at Toria and then raised his eyes to the ceiling. Egert was not blind; he had no problem reading in this action the student's utmost contempt for his academic knowledge. However, to take notice of the behavior of this ratty, pitiful student was beneath his dignity.

Toria smiled in embarrassment. "I would be quite happy to talk to you about it, but we are very tired from the road, so I suppose it is time for us to go." She stood up smoothly, leaving her glass of wine unfinished.

"Mistress Toria!" Egert jumped up with her. "Perhaps it may be that you will allow me to fulfill my duties as a host tomorrow? If you are really interested in the local sights of interest, I am considered an expert on them, the best in the entire city."

Egert considered Kavarren's sights of interest to consist mainly of taverns and the paddocks of the fighting boars, but the credulous Toria was taken in by his utterly unartful trap. "Is that so?"

The student groaned heavily.

Not paying him the slightest attention, Egert nodded energetically. "Without a doubt. Will you permit me to know your plans for tomorrow?"

"They have yet to be determined," the youth answered morosely. Peering at him through narrowed eyes, Egert noted with amusement that students were capable of becoming angry.

"Mistress Toria"—Egert turned to the girl as if there had never been a student born into the world—"tomorrow I ask that you plan for a sightseeing tour, dinner at the finest establishment in Kavarren, and an evening excursion on a boat. The Kava is an extremely picturesque little river, did you notice?"

She somehow seemed to deflate. Her eyes darkened and now they seemed like twin pits beneath a troubled sky.

Egert smiled as charmingly, as sincerely, and as vulnerably as he could. "I didn't understand half your tale. I would truly like to ask you a few questions about this, um, gentleman, who gave the world the Order of Lash. And to show my gratitude for the tale, I, your humble servant, will arrange everything for your pleasure. Everything that you require will be laid at your feet. Until tomorrow!"

He bowed and left; the tall, middle-aged guest followed his exit with a weary gaze.

The custodian of the Town Hall delayed and shook his head for a long time: the book depositories were in a useless state; a large portion of the books had been destroyed in a fire, which had occurred about thirty years ago. He worried that a beam might very well fall on the heads of the young people. The researchers, however, were adamant, and in the end they were allowed access to the treasures they wished to see.

Of those treasures, however, there remained only pitiful crumbs: those very few that the fire had spared had become fat with an entire generation of rats. Raking through the rubbish and litter, the researchers kept exploding into exclamations of despair. Egert, appearing in the book depository with an enormous bouquet of roses, found the young couple just at the moment when, amidst the general ruin, they finally found a corner that had survived more or less intact.

They completely ignored Egert's arrival. The student was hanging somewhere under the ceiling, swaying on a broken-down stepladder; Toria was craning her neck to watch him, and in her pose Egert saw something akin to worship. Tufts of spiderwebs were tangled in her hair, but her eyes were shining and her soft lips were half-open with delight as she listened to the student, who spoke without ceasing.

He was bursting with words like a fountain bursts with water. Reading out incomprehensible passages from a book, he interpreted them for Toria in the same breath. Long, outlandish names rolled off his tongue while he floridly reasoned out runic texts, and from time to time he switched over into some language that Egert did not know. The girl took a heavy, dusty volume from his hand, and her tender fingers caressed its binding so reverently that Egert experienced a moment of irrational jealousy toward the book.

He stood there for nearly half an hour without being honored by so much as a single glance. Annoyed, he placed the bouquet in the nearest corner and left. His wounded pride pricked unpleasantly at his soul.

The young guests returned to the inn just in time for supper, but once that was over Toria did not leave her room, nor did she answer the courteous note Egert sent her.

On the following day, the custodian of the Town Hall had an appointment with the beneficent Lord Soll, and so the young researchers, who turned up for their books, received a bewildering refusal: it was entirely impossible today; the stairs were under repairs; the keys were under guard. The student and Toria, astonished, were forced to return to the inn. Egert sat in the dining room the entire day, but still Toria did not descend the stairs.

It rained all night long. The rain drenched the student, who departed for the Town Hall in the morning and again returned defeated. It was well after dinner when the clouds finally dispersed and the sun began to peek down upon the drenched city; the young couple, having been so inactive for the past two days, decided to go out for a walk.

As if they were afraid to walk very far away from the inn, the student and his fiancée turned back and forth several times along the drying street, completely unaware of how many attentive eyes kept watch over them through the windows of the Faithful Shield. One noted that the student watched over his fiancée far better than the merchant Vapa watched over his wife; another noted that the wife of the merchant could not hold a candle to the visiting beauty; yet another began to laugh.

Then Karver appeared in the path of the two promenaders.

The spectators, glued to the windows of the Faithful Shield, watched as Karver, as if by chance, grazed the student's shoulder and then bowed apologetically, almost to the ground; the student bowed as well, and Karver joyfully started a conversation with him, and after asking most humbly for Toria's permission, led the young man to the opposite side of the street. Waving his arms about, he had herded the student still farther along the street, almost to the corner, when Egert emerged from the doors of the tavern.

Toria answered Egert's formal greeting with a polite yet reserved nod. She did not seem bewildered or fearful; her eyes, as detached as before, looked at Egert attentively, fearlessly, and with patient inquisitiveness.

"Well, you're a cunning one, aren't you," said Egert with rough reproach. "You made a promise, you did. I waited for the continuation of your tale, and you never came down even once!"

She sighed. "Tell the truth. You're not the least bit interested in that."

"Me?" erupted Egert.

Toria looked over her shoulder, searching for her fiancé; catching that tense glance, Egert scowled and began speaking in a low voice.

"What is the point of your seclusion? Are you really preparing yourself for the role of the humble wife, and for such a tyrannical little husband? What's so terrible about a little conversation, or perhaps a stroll? What's wrong with having dinner together, or taking a boat ride? But perhaps I've offended you somehow. Or maybe you don't belong to yourself?"

She turned away from him; Egert feasted his eyes on her profile.

"You are so persistent," she said reprovingly.

"And what would you have me do?" Egert marveled sincerely. "The most beautiful woman in the world is visiting my town."

"Thank you. You have peculiar notions of hospitality. But I must leave you." Toria took a step in the direction where the garrulous Karver had ensnared the student.

Egert grew angry. "You are going to chase after that man? You?"

Flushing, Toria took another step.

Egert blocked her path. "You are like a precious jewel that has chosen a rotten hunk of wood as her setting. Use your eyes! You were born to rule; you are a queen, a goddess, but you—"

The student escaped from the corner; he was red faced and disheveled, as if he had been scuffling, and it seemed likely that something unpleasant had happened between him and Karver, who leapt after him, shouting for the whole street to hear.

"Sir, you aren't even married yet and already you're playing the cuckold! If the woman wants to talk to a man in the street, a man who is pleasing to her, that is no reason for hysterics!"

An artisan passing by burst out laughing. The gray-haired guest, who had just exited the doors of the inn, slowly turned his head toward the group. Lieutenant Dron and the eternally gloomy Lagan emerged onto the front steps of the Faithful Shield.

The student flushed from red to purple; he turned toward Karver as if about to strike him, but then he thought better of it. He turned back and hurried over to the perplexed Toria. He took her forcefully by the hand. "Let's go."

Their route of escape, however, had already been blocked off by Egert. Gazing straight into Toria's eyes, he asked softly, "Are you so submissive as to allow this . . . this creature to lead you away to the gray, spiritless life he has prepared for you?"

Karver shouted at the student, "But you still have time, sir, to fit yourself for horns! Not a week will pass after your happy little wedding before they adorn your learned brow!"

The student had begun to shake slightly; not even Toria's hand, which was holding his wrist in a viselike grip, could restrain this shaking.

"Lord Soll, please allow us to pass."

"In the event that a man should whip out his sword, you, sir, will be able to poke him with your horns," continued Karver. "This should give you with a certain advantage."

The student, as though blind, leapt forward right into Egert. Egert's iron-hard chest repelled him back to his former position.

"What would you call that combat maneuver, master student?" asked Karver. "The Pouncing Pupil? Do they teach that at the university?"

"Lord Soll," said Toria softly, looking Egert straight in the eye, "it seemed to me that you were an honorable man."

Over the course of his, admittedly not very long, life, Egert had had suffi-cient occasion to study women; he had seen numerous coquettes, whose *Be gone!* meant *Come to me, my love* and whose *Foul rogue!* meant *We must talk about this later.* Married women in the company of their spouses had demon-strated their disinterest and then, once the two of them were alone, had thrown themselves on his neck. Egert knew and could read many shades of meaning, but in the eyes of Toria he read not only complete indifference to the splendor of his manliness, but also the furious power of antagonism, of rejection.

Lieutenant Egert Soll was cut to the quick. In front of the entire regiment sitting in the Faithful Shield, a student, almost a eunuch, someone who did not even carry weapons, had been chosen over him, a man who had hereto-fore never known defeat.

Unwillingly stepping to the side, he gritted his teeth and snarled, "Well, my sincerest congratulations! An aristocrat in the embrace of a sniveling bookworm: what a splendid couple! But perhaps your learned spouse is just a screen behind which you hide your many lovers?"

Drawn by the noise in the street, the maidservants and guests were peering out the windows of the inn.

The student released Toria's hand. Ignoring her beseeching look, he drew a deep line in front of Egert's boots with the dusty toe of his shoe: the traditional challenge to a duel.

Egert laughed condescendingly. "What? I don't brawl with women! You, my dear sir, don't even have any weapons!"

Drawing his hand back, the student quickly and audibly slapped Egert across his face.


The excited crowd—guards, guests of the inn, chambermaids, servants, and casual passersby—filled the rear courtyard of the Noble Sword; Karver was there, practically crawling out of his skin, hurrying to clear a space amidst them for the combatants.

Some kind soul had lent the student his sword, but in his hands even that decent blade looked ridiculous, like knight's armor at a grocer's stand. His fiancée seemed ready to break down into tears for the first time since Egert had met her. Toria's cheeks, white as a shroud, were covered in irregular splotches; their jagged pattern concealed her beauty. Biting her lips, she threw herself at the spectators by turns.

"Stop this, you! Merciful Heaven, Dinar! Stop them, someone!"

To stop an honorably proclaimed duel was unlawful and also foolish: all the residents of Kavarren had imbibed that notion with their mother's milk. They simply watched Toria with sympathy and curiosity, and many of the women envied her silently: Just think, to be the reason for a duel!

One chambermaid decided, with sincere goodwill, to comfort the poor girl. Throwing off her arms, Toria, despairing of being able to stop Dinar, decided to leave. But she returned almost immediately, as if on a leash. The crowd parted before her, politely giving way, silently acknowledging her right to watch all the details of the fight. Toria leaned against the wheel of a carriage and remained frozen there as if overtaken by stupor.

The adversaries were ready. They stood opposite each other, enemy against enemy. Egert grinned derisively: there was nothing better than love, except a duel. True, his rival was entirely worthless. Just look at how he wheezes, trying to stand in the correct position! It was apparent that he had taken a fencing lesson or two, but not enough to do him any good.

Egert cast his eyes over the faces in the crowd, searching for Toria. Would she watch? Would she finally understand that she had favored a tiny stream from an overflowing sink over a thundering waterfall? Would she repent?

Instead of Toria, Egert met the eyes of the middle-aged guest, that gray-haired man whose head rose above the crowd like a pine tree towering over an orchard. The guest's gaze, steadfast but expressionless, displeased Egert; he tossed his head and flicked his sword at the student like a stern master flicking a switch.

"Hup, now!"

The student recoiled involuntarily, and the crowd burst into laughter.

"Lay into him, Egert!"

Egert grinned widely. "This is nothing more than a small lesson in good manners."

The student narrowed his eyes, bent his knees as though he were in a fencing class, and sprang forward recklessly, as if he intended to chop Egert up into cabbage. Within a second, he was looking around in amazement, searching for his opponent, while Egert, appearing behind his back, reminded the student of himself with a delicate jab just below his spine.

"Try not to get distracted, now!"

The student whirled around as though stung. Egert bowed politely and retreated a step.

"All is not lost, lad! Gather your strength and give it another shot. The lesson is just beginning!"

The student stood as rigidly as a mast; the tip of his blade was not pointed at the eyes of his opponent, as it should, but rather at the sky. He lunged awkwardly, managing to hit Egert's sword, but then the student's blade swung wide. Its tip hit the sand, and he was barely able to keep his grip on the hilt. The spectators began to applaud. Egert, however, was already bored with this game. He could fence for a hundred hours without rest, if only his hopelessly feeble adversary would not fight so tiresomely.

Egert knew seventeen defenses and twenty-seven attack maneuvers. The entire allure of the sport consisted of connecting these maneuvers so that they created a mosaic tapestry that he wove with his sword, then scattered and reassembled anew. Egert was unable, afterwards, to repeat many of the improvisations that resulted from this weaving: they were born from inspiration, like verse, and they were usually crowned with a wound, if not death. Alas, with this student before him, even with a sword, Egert was limited to using one particular maneuver, a maneuver so simple and vulgar that it resembled smoked herring.

Turning away from yet another clumsy attack, carelessly fending off strong yet inaccurate blows, Egert turned his head in search of Toria. Once he saw her pallid, almost vacant face in the crowd, he mounted his own attack, and the student did not even have time to understand what was happening. Egert dramatically held the tip of his blade near the student's chest, and the audience yelled out rapturously. Only the tall, gray-haired boarder maintained his calm.

This was repeated again and again. The student could have died ten times already, but Lord Soll prolonged the game, playing with the youth like a cat plays with a mouse. The student thrashed about, brandishing his sword. Pebbles skittered away from under his dusty shoes, but his enemy was like a shadow, ever-present and untouchable.

Egert's intentionally pedantic, toxic voice never ceased admonishing the student. "So! Ah-ha! Like this! Why do you squirm so, like a snake in a frying pan? Again! And again! Ha! Yes, you are a lazy, indolent pupil! You must be punished! Now!"

Every cry of *now* was followed by a small jab. The student's coat, lacerated in several places, hung in rags, and sweat poured down his drawn face.

The combatants once again stood facing each other. The student was worn out and bewildered, while Egert was not even out of breath. Looking into his opponent's desolate, hate-filled eyes, Egert sensed his own power, an idle, unhurried power that did not even need to be used, only enjoyed.

"Are you afraid?" he asked in a whisper, and in the same breath he read the answer in the student's eyes: Yes, he was afraid. Terror stood in front of Egert, whose sword was like a serpent's sting pointed at the poor man's chest. Egert's opponent was defenseless against him; he was no longer an opponent, but a victim, and rage had long since given way to anxiety and the desire to ask for mercy, if only his pride would allow it.

"Should I show you mercy?" Egert smiled with just the corner of his mouth. He felt the student's terror on his skin, and this feeling sweetly thrilled his nerves: all the more so since, in the depths of his soul, Egert had already decided not to penalize the boy too harshly.

"Should I show mercy? Well?"

Despair and terror forced the student into a new, hopeless attack. At the exact same moment, Egert's boot came down in a puddle, forsaken by the rain, and lost its solid connection to the ground. The legs of the magnificent Egert splayed apart like the limbs of a newborn colt. He barely kept his balance, and the student's sword grazed the guard's shoulder, slicing off his epaulet. That proud military affectation hung by a thread, like a dead spider, and the crowd—that cursed crowd, always on the side of the victor—broke out into delighted howls.

"Ha, Egert! He got a hit!"

"Keep at it! Keep at it! He'll fall back!"

"Bravo, student! Teach him a lesson! Thrash him!"

When guards who had been observed in some villainy or cowardice, or who had been convicted of treason, were expelled from the regiment, they suffered a shameful punishment: Their epaulets were publicly shorn from their shoulders. Without knowing it, the student had brought great shame upon Egert, who saw his comrades exchanging glances, smirking and whispering amongst themselves—for shame!

Everything further transpired instantaneously, in the space of a breath.

Forgetting himself in his fury, Egert sprang forward. The student, absurdly throwing up his sword, leapt forward to meet him—and froze, his astonished eyes staring into the guard's. Egert's family sword blossomed from his back; it was not lustrous as usual, but dark red, almost black. Standing for a second more, the student fell down as awkwardly as he had fought. The crowd became quiet; a blind man would have thought that there was not a single soul in the back courtyard of the tavern. The student slumped heavily onto the trampled dirt, and Egert's unmercifully long blade slipped out of his chest like a snake.

"He impaled himself," said Lieutenant Dron loudly.

Egert stood, his blood-soaked sword lowered down toward the ground, and stared dully at the form in front of him. The crowd shuffled slightly, letting Toria through.

She walked carefully, as if on a wire. Paying no heed to Egert, she approached the youth on tiptoe, as though she were afraid to wake him. "Dinar?"

The young man did not answer.

"Dinar?"

The crowd dispersed, averting their eyes. A reddish black stain crept out from under the lad's dark coat. The innkeeper sniveled in a low voice, "Oh, these duels! Young blood is hot, everyone knows it. What should I do now? Well, what am I going to do?"

Egert spit to get rid of a metallic taste in his mouth. Glorious Heaven, why did it go so wrong?

"Dinar!" Toria gazed pleadingly into the young man's face.

The courtyard emptied slowly; as he was leaving, the tall gray-haired boarder cast a glance in the direction of Egert, a glance that was intent yet incomprehensible.


The student was buried quickly, but with all the proper decorum, at the city's expense. The city was flush with gossip for a week. Toria addressed a complaint to the mayor. He received her, but only so that he could express his condolences and lift his hands in dismay: the duel proceeded according to all the proper rules, and although it is extremely unfortunate that the youth died, did not he himself challenge Lord Soll? Alas, my dear lady, this unfortunate incident can in no way be called a murder. Lord Soll is not under arrest. He fought on the field of honor, and he too might have been killed. And if the deceased gentleman student did not carry weapons and did not know how to wield them, well then, this misfortune falls to the student and is in no way the fault of Lieutenant Soll. . . .

Four days had passed from the day of the duel, three from the day of the burial. In the gray early morning, Toria abandoned the city.

The week of her stay in Kavarren lay on her face in black, funereal shadows. The student's bundle dragged on her arm as she plodded out to the carriage waiting by the entrance; her eyes, extinguished, ringed with dark shadows, watched the ground as she walked, which is why she did not immediately recognize the man who courteously lowered the running board of the coach.

Someone's hand helped her cast the bundle onto the seat. Mechanically offering thanks, Toria raised her eyes and came face-to-face with Egert Soll.

Egert had been watching over the fiancée of the student he killed, though he himself did not know why. It is possible that he wanted to apologize and to express his sympathy, but it is more likely that he entertained certain vague hopes in regards to Toria. As a worshipper of risk and danger, he was accustomed to taking a relaxed approach to death, his own and others'. Should not the victor have a right to count on an allotment of the relinquished inheritance of his vanquished foe? What could be more natural?

Then Toria met Egert's gaze.

He was prepared for a display of wrath, despair, or hatred, and he had fortified himself with words appropriate to the situation. He even intended to accept a slap in the face from her hand, but what he saw in Toria's splendid yet heartbroken eyes repelled him backwards like a blow from a steel-clad fist.

The girl looked at Egert with bleak disgust completely lacking in malice, as one might look at vermin. There was no hatred in her, but it seemed as though she might vomit at any moment.

Egert did not remember the route he took as he walked—or did he run?—away, his eyes downcast so that he might never again see or meet or remember such a gaze.


The next day, he was sitting in the Faithful Shield, gloomy, despondent, and full of malice. Karver was hovering next to him, happily chatting away about boars and women: the seasonal boar fights were not far off. Would his father enter Handsome, Butcher, or the young Battle? Incidentally, the lovely Dilia, wife of the captain, had asked about Egert, and it would be quite dangerous to neglect her; she would get her revenge. And why on earth should Egert, who was the center of attention in the city this week, spoil the bright days of such a remarkable life with despondency?

Egert instinctively noticed a certain pleasant agitation in the voice of his friend. It seemed that in the depths of his soul, Karver rejoiced in the knowledge that, although he was victorious in the field of battle, Egert had come in second in the field of love and was therefore equal to other mortals. It is possible that, in judging him this way, Egert wrongly accused Karver in his mind, but that was neither here nor there: the chatter of his friend wearied Egert. With the nail of his index finger, he carved out a furrow in the blackened tabletop. Yes, he agreed with everything Karver had to say, but for Heaven's sake, let him shut up for a minute and give his lieutenant the opportunity to finish his mug in peace!

Just then the door opened, thrusting a waft of cool air and a ray of light into the stuffy tavern. The newcomer stood on the threshold and, after looking around to be sure he had the right place, he entered.

Egert recognized him. He was that strange gray-haired man who had been staying at the Noble Sword for the last ten days. Walking past the guards, he pulled out the chair at a vacant table nearby and heavily lowered himself into the seat.

Not knowing exactly why, Egert watched him out of the corner of his eye in the feeble light of the crowded tavern. It was the first time he managed to get a close look at the stranger's face.

The age of the grizzled boarder was impossible to determine: he could have been anywhere from forty to ninety years old. Two deep, vertical lines intersected his cheeks and lost themselves in the corners of his chapped lips. His long, thin, yellow nose flared continually, as if it were about to fly away. His eyes, clear and set far apart, seemed completely unconcerned with the world around him. Examining him, Egert saw his large, leathery eyelids, devoid of eyelashes, twitch slightly.

The innkeeper brought the stranger a mug of wine and was about to move off when the stranger unexpectedly stopped him.

"Just a minute, dearest. Don't you see, I've no one to drink with. I understand that you are busy, but all I require is a little company. I want to drink to the glorious guards, the destroyers of the defenseless."

The innkeeper flinched: he understood quite well to whom this toast was directed. Muttering apologies under his breath, the kindly soul scuttled off, and just in time, for Egert too had heard the words that were meant for him.

Unhurriedly placing his mug back on the table, he looked the stranger right in the eyes. As before, they were calm, even indifferent, as though someone else entirely had spoken that disastrous toast.

"And just whom are you drinking to, my dear sir? Whom do you name so?"

"You," the stranger said, undaunted. "I name you, Egert Soll. You are right to go pale."

"Pale?" Egert stood up. He was in his cups, but far from drunk. "What the—" The words strained through his teeth. "I am afraid that someone may come tomorrow wishing to call me the destroyer of feeble old men."

The stranger's face changed oddly. Egert suddenly understood that he was smiling.

"A man chooses who he will be, what his reputation will be. Why don't you slaughter, let's say, women with that sword of yours? Or ten-year-old children? It's possible they might have more success against you than your last victim did."

Egert was rendered speechless; at a loss, he turned toward Karver. But

Karver, who was usually so sharp of tongue, was now, for some reason, wrapped in silence. The customers of the tavern, the innkeeper, who had retreated to the kitchen doorway, and a small, snot-nosed scullion were all keeping their heads down as if they sensed that something extraordinary was about to happen.

"What do you want from me?" Egert forced out, looking into those large, limpid eyes with hatred. "Why are you trying to provoke me into drawing my sword?"

As before, the stranger stretched his long, dry mouth into a smile. His eyes remained cold. "I also have a sword. But I thought you preferred those who don't carry weapons, eh, Soll?"

With great difficulty, Egert forced himself to unclench his fingers, which were fastened to the hilt of his sword.

"Do you like easy victims?" The stranger asked soulfully. "Victims who exude terror? That sweet feeling of power, eh, Soll?"

"He's a madman," Karver said quietly, as if confused. "Egert, let's go, yeah?"

Egert drew a deep breath. The stranger's words affected him deeply, painfully, and far more strongly than he liked. "It is your good fortune," he uttered with difficulty, "that you could be my grandfather. And I don't fight with old men, is that clear?"

"It's clear." The stranger again raised his mug, and turning to Egert, to Karver, and to all those who were listening to their conversation with bated breath, he declared, "I drink to Lieutenant Soll, the embodiment of cowardice, hiding behind a mask of valor."

However, he did not manage to drink his toast, because Egert's sword, flying out of its scabbard, knocked the mug out of his hand. The silver cup bounced along the stone floor and then stopped in a dark red pool of spilled wine.

"Splendid." The stranger contentedly wiped his wet fingers on his napkin, and his enormous nostrils swelled. "Do you have enough courage to take the next step?"

Egert lowered his sword; its tip rasped along the stones, drawing a curvy line at the feet of the stranger.

"Good." The grizzled boarder of the Noble Sword was satisfied, although his gaze, as before, remained entirely indifferent. "Only, I will not fight in a tavern. Name the place and time."

"By the bridge beyond the city gates," Egert forced himself to squeeze the words out. "Tomorrow at dawn."

The stranger took out his purse, extracted a coin from it, and laid it on the table next to the wine-stained napkin. He nodded to the innkeeper and started for the door; Egert just had time to throw words at his back, "Who will be your seconds?"

The boarder of the Noble Sword stopped in the doorway. Over his shoulder he said, "I have no need of seconds. Bring someone for yourself."

Lowering his head under the lintel, the stranger left. The heavy door swung shut.

A good half of all the duels in Kavarren took place by the bridge beyond the city gates. The choice warranted itself: walking only a few steps from the road, duelists found themselves in an unpopulated place, concealed from the road by a wall of old spruces; furthermore, in the early morning dueling hour, the road and bridge were still so deserted that they seemed long since abandoned.

The combatants got to the bridge at almost the same time. Egert arrived a bit in advance of the grizzled stranger, and he stared into the dark water while he waited.

The cloudy spring river carried swollen shards of wood, clumps of river grass, and lifeless shreds of last fall's leaves in its current. Here and there small whirlpools eddied around stones, and Egert liked to peer into the very depths of their black funnels: they reminded him of the intoxicating sensation of danger. The railing of the bridge was completely rotten, but Egert leaned against it with his entire body as if tempting fate.

His adversary finally mounted the bridge, and it seemed to Egert that he was quite out of breath. At this moment, the stranger appeared truly old, much older than Egert's father, and Egert was stunned: Would there really be a duel? But meeting those eyes, cold and clear as ice, he immediately forgot that thought.

"Where is your friend?" asked the stranger.

Egert had been beyond stern when he forbade Karver to accompany him. If his opponent chose to defy the rules and forgo a second, why on earth should he, Egert, behave any differently?

"And if I should suddenly attack you with a dishonorable maneuver?" asked the grizzled man, not taking his eyes off Egert.

Egert sneered. He could have said that he had little fear of pushy old men and their dishonorable ways, that he had little use for empty chatter, and that he had conquered numerous opponents in his short life, but he saved his breath, contenting himself with this eloquent sneer.

Without uttering another word, the duelists left the road. Egert walked in front, carelessly exposing his back to his opponent, by which action he meant to shame the stranger, to demonstrate his complete dismissal of any villainy. They passed by the spruce grove and came out into a clearing, circular like an arena and tramped down by the boots of countless generations of Kavarren's duelists.

It was damp there from the river. Removing his uniform jacket with its firmly sewn epaulets, Egert regretfully thought that the spring this year had been extremely cold and long, and that the outing he had planned for the day after tomorrow would have to be deferred until the days became warmer. The dew weighed the grass down to the ground and rolled down the tree trunks in large drops. It seemed as though the trees were weeping for someone. Egert's well-made boots were also covered in drops of dew.

The adversaries stood opposite each other. Egert realized with amazement that for the first time in his entire dueling experience he was contending with a rival about whom, all else being even, nothing was known. However, this did not bother Egert at all: he was about to learn everything he needed to know.

They both drew their swords: Egert indolently, his opponent calmly and indifferently, like everything else he did. The stranger did not hurry to attack; he simply stood and looked Egert in the eyes. The tip of his sword also looked Egert in the eyes, intently, seriously, and just by the way the stranger stood in his pose, Egert understood that this time he would have need of all seventeen of his defenses.

Wishing to test his opponent, he embarked upon a trial attack, which was repelled leisurely. Egert tried another, and in similar fashion the stranger deliberately repulsed the rather cunning strike that consummated Egert's short, newly minted combination.

"Congratulations," muttered Egert, "you're not bad for your age." His next combination was artfully composed and brilliantly executed, but the grizzled stranger just as dispassionately fended off the entire series.

Not without pleasure, Egert realized that his opponent was worthy of his attention and that his victory would not be easy, but that would make it all the more honorable. In the depths of his soul he bitterly repented that there were no spectators around who could appreciate his brilliant improvisations, but at that very moment the stranger attacked.

Egert was barely able to turn the attack aside; all seventeen of his defenses were wiped out as he impotently switched from one to the next. Blows fell upon him one after the other, unexpected, insidious, unrelentingly intense, and as he furiously defended against them, Egert saw steel very close to his face more than once.

Then, just as suddenly, the attack stopped. The stranger retreated a step as if he wished to better examine Egert from head to toe.

Egert was breathing heavily, his wet hair was sticking to his temples, trickles of sweat were pouring down his back, and his sword arm was ringing like a copper bell.

"Not bad," he gasped, looking into those clear eyes. "Well, you never said you were—what are you, a fencing master gone into retirement?"

With these words he sprang forward and, had there been any witnesses to this battle, they would have confirmed without reservation that the swordsman Egert had never before produced anything like these magnificent combinations.

He hopped like a grasshopper, simultaneously attacking from the right and left, from above and below, planning out his moves twenty steps in advance; he was fast and technically flawless; he was at the peak of his form—and yet, he did not achieve a single success, however small.

It was as if all his blows came up against a stone wall. A bull calf might feel something similar the first time he contended with an oak tree. Not a single combination unwound to its finish; his opponent, as if he knew Egert's thoughts in advance, turned all his plans inside out, passing into counterattack, and Egert felt the stranger's blade touch his chest, his stomach, his face. Egert recognized, finally, the game of cat and mouse that he himself had played with the student; it was crystal clear that Egert could have been killed a good ten times, but for some reason he remained among the living.

"Interesting," he wheezed, retreating two steps. "I'd like to know to whom you sold your soul . . . for this . . ."

"Are you afraid?" asked the stranger. These were his first words since the beginning of the fight.

Egert studied this indifferent old man endowed with unprecedented strength; he studied his rugged, lined face and enormous, cold, lashless eyes.

The stranger was not even breathing hard: his breath, just like his voice and his gaze, remained even.

"Are you afraid?"

"No," Egert responded contemptuously, and as Glorious Heaven was his witness, it was the purest truth. Even in the face of inevitable death, Egert did not experience trepidation.

The stranger understood this; his lips elongated the way they had in the tavern. "Well . . ."

Ringing, their blades crossed. The stranger performed a subtle circular motion with his blade, and Egert shrieked in pain as his wrist bent backwards. His fingers opened of their own accord, and his hereditary sword flew through the steel gray sky in an arc, thudded into a pile of last year's leaves, and sank from sight.

Clutching his injured wrist, Egert retreated, not meeting his opponent's eyes. He was mortified that the feeble old man could have quickly disarmed him in the very first minute of the battle by this maneuver, and that the battle they had just had was nothing more than a farce, a game, like suicide chess.

The stranger looked at him calmly, without speaking.

"Are you just going to stand there?" asked Egert, outraged but not frightened. "What comes next?"

The stranger remained silent, and Egert realized that his own bravery and scorn of death were a weapon he could use to debase his conqueror.

"Well, go ahead and kill me," he laughed. "What else can you do to me? I'm not some abject student who trembles in the face of death. You want to see the truth of it? Strike me!"

Something changed in the stranger's face. He stepped forward, and Egert was shocked to realize that the other man really did want to strike him down.

Killing an unarmed man was, to Egert's eyes, the greatest possible infamy. He smirked as scornfully as he could. The vanquisher lifted his blade. Not turning his eyes away, Egert gazed intrepidly at the naked edge near his face.

"Well?"

The stranger struck.

Egert saw how the steel edge of the sword swept through the air like the shining blade of a fan. He awaited the blow and death, but instead he felt a sharp pain on his cheek.

Not understanding what had happened, he raised his hand to his face. Warm liquid flowed down his chin. The cuff of his shirt was immediately stained with blood. In passing, Egert gave thanks that he had taken off his coat and thus saved it from being ruined.

He raised his eyes toward the stranger, and saw his back. He was sheathing his sword in its scabbard as he walked leisurely away.

"Hey!" shouted Egert, scrambling to his feet like a fool. "Don't you have anything else to say, you long-toothed louse?"

But the grizzled boarder of the Noble Sword did not look back. And so he left, without turning around a single time.

Pressing a kerchief to his cheek, he picked up his family sword and tossed his coat over his shoulder. Egert was wholeheartedly grateful that he had come to the duel without Karver. A whipping was a whipping, even if the hoary stranger had been as skilled with a blade as Khars, Protector of Warriors. All the same, he was not Khars. The Protector of Warriors valued tradition; there was no way that he would have ended a duel in such a strange and absurd way.

Dragging himself to the shore of the river, Egert got on all fours and peered into the dark, perpetually rippling mirror of the water. A long, deep gash, reflected in the water, loomed on the cheek of Egert Soll. It ran from his cheekbone to his chin. At the sight of it, the reflection pursed its lips incredulously. A few warm, red drops fell and dissolved into the cold water.

# 2

When he returned to town, Egert really did not want to meet any of his acquaintances, which is probably exactly why he found Karver, who was extremely overwrought, at the first intersection.

"That graybeard returned to the inn as whole as a full moon. I was wondering . . . What's that on your face?"

"A cat scratched me," Egert spat through his teeth.

"Ah," drawled Karver ruefully. "I was thinking about going down to the bridge."

"What, to consign my cold, dead body to the ground?" Egert tried to stifle his irritation. The deep gash on his cheek had stopped bleeding, but it burned as if it were a red-hot rod resting against his face.

"Well," drawled Karver equivocally and in the same breath added, lowering his voice. "The old man; he left right away. He already had his horse saddled."

"What do I care? One less madman in town," Egert hissed.

"I told you that right away." Karver shook his head soberly. "A lunatic, you know? You could see it in his eyes. There was something completely deranged in those eyes, did you notice?"

It was obvious that Karver was not at all averse to discussing lunatics in general and the stranger in particular. Of course, he wanted to be privy to the details of the duel, and the next words out of his mouth would almost certainly have been an invitation to the tavern, but for the present, bitter disappointment awaited Karver. Without appeasing his curiosity even the slightest bit, Egert hurriedly, and somewhat dryly, said his good-byes.

The Soll family emblem that graced the iron-bound gates had been created to evoke pride in the family's friends and terror in their enemies. The belligerent animal that was depicted there did not have a name, but it was furnished with a forked tongue, steel jaws, and two swords held in razor-sharp talons.

Dragging his feet with difficulty, Egert walked up to the high entrance, where a servant stood ready to accept the cloak and sword of the young gentleman, but on that unhappy morning Egert had one but not the other; therefore, the young gentleman simply nodded in answer to the deep, deferential bow of the servant.

Egert's room, like nearly all the rooms in the Soll family manor, was decorated with tapestries that depicted various species of fighting boars. A few sentimental novels, interspersed with textbooks on hunting, languished on the small bookcase; Egert had never opened either the novels or the textbooks. A portrait hung on the wall between two narrow windows. The portrait was of Egert's mother when she was young and beautiful; she was holding a curly-haired blond child snuggled in her lap. The artist, who had painted the picture fifteen years ago at the behest of the elder Soll, was nothing more than a fawning toady: Egert's mother was excessively beautiful, with a beauty that was not her own, and the child was simply the embodiment of all that was good and wholesome. The eyes were too blue, the little cheeks were too sweetly chubby, and the little dimple on the chin was too cutely appealing. It seemed that at any moment this wondrous child might take flight and dissolve into the ether.

Egert approached the mirror that stood on the bureau next to his bed. His eyes were no longer blue; they were gray, like an overcast sky. Egert stretched his lips reluctantly: the dimple was gone as if it had never been, but the wound snaked across his cheek, long, stinging, and bloody.

At his summons the old first maid, who had long ago been entrusted with all the workings of the house, appeared. She groaned, chewed her lips, brought out a jar of ointment, and applied it to the wound. The pain subsided. With the help of another servant, Egert got his boots off, divested himself of his coat, and overcome, fell into his couch. He was exhausted.

It came time for dinner, but Egert did not descend to the dining room; instead, he informed his mother that he had already eaten at the tavern. Truthfully, he did want to go to the tavern; he already regretted the fact that he had not stayed and had a few drinks with Karver. He even stood up, planning to go out, but then he paused and sat down again.

Very soon his head started to spin. Then the blond boy in the portrait, that delightful boy with the clean cheeks, unstained by a sword, nodded his head and smiled meaningfully.

Evening was drawing close; the hour had arrived when the day was not yet dead but the night was not yet born. Beyond the window the sky faded. Shadows crept out of the corners, and the room transformed. Studying the muzzles of the boars on the tapestries, still visible in the twilight, Egert felt a faint, vague uneasiness.

He cautiously paid heed to this awkward, uncomfortable, tenacious feeling. It was as if there was an expectation, an expectation of something that had neither form nor name, something shadowy but inescapable. The boars bared their teeth at him; the fair-haired boy, snuggled in the lap of his mother, smiled; the edge of the valance over the bed quivered sluggishly; and Egert suddenly felt cold in his warm couch.

He stood up, trying to free himself from the unpleasant, uncertain anxiety. He wanted to call for someone, but then he thought better of the idea. He sat down again, agonizingly trying to identify the cause of his anxiety and to determine where the threat was coming from. He sprang up again to go into his drawing room and there, to his joy, was a servant bringing in lighted candles. An ancient, many-armed candelabrum was standing on the table, the room was brightly lit, the twilight had already given way to night, and Egert immediately forgot about the strange sensation that had swept over him at the juncture between day and night.

That night he slept without dreams.


Far from Kavarren, in a room filled with harsh incense, two people talked, their hands resting on a tabletop of polished wood. One set of hands was senile, with long nervous fingers, and the other young, white and strong, with a tattoo on the wrist:

"The mage refused, Your Lordship."

"I am disappointed, my brother. You failed to persuade him."

"This mage is a proud man. Money is not important to him—perhaps he is well-to-do. He does not need power, and he did not want to be introduced to our Secret. He did not believe us."

"You failed me, my brother."

"We tried . . . we did everything we could . . . but . . . but we failed, Your Lordship," the younger man replied, and his voice audibly cracked. "But we will find another way. We will manage without the mage."

The old man kept silent for a long while. The gray mane of his hair hid his face; clever, sharp eyes looked from under the white eyebrows.

"I rely on you, my brother," he said finally, and his thin fingers were bound into the locks of his hair. "We cannot be delayed any longer. The world gets older; people become impudent. Our brotherhood is losing influence."

"Fragile peace will be changed by a new one," the young man said confidently.

"Fragile peace will be changed by a new one," echoed the old man. "You have to hurry, Fagirra. The End of Time is on the threshold."

After leaving the room, the man with the tattoo walked along the rock terrace and stood for some time, inhaling the smoky air the city. Then he pulled the gray hood onto his head, nodded to the guards at the gate, and found his way to a bustling street via a dark lane. Two women with baskets, returning from the market, bowed stiffly to him and hurried to the other side of the street.

He walked, wrapped in his hooded robe with his face covered. When he stared at someone's back the person would shudder, look back, bow, or dive into the crowd. But people seemed to bow with less respect than before, and some people did not bow at all—they looked at him sullenly, and the young ones—some of them even glared at him with naked challenge. The lesson will have to be severe, he thought with a sigh. Cruelty will be necessary. He walked on.

He came to a small river shining in the sun under the humpbacked bridge in a deserted section of the city. A poor man, still as a statue, sat close by. His dry hand projected like a dead branch, vainly expecting alms.

The man in the hooded robe slowed his steps, almost completely hidden in the shade.

A passerby emerged at the opposite end of the lane. How could this village fellow have strayed there—perhaps he was lost, perhaps someone gave him bad directions? He looked every inch a young merchant from the suburbs who had sold off his goods and was so happy with life that he glanced kindly at the poor man.

"Take a coin, drink to my luck. . . ."

"Thank you," answered the poor man slowly.

Suddenly the beggar's hand gripped the wrist of the merchant with surprising force. A broad-shouldered, red-faced confederate emerged from an alleyway and caught the purse, which was snatched from the passerby's waist seconds earlier by the poor man. The merchant tried to shout, but the bulky fellow threw a rope around his neck.

Everything ended very rapidly. The body of the unlucky merchant, "relieved" of purse, tobacco pouch, and thin neckkerchief, was packed into a bag—not to be distinguished from hundreds of other bags, which were in abundance in the commercial streets. The bulky fellow and beggar, breathing heavily, finished their job when a shadow appeared on the road.

Both raised their eyes and started back in horror.

The gray-robed man smiled from under the hood. In his hand—with the tattoo on the wrist—coins tinkled.

"Tail, Nutty, be moderately greedy," said the man in a soft voice that made the killers tremble. "I require your assistance."


A week went by, and the city thankfully forgot about the tragic incident associated with the name of Egert Soll. Grass began to grow on the student's grave, it was announced that a new arena for the boar fights would be erected on the shore of the Kava river, and the captain of the guards, the husband of the beautiful Dilia, proclaimed that there would be a parade before the guards set out into the countryside for their upcoming drills, which were pompously termed military field maneuvers.

The maneuvers took place every year. They were implemented to remind the gentlemen of the guards that they were not simply a riotous assembly of carousers and duelists, but a military unit. Egert loved these drills because they naturally afforded him the chance to boast of his prowess, and he always looked forward to their approach.

This time he was not looking forward to them.

His wound had scabbed over; it almost did not hurt anymore. His manservant had caught the trick of shaving Egert with special care: hair on one's cheeks and chin was considered incompatible with aristocratic birth, so Egert did not consider, even for a moment, hiding his wound with a beard. Little by little, those around him became accustomed to his new appearance, and he himself often forgot to think about his wound, but with every passing day the strange anxiety, which had taken up residence in his soul, grew steadily, until it began to turn into a flurry of alarm.

During the day he felt tolerably well, but as soon as darkness settled in, the alarm unaccountably crept out of shadowy corners and chased him home, where at the command of the young master, his servant brought almost all the candles in the house into his rooms. However, even though Egert's rooms blazed with light like a ballroom, at times it still seemed to him that the boars, their eyes full of blood, might trot right out of the tapestries.

One evening he found a means of combating this strange affliction: He ordered his servant to turn down the bed before sunset. He lay down, and although he did not succeed in falling asleep right away, Egert stubbornly refused to open his clenched eyes. Finally, he slid into slumber and then into a dream.

Glorious Heaven, it would have been better to stand on guard the whole night.

In the desolate predawn hour a dream came to him. He had already had many dreams that night, simple, ordinary, more or less pleasant dreams: women, horses, acquaintances, cockroaches. Waking up, he forgot his dreams sooner than he realized he had dreamed; this time he awoke in the middle of the night, his sweaty nightshirt molded to his body, shaking like a puppy left out in the rain.

It was likely influenced by some long-forgotten tale about the incursion of the black plague that arose from the furthest reaches of his memory, one of those horrible tales of the elders, about which he had laughed when he was still an adolescent. In his dream he saw a strange creature in a blackened, shapeless garment mounting the terraced steps of his house, its face muffled with rags blackened with pitch. In the hands of this visitor there was a tool that resembled a pitchfork, with extremely long, inverted tines; it was like an enormous bird claw, clutched tight with spasms. The manor was empty. The visitor climbed to the drawing room, where the lid of the harpsichord was thrown up, the candles were burnt down to their stubs, and Egert's mother sat with her hands resting on the keys: yellow, desiccated, dead hands. The visitor lifted up his pitchfork, and Mother toppled to the side like a wooden figurine. The pitch-covered creature raked the dead body with his tool like a gardener rakes up last year's leaves.

Egert could not remain in the dark for a second longer: Don't remember that dream, forget, forget! He lit a candle; then, burning himself, he lit another. The portrait gathered shape out of the darkness: a blond boy in the lap of a woman. Egert froze for a second, peering into the face of his young mother, as if begging for protection like a child. A cricket sang somewhere nearby; the dead hours of night stood beyond the window. Egert clutched the candelabrum to his chest and stepped closer to the portrait, and in the twinkling of an eye, the face of the woman in the portrait twitched with a dreadful malice, turned blue, broke into a grin. . . .

With a scream he awoke for a second time, this time in truth. Beyond the windows was the same old night, deep, sultry, and clammy.

He lit the candles with trembling hands. Shuffling his bare feet, he drifted around the room from corner to corner, clutching his shivering shoulders with his hands. What if this were yet another dream? What if he was doomed until the end of his years to live in ghastly dreams and to awake only to exchange one nightmare for another? What would happen tomorrow? What dreams would tomorrow bring?

Dawn found him lying in his couch, doubled up, haggard, and trembling.

A few days later, it was his turn to do his duty on night patrol. He rejoiced; since that unforgettable dream, the very sight of his bed was disagreeable to him. It was far better to spend the night in the saddle with his weapons at hand than to struggle against the treacherous desire to leave the candles burning until morning!

There were five of them on guard: Egert who, as a lieutenant, was the leader of the patrol; Karver; Lagan; and two very young guards, about sixteen years old.

The patrol was a traditional part of the nighttime existence of Kavarren. Any shopkeeper would declare without pride that he slept more peacefully when he could hear the *clip-clop* of hooves and the voices of the sentries beneath his windows. There was rarely anything serious to attend to; there were just not enough nocturnal thieves, and those who did decide to thieve went about their work quietly and apprehensively: the gentlemen of the guards were very serious about their task.

Having received, as was usual, parting words from their captain, the guards set out. Egert and Karver rode in front, and behind them rode Lagan and the two younglings, Ol and Bonifor. Having taken a turn through the streets that surrounded the Town Hall, they made their way toward the city gates. One after another, the lights in the windows went out. The rasps of latching dead bolts and the clatters of shutters swinging shut could be heard from all around. The tavern by the gate was wide awake; the cavalcade hovered in front of the wide oak doors, trying to decide whether or not to stop in for a minute and visit the landlady who ruled over the lovely Ita and Feta. In the end, duty triumphed over temptation and the patrol was about to continue on its way when a drunk, lurching, stumbled out of the doors of the tavern.

In the darkness and in his intoxication, the reveler had neither family nor name: it was impossible to determine whether he was an aristocrat or a commoner. Jauntily whooping, Karver rode his horse toward the drunk. Cantering at nearly full tilt, he raised his steed onto its hind legs right in front of the stupefied drunkard, not touching the poor man, but letting the hot breath of his horse pour over him and thus terrifying him half to death. The guards laughed. Emitting a strange, distressed cry, the drunk sank down onto the pavement, but Karver was satisfied, and he returned to his companions, all the while peering over at Egert. Egert had once taught his friend that particular jest.

They moved on. The town lay in darkness. Only the torches in the hands of the patrol and the rare stars that shone weakly through the openings in the clouds illuminated the black façades of the sleeping houses. They rode silently. The pavement rang out under the hooves of their horses, and Egert, who found it unpleasant to watch the shadows that danced along the street, focused on the worn stones passing by under his horse.

The pavement below him suddenly seemed like a river undergoing the first thaw of the year: the cobblestones thronged without order; they cracked and jutted over one another, raising their jagged edges as if waiting for victims. Egert felt a chill, and he suddenly understood something he had never realized before; he understood and was astounded by his former blindness: the stones of the pavement were hostile, deadly, and dangerous, and a man who fell on them from a height, even if from the back of a horse, would most certainly be doomed.

The cavalcade continued on its way, and Egert's stallion clip-clopped his hooves along with all the others, but his rider could no longer see anything around him. Squeezing the reins with sweaty palms, Egert Soll, a natural-born horseman, nearly died from the fear of falling off his horse.

The crunch of a broken neck kept repeating in his ears. The stones of the pavement thrust upward lasciviously, as if anticipating the moment when the head of the brave lieutenant would burst like a ripe melon on their burnished edges. An avalanche of sweat rolled down Egert's back even though the night was brisk, almost cold. In the space of two blocks, he managed to die a thousand times until, finally, his horse began to sense that something was wrong, as if the perturbation of his rider had been transferred to him as well.

The cavalcade whirled around suddenly. The agitated stallion jerked, and this unexpected movement was enough to unseat the celebrated equestrian Egert.

Egert did not understand how it happened. He had long ago forgotten how to fall from a horse; the last time it had happened to him, he was only ten years old. He felt only a momentary horror; then the black sky with its smattering of stars flashed before his eyes and was followed by a painful but, to Egert's astonishment, nonfatal blow.

He was lying on his side. All he could see in front of him were his horse's hooves and the torch that had flown from his hand as he fell. It now sputtered in a puddle to his left. He heard astounded questions somewhere in the distance, which caused him to comprehend suddenly what had happened. Egert was thankful for the blessing of being able to pretend he had lost consciousness.

What could possibly cause a lieutenant of the guards, especially Egert Soll, to fall from a horse that was going no faster than a walk? Only death, thought Egert as he lay there, and he wished to die.

"Egert! Hey, help me, Lagan! It's like he's dead! What happened?"

He felt someone's hands grasp him by the shoulders and turn him over so he was facing upward, but he did not give any signs of life.

"The canteen, Bonifor, the canteen, quickly!"

A small stream of water spilled over his face. After waiting a bit longer, he groaned and opened his eyes.

In the light of the torches, he could see Karver, Lagan, Ol, and Bonifor bending over him; their faces were all surprised, and those of the younger guards were still frightened.

"He's alive," Ol noted with relief.

"How did this happen to him?" Lagan asked stolidly. "Egert, are you drunk, or what?"

"When we set off for the night, he was sober," Karver retorted. "Unless, while we were riding, he somehow managed to . . ."

"While on duty?" asked Lagan good-naturedly.

"Well, he doesn't smell of drink," growled Bonifor.

Egert was quite embarrassed to be lying on his back and serving as an object of general interest; besides, the pavement stones, which had waited for their chance, were sticking into his back. Fidgeting, he raised himself up onto his elbow, and at the same time a few hands immediately helped him stand up.

"What's wrong with you?" Karver asked finally.

Egert did not know what was wrong with him, but he had no plans to give the other guards a detailed account of what had happened.

"I don't remember," he lied, trying to make his voice sound as hoarse as possible. "I remember we were riding. Then everything went dark, obscure, and then I was lying on the ground."

The other guards exchanged looks.

"That's not good," said Lagan. "You should go see a doctor."

Egert did not answer. Suppressing a shiver, he reluctantly climbed back on his horse. The night patrol continued, but until the early morning hours, Egert kept catching inquisitive glances thrown at him by his comrades, as if they were waiting for him to fall from his horse again.


A few days later, the regiment went out on maneuvers.

Their send-off was accompanied by all sorts of pomp: as was customary, the maneuvers were preceded by a parade. Almost the entire population of Kavarren gathered on the embankments; moreover, the heads of the esteemed families appeared with miniature banners of their Houses, and their drawn swords, held up like the batons of bandleaders, served as banner poles. The mayor was robed in a mantle embroidered with heraldic animals. Boys whose names had been entered into the roster of the regiment but who had not yet reached manhood were formed into a column and marched back and forth several times. A fifteen-year-old youth marched at the head of the column while a three-year-old lad in a little uniform with a wooden knife stuck in his belt brought up the hind end. The difference in the length of the strides of these future guards was obvious; the tiny lad was panting heavily, and he foundered a number of times, getting tangled in his baldric. However, he never cried; he was well aware of the honor he had been favored with today.

Finally, the heroes of the day appeared. Led by their captain, the guards solemnly trotted along the street, each on his own sleek, well-groomed horse, and in the right hand of each was his sword, held up in salutation. Bold girls from the crowd jumped out toward the nearest horses, throwing crowns of violets onto the blades of the guards: each of these wreaths signified a girl's tender, friendly feeling for a guard. The majority of these wreaths fell to the captain, as was proper, but Egert, who was looking pale and not very healthy this morning, also received many. Throwing flowers and flinging up their hats, the crowd spun around them; they accompanied the guards as if the regiment were going to war, even though each knew that after three days it would quietly return, whole and unharmed, to the town.

The citizens remained to celebrate, but the guards passed through the city gates and set out on the high road toward the place where a military encampment had been prepared the week before.

Spring was finally displaying its true glory. Egert sat in his saddle with his back hunched, not at all heartened by the delightful, sunny landscape that stretched out to the right and left of the road. He had spent the night before without sleep; well before midnight, he had been visited by the usual nightmare. Replacing candles in the candelabra as they burned down, he had waited for dawn. The parade did not lift his spirits as expected, but instead brought a new shock: Egert discovered that the very sight of a drawn sword was exceedingly objectionable to him. Glorious Heaven! The sight of a naked blade, which always caresses the hearts of swordsmen and duelists alike, no longer called up sweet thoughts of glory and victory. Gazing at the tapered steel, Egert was stunned; he now thought only of lacerated skin, of exposed bone, of blood, and of pain, after which death would close in.

His comrades-in-arms looked askance at him; the official story was that he was grievously in love. His comrades discussed the possible objects of this unfortunate passion, and most of the more astute assumed that the cold and splendid Toria, fiancée of the slain student, had captured the heart of the lieutenant. Only Karver took no part at all in these discussions; he merely observed silently from a distance.

Turning away from the road, they galloped to the edge of a deep gully; clods of earth showered down into the chasm from under the hooves of the horses. The captain hollered out a command. Egert flinched, catching sight of a log, polished so there was not a single knot, that extended from one edge of the ravine to the other.

Once, on a dare, Egert had danced in the very middle of this beam, directly over the deepest part of the ravine. Every time Egert's feet had trod on the smooth, slippery surface, his soul had been transfixed by an all-encompassing rapture at the proximity of danger and an awareness of his own courage. Not satisfied with this risk alone, he compelled others to risk themselves; using his power as a lieutenant and the magical impact of the word *coward*, he arranged a fight on the log. Someone had slipped, fallen to the bottom of the ravine, and broken his leg. Egert did not remember the name of that poor bastard, but from that time on, the man did not walk very well and had to be forced from the regiment.

Egert recalled all this in the second it took for the guards to dismount next to the log at the command of the captain.

They formed a line. The captain put the youngest, most inexperienced guards to the side, and Lieutenant Dron, who had been declared the instructor of the youths, proceeded to explain to them the essence of the test with an air of importance. Meanwhile the captain, not wishing to lose a single minute, commanded the others to begin.

The requirement was simple: Cross to the far side and wait there for the others. The young sword-bearers, who had been brought on maneuvers expressly for such small services, were to lead the horses back to the camp. Egert numbly handed his reins to an adolescent who was gazing up at him in adoration.

In strict order, one after the other, the guards overcame the obstacle, some with bravado, some with badly concealed nervousness, some running, some with anxious, mincing steps. Egert brought up the rear of the column, watching as the boots of his comrades intrepidly trampled the smooth trunk of the log. He tried with all his might to figure out where this clammy feeling in his chest and this painful weakness in his knees came from.

Having never before experienced real terror in the face of danger, Egert did not immediately understand that he was simply afraid, so intensely afraid that his legs became weak and his stomach cramped painfully.

The line of guards on the near side of the ravine slowly diminished. The youths who had passed though the ordeal for the first time thronged joyfully on the opposite side, yelling encouragement to those who were treading on the beam. Egert's turn got closer. The squires, who had long since fulfilled their duty of stabling the horses, had returned; they now waited for the rare opportunity of seeing a new feat of Lieutenant Soll.

Karver, who was last in line before Egert, stepped out onto the log. At first he walked carelessly, even flippantly, but somewhere near the middle, he missed a step and, nervously throwing his arms out to the side, finished his passage. The former Egert Soll would not have let this opportunity to whistle condescendingly at his friend's back pass, but this Egert, who was now expected to step out onto the log, could only take a deep breath.

All the guards were drawn up on the opposite bank, and all, to a man, were watching Egert inquisitively.

He forced himself to step forward. Dear Heaven, why are my knees shaking so!

His boot was planted unsteadily on the very edge of the beam. It was impossible to cross over to the opposite side. The beam was smooth; his legs would certainly slip off it; in the best-case scenario, Egert would falter, but in the worst case . . .

They were all waiting. The beginning of Egert's stunt was already quite unusual.

Licking his dry lips, he took a step and staggered, waving his hands in the air. On the far side, they laughed, assuming that he was adroitly feigning clumsiness.

He took yet another half step and caught a clear glimpse of the floor of the ravine and of the sharp rocks at its bottom, and of his own mutilated body, dashed upon the rocks.

And then, raising melancholy eyes to the path laid out before him over the abyss, he made a decision.

He decided, and he jumped backwards quickly, grasping at his chest with a few theatrical gestures. He jerked as if he were having a convulsion, staggering and deftly jumping down off the log; then he fell to the ground as though dead.

Twitching in a heap of last year's leaves, Egert feverishly tried to remember the symptoms of the horrible illnesses about which he had once heard: falling sickness, seizures. It would be good if he could froth at the mouth, but his mouth was as dry as an abandoned well. He was just going to have to make up for the lack of symptoms with inconceivably violent convulsions of his body.

The astonishment and laughter on the other side of the ravine changed into cries of horror; the first to reach him was that adolescent to whom Egert had entrusted his stallion. Glorious Heaven! Egert's ears burned from shame and mortification, but there was no choice, so he flopped like a fish out of water; he wheezed and gasped while the captain, Karver, and Dron surrounded him on all sides. For about ten minutes, they tried to bring him to his senses, but it was all in vain; clenching his teeth and rolling his eyes back into his skull, Egert assiduously portrayed a dying man, except that a man who was really dying in this situation would have gone cold and turned blue, whereas Egert was hot and red from the unparalleled, fiery shame.

Alarmed by the unexpected illness of Lieutenant Soll, the captain sent him back to town straightaway. He would have accompanied him, but Egert managed to refuse. The captain thought to himself that even in this grave illness, Egert displayed an uncommon bravery.

Egert's father worked himself up into a lather no less intense than the captain's. No sooner had Egert pulled off his boots and collapsed into his couch than a knock, polite yet adamant, came at his door. The elder Soll and a short, hollow-seeming man in a smock that extended down to his ankles, a doctor, appeared on the threshold.

Egert had no other option but to force out a report of his indisposition and to hand himself over for examination.

The doctor tapped him thoroughly with a hammer; he probed, listened, and nearly sniffed Egert all over, and then he peered inquisitively into Egert's eyes for a long moment, extending his lower eyelid for this purpose. Still gritting his teeth, Egert gave answers to extremely detailed questions, a few of which forced him to blush: No, not ill. No. No. Clear. Every morning. Wounds? Perhaps a few trifling scratches. The gash on your cheek? An unfortunate incident; nothing to worry about.

The elder Soll was nervous; he rubbed his hands together so torturously that they threatened to be chafed until they bled. Wishing to peer down Egert's throat, the physician nearly ripped out his tongue. Then he dried his hands on a snow-white handkerchief, and letting out a sigh, recommended the usual remedy of doctors who have come up against a brick wall: bloodletting.

Soon a large copper basin was delivered to the room. The leech opened a black valise and set out scalpels and lancets, gleaming like a fine spring day, on the clean tablecloth. Small round jars clanked in the little bag, and the old first maid dragged out fresh linen.

All these preparations drove Egert into a desolate, black anxiety; he began to think that it might be better if he returned to the maneuvers. His father, heartened that there was some way to help his stricken son, solicitously assisted him in taking off his shirt.

The preparations were finished. However, when Egert saw the businesslike blade in the inexorable healer's hand, it became very clear that bloodletting would not do.

"Oh, my son!" muttered his father perplexedly. "Glorious Heaven, you really are very ill."

Cowering in the corner with a heavy candlestick held in front of him, Egert breathed heavily. "I don't want it! Leave me in peace."

The old first maid pensively chewed her lips. A pale, middle-aged woman stood at the threshold of the room. It was Egert's mother.

Looking around at those present and then taking another appraising glance at Egert, who was naked to his waist, his round muscles protruding prominently, straining against his fair skin, the doctor dolefully shrugged his shoulders. "Alas, gentlemen."

The instruments were returned to the valise. The bewildered elder Soll vainly tried to extract an explanation from the physician about the meaning of his *alas*. Did it mean that Egert's illness was already too far advanced?

Having gathered his things, the doctor glanced at Egert once more, shook his head, and announced, appealing more to the boars on the tapestries than to the Soll family, "The young man, humph, he is extremely healthy. Yes, masters. But if something is troubling the young man, it is not a medical problem, kind masters. Not medical."


Glorious Heaven! Stalwart Khars, Protector of Warriors, how could you allow this?

Lieutenant Egert Soll was mortally wounded; his stricken sense of self whimpered plaintively. The most extraordinary and distasteful thing was that Egert's pride had been wounded not from without, but from within.

He stood in front of the mirror for a solid hour, performing his own medical inquest. The same old familiar Egert looked out at him from the depths of the mirror: gray blue eyes, blond hair, and now the scratch that had taken up residence on his cheek. Prodding the wound with his finger, Egert decided that it would scar. Henceforth, Egert Soll would display a distinctive mark. Well, a scar on a man's face is more a mark of prowess than a defect.

He breathed on the mirror and traced an oblique cross in the circle of mist created by his breath. It was too soon to lose heart; if all the events of recent days were simply caused by an illness, then he knew a surefire way to cure it.

Changing his linen shirt for a silk one and ignoring the pleas of his distraught father, Egert left the house.

All the guards knew that the wife of the captain, the beauty Dilia, graced Lieutenant Soll with her favors. It was a wonder that so far the captain himself knew nothing about it.

His visits to Dilia conferred a twofold pleasure to Egert: delighting in the ardent embraces of the captain's wife, he also relished the risk and the awareness he had of his own audacity. He especially enjoyed kissing Dilia when he could hear the steps of the captain on the stairs, coming ever closer, closer. Egert understood very well what would happen should the captain, a decent yet jealous man, find his lieutenant in Dilia's lace-covered bed. The steel nerves of the beauty never succumbed when her perpetually absent, suspicious husband knocked on the door to her bedroom. Egert would laugh and, still laughing, escape out the window, grabbing his clothes from the hook by the fireplace as he went. And never, not even a single time, did that infernal rogue Egert drop so much as a button or a clasp, and not a single sound did he make as he slipped over the windowsill. Silent, Dilia would simultaneously hear a rustle under the window and the heavy steps of her husband as he came to her bed. And strangely, this vigilant husband never caught the scent of another man in his conjugal bed.

His visits to Dilia always encouraged Egert, and so he went to her now, expecting to cure his strange affliction by resting his head on her breast.

The evening was setting in; twilight, as before, discomforted Egert, but the thought of his imminent bliss helped him to overcome his fears. The chambermaid, as usual, was bribed. Dilia, her beauty hidden only by a lacy dressing gown, met Egert with wide-open eyes.

"Heavens, what about the maneuvers?"

However, her astonishment almost immediately gave way to a smile that was both gracious and covetous. The beauty was flattered. Only a true cavalier would secretly slip out of a military camp for the sake of a rendezvous with his beloved!

The chambermaid brought in wine on a tray and fruit in a little bowl decorated with peacock feathers, the emblem of passionate love. Dilia, pleased, spread herself out on the bed like a well-fed cat.

"Oh, Egert. And here I was, ready to think the worst of you!" She smiled delicately. "Your duels mean more to you than your love. I'm quite jealous of your duels, Egert!" The captain's wife tossed her head so that her dark curls would spread out over the pillow as alluringly as possible. "Just because you killed some student, is that really a reason to neglect your Dilia for so long?"

Trying not to look into the shadowy corners of the bedroom, Egert muttered a sugary compliment. Dilia purred and continued, threading her voice with velvet undertones. "But now, your conduct gives me the chance to forgive you. I know what these maneuvers mean to a guard. You have sacrificed your beloved games and you should be rewarded." Dilia leaned forward, her lips half-open, and Egert caught the heady scent of roses wafting from her skin. "You should be properly rewarded."

He took a deep breath; tender little fingers were already struggling with the buttons of his uniform.

"Let my husband sleep in a bunk and be food for mosquitoes, yes, Egert? We have the entire night and tomorrow and the day after tomorrow. Isn't that right, Egert? That scar, it suits you so well. This will be our best time ever."

She helped him undress or, more accurately, he helped her to undress him. Vanishing into the bed, he felt how her body, smooth as silk, burned like fire. Sliding his palms down her taut sides, Egert shivered: he had stumbled upon something iron, warmed by the beauty's hot blood.

Dilia burst out into sonorous laughter. "It's a chastity belt! A little gift from your captain, Egert!"

Before he really had time to understand her words, she shifted and fished a small, steel key out from under a pillow.

For a few minutes, Egert was able to forget about his worries. Chuckling, he listened to the tale of how this enchanted key had been born, fully formed, from a bar of soap. Before his excursion, the captain had decided to take a bath. Dilia, with touching concern, had asked if she could help him. When the cuckold had finally succumbed to the lapping of the warm water and the tender caresses of her soft palms, she slyly plucked the key from the chain that was hanging around the captain's neck and pressed it into a bar of soap. The captain set off for the maneuvers, clean and satisfied that all would be well at home while he was gone.

The chastity belt fell to the floor with a thud like a small, iron fetus.

There was a breathless silence in the house. The servants had apparently left for the night, and the chambermaid had gone to bed. Caressing the wife of his captain, Egert could not chase away the thought that it took less than two hours to travel from the guards' field camp to town.

"Egert," whispered the beauty passionately, and a voluptuous smile revealed her gleaming teeth. "It's been so long, Egert. Embrace me."

Egert obediently embraced her, and a poignant wave of passion surged through him. The beauty groaned: Egert's kiss seemed to reach right down through her. Moving against each other smoothly and rhythmically, they were both about to ascend on the wings of bliss when Egert's sensitive ear caught the sound of a rustle beyond the door.

Thus does white-hot steel suffer when it is tossed into icy water. Egert froze, his skin immediately covered in large beads of sweat.

The captain's wife, having moaned a few more times in solitude, opened her eyes in astonishment. "Egert?"

He swallowed sticky, viscous spittle. The rustle repeated itself.

"It's just mice." Dilia breathed a sigh of relief. "What's wrong, my love?"

Egert did not know what was wrong with him. The image of the captain, hunkering down in front of the door and peering through the keyhole, arose before his eyes. "I'll take a look," gasped Egert. He grabbed a candlestick and hastened to the door.

A small gray mouse skipped backwards but, being somewhat more daring than Lieutenant Soll, did not immediately dash into its hole. Instead it stopped just at the threshold, its inquisitive black eyes glittering up at Egert.

Egert wanted to kill it.

Dilia waited for him with an indulgent grin on her face. "Oh, these guards! Why this whimsy, Egert? Why are you teasing me? Come to me, my lieutenant."

And again she wrapped her arms around him, but Egert, expertly caressing this swooning, feminine body, remained cold and unresponsive.

Then, bringing her lips right up to his ear, Dilia began to whisper tenderly, "We're alone, alone in this house. Your captain is now far away, Egert. You don't hear his steps on the stairs. He's there in the camp, in his tent, guarding his flock. He's a stalwart captain; he checks on the sentries every hour. Hold me, my valiant Egert: we have the whole night ahead of us."

Lulled by her whispers, he finally stopped listening so attentively, and his young passion again took the upper hand. His body found its former strength and tension. It burned. It came back to life. Dilia purred and bit down on his shoulder; Egert sank into her with uncontrollable greed. The sweetest moment was near when the front door banged open; the sounds of furtive footsteps could be heard from below.

The world went dark in front of Egert's eyes; all his blood, set on fire by passion, rushed away from his face, which gleamed milky white in the half-darkness. Cold sweat dropped onto the delicate skin of the beauty under him. Shivering as if from fever, Egert slithered off her and crawled to the side of the bed.

Subdued voices chattered below. Dishes clinked in the kitchen. It was amazing how sharp Egert's hearing was at that moment! Again footsteps, a hushed curse, a hiss calling for silence . . .

"It's the servants returning," Dilia explained languorously. "Really, Egert, this isn't the way to behave toward a woman in love."

Sitting on the edge of the bed, Egert wrapped his naked arms around his chest. Heaven, why was he such a disgrace! He wanted to flee without looking back, but the thought of running and thereby leaving Dilia at a loss caused his jaw to clench.

"What's wrong with you, my dear friend?" the captain's wife asked quietly from behind his back.

He wanted to lash out at himself, beat away this horror, but instead he unclenched his teeth, scarcely feeling the pain in his jaw.

"Egert"—bitter pique slithered into Dilia's voice—"don't you love me anymore?"

I'm sick, Egert wanted to say, but then he thought better of it and kept quiet. Heaven, that would be an idiotic thing to do!

"I love you," he said hoarsely.

The servants below finally settled down, and the house was once again steeped in silence.

"Did I take off my chastity belt for nothing?" Dilia's words, venomous as a poisoned dart, stabbed Egert's naked back.

And again, he conquered himself. Cold and clammy, he crawled back under the blanket: Dilia might as well have been lying next to a frog or a newt. The beauty, insulted, pulled back, but Egert drew her to himself with wooden arms.

Miraculously, his body was still strong and voracious. Having twice survived a shock, it still again desired love, like a bonfire, mercilessly doused with water, can still restore itself from a single spark.

Dilia revived as well, meeting him halfway; within a few minutes, the room resounded with lustful growls. Egert was intent on his goal, no longer thinking of pleasure: the sooner he could get this business over with and reclaim whatever small shreds of his former reputation that were left, the better. Only a few seconds remained until the desired end. The entire house was sunk in silence, the town was sleeping, tranquillity covered the entire midnight world, and it seemed there was nothing that could keep Egert from finishing what he had started, when once again the image of the captain, rushing into the room accompanied by Dron and the guards, reared up in his imagination. The picture was so clear and vivid that Egert even saw the streaks of red in their bloodshot eyes, and he could practically feel a rough, gnarled hand seizing the edge of the blanket. Egert winced, imagining the kick that would come next.

He went limp, like a disemboweled carcass. It was all in vain; any further effort on his part was fruitless, and further repetitions of the scene would only be despicable and ludicrous. Egert Soll, the premier lover in town, was doomed to failure.

Dilia began to laugh mockingly.

Egert sprang up, scooped his clothes up into his arms, and dashed to the window. Along the way, he lost half his wardrobe, knocked the tray with wine and fruit onto the floor, and overturned a table. Flying up onto the windowsill, his heart failed him at the sight of the height of the second story, but it was already too late; he could no longer stop himself. Flying through the window with a burst of speed, the magnificent Egert Soll tumbled into a flower bed like a stone, destroying the rhododendrons and earning the eternal damnation of the gardener. Dressing as he fled, getting tangled in a heap of sleeves and trousers, weeping from shame and pain, Egert rushed toward his home, and it was lucky that there were still a few hours left until dawn and no one saw the renowned lieutenant in such a pitiful state.

When they returned to the city, the first thing the guards did was inquire after the health of Lieutenant Soll. With a bitter smile, a pale, haggard Egert assured the messengers who arrived at his house that he was on the mend.

Gossip about his failure with Dilia became the property of wicked tongues the very next day; it was passed on with relish and satisfaction, but in their heart of hearts no one really believed it. They thought it more likely that the infamous captain's wife was getting revenge for a lovers' quarrel.

Egert could only find comfort in solitude. He spent days on end either locked away in his room or roaming the deserted streets. It was during one of these rambles that a simple and horrifying thought occurred to him for the first time: What if what was happening to him was not a happenstance or a momentary indisposition? What if this neurosis dragged out even longer, for months, years, forever?

Egert temporarily freed himself from mustering and patrols, he diligently avoided the company of his comrades, it terrified him to think of visiting a woman, and his forgotten sword stood in the corner of his room like a disciplined child. The sighs of the elder Soll could be heard around the entire house. He understood as well as his son that Egert could not go on like this: he either had to get better or leave the regiment.

From time to time, Egert's mother would appear at the door to her son's room. Having stood there a few minutes, she would slowly make her way back to her own room. One time, however, encountering Egert in his sitting room, she did not remain silent as usual, but cautiously grasped the collar of his shirt.

"My son, what is wrong with you?" Raising herself up on her toes, she laid a hand on his forehead as if checking him for fever.

The last time she had asked him about anything was about five years ago. He had long ago gotten out of the habit of talking with his mother, and he had forgotten the touch of her tiny, dry fingers on his brow.

"Egert, what happened?"

At a loss, he could not squeeze out a single word.

From that time onward, he began to avoid his mother as well. His solitary outings became bleaker and bleaker until, one day, not even knowing how he got there, Egert stumbled upon the town cemetery.

He had not visited the cemetery since he was a child; fortunately for him, all his relatives and friends were still alive. Egert had never understood why people would want to visit this abode of the dead. Now, passing through the boundary hedge, a shudder coursed through him and he stopped. The cemetery seemed strange to him, frightening, as if it did not belong in this world.

The crippled caretaker peered out of his little hut and then disappeared.

Egert shivered. He wanted to leave, but instead he slowly made his way along the paths that wound among the memorials.

The graves of the richer folk were marked with marble while those of the poorer, with granite: small statues, hewn from stone, topped both kinds. Almost all of them depicted forlorn, weary birds perching on the gravestones, according to the tradition of Kavarren.

Egert walked on and on; he had long ago started to feel ill at ease, but he kept reading the partially effaced inscriptions on the headstones as though he were enchanted. It started to rain. The drops flowed along the stone beaks and drooping wings of the birds, and little rivulets ran through the lifeless claws that hooked into the headstones. The day had passed into a gray fog, and from out of that veil, limp marble eagles lurched toward Egert; tiny swallows with raised wings and cranes with lowered necks loomed and then passed. Entire families reposed in these vast enclosures. On one headstone, two nestling doves sat motionlessly. On another, a small, haggard wren bowed its head limply, and the inscription on the stone, inundated with water, compelled Egert to pause:

I shall take wing once more.

Water streamed over Egert's face. Exhausted, he decided to leave. As he approached the exit, a gray, moist vapor began to rise from the ground.

At the very edge of the cemetery, he stopped.

To the side of the path loomed a fresh grave without a monument, covered with a slick, granite slab. Letters bled through the puddles on the gray slab: DINAR DARRAN.

That was it. No other words, no symbols, no message. But perhaps this is an entirely different person, thought Egert anxiously. Maybe this is another Dinar.

Scarcely aware that his feet were moving, he drew nearer to the grave. Dinar Darran. A carriage by the entrance to the Noble Sword and a girl of strange, perfect beauty. A curved line drawn right in front of Egert's boots and the formless red splotches on her face: "Dinar!"

Egert flinched. Toria's voice rang so clearly in his ears, like the crash of shattered glass: "Dinar? Dinar? Dinar!"

A tired stone bird would never alight on this grave.

The caretaker once again leaned out of his hut, staring at Egert in alert astonishment.

Egert turned away from the grave and fled from the cemetery as fast as he could.

Far from Kavarren, in a dark and empty alley, a poor man sat still as a statue. The smell of rotten fish coming from the river was thick in the air.

Steps echoed down the lane, and a young fellow of about seventeen, fat-cheeked and plump as a roll, came into view. Clearly he was lost; it seemed that someone sent him in a wrong direction. After reaching the place where the poor man was seated, the fellow slowed down:

"Hmmm . . ."

He was confused . . . or was frightened; there, in the alley, it was quiet and desolate.

"Sir, could you tell me . . . where I can find the tavern called the One-Eyed Fly?"

The beggar stretched out his palm. The man hesitatingly took out a small coin, put it back, and took out a smaller one: "Here, send your blessings for my mother, she—"

The poor man suddenly caught the wrist of the young fellow in a viselike grip. A beefy fellow appeared behind the back of the unlucky passerby and wound a thick hemp cord tight on his pink neck. The man wheezed.

"Freeze! Guards!"

The young man who was more dead than alive struggled, and suddenly no one was holding him. The rope, which had been stuck around his throat, came loose, the darkness in front of his eyes cleared away, and the man found himself on all fours. Coughing, he removed the rope and realized he was alive, he had been saved.

Footsteps ran away down the alley. The man started to flee from this terrible place, and he almost bumped into a man wearing a gray hooded robe.

"Oh . . ." From the fire right into the flame; the man with fat cheeks startled back, without knowing where to go.

"Do not be afraid." The robed man removed the hood, revealing a bright, honest face. "I must have frightened them off. Robbers are afraid of Lash and those who serve him."

"Th-thanks," answered the young man, stepping back. Both his knees and elbows were shaking.

"There is nothing to worry about," the man spoke softly but persistently. "Let's get away from here. How did you find yourself in this dangerous alley? Let's go, let's go . . ."

The young man did not intend to go anywhere with the man in the hooded robe. Yet somehow he decided to follow him. His feet started to move and, step by step, they walked along uninhabited side streets. Soon they were seated on the rear porch of a small bakery at a secluded table.

"Well, sir, I am a student. No, sir, I only recently began studies at the university. My father works as a public notary, he is an educated man, it goes without saying, and he decided that I should also study science. I was a good student. . . . Actually, I still am."

The young man with fat cheeks was deceiving. His father was a modest clerk, and his sisters wore secondhand dresses one after another, because there was never enough money in their family. There was even less hope.

"Dean Luayan? Yes, he is a great mage, great scientist. . . . Yes, it goes without saying, we are close friends!"

The man in the robe shook his head sadly. The son of the clerk suddenly felt shriveled.

"I mean . . . I wanted to say . . . I attend the dean's lectures every week."

And I understand nothing, the young student thought.

The robed man put his white hands on the edge of the table—the tattoo on his wrist was visible—and he started to speak. Each of his words was as cold and sharp as an icy asterisk. Each word scolded his listener to the bones.

The fat-cheeked son of a clerk sat leaning on the tabletop. His blue eyes were rounded and resembled the peas on the dress of a fashion-model.

"The end is coming . . . very soon," the man in the gray robe said.

"Why?" said the student. "The End of Time . . . Indeed this has no . . ." He met the glance of his interlocutor and finished his sentence in a whisper: ". . . scientific explanation."

"No one in the world can understand all the sciences." The man in the hooded robe sounded as if he regretted it. "Even Dean Luayan . . . by the way, don't tell him anything about our conversation."

"But why not?"

The man in the gray robe glared angrily. Soon the table began to tremble, shaking the beer in their mugs. The confusion on the young man's face was replaced by panic.

"But you do not have to fear." The man with the tattoo raised the corners of his lips. "If you do everything as it needs to be done, Lash will protect you. Everybody who has faith in us will be saved."

"I will do everything which has to be done. What about others? Those the Order will not save?"

"The Order will save the ones who deserve it," the man in the hooded robe responded dryly. "The others will cry bitterly until they die."


Days passed by. From time to time, a messenger would come from the captain, always carrying the same question: How did Lieutenant Soll feel and was he able to take up his duties once more? The messenger would return, always carrying the same answer: The lieutenant was feeling better, but he could not yet resume his duties.

Karver also came to the house a few times. Each time he was forced to listen to the same excuse, delivered through a servant: The young gentleman, alas, was too weak and could not meet with his old friend.

Kavarren's guards gradually became accustomed to having their carousals without Egert; at first they were all excited by the tale of his fateful love, but the subject soon withered away of its own accord. The serving girl Feta, who worked in the tavern by the town gates, sighed secretly and wiped her little eyes, but she was soon comforted, for even without the glorious Egert Soll, there were enough splendid gentlemen with epaulets on their shoulders to go around.

Finally, the messenger from the captain asked his eternal question slightly differently: Would Lieutenant Soll ever resume his duties? After hesitating, Egert answered in the affirmative.

He was told to report to a unit that was engaged in mock battles the next day. These engagements, which were of necessity undertaken with blunt weapons, had always seemed ridiculous to Egert: How could one get a taste of danger while holding in one's hand blunt, toothless steel? Now, just the thought of having to stand face-to-face with an armed opponent was enough to cast Egert into a fit of trembling.

In the morning, after a sleepless night, he sent a servant to the regiment with a message that the illness of Lieutenant Soll had returned, worse than before. The courier was just about to leave the house, but he never managed to pass the threshold, because Egert's father, stern and full of indignation, ruthlessly intercepted his son's message.

"My son!" Veins bulged on the temples of the elder Soll as he stood, glowering like a storm cloud, at the entrance to Egert's room. "My son, the time has come for you to explain." He took a breath. "I always saw in my son, above all else, a man. What is the meaning of your strange illness? Are you intentionally abandoning your regiment, service in which is the duty of all young men of noble birth? If this is not the case, and I truly hope it is not, then how do you explain your reluctance to appear at training?"

Egert looked at his father, no longer so young or so healthy; he saw the tendons that were drawn tight across his wrinkled neck, the deep creases between the imperiously drawn brows and the indignantly glittering eyes. His father continued, "Glorious Heaven! I've been watching you the last few weeks. And if you were not my son, if I hadn't known you before, I swear to Khars, I'd think that the name of your affliction was cowardice!"

Egert jerked back, as though he had been slapped in the face. His entire existence cried out from grief and insult, but the word had been spoken, and deep in his heart Egert knew that what his father said was true.

"There has never been a coward in the Soll family," said his father in a constrained whisper. "You must take yourself in hand, otherwise . . ."

The eldest Soll wanted to say something far too terrible, so terrible that his lips trembled with ire and the vein on his temple throbbed even more vigorously: he wanted to offer the prospect of a paternal curse and expulsion from the family home. However, he decided not to issue this threat and instead repeated meaningfully, "There has never been a coward in the Soll family!"

"Leave him alone." The words came from behind the enormous back of the elder Soll.

Egert's mother, a pale woman with perpetually hunched shoulders, did not often take the liberty of interrupting the conversations of men.

"Leave him alone. Whatever may have happened to our son, for the first time in years—"

She stopped short. She wanted to say that for the first time in years, she did not sense in her son the harsh and predatory tendency that frightened her and transformed her own child into something foreign and offensive, but she too decided not to say this aloud and only looked at Egert longingly and sympathetically.

Egert grabbed his sword and left the house in haste.

That day, the mock swordfights went on without Lieutenant Soll because, after exiting the gates of his house, he did not make his way to the regiment. Instead, he wandered the empty streets in the direction of the city gates.

He stopped in front of the tavern; there is no telling what compelled him to turn toward the wide, well-known door.

At that early morning hour, the tavern was empty, but a bent back could be glimpsed among the far-off tables. Egert walked closer. Without unbending, the back crawled along the floor, sweeping and humming a tune without words or melody. When Egert pulled out a chair and sat down, the humming broke off, the back straightened, and the maidservant Feta, red and breathless from happiness, let a shaggy mop fall to the floor.

"Lord Egert!"

Forcing a smile, Egert ordered some wine.

Square spots of sunlight lay on the tables, the floor, and the carved backs of the chairs. A fly buzzed weakly, bumping its brow against the glass of a square window. Chewing on the edge of his mug, Egert stared dully at the carved patterns on the tabletop.

The word had been spoken, and now Egert repeated it to himself, wincing from pain. Cowardice. Glorious Heaven, he was a coward! His heart had already failed him innumerable times, and there were witnesses to his fear, the most important of whom was Lieutenant Soll, the former Lieutenant Soll, a hero and the embodiment of fearlessness!

He stopped chewing on his mug and started in on his fingernails. Cowards were disgusting and despicable. More than once, Egert had observed others being cowards; he had seen the outward signs of their fear: pallor, uncertainty, trembling knees. He now knew how his own cowardice looked. Fear was a monstrosity, worthless and insignificant when viewed from the outside, but when seen from within, it was an executioner, a tormentor of irresistible power.

Egert tossed his head. Was it possible that Karver, for example, experienced something similar when he got scared? Perhaps all people did?

For the tenth time, Feta appeared with a rag in hand, scrubbing away Lord Soll's table until it shone. Finally, he answered her shy, ingratiating glance.

"Don't fidget so, you little plover. Take a seat next to me."

She sat with such alacrity that the oak chair creaked. "What is my lord's pleasure?"

He recalled how the knives and daggers he had thrown at her had rooted themselves in the lintel above her head; he recalled it and was covered in cold horror.

Groaning compassionately, she immediately responded to his sudden pallor. "Lord Soll, you've been ill for so long!"

"Feta," he asked, lowering his eyes, "are you afraid of anything?"

She smiled happily, deciding that Lord Soll was, apparently, flirting with her. "I'm afraid that someday I might displease Lord Soll and then the land-lady would fire me."

"Indeed," breathed Egert patiently, "but are you afraid of anything else?"

Feta blinked at him, not understanding.

"Well, darkness, for example," prompted Egert. "Are you afraid of the dark?"

Feta's face darkened, as though she was remembering something. She mut-tered grudgingly, "Yes. But why do you ask, Lord Egert?"

"And heights?" It seemed he had not noticed her question.

"I'm afraid of heights too," she confessed quietly.

There was an oppressive pause that went on for some time; Feta stared at the table. Just when Egert became sure that he would not hear another word out of her, the girl shivered and whispered, "And, you know, especially thun-der, when it goes off without warning. Ita told me that in our village there was one little girl who was killed dead by thunder. . . ." Her breath faltered. She put her palms to her cheeks and added, blushing painfully, "But what I am most afraid of is . . . getting pregnant."

Egert was taken aback; frightened by her own candor, Feta began to babble, as if trying to smooth out the awkwardness with a flood of words.

"I'm afraid of bedbugs, cockroaches, tramps, mute beggars, landladies, and mice. But mice aren't all that terrifying: I can get over that fear."

"Get over it?" echoed Egert. "But how do you . . . What do you feel, when you are scared?"

She smiled tentatively. "Afraid, and everything. Inside, it's as if everything gets weak and all." She suddenly blushed hotly, and under the veneer of her inability to explain there remained one more important sign of fear.

"Feta," asked Egert quietly, "were you afraid when I threw knives at you?"

She shivered as if remembering the best day of her life. "Of course not! I know that Lord Egert has a steady hand."

The landlady snarled from the kitchen, and Feta, making her apologies, flitted away.

The square patches of sunlight slowly crawled from the table to the floor, then from the floor onto a chair. Egert sat, hunched over, and traced the edge of his empty mug with his finger.

Feta could not understand him. No one alive could understand him. The ordinary world in which he, by right, was sovereign and master, that warm, dependable world had been wrenched inside out; it now stared hard at Egert through the tips of swords, the jagged edges of stones, medicinal lancets. Shadows dwelled in this new world, and the nighttime visions that had already caused Egert so many sleepless nights in his blazing rooms. In this new world he was insignificant and piteous, as helpless as a fly with its wings ripped off. What would happen when others found out?

The heavy door crashed open. The gentlemen of the guards poured into the tavern, and Karver was among them.

Egert remained sitting where he was, though he did perk up involuntarily, as though he was about to flee. The guards surrounded him instantly. Egert's ears began to ring from all the boisterous greetings, and his shoulder ached painfully from all the hearty punches.

"Here we were, talking about you!" trumpeted Dron's voice over all the others. "As they say, 'You gossip about a wasp, and behold, the wasp takes wing.'"

"They said that you were on the verge of death," one of the younger guards reported merrily.

"Don't hold your breath!" laughed Lagan. "We'll all die sooner. But if you're sitting in a tavern, that must mean you're better."

"He is sitting in a tavern and avoiding his friends," mourned Karver bitterly, earning a few reproachful glances.

Egert met his friend's gaze reluctantly, and he was surprised at what he saw there. Karver was watching his masterful friend with a strange expression on his face; it was as though he had just asked a question and was patiently awaiting the answer.

Feta and Ita were already bustling around the new guests. Someone raised his glass to the renewed health of Lieutenant Soll. They drank, but Egert choked on the wine. From the corner of his eye, he could see that Karver had not stopped examining him with that inquisitive gaze.

"What are you, some kind of hermit crab, hiding away all quiet?" asked Lagan cheerfully. "A guard without good company withers and fades like a rose in a chamber pot."

The young Ol and Bonifor laughed far too loudly for the quality of the joke.

"I swear by my spurs, he must have been writing a novel in letters," proposed Dron. "Sometimes, I'd pass by on patrol and see that his rooms were lit until morning."

"Really?" marveled Karver, but the others just clicked their tongues.

"I'd like to know if there's some beauty to whom Egert devotes these vigils," drawled one of the guards in a faux romantic voice.

Egert sat in the middle of the joyful din, smiling sourly and uncertainly. Karver's intent gaze was discomforting him.

"Dilia sends her regards," Karver remarked carelessly. "She stopped by the tilting yard and, among other things, inquired why the fights were taking place without Egert."

"By the way, what should we tell the captain?" Dron asked suddenly.

Egert gritted his teeth. More than anything else, he wanted to disappear from this place, but to leave now would be an insult to the general merriment and the guards' benevolent attitude toward him.

"Wine!" he yelled out to the landlady.

In the course of the next two hours, Egert Soll made the most important discovery of his life: Alcohol, if drunk in sufficient quantities, can suppress both spiritual unrest and fear.

Toward dusk, the crowd of guards, fairly thinned out by this time, spilled out onto the streets and stumbled away from the Faithful Shield. Egert hollered and laughed no less than the others. From time to time he caught the alert glances of Karver from the corner of his eye, but the inebriated Egert no longer cared: he was enjoying the long-awaited awareness, however false, of his own strength, freedom, and daring.

All the townsfolk who came across this gloriously drunken company shrank back toward the curbs, not at all desirous of crossing paths with the gentlemen of the guards. On the embankment, a lamplighter was kindling the streetlights: the revelers nearly knocked his ladder out from under him. Egert roared with laughter. The streetlamps danced in front of his eyes; they circled in a waltz, bowing and curtseying. The thick air of late spring was full of smells, and Egert gathered them in with his nose and mouth, experiencing with every swallow the fragrance of the sun-warmed river, the freshness of grass, wet stone, pitch, someone's perfume, and even warm manure. Embracing Karver with his left arm and, one by one, all the other guards with his right, he unquestioningly accepted that his illness had left him, and that like any cured invalid, he had the right to an especially intense joy for life.

Opposite the entrance to the Faithful Shield, not far from the place where the student and his fiancée, Toria, had first alighted from their carriage, there was a puddle standing in a pothole. The puddle was as deep as regret and as greasy as a feast day broth. Neither the wind nor the sun had dried up this puddle; though it had shrunk slightly, it had preserved itself from the early spring until the very threshold of summer, and it could be expected that such unusual persistence would help it remain there until the fall.

The puddle caught the fading, evening sky on its black, oily surface. A drunken tailor wobbled on its edge.

That this man was indeed a tailor was clear from the very first glance: a well-thumbed measuring tape was draped around his slender neck in a loose knot, and he was wearing a large canvas apron smeared with chalk. His flaxen hair was mussed into two tufts that sprang up behind his ears. Too young to be a master, the apprentice tailor peered at the puddle and hiccuped quietly.

Karver laughed out loud. The others joined in his laughter, but with that the matter should have ended. The apprentice raised his cloudy eyes and said nothing, and the guards, passing to the side of the puddle, walked toward the doors of the tavern.

Of course, just as Egert was walking by the befuddled tailor, the apprentice lost his balance and took a sweeping step forward. His heavy wooden clog crashed down into the very middle of the puddle, raising a violent fountain of fetid muck, a large part of which landed on Lieutenant Egert Soll.

Egert was doused nearly from head to toe; the dirty grime splattered over his coat and his shirt, his neck and his face. Feeling large, cold globs of mud slither down his cheeks, Egert froze on the spot, unable to take his glassy gaze from the soused apprentice.

The guards surrounded the tailor in a dense ring; while they watched Egert warily, they regarded the lad with curiosity and interest. However, the journeyman was far drunker than Lieutenant Soll and thus far more daring: he was not at all afraid of the gentlemen of the guards, though it is possible that he simply did not notice them. With purely scientific interest, he examined his clog, which had disturbed the surface of the puddle and flung mud at Egert.

"Shove him in, the pig," Dron advised good-naturedly. Young Bonifor darted forward, anticipating the amusement this entertainment would bring.

"May I do it?"

"This is Egert's man," Karver commented dispassionately.

Lieutenant Soll grinned fiercely, took a step toward the tailor, and immediately sobered up. Reality descended upon him, grinding down the spring, freedom, and his newborn courage; Egert faltered from the sudden thought that he would once again exhibit his fear. And indeed, as soon as he thought about fear, a dreary weakness burrowed into his belly. All he had to do was simply extend his hand and seize the lad by the collar, but his hand was drenched in sweat and had no intention of complying.

Great Khars, help me!

Shaking all over from the effort, Egert reached out for the scruff of the apprentice. He grasped the collar of the tailor's jacket with his damp palm, but at that very second the boy roused himself, throwing off Egert's hand.

The guards were silent. Egert felt rivulets of cold sweat chasing one another down his back.

"What a pity," he forced out with great difficulty. "He's just an idiot, a drunk who accidentally . . ."

The guards exchanged glances. The apprentice, meanwhile, if not wishing to contradict Egert's words, then simply desiring to continue his scientific inquiry, deliberately raised his wooden clog over the puddle.

The guards sprang back in time; only Egert, who stood as if transfixed, was inundated with the next, even more plentiful helping of greasy mud. The tailor reeled, maintaining his balance with difficulty. Feasting his eyes on the result of his act, gratified, he smiled like a brewer's horse.

"He'll kill him," observed Dron in an undertone. "Damn!"

Egert's face, ears, and neck burned under the layer of black slurry. Strike! His reason, his experience, and all his common sense insisted on it. Beat him, teach him a lesson, let them pry you off his unresponsive body! What is wrong with you, Egert? This is past endurance, this is the end, the end of everything, kill him!

The guards were silent. The apprentice smiled drunkenly.

Egert fumbled at the hilt of his sword with a wooden hand. Not this! screamed his better judgment. How can you swing your sword at a defenseless man, at a commoner?

. . . at a defenseless man, at a defenseless man . . .

The apprentice raised his foot a third time, now looking Egert straight in the eyes. Apparently, he was so drunk that, regardless of the armed guards surrounding him, he was able to recognize only the pleasure he received from this distinct action: the journey of the muck from the puddle to the face and clothes of a certain gentleman.

The apprentice was still raising his foot a third time, but Lieutenant Dron could no longer contain himself. He darted forward with an inarticulate growl and smashed his fist into the tailor's chin. The astonished apprentice fell backwards without a single sound, and there he remained, stretched out on the ground, sniveling.

Egert took a deep breath. He stood, covered in mud from head to toe, and ten stunned pairs of eyes watched as the mess dripped from the gold braid of his coat.

Dron was the first to break the silence. "You might have killed him, Egert," Dron said, by way of excuse. "You're all wound up. He probably should be killed, but not here, not now. He's beyond drunk, the moron, but you were about to draw on him, a commoner! Egert, can you hear me?"

Egert stood, staring into the puddle just as the apprentice had when they first encountered him. Thank Heaven, Dron had decided that Egert was paralyzed by a fit of rage!

They were pawing at his wet sleeve.

"Egert, are you out of your mind? Dron is right, you shouldn't kill him. If you kill them all, there would be no craftsmen left, right? Let's go, Egert, eh?"

Ol and Bonifor were already waiting at the doors to the tavern, impatiently looking back at the others. Someone took Egert by the arm.

"Just a minute," muttered Karver.

They all looked at him in surprise.

"Just a minute," he repeated, louder this time. "Dron, and you, gentlemen—in your opinion, did Lieutenant Soll behave correctly?"

One of them snorted, "What is this nonsense, what are you doing, talking like this about your superior, asking if it was correct or incorrect? If he had acted, this dolt wouldn't be alive."

"It would have been improper, had he brutalized the lad," remarked Dron in a conciliatory manner. "That's enough, Karver, let it go."

Then something odd happened. Slipping between the guards, Karver suddenly appeared right in that same spot where the now prostrate tailor had stood before. Bending his knees slightly, Karver struck the puddle with his boot.

It became as quiet as a long-forgotten tomb. A convulsion passed through Egert's body as fresh grime adhered to his coat, slicking his scarred cheek with new drops and cementing his blond hair into icy tufts.

"But!" one of the guards said stupidly. "Uh, but what . . ."

"Egert," Karver asked quietly, "are you just going to stand there?"

His voice seemed at once very near and very far away: it was as if Egert's ears were stuffed with cotton.

"He is just going to stand there, gentlemen," Karver promised just as quietly, and once again he doused Egert with stinking slime.

Lagan and Dron grabbed Karver from either side. Without resisting, he allowed them to drag him away from the puddle.

"Don't take on so, gentlemen! Take a look at Egert. He's not trembling with rage. He's ill, after all, and what do you suppose the name of his illness might be?"

Egert could scarcely pry open his lips to force out a pitiful, "Shut up."

Karver was heartened. "Well, well. You're blind, gentlemen. I beg your pardon, but you are as blind as a bunch of moles."

Taking advantage of the fact that Lagan and Dron, perplexed, had released his arms, Karver rushed over and drenched Egert yet again, almost emptying the puddle.

The heads of the curious sprouted out of the windows and doors of the Faithful Shield like mushrooms sticking out of a basket.

"Oh, but he's drunk!" Bonifor cried out in a panic. "How can you? He's a guard!"

"Egert is no longer a guard!" snapped Karver. "His honor is as besmirched as his coat."

Egert then raised his eyes and met Karver's glare.

He was so impossibly observant, this friend and vassal of his. The long years of taking second place had taught him to watch and bide his time.

Now, having guessed, he hit the target squarely. He won, he was victorious, and in his severe eyes, fixed on Egert, Egert read the entire long history of their faithful friendship.

You were always braver than me, said Karver's eyes. You were always stronger and more fortunate, and how was I repaid for my faithfulness and patience? Remember, I tolerated the most caustic and wicked jests; I endured them by rights; I practically rejoiced in your mockery! Life is fickle; now I am braver than you, Egert, and it is only right that now you should . . .

"What? Are you out of your mind, Karver?" several voices cried out at once.

. . . It is only right that now you, Egert, should occupy that place to which your cowardice has committed you.

"This means a duel, Egert!" Dron enunciated the words hoarsely. "You must challenge him!"

Egert saw his friend blink. Somewhere in the depths of his consciousness, a stray thought flew past: What if he had miscalculated after all? What if Egert did challenge him? What if there was a duel?

"This means a duel. . . . A duel, Egert . . . Challenge . . ." Voices floated in the air around Egert's head. "Call him out. This hour or tomorrow, whatever you want. At dawn by the bridge . . . Duel . . . duel . . . duel . . ."

And then Egert experienced that symptom of fear about which Feta had been silent during their conversation: His fear increased at every mention of the word *duel*.

Karver saw this and understood. His eyes, fastened on Egert, flared with an awareness of his complete and utter safety.

Duel . . . Duel . . . Duel . . .

Somewhere deep in Egert's soul, the former Lieutenant Soll thrashed about, ranting with impotent rage, commanding him to draw his sword and trace a line in the dirt in front of Karver's legs, but fear had already mastered the onetime lieutenant; it had broken him, paralyzed him, and was now forcing him into the most shameful of all crimes for a man: the refusal to fight.

Egert took a step backwards. The gloomy sky spun over his head like an insane carousel. Someone gasped, someone gave a warning shout, and then Lieutenant Egert Soll turned around and ran away.

That very same evening, leaving his coat, which was caked in mud, at his ancestral home, and taking with him only a small traveling bag, Egert abandoned his hometown, persecuted by an intolerable terror and an even more oppressive shame.


Far from Kavarren, a merry party took place in the square of a large city.

In the middle of the square stood the statue of a man in a hooded robe, with his face half-hidden by a rocky hood. *Sacred Spirit Lash* was carved on the pedestal; until recently the people of this city approached the sculpture only to bow in respect or—especially in the old times—to place presents at the statue's feet.

But times change and, apparently, change swiftly. The world gets weaker; people become impudent. A half dozen young people, undoubtedly students, had managed to put a colorful female skirt on the statue, and now the most insolent of these puny adolescents had attached a jaunty frilled cap on the head of the Sacred Spirit. Even worse, a mustache was painted on the upper lip of the sculpture with a piece of coal. A man in a gray hooded robe stood in the shade, in a narrow passage between two walls, unnoticed. It was too late to prevent the disgrace, the blasphemy taking place; he could only observe it now.

People were frightened after seeing what the students had done. Respectable and quiet people hurried away from the square. A pious old woman threw a rotten turnip at the impudent youngsters, but she missed, and the turnip splattered on the statue's shoulder; the crowd began to laugh.

The man in the hooded robe looked around. More curiosity seekers were gathering, more merry faces appeared; a cute girl dressed as a servant looked out of a window, giggling in her fist. A prosperous-looking merchant was laughing and pointing. The apprentices stopped and observed this scene with interest. Things were bad, very bad; the servants of Lash were never liked. But to be openly laughed at? Several years ago it was impossible to imagine. Remaining unnoticed, he returned to the alley and waited for the guards in red-and-white uniforms marching toward him. He waved his hand urgently to attract the patrol.

The officer in charge obeyed unwillingly. He approached the man in the gray robe and met his eyes: "What is it?"

"Lash was insulted," said the robed man in a voice that would make even killers feel fear. "This is blasphemy! Witnesses should be considered to be accomplices."

Passersby stepped aside, making room for the patrol. The merry laughter and noise continued in the square, the pranksters and onlookers unaware of the oncoming soldiers. In but a moment, arrests would be made. All of a sudden, "Oink, oink!" was heard.

It came from one of the students sitting on a roof and giving signal to retreat. The young scoundrels rushed in different directions and were lost in the darkness of the side streets. The horrified idlers hurried away at the sight of the uniforms: a wet nurse with a baby, a flower girl, an old grinder . . . The guards, however, did not hurry to catch anyone: the scene of the Sacred Spirit in a skirt, mustache, and cap horrified them. Swords were raised, the cloth was slashed and thrown to the ground, and the statue of the Spirit Lash was quickly freed of the rags and the mustache.

The square was deserted. Windows were slammed shut. The guards turned around; the man in the robe had disappeared as if he had been swallowed by the cobblestones that paved the square.

The guards exchanged glances and continued their patrol, looking more gloomy and stepping heavier than usual. Meanwhile, the man in the gray robe, hiding his face with the hood, moved away. People bowed to him and hurried to disappear from the road—but this respect did not deceive him.

"Oink, oink." The collectors returned yesterday from the suburbs—it was shameful to see what the peasants dared to offer now as gifts to the Order of Lash. Corn and turnips instead of silk, spices, and golden jewelry.

"Oink, oink." Soon, very soon, they will be taught a severe lesson. And they will beg, but it will be too late.

# 3

Night was coming on quickly beyond the foggy window. The coach mournfully slouched over the bumps in the road, and Egert cowered in the corner and stared blankly at the gray, perpetually monotonous wayside disappearing behind him.

Three weeks had passed from the day, or more accurately from the night, of his flight from Kavarren; the feeling of the end of the world and of the end of life that had then overwhelmed Egert and had ripped him away from his home, his city, his uniform, and his own skin—that dreadful, agonizing feeling had now dulled, and Egert simply sat in the dusty corner of the coach, his fist tucked beneath his chin, looking out the window and trying not to think about anything.

His bag would not fit on the baggage rack, so it now crouched between his legs, keeping him from tucking them under the seat below him. The entire baggage compartment was full of bundles and hampers that belonged to a traveling merchant. This merchant, a bilious and sinewy old man, was now sitting across from Egert. Egert knew very well that he had the right to displace the merchant's goods in behalf of his own bag, but he could not force himself to say a single word in his own defense.

The seat next to the old man was occupied by a pretty, young, and somewhat timid person: to all appearances, a maiden who had prematurely flown the coop of her father's nest in order to set out in search of work, a husband, and adventure. Having initially taken an interest in Egert, but having received not even the slightest encouragement from him, the poor girl was now aggrievedly tracing her little finger along the glass of the window.

To the side of Egert sat a dejected person of indeterminate age with a bluish gray nose that hung like a drop and short, ink-stained fingers. Egert privately identified him as a wandering scribe.

The hulk of the coach was swaying smoothly, the merchant was snoozing with his face resting against the windowframe, the young lady was unsuccessfully trying to catch a troublesome fly, the scribe was staring off into space, and Egert, whose back was aching and whose legs were swollen from his uncomfortable posture, was thinking about the past and the future.

Having lived in Kavarren for twenty years and never having gone any considerable distance away from the city, he now had the opportunity to see the world, but this opportunity scared him far more than it pleased him. The world seemed comfortless, a shapeless wasteland of little towns, villages, inns, and roads, along which roamed people: morose, sometimes dangerous, but more often apathetic people who were invariably disagreeable to Egert. Strange people. Egert felt scruffy, haggard, and hunted. Now, covering his eyes in the steadily swaying coach, he once again desperately wished that it would all turn out to be a foolish dream. For a shining moment, he truly believed that he was about to wake up in his bed and that, opening his eyes, he would see the boars on their tapestries. He would summon his manservant, and he would wash his face in clean water over a silver basin. He would be the previous Egert Soll, not this despicable, cowardly vagabond. He believed in this vision so sincerely that his lips cracked open in a smile and his hand went to his cheek as though chasing away slumber.

His fingers stumbled upon the long seam of his scar. Egert flinched and opened his eyes.

The merchant was snoring softly. The girl had finally caught the fly and, clutching the insect in her fist, was listening attentively to the buzzing of the unfortunate captive.

Dear Heaven! Egert's entire life, his entire happy and dignified life, had shattered into a thousand pieces and escaped into an unimaginable abyss. Behind him there was only shame and pain too dreadful to remember; before him lay a gray, cloudy, queasy uncertainty too dreadful to conceive of. Why?

Egert asked himself this question again and again. At the root of all the misfortune that had befallen him lay the strange cowardice that had suddenly awoken in the soul of a brave man; but why? How was such degeneration possible? Where did this affliction come from?

The duel with the stranger. Egert returned to that duel in his mind's eye over and over, and every time, he wondered: Was it really possible that a single defeat could break him so? A single, absurd, incidental defeat that occurred without any witnesses?

He clenched his teeth hard and stared out the window, beyond which the damp, somber forest swept out into the far distances.

The hooves of the horses tramped out an even, steady pace. The peddler awoke and unwrapped a bundle containing a hunk of bread and a smoke-cured leg of chicken. Egert turned away; he was hungry. The girl had finally killed the fly and now also reached for her bundle, from which she extracted a roll and a piece of cheese.

The scribe was apparently considering whether or not it was time for him to sup as well, when the previously steady rhythm of the horses' hooves suddenly became erratic.

The coach started jerking: at first forward, then awkwardly to the side. Up front, the driver screamed something indecipherable but full of terror. The clatter of hooves could be heard from behind and to the side of the coach, and the peddler suddenly went white as chalk. His hand, still clutching the chicken leg, shiny with grease, began to tremble vigorously.

The young girl spun her head from side to side in shock; crumbs from her roll clung to her lips and showed up white against their rosy pink. The scribe gasped. Egert, not understanding what was happening, but sensing that something was not right, pushed his shoulders back into the worn upholstery.

The carriage bounced heavily over something in the road and lost speed so quickly that Egert almost flew forward into the merchant.

"Rein it in!" a man's voice yelled wickedly from behind the coach. "Rein in! Stop!"

The horses started neighing in panic.

"Glorious Heaven!" groaned the merchant. "No, no!"

"What is it?" asked the maiden faintly.

"Highwaymen," explained the scribe calmly, as though he were in an office.

Egert's miserable, timorous heart jumped up into his throat in a single convulsive movement, only to immediately descend into his stomach. He hunkered down onto the seat and firmly squeezed his eyes shut.

The coach shook and then stopped. The driver began to mutter beseechingly, and then he screamed and fell silent. The doors of the coach jerked
from the outside.

"Open up!"

A hand reached out and shook Egert by the shoulder. "Young man!"

He forced himself to open his eyes and saw a pale face with wide-open,
rapidly blinking eyes hovering over him.

"Young man," murmured the girl. "Say that you are my husband. Please,
it could be true."

Following the instinct of the weak, who seek the protection of the strong,
she grabbed Egert's hand: thus does a drowning person pluck at a rotten log.
Her gaze was full of such entreaty, such a zealous request for aid, that Egert
suddenly felt hot all over, as if he had been tossed into a frying pan. His fingers began to fumble at his side, searching for his sword, but they had barely
skimmed the hilt when they jerked back as if burned.

"Young man . . ."

Egert averted his eyes.

The doors jerked again, someone cursed beyond them, and then the light
coming in through the dingy little window was cut off by a shadow.

"Step lively! Open up!"

Egert began to shake from the sound of this voice. Terror rolled over him
in waves, each new wave far exceeding the one that came before. Cold sweat
streamed down his back and sides.

"We need to open the door," observed the scribe impassively.

The peddler was still clutching the chicken leg in his fist. At the scribe's
words, his eyes shot up to the top of his forehead.

The scribe stretched his hand out toward the door latch; at that very moment the girl, having despaired of securing any help from the young man,
caught sight of the dark hollow underneath the opposite bench.

"Just a minute," said the scribe in a conciliatory tone to those who were
waiting outside. "The latch is jammed, just a minute."

With a dexterous movement, the girl rolled under the bench. The shabby
cloth that covered the seat concealed her completely from any passing glance.

Egert did not recall very well what happened next.

Befuddled by terror, his mind suddenly saw a way out, a slender hope for
salvation. The hope was, of course, a sham, but Egert's clouded brain did not

understand this; it was overwhelmed with a single, tremendous wish, border-
ing on insanity: to hide!

He dragged the girl out from under the bench like a hound dragging a fox
from its hole. Of course, she struggled; she bit him on the elbow, writhing in
his arms, trying to crawl back under the bench, but Egert was stronger. Col-
lapsing from terror, he crawled under the bench and squeezed himself into the
darkest corner. Only then did he realize what had happened.

The only reason he did not immediately die from shame was that the door
finally swept open and a new wave of fear robbed Egert of the ability to consider his actions. All the passengers were ordered out of the coach. Through
the black shroud that clouded his eyes, Egert first saw massive steel-toed
boots step onto the floor of the coach; then a hairy hand descended to the
floor, propping up the black beard and blazing eyes of a man who said, "Ha!
Indeed, there he is; the little fawn!"

Egert's mind once again collapsed.

He did not even resist as he was dragged from the coach. The horses were
tossing their heads in terror, rolling their eyes at the vast tree trunk that had
been laid across the road to intercept their path. The coachman, smiling
mournfully, his eyes swollen and streaming with tears, was obligingly allowing himself to be tied up. The baskets and bundles of the merchant were flying
from the baggage compartment; a portion of them, disemboweled like rabbit
skins at a bazaar, had already tumbled to the ground nearby.

They patted Egert down, but the only loot they got from him was his family sword and the gilded buttons on his jacket. They collected a purse from
the scribe. The merchant, trembling and sniveling, watched as they broke
open the lock of a potbellied chest. Two of the highwaymen held the girl by
her arms; she kept twisting her head from side to side, shifting her gaze from
one to the other and pleading inaudibly.

There were five or six bandits, but Egert was in no condition to remember
a single face. Having finished their pillage, they divided their loot among
their saddlebags and flocked around the coach. They tied the scribe to the
merchant, and the driver to the tree trunk lying in the road, but they did not
bother to tie Egert up. It was obvious he would not run away: his legs refused
to work.

The bandits gathered in a circle and one by one thrust their hands into a
cap. Egert dimly realized that they were drawing lots. The black-bearded

robber nodded contentedly, and the two who were holding the girl released her elbows. Black-beard took her by the shoulder proprietarily and led her into the coach.

Egert saw her wide eyes and trembling lips. She walked without resisting, only ceaselessly repeating some entreaty directed at her tormentors. Black-beard shoved her into the carriage, while the others expectantly arrayed themselves on the grass surrounding it. The coach teetered; the carriage springs screeched, flexing rhythmically, and a thin, high voice cried out plaintively from within.

The bandits drew lots again and again. Egert lost track of time. His mind began to bifurcate: over and over he flung himself at the bandits, crushing their ribs and snapping their necks, and then he would suddenly realize that he was sprawled out the ground as before, clutching at the grass with cramped fingers and rhythmically rocking back and forth. He was loose, but he was tied hand and foot by this morbid, fiery terror.

And then he once again dissolved; he lost his memory and his ability to reason. Branches were lashing at his face: it seems he was running after all, except that his legs refused to obey him, like in a bad dream, and continually threatened to collapse under him. At that moment, he was tormented by a desire far greater than the pain and fear, the desire to cease to exist, to not be, to have never been born. Who was he now, Glorious Heaven? Who was he after all this? What crime was more dreadful than that which the monstrosity of fear, having taken up residence in his soul against his will and lacerating him from the inside, had already committed?

And once again the darkness came, and everything ended.

The ancient hermit who lived in the mud hut by the stream would occasionally find people in the forest.

Once, on a brisk winter's morning, he found a young girl, about fourteen, in a thicket. White and hard as a statue, she was propped up against a tree trunk, and in her hands she held an empty basket. The hermit had never found out who she was or what brought her to ruin.

Another time he found a young lady in the forest. She was bloody, covered in bruises and suffering from delirium. He carried her to his little mud hut, but the next day he was forced to bury her as well.

The third time, the hermit's discovery turned out to be a man.

He was a handsome and strong young man who was far taller and heavier than the hermit himself and thus quite difficult to drag through the forest. Trying to catch his breath, the elder was washing him with water from the river when the foundling groaned and opened his eyes.

The hermit rejoiced: At the very least, he would not have to bury this one! He flung his arms up and bellowed. Deprived of the gift of speech since birth, only thus could he give expression to his feelings.

River weeds trailed across the surface of the little stream. Their dark green tips, stretching out as if in supplication, were trying to sail away along the current, but their roots, bogged down in the obscure, earthy depths, restrained them. Dragonflies hung motionless over the stream, enormous, mindless dragonflies, opalescent as a lady's finery.

For days on end, Egert Soll sat by the water, watching the trailing weeds and the dragonflies. Now and then he enlivened this spectacle by leaning over the dark mirror of the water and peering at the lean, vagabond scar reflected there. Sparse, sandy brown stubble could not hide the mark.

The hermit did not seem at all dangerous, but Egert still required an entire week to train himself not to shrink back at his approach. The kindhearted elder constructed a bed for his guest out of dried grass and shared his food with him, which consisted of fish, mushrooms, and cakes. Where these latter were baked was a mystery to Egert, but they appeared with enviable constancy. Very little was required of Egert in exchange: the hermit indicated that he should gather brushwood from the opposite shore of the stream or split the firewood that was piled up by the side of the hut. However, it became clear almost immediately that these tasks were beyond Egert.

A flimsy little bridge crossed the stream: three thin boles, lashed together with ropes. The stream only came up to Egert's waist at this crossing, and the bridge lay only inches above the water, but all the same Egert was afraid to entrust the quivering beams with the weight of his body.

The hermit watched from afar as the strong young man unsuccessfully tried to overcome the obstacles that arose before him. A step, at most two, along the bridge and a disgraceful flight backwards were all he could manage at first. Tying his boots around his neck, Egert tried to ford across the brook, but once again had to retreat because the icy water gave him a cramp in his leg. No one will ever know what the hermit thought about all this, for he was mute and accustomed to keeping his thoughts to himself.

Egert made it across the river the following day. Clutching at the beams with a viselike grip, he crawled across on all fours; only when he reached solid ground did the former guard—soaked, shivering, his heart pounding furiously—decide to open his eyes.

The old man watched all this from his hut, but Egert no longer had the strength to be ashamed. He was a mute witness: the same as the pines, as the sky, as the stream.

Egert had similar problems with splitting the firewood. The stump with its ax planted securely in it instantaneously reminded him of an executioner's block, of beheading, of death: the wide blade of the ax carried within itself pain, lacerated muscles and tendons, hewed bones, and torrents of blood. Vividly, as if in a vision, Egert saw how the ax would slip from the stump and embed itself into his leg, his knee, how it would chop him into pieces, mutilate him, kill him . . .

Egert could not take such an awful weapon in his hands. The patient old man did not insist.

Thus, day after day passed by. Sitting by the stream, looking at the water and the dragonflies, Egert frequently remembered everything that had transformed Lieutenant Soll from a splendidly valiant man into an abject, cowardly tramp.

He would have been happier not to remember. He envied the hermit fiercely: it seemed as though he could think about nothing at all for hours on end while an expression of ethereal unconcern and heavenly peace lay on his pitted, sparsely bearded face. Such happiness was inaccessible to Egert, and shame, red-hot as if from the coals of a fire, at times compelled him to beat his head on the ground.

The hermit would withdraw a ways every time he observed in Egert's eyes the onset of these convulsions of grief, these assaults of shame and despair. He would walk away, and with an attentive yet unintelligible expression on his pocked face, he would watch Egert from afar.

Not only memories tormented Egert: never in all his days had he slept on straw, eaten dried mushrooms, or gone without a change of linen. Egert grew thin and lean, his eyes began to cave in, and his beautiful blond hair became stuck in matted clumps; giving in one day, he cut off his long tresses with the hermit's knife. His stomach ached and growled from the unfamiliar food. His lips cracked, and his face sagged. He laundered his shirt in the cold stream and at the same time washed himself, an activity that caused the hermit to marvel: Why did the young man bother with these time-consuming and unpleasant formalities?

The first two weeks were the most difficult. With the onset of darkness, when the forest became a den of murmurs and shadows, Egert hid in the mud hut with his head bundled up in the hermit's burlap sacks like a little boy. Once or twice, a long, plangent howl arose from brush. Stopping up his ears with his palms, Egert shivered until dawn.

However, there were quiet, clear evenings, which Egert ventured to while away together with the silent hermit by a pale campfire, lit near the entrance to the hut. On one of these evenings he raised his head, and there amidst the scatterings of stars, he suddenly saw a familiar constellation.

He was happy until he realized that this constellation repeated the smattering of beauty marks on the neck of a certain woman, a woman whom Egert had known for only a very short time, but whom he could never forget. He grew morbid again because all the memories tied to her name tormented him as much as his affliction.

Then it started to become easier. One day, Egert set off to get some brush, and right as he got to the little bridge, he realized that he had forgotten his rope. He returned to the hut, and surprisingly enough, the complicated and torturous process of fording the stream passed by this time far more easily than usual; in any event, it seemed easier to Egert. Another time, he intentionally returned away from the bridge, and as if he had received an additional charge of bravery, he waded to the other shore almost entirely without the use of his hands, though he was doubled over by the end.

His life became easier from that moment on, though it was still endlessly complicated. An array of fine, precisely defined, and seemingly senseless actions protected him from any imminent danger: to cross over the unsteady little bridge on his way back to the mud hut, he had to touch his palm to a shriveled old tree on the far shore and silently count to twelve. Every evening, he threw three pieces of kindling, one after the other, into the stream to protect himself from nightmares. In this way he gradually overcame himself; he even decided to take up the ax, and with some success he chopped a few logs in front of the surprised and gladdened hermit.

One day, when Egert was, as usual, sitting by the water and asking himself for the hundredth time about the source of the misfortune that had befallen him, the hermit, who until then had never plagued the young man with his company, walked up and put his hand on Egert's shoulder.

Egert flinched; the hermit felt how his muscles tightened under his threadbare shirt. Egert saw what appeared to be compassion in the old man's eyes.

He frowned. "What?"

The hermit warily sat down next to him, and he traced a line with his grimy finger down his own cheek from his temple to his chin.

Egert jerked backwards. He involuntarily raised his hand and touched the slanted scar on his cheek.

The elder began to nod, satisfied that he had been understood. Continuing to nod his head, he chafed his skin with his fingernail until a red stripe, similar to Egert's scar, bled through the sparse gray whiskers on his spotted face.

"Well, what of it?" Egert demanded desolately.

The hermit glanced at Egert and then at the sky. He frowned, shook his fist in front of his own nose, fell back, shut his eyes and again scratched his fingernail down his cheek.

"M-m-m . . ."

Egert was silent; he did not understand. The hermit smiled sorrowfully, shrugged his shoulders, and returned to his hut.


Every once in a while, the hermit would leave for an entire day and return with a basket full of food, which would have seemed simple and coarse to Lieutenant Soll, yet was delicious from the point of view of the tramp Egert. Egert supposed that the old man visited some place where people lived, and that these people were well disposed toward the ancient hermit.

One beautiful day, Egert summoned up the courage to ask the elder to take him along.

They walked for a long time. The hermit, by some unknown signs, ferreted out a scarcely perceptible path, while Egert firmly pressed the pinkie finger of his left hand into the thumb of his right: it seemed to him that this ploy would spare him the fear of lagging behind and getting lost.

Autumn reigned in the forest, not the earliest autumn, but also not the latest; it had not yet had the chance to grow old and wicked as it progressed toward winter. Egert carefully stepped through the yellow shreds of fallen leaves, which seemed to crunch with a weary sigh each time his foot disturbed them. The trees, besieged by a dreary calm, heavily lowered their half-naked, weakened limbs to the ground, and every fold in their coarse bark reminded Egert of his old scar. Pressing the pinkie of his left hand to the thumb of his right, he followed his mute guide, but was not at all happy when the forest finally ended and an isolated hamlet came into sight.

From somewhere beyond the fence resounded the howls and barks of a pack of dogs, which caused Egert to freeze in place. The hermit turned back and mooed encouragingly at him. From the nearest gate in the fence, two teenage boys were dashing toward them, skipping and hopping as they ran; at the sight of them, Egert involuntarily seized the hermit by his shoulder.

Ten paces away, the boys stopped short, gulping air, their eyes and mouths wide open. Finally, the one who was a bit older gleefully cried out, "Look! Elder Chestnut has picked up a stray!"

The little hamlet was small and solitary. It consisted of twenty-odd farmyards, a little turret with a sundial, and the house of the local wisewoman, which was on the outskirts. Life flowed by there lazily and with regularity. The arrival of Egert did not especially surprise anyone except the children: Chestnut had picked up some young man with a scar, and that was all well and good. At the suggestion that he stay on to work and spend the winter at the hamlet, Egert only sullenly shook his head. To winter where it was warm? What for? To grope for human society? Perhaps he would still return home, to Kavarren, where his father and mother, and his room with its fireplace and tapestries were?

Glorious Heaven, after everything that he had done! He no longer had a home. He no longer had a father or a mother; it was past the time to mourn Lieutenant Soll, whose place in the world was now occupied by a nameless young man with a scar.

Winter turned into one long delirium.

Though accustomed to the cold since childhood, Egert still took ill with the arrival of the first frost. More than once over the course of the long winter, the hermit grieved that it was so difficult to hollow out a grave in the frozen earth.

Egert thrashed about on the straw, gasping and coughing. The old man seemed more of a fatalist than a doctor: he swathed Egert in bast matting and gave him herbal infusions to drink, but after assuring himself that his patient had quieted down and fallen asleep, he went into the forest with a spade, justly reasoning that if he chipped away at the ground little by little, the hole might attain the appropriate depth by the time it was needed.

Egert was unaware of this. Opening his eyes, he saw above him first that solicitous, pocked face, then the gloomy beams of the ceiling, then the honeycombed patterns that had been carved into the mud walls. One day he came to consciousness and saw Toria over him.

"Why are you here?" he wanted to ask. His tongue would not obey him, but he asked the question without parting his lips, mute like the hermit.

She did not answer. She was sitting, her back arched and her head lowered toward her shoulders like a mournful stone bird on someone's grave.

"Why are you here?" asked Egert again.

She shifted slightly. "And why are you?"

Fierce, burning flames seared his eyes as if a torch had been set to them.

His mother also came. Egert felt her hand on his forehead, but he could not open his eyelids. Then pain and fear overwhelmed him, and he could not recognize her; he could not recall her face.

The hermit shook his head and shuffled off into the forest, carrying the spade under his arm.

However, as luck would have it, the frosts gave way to warmth and Egert Soll was still alive. One warm spring day, weak as a kitten, he made his way to the door of the hut without any help and raised his face—his wasted face that now seemed to consist only of his eyes and the scar—toward the sun.

The hermit waited a few more days and then, sighing and wiping away sweat, he refilled the vacant grave that had cost him so much labor.


The old wisewoman lived on the outskirts of the tiny hamlet. Egert furtively drew a circle on the path, pressed his left pinkie to his right thumb, and knocked on the gate.

He had been preparing himself for this visit for many days. Time and again the hermit had tried to tell him something, poking at his scar with his finger. Finally, gathering up his courage, Egert set out for the hamlet alone in order to visit the wise woman.

Her courtyard was quiet; it seemed the old woman kept no dogs. A spring wind slowly turned an ungainly weathervane on the roof. The weathervane was a greased wheel with shrunken oddments attached to it, scraps that Egert, upon closer inspection, realized were the skins of frogs.

Finally, Egert heard the shuffling of footsteps. He shivered, but he clenched his teeth and remained where he was.

The gate cracked open with a moan, and a prominent, expressive blue eye, like a glass marble, stared hard at Egert. "Ah, the young stray with the scar."

The gate swung open wider and Egert, overcoming his diffidence, stepped into the yard.

A thatch-roofed hut stood by the fence; on a chain near it—Egert recoiled—sat a wooden beast covered in tar, with curved fangs peeking out of its half-open jaw. Instead of eyes it had black pits. Walking past, Egert broke out into a sweat because he felt a furtive, observant gaze looming in those pits.

"Come in."

Egert entered the house, which was congested with an abundance of superfluous items that seemed randomly strewn about. It was a dark and mysterious house, and the walls were covered with two layers of dried herbs.

"Why have you come, young man?"

The old crone looked at him with one round eye. The other was closed, and the eyelid had grown into her cheek. Egert knew that the old woman never worked wicked magic on anyone; quite the opposite: she was well loved in the village for her rare abilities to heal. He knew this, and all the same he trembled before that steadfast, wooden stare.

"Why have you come?" repeated the wise woman.

"I wanted to ask you something." Egert had to force the words out.

Her eye blinked. "Your fate is crooked."

"Yes."

The old woman meditatively wiped her nose, which was snubbed like a girl's. "We'll see. Let's take a look at you."

Casually stretching out her hand, she took a thick candle from a shelf, lit it by rubbing the wick with her fingers, and though the day was quite bright, brought the flame close to Egert's face.

Egert braced himself. It seemed to him that instead of warmth, cold emanated from the flame.

"Well, aren't you just a big bird," said the old woman pensively. "Your aura is mangled, Egert."

Egert shivered.

"Your scar," continued the old woman, as if talking to herself, "is a mark. Now, who would mark you like that?"

She put her eye very close to Egert's face and suddenly sprang back, her blue eye almost pushing its way out of its socket. "By the frog that enlightens me, by the frog that directs me, by the frog that protects me: Get out, get out!"

And with surprising strength she seized a stupefied Egert by the shoulders and pushed him away. "Out! Go, and don't return! It is not for me to stand against him; I do not have the strength to tussle with him!"

Before he could come to his senses, Egert was already at the gate. His back crashed into the fence.

"Grandmother! Don't chase me away! I—"

"I'll set my dog on you!" snapped the sorceress, and—Glorious Heaven!— the wooden beast slowly turned its tar-covered head.

Egert shot out of the gate like a cork. He would have run away without looking back, but his weakened knees buckled and he sank down into the dust of the road like a sack.

"What am I going to do?" he murmured wearily, turning his face toward a dead beetle lying by the wayside.

The gate screeched again, opening slightly. "Search for a great wizard, an archmage. And never again come to this village, you won't leave alive!"

And the gate slammed shut with a crash.

# PART TWO

*Toria*

# 4

Two slanting rays of sunlight fell from the stained glass windows, bathing the stone floor in a cheerful, dappled glow, causing the austere, somber world of the library to be transformed. The sound of voices wafted smoothly from beyond the thick walls; the headmaster's lecture was just about to begin in the Grand Auditorium. The third window—the one that opened onto the square— had both its shutters flung wide open for the first time since the beginning of winter, and from the square beyond could be heard a noise that was not quite as decorous, but more exuberant: songs and shouts, the patter of hooves and wheels, laughter, the tinkle of bells, and the neighs of horses.

The work was close to finished: the long list was riddled with check marks, and the book cart sagged dolefully under the unbelievable weight of the tomes collected from the shelves. Toria stepped onto the ladder, but instead of going up she suddenly closed her eyes and pressed her face against the warm wood, worn smooth by many centuries of palms.

It was once again spring. Once again, the window cracked open onto the square, and the tart smell of ancient books, so beloved by her, mingled with the scents of dust, grass, and black earth, all warmed by the sun. Soon the river would warm up and strawberries would begin to flower. It was strange and astonishing, but she had the desire to loll about in the grass, to lie there, feeling the trampled stalks with her cheek and gazing about thoughtlessly, like a bee crawling around the velvety interior of a flower; to follow the ants with her eyes as they blazed a path along a stem. . . .

But Dinar was no more. He had been in the ground for a year already. The ants wandering in the grass now wandered over Dinar. Here the books were piled high, the sun shone beyond the window, boatmen shouted to each other by the river, but Dinar was not anywhere because that deep, black hole in the ground, which she remembered through a fog of horror and disbelief, that pit into which foreign people had lowered a wooden box—was that really Dinar? No, she would never again go to his grave; he was not there, that man, whom they buried. It was not him.

Toria took a faltering breath and opened her eyes. The mottled spots of sunlight had moved closer to the wall; in the corner of one of them sat a white cat, shining with the radiance of the light, mottled and patched like a jester. This cat was the guardian of the library; he protected it from rats and mice. Two round, yellow eyes gazed at Toria with reproach.

Despite herself, she smiled. She tested whether the stepladder was stable, picked up the hem of her dark skirt, and confidently climbed up the rungs, as she had already done a thousand times before.

Her left knee suffered from a blunt, weak ache. A week ago Toria had stumbled on the ladder and fallen, grazing her leg and ripping open her stocking. The elderly serving woman, who came twice a week to clean the annex, had darned the stocking. Whenever she was left alone with Toria, this good woman immediately began to sigh and lift her hands in dismay. "How can it be, you sweet young thing, such a beauty! And already for a year now wearing only one and the same dress! We'll just have to find some money for a pair of silk stockings . . . and for a bonnet, and slippers. . . . A beauty without new clothes, that's like a jewel without a setting!"

Toria smirked and licked her lips. A solid scar protruded from her lower lip. Then, a year ago, she had bitten it until she bled.

The hum of voices from beyond the wall quieted: undoubtedly the headmaster had mounted the rostrum. Today he would be teaching the students about the remarkable events that occurred, according to scholars, at the edge of the world, at the very Doors of Creation.

Toria grinned again. It was not given to any man to know what really happened at the Doors. As her father said, "Whoever has stood at the threshold can no longer speak to us."

Well, that's the last shelf. A thread of dust-laden cobweb waved laboriously over Toria's head. Spiders were permitted to live under the ceiling; her father joked that after he died, he would become a spider, and he too would guard the library.

Toria looked down intrepidly. She was not at all afraid of heights, so she felt neither agitation nor excitement. She stretched out her hand toward a row of gilded spines, but she changed her mind and turned away from the shelf.

Here, right under the ceiling, was a small, circular window that allowed one to look out from the library into the Auditorium. Toria used to perch here so that, amidst the sea of inclined heads, she might find one: a dark, disheveled, touchingly serious head. It was a game. Dinar was supposed to feel her gaze and raise his eyes to her.

Toria realized that the thought of Dinar no longer summoned an attack of sharp, bitter despair. She remembered him with sorrow, but no longer with that pain, which had for so long filled her days, her nights, and again her days.

Her father had told her that it would be this way. She had not believed him; she could not believe him, but her father had, once again, been right. As always.

Recalling her father, she turned back to the books.

There it was: a massive tome in a simple black binding. The spine seemed warm, and the embossed silver letters gleamed faintly. *On Prophecies.*

Goose bumps jumped up all over Toria's skin: only one copy of this book existed. Many centuries ago, an archmage had dedicated his entire life to this book. Now Toria would take it and bring it to her father; he would write a new chapter in his work, and after several centuries someone else might similarly, reverently take her father's book from a shelf and learn what the life of Dean Luayan had been dedicated to.

Carefully descending, Toria put the last check on her list; the history of prophecy was set down on the book cart.

So, for today the work was finished. A fresh wind broke in through the window, disturbing the dust of the books and forcing three small sneezes from the guard cat. Toria absentmindedly tucked away a lock of hair that had swept across her forehead and gazed out at the square.

The hot sunlight dazzled her, and the many-voiced hum deafened her. The square spun about like a carousel bedecked in ribbons. The merchants, carrying trays, were calling out their wares; the many-colored parasols of the promenading ladies were weaving through the crowd; and a patrol was passing by, the lead officer of which, in his red uniform with white stripes, deliberately and harshly contracted his brow, shaven according to custom, but at the same time did not stop himself from looking back at any especially lovely flower girl. Street urchins prowled under the feet of the walkers, the buyers and all those rushing people going about their own business, and above the crowd, as majestically as sailing vessels, magnificent sedans borne by lackeys drifted by.

The courthouse, squat and ill favored, seemed like an old toad in the sun's rays: a withered toad that had crawled out into the light and was warming its wrinkled sides in the sun. Toria, as usual, stole a glance at the round pedestal in front of the iron doors of the court. Two menacing words were emblazoned on the doors, DREAD JUSTICE! and on the pedestal there was a small gallows with a stuffed manikin hanging from a noose.

A tower with grated windows soared up next to the courthouse; some guards drowsed by the entrance to the tower, and a bit farther on three men in gray hooded robes were having a dignified conversation: these were the acolytes of the Sacred Spirit Lash. The sky hung above the square like an enormous blue banner.

Toria breathed blissfully; the sun lay on her face like a warm hand. The cat hopped onto the windowsill and sat next to her. Toria rested her hand on the back of its neck, and suddenly felt an unparalleled sense of her own kinship with this square, with this city, with the books, with the cat, with the university. And then she smiled happily, for perhaps the very first time in this last, black year.

The crowd clamored, the crowd bubbled like a motley stew boiling in a cauldron, and Toria's gaze nonchalantly slid over the hats and the parasols, over the uniforms, the bouquets, the trays of pies, over the dirty faces and the well-groomed ones, over the pomaded hair, the lace, the patches, the spurs until, amidst this hectic mass of humanity, one exceedingly strange man caught her attention.

Toria narrowed her eyes. The man was hidden from her gaze now and again by the crush of people, but this did not stop her from noticing, however far away she was, a certain incongruity in his bearing. It seemed like he was not walking through a populated square, but cautiously moving from hillock to hillock in a bog full of quicksand.

Astonished, Toria watched him even more attentively. The man was moving through a complicated, predetermined route: having made his way to a lamppost, he caught hold of it with his hands and stood against it for a moment, lowering his head as if he were taking a nap. Then, having determined the next leg of his arduous path, he moved on slowly, as if forcing himself.

He was completely uninterested in what was going on around him, even though, judging from his appearance, he was definitely not a sophisticated city-dweller. If anything, he was a vagrant who had worn out the majority of his clothes walking along the country roads. Catching sight of the red-and-white patrol with their swords and spurs caused him to jump so forcefully that he bumped into a seller of baked apples and nearly knocked him to the ground. Toria could hear shouts and abuse coming from the apple seller as the strange tramp jumped yet again, trying to get out of the way.

However complex, unnatural, and winding the man's path was, his goal appeared to be the university. Slowly but surely, the stranger came ever closer and closer, until she was finally able to make out his face.

Her heart beat painfully, violently; it stopped, and then it leapt wildly as if it were a hammer muffled in rags, beating against a wooden anvil. Toria did not yet understand what was happening, but the warm, spring day suddenly felt bleakly cold.

She recognized the face of the strange man, or so it seemed to her in that first second. In the next moment, chewing the scar on her lower lip, she was already telling herself silently, It's not him.

It was not him. He did not have a scar on his cheek, but more important: his eyes could never contain such grief, or such a hunted look. It could not be him: this man was dirty, scruffy, and atrophied, while he shone with self-satisfaction and good fortune; he fairly burst with the sense of his own attractiveness and irresistibility and was, indeed, handsome—Toria twisted her lips in disgust—he was handsome, while this one . . .

The tramp came even closer. The spring wind tousled his disheveled blond hair. He stood irresolute and tense in front of the university building as if he could not decide whether or not to approach the doors.

It is not him, said Toria to herself. Not him, she repeated fiercely, but her heart was beating ever faster and wilder. That shrunken, sallow face with that horrible scar running along the entire cheek, that uncertainty in every movement, those foul rags . . .

Toria leaned forward, peering at the stranger intensely, as though desiring to encompass him with just a single look. The stranger sensed her gaze. He shuddered and raised his head.

Egert Soll was standing under the window: in the blink of an eye, no doubt whatsoever remained in Toria. Her fingers gripped the windowsill, driving a splinter under one of her fingernails, but she did not feel the pain. The man standing below the window blanched deathly pale beneath his layer of dust and his sunburn.

It seemed as though nothing could appear more terrible to his eyes than the sight of this young woman in a high window; it was so terrible that it compelled him to shake, as if an abyss had suddenly opened right in front of him, and from that abyss the jaws, dripping with bile, of the mother of all monsters had reached out for him. For several seconds he stood as if frozen in place, and then he suddenly turned and dashed off. Disturbed flower girls yelled after him in the crowd. An instant, and he was no longer even in the square, which continued to spin festively like a carousel.

Toria stood by the window for a long time, thoughtlessly sucking on her wounded finger. Then, abandoning the cart laden with books, she turned around and slowly walked out of the library.

Egert had entered the city at dawn, just as the city gates were being raised. His defensive rituals, invented by him in droves, somehow helped him cope with his terror: gripping a button that had escaped from his shirt in his sweaty fist, he planned out his route in advance, moving from landmark to landmark, from beacon to beacon; by this method, of course, his route was significantly lengthened, but it also secured a hope in his soul that he would manage to avoid any danger.

Kavarren—massive, splendid Kavarren—was, in truth, a tiny, quiet little provincial town: Egert understood this now as he wandered through the noisy streets, dense with people and carts. Egert had been living in solitude for so long that the mass of people caused his head to spin; he kept having to lean against walls and lampposts so that he could rest a bit, squeezing shut his bloodshot eyes.

The hermit showed him the best way to the city, and gave him cheese and griddle cakes for his journey. The road to the city had been long and full of apprehension and fear. The cakes had been finished the day before yesterday, and Egert was now suffering from hunger as well as fear.

The goal of his agonizing pilgrimage was the university: Egert had been told that he could find a genuine archmage there. Unfortunately, Egert had not been able to discover either his name or his title. The kindhearted passersby, whom Egert finally resolved to question, unanimously directed him to the main square: there, they said, was the university and also other curiosities that might appeal to a traveler. Squeezing his button and scurrying from landmark to landmark, Egert moved on.

The main square was like a seething cauldron; trying as hard as he could to fight his dizziness, Egert weaved his way through the crowd. Details detached themselves from the throng and penetrated his eyes: an enormous mouth smeared with cream, a lost horseshoe, the wide-open eyes of a mule, a stunted scrub of grass in the crack between cobblestones . . . Then he stumbled into a round black pedestal, raised his head, and to his horror discovered that he was standing beneath a miniature gallows, where an executed dummy with glassy eyes was gazing down at him apathetically.

Recoiling, he nearly ran into a man in a gray hood. The man turned around in surprise, but Egert could not make out his face, hidden by the hood. He struggled through the crowd once again, and this time the crooked path from marker to marker deposited Egert in the middle of a patrol: five well-armed men in red-and-white uniforms, disagreeable and menacing, who were just waiting for the chance to seize a helpless tramp. Egert darted away, his mind full of a vision of prison, the whip, and hard labor.

Five or six men in gray hooded robes were standing in a huddled circle, conversing about something. Egert noticed that the crowd split around them, like a seething river breaks away from a rocky island. The faces of the robed men were lost in the shadows of their hoods, and this gave the gray figures a very sinister appearance. Egert was far more terrified of them than of the guards and adjusted his path so that he stayed at least ten feet away from the group.

There, finally, was the university building. Egert stopped to catch his breath. By the entrance to this sanctuary of learning, frozen in majestic poses, were an iron snake and a wooden monkey. Egert marveled at the sight; he did not know that these images symbolized wisdom and the pursuit of knowledge.

He simply had to ascend the steps and take hold of the brightly finished copper door handle, but Egert stood, unable to take even a step. The building oppressed him with its grandeur: there, beyond the door, secrets were hidden; there, the "archmage" awaited Egert, and who knew what the forthcoming meeting might have in store for this miserable vagabond. The gossip that all students were castrated for the glory of knowledge suddenly came to mind; it seemed to the dazed Egert that the iron snake was looking at him keenly and wickedly, and that the monkey was grinning obscenely.

Covered in clammy sweat, Egert was still standing in the same place when a new, even more disquieting feeling compelled him to shiver and raise his head.

A pale, dark-haired woman was steadily and intently staring down at Egert from a high, wide window.


"What is this?"

The fat-cheeked student turned even more pale: "This . . . I brought it for you. That's what you . . . requested."

"I requested the books, my friend."

It was dark in the room, and only one bright spot—a ray of sunlight from the sole narrow window—was on the table. A heap of paper wrapped by a ribbon lay on the table under the sun's ray, and dust specks were flying above the yellow pages.

"Mr. Fagirra," mumbled the student, "there was no way to carry the books out. Even the smallest . . . magic book cannot be taken out."

"Brother Fagirra."

"What? But . . . Excuse me, Brother Fagirra, I . . . honestly, I have done everything. The dean is suspicious, Mr. . . . Brother Fagirra. I brought . . . here is what I managed to get. Here are the notes."

"Well."

"One of the students made notes . . . made notes of what was in the books in the library that you wanted me to get."

"This is not enough, my friend."

"This all that I could get, Brother Fagirra."

"I fear that the End of Time will bring much sorrow to you."

The cheeks of the young fellow, recently so round, became sunken: "No. Please. Just give me another chance!"

The man with the tattoo on his wrist only raised the corners of his lips: "It is good. From this day, you will report to me about everything that happens at the university."


Egert dashed through the crowd, deaf to the curses of the upset hawkers, insensible to the fingers snatching at his tattered shirt or the irritated pokes he received while running past. He ran away from the square, from the university with its wide window where the face of Toria remained, still white as a ghost: Toria, the fiancée of the student he had killed. Flee! This was an evil, unlucky portent; he should never have come to this city. He had to get to the gates as quickly as possible; he had to escape from the net of these narrow, winding, overcrowded streets.

But the world of this enormous city, indifferent, satisfied, and lazily festive, had already possessed Egert as if he were its own rightful victim. It seemed to Egert that the city was gradually digesting him like a massive stomach, desiring to dissolve, destroy, and absorb him into itself.

"You, tramp, step aside!"

Huge wheels roared along the cobbled pavement; an arrogant face in the velvet semidarkness of a carriage sailed over Egert's head, and lowering his eyes, he saw an opalescent beetle flattened into a disk in the furrow left by the wheels.

"You, vagrant, get out of the road! Out of the road!"

Housewives joyfully called out to one another from windows, and from time to time a cascade of slops descended onto the pavement: then the exchanges turned into bickering.

The merchants were slaving away.

"Here, I've got combs, bone combs, turtle shell combs! And look at this miraculous potion: Smear it on your head and your hair will grow; dab it on your armpits and the hair will fall out!"

"Barbers! Jars, leeches, bloodletting! Razors! We'll shave you!"

A mob of street urchins were taunting a modest young lad who was dressed as neat as a pin. Beggars were huddled along walls covered with bas-relief sculptures; the wind played with the tattered ends of their rags, and their motionless, outstretched palms seemed like the dark leaves of an outlandish shrub. Penetrating calls of "Alms, alms . . ." hovered over the street, although the parched lips of the beggars hardly moved at all; only their eyes, dreary and yet at the same time covetous, caught the glances of the passersby: "Alms, alms . . ."

Away, away, off to the gate! Egert swerved onto a street that seemed familiar to him, but it betrayed him; it deposited him at a stone-dressed canal that ran straight away to either side. An odor of fungus and mold rose up from the green water. A wide bridge bulged over the canal. Egert had no memory of this place; he had never been here; he had definitely gone astray.

He decided to ask the way to the city gates. The first person to whom he dared to turn was a dignified, amiable housewife in a starched cap; with delight and in detail, she described the route to the city gates to him. Following her instructions, he passed through two or three alleyways, diligently walked through a populated intersection, turned where he had been ordered and suddenly came out near the very same humpbacked bridge that ran over the very same canal. Water striders were gliding along the surface of the stale water.

Remembering the misleading words of the woman in the starched cap, Egert again gathered his courage and asked a lean, poorly dressed young maidservant for help. She blushed, and by the furtive pleasure in her modestly lowered little eyes, Egert suddenly realized that for this pitiful creature he was not at all a filthy beggar, but a presentable young man, even a handsome man, potentially a lover. For some reason this realization brought Egert not pleasure, but pain; the girl, in the interim, had seriously and painstakingly explained to him how to get to the gates, and her explanation was completely contrary to the instructions of the housewife in the cap.

Hurriedly thanking the somewhat disappointed serving girl, Egert once again set out on his way. Looking around intently, he walked past a chandler and a pub, past an apothecary with live leeches in jars and bottled tonics, and past a button manufacturer with a shop window that dazzled the eye: hundreds of silver, mother-of-pearl, and bone circles ogled him from the display. He walked through a gloomy alleyway, sided by the looming, blank walls of houses. It turned out to be the territory of a procuress: in the semidarkness, first one then another sweet-eyed face approached Egert and, unerringly identifying him as a bum and not a prospective client, indifferently turned away.

The alleyway led Egert onto a circus; in its center was a statue on a low pedestal. The head of the statue was covered by a stone hood. Recalling the people in gray, who had terrified him in the main square, Egert hesitated to walk closer to the statue and read the inscription carved in the stone:

The Sacred Spirit Lash

He had heard about the Sacred Spirit when he was a child, but he had imagined him to be more majestic than this. Regardless, he did not have any time for reflection at the moment. Drawing a deep breath, he once again asked for directions, this time from a young, mild-mannered lemonade vendor. According to the lad, the city gates were but a stone's throw away. Inspired, Egert walked on along a wide but not very busy street. He passed by the house of a bonesetter, which had a pair of crutches of considerable size pegged to the door; past the house of a horse doctor, which had a sign deco-

rated with three horsetails; and past a bakery. Finally, bewildered, he walked
out at the very same arched bridge over the musty canal.

It seemed as if some unknown force was grimly determined to keep Egert
going around in circles. Overcome, he leaned against the wide stone railing;
somewhere over his head a shutter smacked loudly against a wall and a window swept open. Egert looked up.

A girl stood in the small, dark window. Egert's vision darkened as he saw
cheeks, pale as if carved from marble, dark hair, a constellation of beauty
marks on her neck. He winced, and then in the next instant he realized that
this was not Toria, that the face, gazing indifferently out the window, was
round and pockmarked, and that the hair was the color of rotten straw.

He turned and laboriously walked away. At an intersection he asked directions in turn of two passersby: affable and wishing him well, they each pointed
him in exactly opposite directions.

Gritting his teeth, he started walking, deciding to rely only on instinct and
luck. Having passed by a few blocks, he suddenly noticed a pair of street urchins who were obviously following him, though still at a safe distance.

He looked back with increasing frequency. The grubby, determined faces
of the urchins flickered in the crowd, all the time getting closer and closer.
Cowering inwardly, Egert swerved once, and then again and again, but
the urchins kept pace with him, walking ever faster, their hungry mouths
widely and insolently grinning. By now an entire horde was merrily following Egert.

Egert kept increasing his pace. The usual terror had already blossomed
within him: it squeezed his throat with cold jaws; it stuffed his rebellious legs
with cotton padding. Egert was keenly aware that he was a victim, and it was
as if this awareness had been imparted to his juvenile pursuers. It impelled
them to chase him.

The hunt had begun.

Egert was not at all surprised when the first stone hit him in the shoulder
blade. Quite the contrary: he was relieved that he no longer had to wait for
that blow because it was already inflicted. But the first stone was followed by
a second and a third.

"Yoo-hoo!" They merrily mocked as they jogged along the street. The
passersby looked around, displeased, and then went about their business.

"Yoo-hoo! Hey, Uncle, give us a bit of smoke, just a pinch. Hey, Uncle,
over here!"

Egert was almost running. Only a small remnant of his pride prevented him from simply taking to his heels.

"Hey, Uncle! You, with the hole in your pants. Look over here!"

A few small pebbles accurately pecked at his legs, his back, and the back of his head. A minute passed and his pursuers had caught up to him; one of their dirty hands grabbed his sleeve, and the shabby threads holding it together ripped.

"Hey, you! What, you don't want to talk to us?"

Egert stopped. They surrounded him. Most of the boys were around eight years old, but there were a few who were a bit older and two or three who might have been as old as fourteen. Grinning expansively, showing black pits in the place where some of their teeth should have been, wiping snotty noses on their sleeves, staring with hostile, narrowed eyes, the gang of hunters took pleasure in Egert's bewilderment, which was all the more sweet since the eldest of these hunters barely stood as tall as their prey's armpit.

"Uncle, buy us a loaf. Give us some money, eh?"

Something sharp pricked him from behind, either a pin or a needle. Egert jerked, and the horde broke out into merry laughter.

"See that? See how he jumped?"

They pricked him again. Tears of pain welled up in Egert's eyes.

A strong man, an adult, was standing in a circle of urchins who were young and weak but reveling in the sense of their ability to act with impunity. Who knows how, but these little beasts had unerringly exposed Egert as a coward, as a victim, as prey, and they were inspired to carry out the unwritten law by which every victim is tried and found guilty.

"Do it again! Make him hop! Silly uncle! Hey, where are you going?"

The last prick of the needle had been intolerable. Egert plunged straight though the gang, knocking one of them from his feet. As he ran away, stones, clumps of mud, and taunts flew after him.

"Oi-oi-oi-oi! Get him! Go on, get him!"

The long-legged Egert could run faster than even the most brazen urchin in the city, but the street wound about, turning into blind alleys that teemed with closed gates. The hunters dashed in front of Egert, cutting across his path from the routes known only to them, flinging stones and mud, screaming incessantly, chirruping and hallooing. At some point it began to seem to Egert that all of this was not really happening to him, that he was watching someone else's abominable nightmare through thick, cloudy glass, but then a stone struck him painfully in the knee, and a different, bitter, overwhelming emotion surged through him, replacing his detachment: This is how it is now, this is his life, his fate, his being.

Finally, he somehow pried himself away from his pursuers.

He found himself in a blighted slum, where a wizened, toothless old crone, holding an enormous snuffbox under her nose, pointed her crooked finger farther into the labyrinth of muddy alleyways. As he traversed them he felt a blunt, apathetic weariness that also dulled his fear, and then he felt fleeting joy at the sight of a square and the city gates.

The gates were closing.

The doors were slowly crawling toward each other. At the bottom of each door he could plainly see three guards, flushed from the strain of pushing them closed. A small shred of sky and the ribbon of the road were visible through the swiftly contracting opening.

What is going on? Egert thought.

With his last strength he ran across the square, but the gap was still narrowing, and then the gates closed with a crash. A chain clinked, threaded through the steel rings of the doors, and as solemnly as a flag, an enormous black lock was raised up onto the chain.

Egert stood in front of the magnificent steel gates decorated with figures of dragons and snakes. Their raised snouts were turned toward him; they watched him morosely and vacantly. Only now did Egert fully comprehend that the doors had been pushed shut, that night was approaching, and that the gates usually remained closed until morning.

"You, there!" The stern bark compelled him to cringe. "What do you want?"

"I must go out," he mumbled inaudibly.

"What?"

"I need to go through, out of the city."

The guard—a sweaty, round-cheeked man who did not seem malicious— smirked. "In the morning, my friend. You were late; that's the way it is. And really, when you really think about it, why would you want to go out there at night? You never know what might happen. So, my boy, you'll just have to wait. We'll open the gates at dawn."

Without saying another word, Egert walked away. It no longer mattered to him.

In the morning the gates would get stuck, or the sun would not rise, or something else would happen. If the unknown and hostile force, the force that had been toying with him all day from the time of his fateful meeting with Toria, if that force did not want Egert to leave the city, then he was not going to be able to leave of his own free will: he would die a beggarly death here, the death of a coward.

The square in front of the gates had emptied. Egert urgently wanted to lie down; it did not matter where, just so long as he could lie down, close his eyes, and not think about anything.

Barely moving his legs, he shuffled away from the gates.

A noisy cavalcade of five or six young horsemen on well-groomed steeds flew toward him from a wide side street. With a practiced eye, Egert absently identified the breed of each horse and noticed how splendidly each of the riders kept his seat. He stood still, waiting for them to pass by, but one of the youths, who was riding a tall, raven-colored stallion, broke away from the company and rode straight toward Egert.

This happened in the blink of an eye—and for all eternity. Egert lost the ability to move.

His legs grew into the pavement of the square, became numb, put down roots: thus must a tree feel, watching the approach of a lumberjack. The horse cantered easily, beautifully, as if on air, but the ground shook loudly from its strong, murderous hooves. Egert saw the black muzzle of the stallion, its wild eyes, the string of saliva hanging from its lower lip, and its chest, as wide as the sky and as heavy as a hammer, was ready to crush him with one blow.

He felt the steam of hot breath in his face, and slowly, so slowly, as if underwater, the stallion rose up on his hind legs.

Egert stared as the glossy muzzle froze right in front of his face. The hooves were thrown up, and the round heads of nails gleamed on newly shod, well-made horseshoes. Then the horseshoes flew up over his head, and the horse's belly opened up before Egert's eyes: the belly of a well-cared-for stallion, with a shaggy crest running down the middle. The horseshoes above his head were kneading the sky, preparing to descend from the heights and splatter the contents of a human head across the cobblestones.

Egert's mind collapsed; he was aware of nothing for the space of five seconds.

As before, Egert was standing in the middle of the square. The patter of hooves and trills of laughter were fading away down an alleyway, and a fine trickle of warm urine was leaking down Egert's leg.

Death would be better than this.

The guards were snorting with laughter behind him, and their laughter reverberated inside Egert's head. All the will of Egert Soll, all his remaining respect for himself, all his mutilated yet still living pride, and all his being screamed, slowly writhing in the inferno of this inconceivable, incredible degradation.

The vacant sky above his head and the empty square beneath his feet both whirled like grindstones, and these two black stones scraped against each other as if wishing to grind to dust the bones of this man who had dared to come between them.

Egert, said his will and his pride. This is the end, Egert. Remember the slimy filth on your face, remember the girl in the coach. . . . Remember your true self, Egert Soll, remember and answer this: Why do you, a man, consent to live in this repulsive, perpetually fearful manner? You have come to the edge: another step, and all your life, all your bright reminiscences, all the memories of your mother and father will curse you, will disown you for eternity. While you still recall what a man should be, put a stop to this despicable monstrosity that has possessed you!

The guards had long ago settled down and forgotten about Egert. Night had already set in: gloomy, moonless, lit only by a few streetlamps. Under one of these streetlamps loomed a wide, squat bit of masonry; it was a well, from which travelers who had just arrived in town usually watered their exhausted horses. Now it was completely lifeless.

Egert walked over to it. A waft of frigid air arose from the well, but Egert forced himself to gaze down into its humid depths. The circular, mirrorlike surface of the water reflected the dim streetlamp, the black sky, and the human silhouette that looked like it was cut out of a soot-black sheet of tin.

He worked quickly. He found a fragment of cobblestone nearby, as cold and heavy as a tombstone. He needed to tie the stone to his neck somehow, but he did not have any rope and his belt kept slipping off it. Fussing and sniveling from terror, Egert finally unbuttoned his shirt and stuffed the cobblestone into the cavity. The feel of the cold stone against his bare chest caused him to squirm.

Holding the stone to his chest with both his arms, he once again walked over to the well. He stood next to it for about two minutes, panting. The city was sleeping; somewhere in the dark heights an unseen weathervane screeched in the nighttime wind, and from afar could be heard the cry of the night watch, "Rest in peace, honest townsfolk!"

May you rest in peace, said Egert to himself. Clutching the stone to his chest like a beloved kitten, he swung a leg, stiff as a board, over the side of the well.

He sat on the stone masonry at the top; he exerted himself again, and his other leg, rebellious and numb, hung over the water. Egert swung around so that his stomach was on the edge of the well; his legs dangled inside without any purchase. Now all he had to do was brace himself and push off from the wall of the well with his hands and knees; then his body would fall over backwards, splash into the water, and the stone secreted in his bosom would immediately drag him to the bottom. The water would wash away all Egert's fear and degradation, all he had to do was . . .

His muscles seized up. Desperately attempting to suppress his terror, he tried to unclench his blue fingers, but they clawed at the masonry with a death grip. If only there were someone there who could crack a whip at his hands! But Egert had no one to help him, and the stone in his shirt pressed against the wall of the well; it prevented him from reaching out to his fingers with his teeth and biting them to force them to unclench. Just a bit more strength, just a bit . . .

But then his terror of death finally tore through the barrier he had momentarily erected in his mind.

Egert clung to the wall of the well with his entire body—his elbows, the soles of his feet, his knees—unable to recall or command himself. He surged upward, gasping for air, willing himself to tear out of his own skin and flee, flee, save himself! Stifled by fear, he tumbled out of the well onto the ground. The cobblestone skidded out of his shirt and Egert, still frantic, crawled away, trembling and weeping.

A guard glanced out of the striped kiosk by the gate and, not seeing anyone or anything, calmly ducked back inside. "Rest in peace, honest townsfolk," resounded from the watch.

Leaning against a lamppost, Egert finally managed to pull himself together. Only now did he acknowledge the profundity of the trap he was captured in.

He had no mastery over himself. Terror made his life unbearable and his death unattainable. He could not escape. All his mortal years, all his long life until old age he would be afraid, afraid, and he would grovel and betray himself, and he would suffer shame and hate himself, and he would rot alive until he lost his mind.

"*No!*" Egert's soul screamed. "No."

His shirt had already lost all its buttons. Egert cradled the cobblestone to his chest like a mother holding her beloved child, dashed toward the well, and leapt for the edge.

He stopped short with a fraction of a second to spare. Catching a glimpse of the dark water below, the fear of death broke his will as easily as a child breaks a match. It allowed him to come to his senses only when he was already on the ground, shaking and squirming like a newborn rat.

He wept and gnawed at his fingers. He called out to the heavens for help, but the heavens remained dark, as is sometimes the case at night. He wanted to die: he tried to force his heart to stop by strength of will, but his heart paid him no heed and beat as before, albeit irregularly and painfully.

Then he felt a gaze on him.

Never before had he so keenly, so markedly felt his skin crawl with another's gaze; he cowered, trying not to move, but the gaze, despite his hope, did not disappear. The gaze slid over his shoulders like a heavy palm. Egert clenched his teeth and slowly raised his head.

About five steps away from him stood a gray-haired man doused in the glow of the streetlamp. His face was elderly, beardless, and covered in a network of wrinkles; it seemed impenetrable, like a mask. The man stood motionless and examined Egert with an inscrutable expression in his tranquil, narrowed eyes.

Egert caught his breath: it was instantly clear to him that this stranger would not insult him or beat him, but at the same time in the depths of his soul rumbled a completely different anxiety, not at all like his usual terror. He wanted this witness of his shame and desperation to disappear as quickly as possible into the night. Trying to convey the fact that the presence of this other man was unwelcome, Egert turned his back on him.

Another minute passed. The intent gaze did not leave Egert in peace for a second.

Egert felt tormented, like he was on a burning stove. Finally, his patience dried up and he decided to speak. "I . . ."

He fell silent, unable to find the words. The strange man apparently had no thought to help him get the words out.

"You . . ." Egert spoke again, and in that moment he had an idea, a simple and brilliant idea. "You," he said more firmly. "You might be able to help me."

The stranger blinked. He politely asked, "Help?"

Getting up with great difficulty, Egert walked over to the well and once again took the cobblestone in his hand. "You could push me. Just a little push. There. Into the water."

The nighttime passerby did not answer, so Egert added quickly, "This is happening, you know? I really need to—I really need you to help me, please."

The stranger transferred his intent gaze from the cobblestone to Egert's face, then to the well, and once again to Egert.

"I really need help," pleaded Egert. "It's necessary. I can't do anything else. But I can't do it myself. Please."

"I really don't think I can help you," uttered the stranger slowly.

Hope, which had flared up in Egert's soul, extinguished. "Then . . . ," he said quietly. "Then please leave. I have to try again."

The stranger shook his head. "I don't think so. I don't think that you'll succeed in this, Egert."

Egert dropped the cobblestone. Scarcely able to swallow his sticky saliva, he stared at the stranger in horror.

"You are indeed Egert Soll; I'm not mistaken, am I?" asked the strange man as if nothing was the matter.

Egert could have sworn that he had never met this man before.

As if reading his mind, the stranger smiled briefly. "My name is Luayan. I am Dean Luayan from the university."

Egert was silent; before his eyes flashed an image of the imposing building and the girl in a high window.

The dean, meanwhile, leisurely walked over to the well and settled himself on its edge as informally as a child. "Well then, let's have a talk, Egert."

"How do you know my name?" Egert forced the words out. In the light of the streetlamp the white teeth of the dean flashed; he smiled and shook his head, as if shocked at the naïveté of the question. And then, shivering at his sudden guess, Egert asked through numbed lips, "Are you a wizard?"

"I am a mage," corrected the dean, "a mage and a teacher. And you, Egert, who are you?"

Without blinking, Egert stared at the tranquil, inscrutable face. He had come to this city to meet this mage, and he had hoped for and feared this meeting. But the appearance of Toria, high up in that window, had muddled and changed everything. He had surrendered hope; he had forgotten all about it, and now here he was, speechless, standing in front of a graying man in dark, strangely cut clothes, standing in front of the witness, whether intentional or accidental, of his pitiful attempts at suicide, and his tongue was stuck on the roof of his mouth: How could he possibly find an answer to the dean's remorseless question?

The dean sighed. "Well, Egert? I know something about who you were. But now?"

"Now." Egert could not hear himself and so began anew. "Now I want to die."

The dean smiled somewhat scornfully, it seemed to Egert. "There is no way, Egert. The man who marked you with that scar does not leave loopholes."

Egert's shaking hand touched the scar on his cheek.

The dean gently rose up: he was only a hairsbreadth shorter than Egert, who was quite tall. "Do you know what that scar signifies, Egert?"

He came close, so close in fact that Egert recoiled; the dean screwed up his face peevishly.

"Don't be afraid."

Firm fingers carefully grasped Egert by his chin and turned his head so that his scarred cheek was exposed to the light from the streetlamp. The silence lasted for a few lingering seconds; finally the dean let go of Egert's chin, sighed as if preoccupied, returned to the well, and once again sat down on the stonework.

Egert stood there, more dead than alive. His interlocutor rubbed his temples, looked to the side, and said, "A curse has been laid upon you, Egert, a serious, frightful curse. The scar is but the imprint of it, the mark, the symbol. Only one man can leave such a reminder of himself, but as I know very well, he very rarely condescends to interfere in the business of others. You must have seriously annoyed him, eh, Egert?"

"Who?" whispered Egert, not understanding even half of what the dean had just said.

The dean sighed again: wearily, patiently. "Do you remember the man who wounded you?"

Egert stood, staring at the ground; finally he shivered and raised his head. "A curse?"

The dean twitched the corner of his mouth. "You really didn't guess?"

Egert remembered the old hermit and the village wise woman, who had been so horrified when she examined Egert's scar more closely.

"I guessed," he murmured, lowering his eyes yet again.

The lamplight flickered in a gust of wind.

"I guessed," repeated Egert. "He was old, or so he seemed. He fought like . . . Now I understand. Was he a wizard? I mean, was he also a mage?"

"Just how did you annoy him, Egert?" asked the dean, knitting his brows together.

Egert soundlessly moved his lips: that final duel, that fight with the grizzled boarder of the Noble Sword flashed before his eyes.

"No," he said finally. "I—there's no way. I didn't want to duel, he himself . . ."

The dean leaned forward. "Understand this, Egert: This man does not bother himself with trifles. You did something that, in his opinion, was worthy of a grave punishment. I am now asking you, what was it?"

Egert could not speak. Memories invaded him all at once, without distinction, descending upon him, deafening him with the ring of steel, the laugh of Karver, the din of the crowd, the voice of Toria screaming "Dinar!"

The grizzled stranger had been there. Oh yes, he had been there, and as he was leaving he had graced Egert with a long look.

Later, at the tavern by the gates, what was it that strange man said? Egert broke out into sweat; he remembered the words of the stranger quite distinctly, as if they had just been spoken: I drink to Lieutenant Soll, the embodiment of cowardice, hiding behind a mask of valor.

"Who is he?" Egert asked desolately. The dean remained silent; Egert raised his head and understood that he was waiting for an answer to the question he had already asked twice.

"I killed a man, in a duel," said Egert with just as much desolation in his voice. "The duel was fought according to the rules."

"Is that all?" asked the dean dryly.

Egert winced painfully. "It was all so haphazard and stupid. That lad, he didn't even carry a sword. I didn't want it. I didn't want it to happen that way."

He glanced desperately at the dean's eyes and saw that the flecks of light from the streetlamp on his severe face had faded. The black sky over the square had become gray, and the even silhouettes of the houses were beginning to appear from the receding shadows.

"So you paid the price," said the dean just as dryly, "for your thoughtless savagery. The man who put that curse on you has doomed you to eternal cowardice. It is possible that he wasn't even thinking about punishment but simply decided to neutralize you, to protect those who aren't like you, those who live differently, who cannot or will not arm themselves."

Dawn broke out over the city. The dean stood up, this time heavily, as if Egert's tale had fatigued him beyond measure.

"Dean Luayan!" exclaimed Egert, shrouded in despair at the thought that the dean might simply turn and walk away. "Dean Luayan, you are indeed an archmage. I—I have been through so much. I've been seeking. I wanted to seek help from you. I beg you; tell me what I must do. I swear I'll do anything, just please take this, this scar from me!"

The streetlamp sputtered and went out. The sleepy guard emerged from the striped kiosk by the gates and glanced with amusement at the tramp who was conversing with a gentleman of such decorous appearance in the middle of the square. Shutters swung open here and there with crashes, the dairywoman cried out resonantly, and the square suddenly came to life, filling up with various people yawning tiredly while they waited: soon the gates would open.

The dean shook his head in defeat. "Egert, you just don't understand; you don't understand who it is fate has brought you into contact with. A curse that is laid upon a person by the Wanderer can only be removed by the Wanderer."

The lock of the gates solemnly slithered down, and people started surging forward. The steel chain rattled in the rings; the guard—a new one had only just arrived to relieve the old—set about making himself comfortable. The gates emitted a majestic groan and smoothly, almost gracefully, proceeded to open.

"Then what should I do now?" asked Egert in a whisper. "Should I search for him, this Wanderer? Who is he? Where can I find him?"

The rooftops were bathed in sunlight. Yellow and white specks of light danced on tin and copper weathervanes.

"Who he is, no one really knows," said the dean, almost smiling. "As for looking for him: What makes you so sure that he would even talk to you?"

Egert's head jerked up. "But, that's just, just . . . He's treated me so badly! What he did to me, and he wouldn't even talk to me?" Egert shook, he was almost in a rage. "All because of a student? Yes, I killed him! But it was a duel, and with the Wanderer, there was also a duel: he should have killed me! I stood before him defenseless. Death for death. But what he did is worse than death and now I envy the student! He died with a sword in his hand, respecting himself. He had a future and he was loved."

Egert stopped short. It seemed to him that a shadow had flitted across the dean's face. Cold sparks blazed in the depths of his narrow eyes, and under his glare Egert's short burst of anger faded away, just as unexpectedly as it had flared up.

"I must find the Wanderer," said Egert vaguely. "I'll take myself away, find him or . . . or, perhaps, I'll die along the way."

Hope rang out in these final words, but the dean shook his head with a smile. "'Anything is possible,' said the fish to the frying pan."

Then he turned and started walking away. Egert stared helplessly at his back.

A new day was dawning; by the gates, a trumpet piped up thinly. The city broke open its jaws, forged from steel, so that the dust of the road could sink into the paved streets, so that any family man could set out for the far distances.

The departing dean suddenly stopped. Turning his face over his shoulder, he rubbed his temple as if he could not find the right words. He smiled at his own discomfort. Egert watched him with wide-open eyes.

The dean returned unhurriedly, as if in a reverie. "In any event, it is entirely unnecessary to search for the Wanderer." He coughed and staggered a bit, and then said slowly, as if weighing each word, "Every year, on the eve of the Day of Jubilation, he appears in the city."

Egert was stunned. He licked his dry lips and asked in a whisper, "And I will meet him?"

"Not necessarily." The dean smiled. "But it is possible."

Egert felt his heart pounding ferociously. "And the Day of Jubilation, when is that?"

"In the autumn."

Egert felt his heart pound one more time and then freeze. "That's so long," he whispered, nearly crying. "So long."

The dean again rubbed his temple pensively and smiled with just the corner of his mouth. Then, as if he had reached a decision, he took Egert by the elbow. "How about this, Egert: I'll give you a place as an auditor at the university, but you'll get room and board like a full-time student. Half a year remains until this possible meeting with your friend, the Wanderer. It would be good for you to spend this time sensibly so that, should he, in the end, indeed deign to give you an audience . . . I'm not promising you anything; I simply want to help you. Do you understand?"

Egert did not say anything. The dean's offer seemed to come out of nowhere, and it stunned him a bit. The image of a pale woman in a window drifted through the depths of his consciousness.

"And of course," added the dean, seeing his perplexity, "of course, no one and nothing at the university will harm you. Do you hear me, Egert?"

Wagons were driving through the open gates; peasants from the surrounding villages were swinging their heads back and forth, struggling through the mass of impudent street urchins, whose eyes unerringly saw and whose hands unerringly grasped anything from the carts that lay in temptation's way. Egert recalled yesterday's little adventure with these same urchins and scowled.

"What are you pondering for so long?" The dean seemed mildly surprised that his offer had not been snatched up immediately.

"Huh?" Egert jumped, caught in his thoughts. "Well, really, I . . . But didn't I say? I agree."

# 5

Two beds with high backs and an old table beneath the little window were all that would fit in the tiny, damp room with the narrow arched ceiling. The small window looked out onto the interior courtyard of the university. Right now it was empty except for the indefatigable old woman who came to clean twice a week; she was pacing back and forth with a duster and a broom.

Egert climbed down from the windowsill and returned to his bed. At the moment, he had more than enough time to lie on his back, stare at the gray arches of the ceiling, and think.

Spring would soon be over, summer would pass by, and then fall would set in. Yet again, Egert counted the remaining months on his fingers. The Day of Jubilation would arrive and a man would come to the city; a man with perfectly clear eyes lacking eyelashes, with fidgety nostrils on his long nose, with a biting sword in his scabbard; a man invested with an unknown but entirely relentless power.

Egert sighed and turned his face to the wall. A small spider was running across the dark stone, throwing its thin, articulated legs up high.

The university was full of students from all walks of life: the poorer among them had their room and board in this wing. The young men who were a bit richer—and there were many of them—rented rooms in the city. Egert avoided both rich and poor. He had written to his father a few days after his installation in the university; without explaining anything, Egert had informed his father that he was alive and well, and had asked for money to be sent.

The answer had come sooner than Egert expected: the post was obviously in good working order. Egert received from home neither reproach nor consolation, nor even a single word on a scrap of paper, but he could now pay for his room and board, exchange his frayed clothing for new, and have his boots fixed. The designation of auditor did not give him the right to wear the pride of the other students: a tricornered hat with silver fringe.

However, he was not even the slightest bit occupied with caps and fringe. Staring at the wall of the damp little room, he saw his home with the family emblem on the gates: there, a rider is bringing a letter; there, his father holds a piece of creased paper in his hands; there, those hands are shaking; and there, standing on the threshold, is his mother, exhausted, graying, her shawl slipping from her shoulder.

It might have been that way, but then again, it might not have. Perhaps his father's hands did not shake when he discovered the name of his son under the sealing wax. Perhaps he had merely twitched an eyebrow and then growled at a servant to send money to this abomination who had blackened the honor of the family.

The door opened behind Egert's back. Shivering as usual, he sat up on his bed.

Egert's roommate, the son of an apothecary in a neighboring village, grinned merrily.

His name was Gaetan, but the entire university and the entire city, both to his face and behind his back, called him Fox. The youth—he was four years younger than Egert—seemed very young for his years: he was short of stature with narrow shoulders and a childish, open face with high cheekbones. Fox's perky, upturned nose was covered in a mass of freckles, and his small honey-colored eyes had the ability to instantly transform his face from its habitually impish expression into a visage of touching naïveté.

Fox was the only person in the entire university—not counting Dean Luayan, of course—with whom Egert Soll managed to speak more than two words in all the time he had been there. On the very first day, overcoming his awkwardness, Egert had asked his roommate if he had seen a girl here, a young girl with dark hair. It was difficult to ask the question, but Egert sensed that remaining in the dark would be even worse. At first he was sure that Fox would laugh and declare that in such a respectable educational institution there were no girls; and he did, in truth, laugh.

"What are you on about, brother? That bird flies so far above your reach! Her name's Toria; she's the dean's daughter. Beautiful, eh?"

Fox kept talking, but Egert could hear only the sound of the blood in his ears. His first instinct was to run wherever his feet would take him, but with inconceivable effort he restrained himself, forcing himself to remember the conversation by the well.

The dean is her father. Cursed fate!

He had spent the entire night following this revelation without sleep, even though this was his first night in a long time in a clean bed. He pulled the blanket up over his head to avoid his fear of the darkness, full of whispers. Lying there, he rubbed his bloodshot eyes and thought feverishly. The thought came to him suddenly: What if all of this was an enchantment? What if both the city and the university were enchanted, and the dean had not found him by accident? He had been brought here in a snare, brought here and secured so they could have their revenge.

The next day he crossed the path of the dean in a narrow corridor. The dean asked him something unimportant, and under that tranquil, steadfast gaze, Egert understood: If this were indeed a trap, he was far too weak to escape it.

The other students observed him with curiosity. He had to answer arbitrary questions and repeat his name innumerable times, flinching away from any unexpected contact. His defensive rituals helped a little, but Egert was afraid that others would notice them and ridicule him.

Soon the students decided that Egert was simply an unusually reserved and sullen person, and thereafter they left him alone. Egert was extremely happy with this turn of events. Even attending lectures became a bit less onerous for him.

All the students were placed into four categories, according to the number of years they had spent studying: students of the first level were called Inquirers, in as much as they studied the first year and thrived more in their desire to learn than in any specific field of knowledge; the students of the second level were termed Reasoners; the third-level students were called Aspirants, in as much as they professed a certain amount of erudition; and finally, the fourth-level students were called the Dedicated. According to Fox, far from all the youths who were striving toward wisdom were honored with this last title: the majority of them failed the summer exams and so, half-educated, returned to their homes.

Gaetan himself studied in the second level and was called a Reasoner; it seemed to Egert that, more than anything else, Fox reasoned about the subtleties of merry revels and nocturnal adventures. The students of the various levels willingly rubbed shoulders with one another; every group gathered for lessons specific to their levels, but the general lectures held in the Grand Auditorium were attended by all. At these lectures, each student tried to extract anything that he was able to digest from the learned speech of the teacher, just as in a large peasant family, where the grandfather eats vegetables, the child eats cereal, and the patriarch eats a slab of meat, all extracted from a single dish placed in the center of the table.

Every time he stepped through the door to the lecture hall, Egert set his teeth, wove his fingers into complex patterns inside his pockets, and overcame his fear. The enormous room seemed ominous to him; vapid stone faces watched from the vaulted ceiling, and in their white, blind eyes Egert sensed menace, if not wicked laughter. Cowering in a corner—the bench was uncomfortable, and it quickly caused his legs and back to go numb—Egert gazed dully at the high, intricately carved rostrum. Usually, the meaning of what the lecturer was saying was entirely lost on him only a few minutes after the traditional greeting.

The headmaster possessed a strident voice and an authoritative manner of pontificating; he talked of matters that were so complicated and abstract that Egert, despairing, ceased all attempts at understanding. Having given up, he fidgeted on the bench, listened to some distant whisperings, murmurs, and giggles, watched the dance of dust motes in a column of sunlight, examined the lines on his own hand, sighed, and waited for the end of the lecture. Never knowing why, he would sometimes raise his eyes to the small round window at the very top of the ceiling: the little window that for some reason looked out of the hall into the library.

The corpulent body and stentorian voice of the professor of natural sciences belonged more to a butcher than a scholar; from his speech Egert understood only the introductory phrases, such as, *besides, as we see here,* and *from this it is to be expected that.* From time to time the professor would engage in the most outlandish behavior: he combined liquids in glass cylinders or ignited sparks over a narrow-mouthed burner. He seemed nothing more nor less than an illusionist at a country fair. Sometimes live frogs were brought into the hall and the professor would slaughter them: Egert, who at one time had intrepidly visited a slaughterhouse, closed his eyes and turned away from the sight.

The brotherhood of students followed the speech from the rostrum with

variable attention, some in silence, some fidgeting and whispering strenuously. Among the scholars there were both daydreamers and idiots; however,
even the least of them understood the proceedings far better than Egert.

Dean Luayan's lectures were by far the most interesting. His person called
forth a multitude of strong and conflicting emotions in Egert: fear and hope
and curiosity, the desire to ask for help, and terror at a single glance. Furthermore, no matter how consumed with himself he was, Egert could not help but
notice the special reverence with which the dean was surrounded in the university.

All the whispers and giggles quieted when the dean appeared in the hall;
encountering him in the vaulted corridors—Egert had seen it with his own
eyes—even the headmaster himself hastened to show his consideration and
respect, and the students simply froze as still as rabbits before a snake: they
considered themselves lucky for every personal response they received when
they greeted him and doubly lucky when they were deemed worthy of the
dean's smile.

Dean Luayan was a mage, and the students gossiped and whispered about
this, but in his lectures he neither taught nor performed magic. He lectured on
ancient times, on long-destroyed cities, and on wars that had once devastated
entire countries. Egert listened as well as he could, but too often unknown
names and dates were repeated, and Egert grew tired, unable to retain any of
it. He would lose the thread of the lecture, and abandoned in a maze of facts,
he despaired of ever understanding. One day, he decided to ask Fox if the
dean ever taught the students magic. As an answer Egert received a sympa-
thetic glance and an eloquent but not entirely decent gesture, both of which
signified that Egert, to put it mildly, was not in his right mind.

None of the students carried arms, but even though Egert had always felt
naked without the weight of steel on his belt, not one of these studious youths
yearned to hold a lethal weapon. Full of spirit, the residents of the annex went
out into the town almost every evening, and their boisterous return interrupted Egert's light sleep sometimes at midnight, and sometimes in the small
hours of the morning. Under the arches of the university they sang the school
song, well known to all the students except Egert. Their individual lives shone
with knowledge and energy, but it was all alien to Egert, because he was a
stranger, an outsider, a foreigner, down to the last blond hair on his head.

Fox had perched with his thin backside on the table. He started to groan, as
if he were reading an especially boring lecture, and then he peered at Egert.

Egert smiled wanly in answer to the interrogative gaze of those mischievous, honey-colored eyes.

"Are you daydreaming?" asked Fox in a businesslike manner. "Daydreams are good for breakfast, but for dinner you need something richer, yes?"

Egert smiled again, painfully. He was a little bit afraid of Fox: the freckle-faced son of an apothecary was sarcastic and mocking, and as ruthless as a wasp. He entirely merited his nickname, and rumors of his pranks had reached the ears of even the reclusive Egert. Besides rumors, one of his escapades had recently unfolded right in front of Egert's eyes.

Among the students there was a certain Gonza, an eternally acrimonious lad who was dissatisfied with everything, the son of an impoverished aristo-crat from a sleepy province. Egert did not know at the time why Fox had chosen him specifically as a target, but one day, as he entered the lecture hall, Egert found the place full of a somewhat overwrought yet carefully concealed merriment. The students kept winking at one another and pursing their lips to keep from bursting out into laughter. Egert, as usual, slunk over into his cor-ner, from where he could see that Fox, of course, was the focal point of the general excitement.

Gonza entered, and the normal, businesslike bustle was restored in the hall. Gonza's bench mate greeted him and in the same breath recoiled in sur-prise. He said something in a low voice. Gonza stared at him in astonishment.

The essence of Fox's plan was revealed to Egert later, but in the meantime Fox looked around just like everyone else, directed his gaze at Gonza, wid-ened his eyes, and started to whisper loudly to his neighbor. Gonza fidgeted, winced, and for some reason grabbed his nose with his hand.

The plan was simple: All his fellow students—some with sympathy, some with malice, some solicitously, some in shock—questioned the stunned Gonza, asking him what had happened to his nose; how could it have grown by nearly a fourth of its size?

Gonza tried to put it off with a joke. He bared his teeth in the semblance of a grin, but his eyes darkened. The next day the trick repeated the same as be-fore; meeting Gonza in the corridor, students frowned and averted their eyes.

Angry and bewildered, the poor lad finally turned to Egert. "Listen here, my dear man. If you would be so kind as to tell me: Is there something wrong with my nose?"

Egert shifted from foot to foot, looking into his questioning eyes, and fi-nally spat out, "It's kind of on the longish side."

Gonza spit angrily and in the evening—as a laughing Fox later told Egert, who had become a sort of accomplice in the prank—in the evening the unhappy provincial lord managed to get his hands on a length of string. He carefully measured his wretched nose to its very tip. Unfortunately for him, he left his measuring string lying around in his room, right under his feather mattress where anyone could find it. Fox, of course, paid the room a visit in the absence of its owner and shortened the ill-fated measure by just a bit.

Heaven, what happened to Gonza when he took it into his head to carry out another measurement! Almost the entire university, crouching beneath the window of his room, heard the woeful, horrified shriek: The measuring string was too short; his unfortunate nose had grown a full half a fingernail's width!

Egert flinched and ceased remembering. A long, drawn-out wail carried from the square. It sounded like the voice of an ancient monster, fettered by stone walls, a monster languishing and alone. Every time he heard the sound of this voice, Egert's skin broke out in goose bumps even though Fox had long ago explained to him that it was nothing more than the ordinary ritual in the Tower of Lash: the gray hoods adored mystery and who knew what went on in those ceremonies of theirs. This howl broke out of the Tower sometimes once a day, sometimes twice, and occasionally there was silence from within for a whole week. The townsfolk were used to the strange sounds and paid them little attention, and it seemed to Egert that he alone wanted to put his hands over his ears every time he heard it.

And so now, having jerked involuntarily, he received a sneer from Fox. "My old dog was just the same, though it was whistles that she didn't like. She'd hear them and start howling; it was like she immediately went out of her mind. Sort of like you, except you howl kind of shyly."

The sound broke off. Egert took a breath. "You . . . you don't know what they, I mean, what are they doing in that Tower?"

The acolytes of Lash were easy to recognize from afar: they were appareled in gray robes with hoods that fell over their faces. They filled the townsfolk with trepidation and awe, sentiments in which Egert partook fully.

Fox wrinkled his nose. He said pensively, "Well, I suppose they have quite a bit to do. For one, there must be an awful lot of laundry: those long robes sweep all over the pavement; they must get all kinds of shit stuck to them. It's a dreadful business, getting rid of all those stains."

Egert repressed a shudder. He asked dimly, "But the sound? That howl?"

Fox shoke theatrically. "That's their laundress: whenever she finds a hole in a hood she immediately starts to wail. She curses, you know."

"What do you know?" asked Egert, gritting his teeth.

"You've just got to go to lectures," laughed Fox.

Egert sighed. For the last few days he had not gone to any lectures. He was tired, he'd given up, he'd had enough, but he did not have the strength or the ability to explain it to Fox.

Gaetan extracted an impossible quantity of green cucumbers from the pocket of his jacket. Critically examining the cucumbers, he nodded to Egert to see if he wanted one. Egert regarded the cucumbers with poorly concealed distrust.

Fox grinned with his entire sharp-toothed mouth, and his eyes flared with the expectation of mischief. Rapidly loosening his belt, Fox slipped a cucumber into his trousers. Huffing, he adjusted the vegetable so it fit naturally.

"Oh! Tonight we'll dance with my love, Farri!"

Embracing an imaginary partner, he danced a few steps with his face set in a romantic expression; the hidden cucumber shook in time to his steps as, apparently, he had intended it to.

"It'll work," remarked Fox, "just so long as I hold her firmly. Let's just hope it doesn't fall out. Well, I'm off."

Stuffing the cucumbers in his pocket, he drew his patched cloak closed. As he walked out the door, he tossed over his shoulder, "By the way, Dean Luayan asked about you. Have a good evening."

Egert sat and listened as Fox's loud steps withdrew down the vaulted corridor. Both Gaetan with his ridiculous cucumbers and the Tower of Lash with its strange yowl instantly fled from his thoughts.

Dean Luayan asked about you.

The dean seemed to relate to Egert exactly the same as he did to all the others; it was as if he had never brought him to the university at dawn, as if they had never had that difficult conversation by the well. Egert was simply an auditor, but one who lived in the annex like a student, and since no one brought up the subject of tuition, he too avoided talking about it with the elderly bursar. The dean, his benefactor, nodded affably to Egert whenever they met, but meanwhile Toria was his daughter, and the slain Dinar was meant to be his son-in-law.

From the time of his arrival at the university, the dean had shown no interest in him, so why was he doing so now? Did he notice that Egert was not going to lectures? Or was it about that encounter, that memorable encounter in the corridor?

It happened four days ago.

Egert arrived at the lecture later than usual. The booming voice of the headmaster wafted through the closed doors. Egert realized that he was too late, but he felt neither chagrin nor regret at this fact, only tired relief. He was turning to walk away when he heard wooden wheels rolling across the stone floor.

The low sound startled him. From around the corner appeared a trolley: a small table on wheels. The table was sagging under a weight of books. As if bewitched, Egert could not tear his eyes away from the glimmering gold spines of the books. On the very top lay a small volume, sealed with a silver clasp and a small, lusterless lock; for some time Egert stared at it, dazed, and then he twitched as if he had been shocked and raised his eyes.

Toria was standing directly in front of him. He could see every small line on her face, though it was as beautiful as before. The high collar of her black dress covered her neck, her hair was collected in a simple, one might even say careless, upsweep, and only one wayward tress, which had somehow managed to escape, fell on her pure, ivory forehead.

Egert wished the flagstones of the floor would open up and swallow him, hide him from her aloof, only slightly strained gaze. The first time he had met Toria, in Kavarren, she had looked calm and perhaps a bit detached; their second encounter, which had resulted in his duel with the student, had twisted her about in a whirlwind of despair, grief, and loss. The third time they had met—Egert flinched at the memory—she had cast her eyes at him, and he had read there only loathing and cold disgust devoid of malice.

Glorious Heaven! He was the very embodiment of cowardice: the thing he was most frightened of on this earth was to once again meet with her face-to-face!

Toria did not lower her eyes, and no matter how much he wanted to, he could not turn away. He watched as the tense aloofness in her eyes changed into cold amazement, and two vertical lines appeared on her forehead; then Toria nudged the trolley forward a bit and looked at Egert questioningly. He stood as still as a pillar, unable to tear himself from the spot where he was standing. She sighed, and the corner of her mouth twitched in exactly the same way as the dean's did: it was as if she was slightly annoyed by Egert's lack of comprehension. Only then did he realize that he had blocked the path of the trolley. He leapt to the side, pressing his back up against the wall. The nape of his neck squeezed against cold stone as he pressed his entire sweaty, shaking body against it. Toria simply walked by, and as she did, he smelled her scent, the intense scent of freshly cut grass.

The sound of the trolley had long since disappeared in the depths of the corridors, but he still stood there, pressing his back against the wall and staring in the direction it had gone.

She entered her father's study, silently closing the door behind her. The dean was sitting behind his enormous writing desk; three candles in a tall candelabrum woefully dropped globules of wax onto the dark, pitted surface of the desk. His goose quill scratched softly. Dozens of bookmarks, lovingly prepared by Toria, hung their colored tassels out of the multitude of books.

Toria stood silently behind him as he wrote.

This not entirely decorous habit had been preserved in Toria from her earliest years: to sneak up on her father while he was absorbed in his work and, peering over his shoulder, to watch in fascination as the black tip of his quill danced across a clean sheet of paper. Her mother had scolded her for this habit: snooping was unladylike, and more important, she was disturbing her father's work. Her father, on the other hand, only chuckled at her when he caught her behind him. It was how she had learned to read, peering over his shoulder.

At the moment, the dean was working on his labor of love: annotation to the latest chapter from his history of mages. Toria understood that he was writing an annotation because she saw two slanting crosses at the head of the page, but the meaning of what he was writing was not immediately clear to her. For a while she merely watched with a certain amount of detached admiration as his pen danced its way across the page; finally, however, the black lines of the letters formed themselves into words for her to read:

> . . . *idle speculation. It appears, however, that the less power a mage is allotted, the more avidly he strives to supplement this lack with superficial effects. The author of these lines was once acquainted with an old witch who levied a strange tax upon an entire village: they were required to gather the hearts of all the rats in the village, without exception, and*

*give them to her. Undoubtedly, the old woman would say she had complicated and mysterious reasons for this incredibly strange requirement. It appears to this author, however, that the slaughtered rats served only one true purpose: to cause the hearts of the peasants to tremble with fear at the very mention of the sorceress who ruled over them. History is full of examples like this, some far more serious, and it is not only uneducated peasants who have been mystified by various kinds of cheap tricks, such as the one just mentioned. Recall what Balthazar Est wrote in his* Meager Notations, *which, by the way, were far from meager: "If black, evil-looking clouds hover over the dwelling of a mage day and night; if the windows of his laboratory glow with a bloodred light; if one meets a chained dragon, uncared for and thus all the more malodorous, in his antechamber instead of servants; and if finally the one who comes to meet you has glowing eyes and carries a ponderous staff in his hand, then you can be quite sure that standing before you is an insignificant dabbler who is ashamed of his own weakness. The most worthless of all the mages I have known never crawled out from under his robe, which was covered in runes. I believe he even slept in it. The most powerful and terrible of my brethren, whose name I am even reluctant to write, preferred to wear spacious, well-worn shirts—"*

The dean paused and let his quill drop.

"You're quoting him from memory?" marveled Toria.

The dean grinned with a certain amount of complacency.

"I saw him," said Toria quietly.

The dean understood that she was definitely not talking about the archmage, Balthazar Est.

One of the candles started to splutter; Toria drew herself up, took a small pair of scissors from the table, and precisely trimmed the wick. She asked in a soft voice, "By the way, who is this powerful and terrible mage who, according to Master Est, liked old castoffs?"

The dean grinned again. "That was Est's teacher. He died about a hundred years ago."

He fell silent and eyed his daughter questioningly. Toria seemed distracted, but the dean saw that all her thoughts were spinning, like a dog on a lead, around one vitally important subject. And in the end her thoughts about this subject found form in words that seemed to escape from her lips, "Egert Soll."

Toria faltered. Her father benevolently waited for the continuation. She removed a heavy folio from the trolley and put it on a cleared corner of the desk then perched next to it, her feet off the ground.

"The impression I get about the scar and all the rest of it is . . . You can't even imagine how much he has changed. You didn't see him before . . ." She fell silent, swaying her foot in its little slipper. "Soll was a magnificent, puffed-up blowhard. Now there's nothing left of that, just an empty shell, a vile skin. Really, Father, why would y—?" cutting off the word half-spoken, she eloquently, with exaggerated bewilderment, shrugged her shoulders.

"I understand." The dean smiled again, but this time sadly. "You'll never be able to forgive him, of course."

Toria tossed her head. "That's beside the point. It's not a matter of forgiving or not forgiving. What if a tree had fallen on Dinar or a rock from a cliff? Could I really hate a stone?"

The dean whistled under his breath. "So in your opinion, Egert Soll is not responsible for his conduct, like an animal? Or like a tree or a stone, as you said?"

Toria stood up, apparently dissatisfied with her inability to express herself. She crossly ripped off a thread that was dangling from her sleeve. "That's not what I meant to say. He's not worthy of my hatred. I neither wish to forgive him nor not to forgive him. He is a void, you understand? He is of absolutely no interest. I have observed him, and not just once or twice."

Toria bit her lip; she truly had often found it necessary to climb up to the top of the heavy stepladder so that she could peer through the small round window between the library and the Grand Auditorium. Egert always sat in exactly the same place, in a dark corner far from the rostrum. His vain attempts to extract some meaning out of the lectures, his subsequent desperation, and the apathetic indifference that always succeeded it had been quite evident to the observer. Pursing her lips, Toria had tried to suppress the hatred within herself and to observe Egert Soll with the dispassionate gaze of a researcher; sometimes she had even experienced a sort of queasy pity for him. But there were also times when her anger broke through, and then, who knows why, Soll would suddenly raise his head and look at the window, not seeing Toria behind it, even though he seemed to be staring straight into her eyes.

"If you had seen him there, by the well," said the dean softly. "If you had seen how the curse worked its will upon him. Believe me, this man suffers deeply."

Toria clutched the lock of hair that had fallen across her forehead and jerked it painfully. Memories flickered before her eyes, eclipsing one another: memories of things it would be best to forget.

Egert had laughed that day: all too well did Toria remember that laughter and the regard of his narrowed, condescending eyes; all too well did she remember that painfully long, fatal game he had played with Dinar; all too well did she remember the black tip of the blade that stuck out of the back of her beloved, and the pool of blood on the wet sand.

The dean waited patiently while his daughter gathered her thoughts.

"I understand," said Toria finally, "that he intrigues you as an exhibit or an artifact, as a man who has been marked by the Wanderer and as the bearer of his curse. But for me, he is nothing more than an executioner whose hand has been cut off. And so, the fact that he now lives there, in the annex, and walks along the same corridors as Dinar once did, that, on top of everything else—" She winced, screwing up her face as if she tasted something rotten. She fell silent. She twirled a lock of hair in her fingers then absently pushed it back into the rest of her hair. The lock immediately broke free again.

"It is unpleasant for you, I know," said her father softly. "It is offensive and painful. But please believe me, it has to be so. Believe me, trust me, and endure it, please."

Toria tugged pensively at the disobedient curl; then, stretching out her hand, she took a knife from the table and, just as pensively, cut off the annoying lock of hair.

She was used to trusting her father completely and in everything. People and animals trusted her father; even snakes trusted her father: she had first witnessed this trust as a young girl, when her father had induced an adder to come out of a haystack where the village boys had been playing. The adder itself was quite terrified; Luayan, who at that time was not yet a dean, sharply scolded the peasant who, horror-stricken, wished to kill the adder; then he tucked the snake into one of his large pockets and thus carried it away into the forest. Toria walked alongside him and was not the slightest bit afraid: to her it was clearer than clear that everything her father did was correct and that he could never house danger within himself. Setting the snake down in a swath of grass, her father took a long time roughly explaining something to it: young

Toria thought he was probably teaching it that it should not bite people. The snake did not dare to slither away without having received the express permission of her father. When Toria excitedly told her mother about all of this, her mother simply frowned and pursed her lips: her mother, unlike everyone else, did not trust her father completely.

Toria had trouble remembering the vague arguments that occasionally bedeviled the small family. It is possible that her father, looking ahead, tried to ensure that his daughter remembered only what was good about her mother; nevertheless, Toria recalled every detail of the disastrous winter evening that had taken her mother away from her.

It was only much later that she began to understand what was meant by that single word—*he*—that was uttered by her father first derisively, then furiously, and finally desolately; in the mouth of her mother, that word always sounded the same, like a challenge. That evening, having argued with her husband, Toria's mother was planning to go to him, but then, for the first time after a long period of dismissive sufferance of his wife's indiscretion, Luayan rebelled.

That is to say that it appeared that he rebelled: in truth, he felt or simply knew what would happen next. He implored, then threatened, and then locked his wife in a room, but she raged at him and threw such words into his face that Toria, trembling with dread in her bed behind the curtains, was steeped in tears of terror and distress. At some point Luayan's forbearance broke down, and he allowed his wife to leave; he simply allowed her to leave. The slamming door almost came off its hinges, so powerful was that parting blow.

"I couldn't bear listening to her," the dean bitterly said to his grown daughter many years later. "I couldn't bear . . ."

Toria, aware of the pain and guilt her father felt, firmly pressed her face to his chest.

Luayan did not sleep that entire night: young Toria, awakening from time to time, saw the lamp burning on the table and her father pacing around the room. Toward morning, without saying a word, he dressed and rushed outside as if he was hurrying to help someone, but it was too late. Even mages cannot quicken the dead, and Toria's mother was already dead when her husband freed her from a high snowdrift on the forest road.

"I couldn't bear listening to her. I was blinded by pride and resentment, but what was the use of taking offense at that woman?"

"You are not responsible," insisted Toria.

But her father averted his face. "I am responsible."


Fox returned after midnight.

At first muted giggles and unintelligible chatter could be heard below the window; then someone began to sing a mournful song, which was almost immediately cut short by a gasp, as if the singer had received a friendly punch on the back.

A brief silence followed, which was then exchanged for rustles in the corridor; the door squeaked open, and Fox stumbled into the room in complete darkness.

The wooden bed groaned under the weight of his gaunt body. Fabric rustled, and first one boot and then the other fell onto the floor. Fox stretched and yawned contentedly, recalling, apparently, tonight's adventure and the complete success of his gigantic cucumber. Already drifting off into sleep, he suddenly heard Egert say softly, "Gaetan."

Fox's bed squeaked. Surprised, he turned over onto his side. "And why is it that you're not sleeping, eh?" The diffuse good-natured quality of his voice betrayed just how much wine he had drunk.

"Gaetan," Egert repeated with a sigh. "Tell me what you know about the dean."

The room became quiet, very quiet; somewhere in the distance a cricket chirped. A shutter banged, and once again there was silence.

"You're such an idiot, Egert," said Fox, his voice already different, more sober. "You've found a wonderful topic for the early hours of the morning." He paused, sniffed angrily, and then added testily, "And anyway, you'd know better. After all, it seems you know each other."

"So it seems," whispered Egert.

"Well, there you go. Now sleep." The bed under Fox fairly screamed, so adamantly did he turn his face to the wall.

A moth was fluttering against the glass; the drumming of its tiny wings broke off and then came to life with renewed vigor. It did not matter if he closed his eyes or kept them wide open: the pervasive dark was as thick as wax, and it seemed to crawl over his eyes. Egert quieted, but as always in the dark, he felt very ill at ease.

Gaetan's bed came alive again, but the squeak was cut short as it reached its highest pitch. "And what are you to the dean, anyway?" Fox asked the darkness in a hissing whisper. "What does he have to do with you? And what do you have to do with him? Well?"

Egert pulled his blanket up to his chin. Addressing himself to the invisible ceiling, he said, "He promised to help me. And I . . . I don't know. I'm afraid of him. And then, she still . . ."

"She? Who's she?" promptly asked the darkness.

"She is Toria." Egert's lips unwillingly formed the name.

"Toria?" asked Fox apprehensively and yet at the same time wistfully. He sighed loudly and sorrowfully said, "Forget about it."

The night watchmen called to one another far away in the city.

"Does he teach her sorcery?" Egert asked, his heart fluttering.

Fox once again crossly turned over in bed. "You were born a fool, and you'll die a fool. He doesn't teach magic to anyone! It's not arithmetic or shoemaking."

The silence settled in once again, broken only by the rustle of the moth and the angry huffing of Fox.

"But he is a mage, right?" asked Egert, overcoming his involuntary timidity. "He's an archmage, right? That's why I . . ."

He wanted to say that that was why he came to the city, to meet the archmage, about whom he had heard on the roads and in the inns along the way; he wanted to say this, but he faltered, afraid to betray himself more than he should. Fortunately, Fox did not notice. His bed gave yet another squeak.

"I—," began Egert again, but Fox unexpectedly interrupted him.

The voice of the freckled boy sounded unusually serious, even a bit emotional. "This is my second year in the university. And all I can tell you is that Dean Luayan, he's . . . it's possible that he's not entirely human." He took a breath. "But he's never worked evil on anyone. No one in the world knows history better than he does, that's for sure. Only, you're right to fear him, Egert. One day—you can't go gossiping about this to anyone—I saw it myself, Egert! An old crone with a drum came to the square. She was a beggar; she drummed and asked for alms. People talked about her, said it was better to keep your distance. But I decided to go take a look at her. I was curious. I was near her when I saw the dean coming. He caught up to the crone, and she suddenly turned around and glared. I was standing to the side, I tell you, but that glare nearly killed me. But the crone stopped drumming; it just spluttered out. She whispered something, and even though I couldn't make out the exact words, they scraped like nails against a chalkboard. Well, then the dean also said something to her. . . . It was such a word. . . . It resounded in my ears for three days. Then he dragged her away, not with his hands, but as if with an invisible rope. And I, a fool, dragged myself after him, although my knees were shaking. They turned into a breezeway and the crone . . . There, where the crone had stood, I swear, was a viper, a heavy, slimy viper, coiled, its jaws open wide toward the dean, and then he raised his hand and from that hand . . ."

Strangely, Fox stopped short and fell silent.

Egert lay still, trying, without much success, to keep himself from shaking nervously. "Well?" he forced out finally.

Fox moved. He stood. He groped for the tinderbox on the table with his hands.

"Well!" moaned Egert.

"Well," Fox echoed dully, striking a spark. "The dean asked: 'What is it that you need?' And the snake hissed, 'The auditor Egert Soll at my mercy.'"

A single candle flared up. Egert, covered in sweat, spit in disgust and at the same time breathed a sigh of relief: he was lying, the cursed joker that he was, he was lying. Probably.

Fox was standing in the middle of the room with the candle, and the black shadows on the walls were quivering: Gaetan's hand was shaking slightly.


Both of them pretended to be sleeping until the dawn broke. In the morning, after spending a few long minutes inspecting the slanting scar on his cheek through the bristles of his beard, Egert forced himself to set out for the lecture.

Dean Luayan descended from his study a bit earlier than usual that day. Seeing him at the end of the corridor, Egert cringed into a dark, dank recess in the wall. Without noticing Egert, or perhaps just giving the impression that he did not notice him, the dean walked by. Just at the moment when he was passing Egert, Fox caught up to him.

Egert could not see him; he could only hear the unusually timid, confused voice of Gaetan: it seemed that he was asking forgiveness for something. "My cursed tongue . . ." came to Egert's ears. "I myself don't know how! I swear to Heaven, from now on I'll be as silent as a fish!"

The dean said something soft and soothing in answer. Fox's voice became more cheerful; as he walked away, his heels clicked on the floor.

The dean stood for a moment in thought; then he turned, and pausing in front of the alcove, he looked to the side and called out quietly, "Egert."

The dean's study was enormous, only a bit smaller than the Grand Auditorium. The sunlight sank down into the shadowy corners of the room: velvet curtains covered the windows like heavy eyelids over inflamed, sleepless eyes, immersing the room in twilight.

"Take a look around, Egert. You're probably curious, so take a look."

In the middle of the study was a writing desk with a three-armed, bronze candelabrum on top; next to the desk, two armchairs with tall, carved backs stood facing each other; and beyond the desk, on a smooth, stark wall, the extended wing of a bird, forged from steel, gleamed wanly.

"That is a memento of my teacher. He was called Orlan. I'll tell you about him later."

Treading carefully, Egert moved along the walls. His pale face, deformed by the scar, was reflected in a slightly frosted glass globe with a sputtering candle inside it. Next to the odd lamp, a crowd of silver figurines stood on a rickety circular table: figurines of people, animals, and huge, dreadful insects. Made with uncommon skill, all the figurines seemed to be staring at the same exact spot. Egert followed the gazes of the silver creatures, which were fixed on the spike of a fabric needle, protruding from a shapeless mass of pine resin.

"You may look, but you may not touch, yes?"

Heaven above, Egert would sooner bite off his fingers than risk letting them touch the stuffed carcasses of giant rats fettered with real chains. The exposed teeth of these long dead rodents seemed still moist with sticky saliva.

Two massive cabinets, as austere and forbidding as guards, were fastened with two pendulous locks. Shelves stretched out along the walls; undoubtedly these held special books, books of magic. Egert shuddered. Dense, black, silky fur grew on the spine of one of these tomes.

Egert no longer desired to look around. Backing away, he awkwardly looked at the dean.

The dean unhurriedly pulled back the edge of one of the curtains, bathing the study in daylight. He sat down in one of the wooden armchairs. "Well, Egert. The time has come for us to have a little chat."

Obeying the dean's extended hand, Egert walked over on shaky legs and crouched on the edge of the other armchair. He could see an azure patch of sky in the corner of the window freed from the curtain.

"Some time ago," the dean began leisurely, "not all that long ago if one judges by the immensity of history, but not at all recently if one judges by the length of a human life, a certain man lived. He was young and prosperous, and he was a mage by the grace of Heaven. As the years went by, he would have become a mage of unprecedented power, had not an unexpected and oppressive rupture occurred in his fate."

The dean paused, as if offering Egert the chance to discern some latent meaning in his words. Egert clutched the wooden armrests with his fingers.

"Thus it happened," continued the dean, "that in his overconfidence and hubris he transgressed the line that separates a trifle from treachery, and he grievously outraged his friends. For his transgression he suffered what might be considered an excessively harsh punishment: he was deprived of the appearance of a man for three years and parted from his gift of magic for all time. But that gift had been a part of his soul, his consciousness, his individuality. And so, abased and renounced, bereft of everything he held dear, he set out on the path of experience."

The dean fell silent, as though he were waiting for Egert to take up the tale and finish it for him, but Egert said nothing, trying to understand what connection the dean's story had to his own destiny.

The dean gave a small, ironic smile. "Yes, Egert, the path of experience. That was his path, and he walked it to its end. You also stand on a similar path, Soll, but your route is different, and no one knows what awaits you at its end. But you must realize that the man I just told you about never killed anyone."

It felt as if a hot iron pierced Egert and swept through his body; however, there was not a shadow of blame or reproach in the dean's tranquil voice. The azure sky in the gleaming gap of the window turned black for a second, and a thought slipped through the abyss of his consciousness: That's it, the most important thing; everything else pales in comparison to that . . . killing. Perhaps the time had come to settle accounts; after all, Toria was the dean's daughter and Dinar would have been his son-in-law.

"But," he spat out, "I really didn't want to. It was an honorable duel. I didn't mean to kill him, Dean Luayan. Before all this . . ."

He faltered, thinking better of what he'd been about to say, but the mage glanced at him, the question in his eyes, and Egert found it necessary to continue.

"I've killed before in duels. Twice, both times fairly. All the people, who died by my sword, they all had kinsmen and friends, but even their kin agreed that death during a duel is not a disgrace and that those who survive aren't murderers."

The dean said nothing. He stood up as if thinking, and walked along the shelves of books, all the while tracing his fingers along their frayed spines. Drawing his head down into his shoulders, Egert watched him, waiting for whatever might happen next: lightning from the dean's outstretched hand or an incantation that would turn him into a frog.

The mage finally turned round. He asked severely, "Imagine that you do finally meet the Wanderer, Soll. What will you say to him? The very same words that I just heard?"

Egert lowered his head even more. He admitted sincerely, "I don't know what I would say to him. I had hoped that you might teach me. But . . ."

He ceased talking because any words he might say would devolve into despicable, inane blather. He would have liked to say that he knew very well that the dean had reason to despise the killer of the student named Dinar, and that it was conceivable that the mercy he had shown to Egert was only a respite before the inevitable punishment. He would have liked to explain that he was sensible to the fact that the father of Toria was in no way obliged to help him in his dealings with the Wanderer; quite the opposite: the dean had a right to regard the curse of cowardice as appropriate. It was only just that Egert should carry the scar on his face until the end of his days. And, finally, Egert would have liked to confess how intensely, albeit hopelessly, he nonetheless reckoned on the dean's help.

He would have liked to say all of this, but his tongue lay in his mouth, sluggish and lacking the will to speak, like a lifeless fish.

The dean walked over to the desk and threw open the lid of a massive writing set. Egert glimpsed a grotesquely shaped inkwell, a sand box with a bronze bead on the lid, a pile of many-colored quills, and a pair of penknives.

The dean smiled ironically. "It was not mere chance that caused me to talk about the mage who was deprived of his gift. It is possible, Egert, that knowledge of his fate may help you in some way. But it is also possible that it may not." The dean took an especially long quill out of the pile, inspected it lovingly, and started sharpening it with one of the penknives. "Half a century ago, Egert, I was a young boy, living in the foothills. My mother, my father, and all my kin perished during the Black Plague, and my teacher, Orlan, became the most important man in my life. His small house clung to the side of a cliff like a bird's nest, and I was a chick in that nest. But then one day my teacher looked into the Mirror of Waters. You see, Egert, a mage who has attained a certain level of power can gather the water from five different springs and perform a conjuration over it, creating the Mirror of Waters, in which he may see that which is hidden from mere sight. My teacher looked into the Mirror, and then he died: his heart burst. I have never been able to discover what or who he saw then. I found myself alone, just thirteen years old. Having buried Orlan according to custom, I did not rush to seek a new teacher, regardless of how young I was. And after some time had passed, I too took it upon myself to create the Mirror of Waters. The Mirror remained dark for a long time, and I was ready to despair, when the surface of the water brightened and I saw—" The dean laid the sharpened quill to the side and took up a new one. "—I saw a man, unknown to me, who stood in front of the immense, wrought iron Doors. The vision lasted only a few moments, but I had time to discern that the rusty bar was partially removed. Egert, have you ever heard of the Doors of Creation?"

The dean paused and looked at Egert inquiringly. Fidgeting in the armchair, Egert felt even more foolish than usual. Shrugging his shoulders, the dean smiled.

"You don't know why I am telling you all of this. It is possible, Egert, that it may be in vain; it is possible that there is no point. But if you wish to speak to the Wanderer . . . Do you really still wish to speak with him?"

The outer door creaked slightly, but to Egert this sound seemed as deafening as a barrage of cannon fire. Toria walked into the study.

Egert cowered in his armchair, but the girl, who had merely paused at the sight of her father's visitor, approached the desk as if it were of no concern and placed a small tray with a slice of bread and a glass of milk on it. Then, exchanging glances with her father, she slowly sat on the edge of the desk, dangling her narrow-tipped slippers over the floor.

"I think I've managed to completely confuse Master Soll with my stories," the dean informed his daughter. Toria smiled sourly.

The dean once again found his tongue, still addressing himself to Egert, who could no longer take in a single word. All he could do was await that blessed moment when it would finally be possible for him to stand up and leave. He never even looked at Toria, but all the same his skin crawled from the indifferent glances that she bestowed upon him from time to time.

Several minutes passed before Egert was able to once again understand what it was the dean had been saying in the interim.

"This is the labor of my life, Soll, the primary text. While it is simply titled *A History of Mages*, it is arguable that before me there has never been another who had the unique ability to link together all that we know about the arch-mages of the past. Many of them exist only in legend, some lived not all that long ago, and some are still alive. I was the student of Orlan—a large chapter is devoted to him—and I knew Lart Legiar personally. These names may mean nothing to you, Soll, but any mage, even the most mediocre, is filled with reverence at the very mention of them."

Egert's head felt as though it were gradually being filled with lead. The room slowly started spinning around him as if around an axis. Only the pale face of Toria, like an elegant alabaster mask, remained stationary.

"I understand that this is difficult for you, Soll." The dean had once again sat in the wooden armchair, and meeting his eyes, Egert's head cleared instantly, as if he had been plunged into icy water. The dean was staring at Egert, as if he could pin him down with his eyes. "I understand. But the path of experience is not easy, Soll. No one can know how your path will end, but I will help you as long as I can manage. Toria—" He turned smoothly toward his daughter. "—that book, the history of curses, is it here or in the library?"

Without saying a word, Toria drew a small leather-bound booklet, the corners of which were reinforced with bronze plates, from a shelf.

"*On Curses?*" she asked in a prosaic tone. "Here it is."

The dean took the book carefully, brushed dust from it with his palm, opened it, and blew on the pages, expelling any remaining motes of dust.

"Here you are, Soll. I am lending you this book in the hope that it will help you to understand more profoundly, to perceive what exactly it was that happened to you. Take your time. You can have it for as long as you need."

"Thank you," said Egert in a voice that was wooden and somehow not his own.

*There once lived a man, and he was harsh and greedy. One day, during a severe frost, a woman with a child at her breast knocked at the door of his house. He thought, "Why is this beggar-woman at my hearth?" He*

*did not let her in. There was a snowstorm, and as she froze in a snow-*
*drift with her dead child in her arms, the woman said one word, terrible*
*to human ears. And that man was cursed: nevermore was he able to*
*light a fire. Whether it was the tiniest spark or a conflagration, a bon-*
*fire or a flame to light his pipe, every flame smoked and expired as soon*
*as he came near it. He became cold and faded, like a flame in a down-*
*pour, and he could not warm himself. He could not warm himself, and,*
*dying, he whispered, "So cold . . ."*

Egert cringed as if from a chill, breathed a sigh, and turned the page.

*In a certain village there was a pestilence, and many people died. Hav-*
*ing heard of the misfortune, a shaman came to the village; he was*
*young, but experienced and skillful. Treating people with herbs, he*
*went from house to house, and the illness should have afflicted him as*
*well, but fortunately it did not touch him. The people were cured. Then*
*they asked themselves, "Whence came this power, bestowed upon the*
*young healer? Whence came this strange vigor in his hands and in his*
*herbs? Why did the pestilence spare him?" The people were afraid of*
*the unknown power and they destroyed the herbalist, hoping to destroy*
*his power with him. However, it happened that after this crime, a reck-*
*oning followed: after only a short amount of time the village was de-*
*serted, and not a soul knew where the people had mislaid themselves.*
*The sages say that they were cursed, that they were all cursed, both the*
*graybeards and the babes, and that they drudge in unknown abysses*
*until the man appears and removes the curse.*

The book was old and every yellowed page contained tales of matters that
were obscure and ghastly. It was difficult for Egert to restrain the nervous
chill that ran through him as he read, but all the same he kept reading, as if his
eyes were riveted to the letters, black as the back of a beetle.

*It happened once that three men stopped a traveler on the road. But he was*
*poor, and the three did not receive any spoils. Then, overcome by spite,*
*they beat him mercilessly. On the brink of death, he said to them, "I was*
*meek and good, and I caused you no evil. Why have you served me thus?*
*I curse and anathematize you: May the earth never again bear you up!"*

*The traveler died, and as soon as his eyes closed the earth went out from under the feet of the brigands.*

*Terror-stricken, they tried to run, but with each step the once firm earth below them yawned ever wider and grasped at their feet, and when they were already up to their knees in earth they cried out for mercy. But the curse had been spoken and the lips of he who had cursed them would remain cold and silent forevermore. The earth would not support the highwaymen. It no longer wished to carry them, and they disappeared up to their waists, and then up to their chests, and then the grass cut short their screaming mouths forever, and only black pits remaining in the ground, and indeed they . . .*

Egert did not read to the end: a dreary sound carried in from the unseen square, the voice of the Tower of the Order of Lash. Egert took a shuddering breath and turned the page.

*A wizard, a decrepit and malicious old man, was passing by a village. It happened that he tripped over a rock lying in the road. He fell and broke his old bones. The sorcerer cried out and cursed the rock: "Henceforth, no people shall settle in this place!" The rock groaned grievously, as if it was in excruciating pain, and daredevils who chose to come close to the place saw black blood trickling from a crevice in drops.*

Egert removed his eyes from the book. A procession of strange and aggrieving stories had been passing before his eyes for the past several days, and any sane man would consider most of these stories to be fairy tales; any sane man, but not the man who wore a slanting scar on his cheek.

*There once was a man who married a beautiful girl and loved her with his entire soul. But his young wife was far too pretty, and an image of her betrayal appeared to the man in a dream. Then, fraught with fear and wrath, he spoke words that turned into a curse, "Let any other man be ruined, upon whom her affectionate, favorable gaze falls even once, and let him die a painful death!"*

*But his young wife remained faithful to him with all her heart and soul, and not a single time did she gaze with tenderness at another man.*

*The years went by, and the couple lived in prosperity and happiness, and their children grew. And so their eldest son matured; he turned from a boy into a youth. And one day, inflamed by his first love, he danced home at dawn. His mother, standing by the porch, gazed at her son and saw his sparkling eyes and his wide shoulders; she saw the lithesome strength and youthful fervor of her son, and her gaze became full of pride, favor, and affection.*

*And the old curse broke free and, without discernment and without mercy, descended upon the youth, regardless of the tears his mother wept. She lost her wits and tore out her eyes, the eyes that had killed her son with a mere glance.*

The grass in the university's interior court was shining under the sun, concealing within its velvety green a horde of vociferous grasshoppers. The invisible insects were in a state of bliss, singing hymns to life. It was just past the lazy midday hour, and a warm wind carried the smells of earth and flowers, but the book, indifferent as a bystander, still lay before Egert on the battered old table.

*A rich and eminent lady had a beautiful daughter who fell in love with an itinerant troubadour. The daughter wanted to run away from home and elope with the vagrant. But their plans went amiss; having discovered the purpose of the enamored couple, the old mother was angered beyond all measure, and being experienced in magic, she spoke a curse, "The man who deflowers my daughter will not know happiness, he will never see the light again, and he will not even remember his own name!"*

*The girl wept bitterly for a long time. The minstrel left for the far reaches of the earth, and there was no longer anyone who dared to covet the hand of the beautiful and wealthy bride. But then one day an arrogant, albeit impoverished, lord announced his intention to take her as his wife. The wedding was performed in a hurry, and on their wedding night the young husband brought to his wife a coarse, lascivious young hostler.*

*And so it happened that the very next day the hostler was struck blind and thus could no longer see the light. He also went mad and for-*

*got his own name, and he shriveled up and thus nevermore did he know happiness. And the young husband began to live with his wife, and he received an abundant dowry. However, his matrimony did not last long because . . .*

A bumblebee, a striped, fluffy ball, flew into the room. It buzzed under the gray arch of the ceiling, bumped into a beam, and fell onto a page that was yellowed with time; then it buzzed aggrievedly and flew back out the window. Egert rubbed his bloodshot eyes with his fists.

Why did Dean Luayan think it was necessary that he read all of this?

In all the centuries sometimes incorrigible evildoers suffered from curses, but at other times they befell people who were not guilty of anything. Egert felt a particular sympathy toward the latter. He too was a victim of a curse; all these people were entwined with him in a common misfortune. The Wanderer happened upon his path, and in passing, with a single slash of his sword, he unrecognizably mutilated Egert's life.

Egert had never before had to sit for so long behind a book. His back was aching, and his tired eyes were watering and smarting from the unfamiliar employment. Pushing aside the thought of rest, Egert sighed and once again pulled the open book toward him.

*A fugitive tramp had taken refuge in the home of a lonely widow. The guards, who served the prince of that realm, were persecuting him, but the woman took pity on him and concealed him in her basement. But when the pursuers, ferocious and well armed, turned up at her house, the widow was frightened. She fainted and thus betrayed the whereabouts of the fugitive. The guards hanged him immediately, but with the noose already around his neck he said to the woman, "What have you done? You are false: let no one trust you until the day of your death!"*

*The tramp died, and the guards buried him right under the widow's window. Ever after, people shunned the miserable woman, for they did not trust her: they did not trust her words, or her eyes, or her voice, or her actions. They did not trust in her kindness and honesty, and she gained a reputation as a wicked, malicious witch throughout the district.*

*But as chance would have it, one day an old man, white-haired as the moon, road through the village on a horse. He visited the house of the despondent woman and told her, "I know why this misfortune has seized you. I know that you have already atoned for your unwitting guilt. Listen to me, and I will tell you how to remove the curse!"*

*She listened well, and waiting until midnight, she went out to the grave under her window, which was overgrown with nettles and thistles. In one hand she carried a jug of water, and in the other she carried a sharp dagger, left behind by the old man. She stood before the grave, raised her face to the moon, and said to the dead man in the ground, "Here is water, and here is sharp steel. Let your thirst be quenched! Take your sorcery from me!"*

*With these words she planted the dagger right in the grave mound; she thrust it deep, right up to its hilt. Then she poured the water out of the jug over the ground and went back into her house. The next morning she looked outside, and saw that a tree was growing on the grave, a young alder. And then the woman understood that the curse was broken, and she rejoiced, and from then onward she began to live peacefully and happily, and she cared for the tree on the grave as for a son.*

With difficulty, Egert tore his eyes away from the even, disinterested lines. *The curse was broken, the curse was broken* repeated over and over in the rustle of the wind, in the warbles of an unseen bird, in someone's distant steps along the echoing corridor of the annex. The curse was broken.

Glorious Heaven! It was worth all the days and nights he had spent stooped over this dreadful book to so fortuitously come upon a story with a happy ending. Wise, a hundred times wise, was Dean Luayan. The curse was broken. *The curse could be broken.*

With an inane smile plastered to his face, he looked out the window. He watched as a shaggy, homeless mutt trampled the grass, scampered after a butterfly. In front of him lay cold nights under bridges and the malicious kicks of a thousand feet, but right now he was frolicking like a puppy, forgetful of everything else under the sun. He was happy.

Happy, thought Egert. Lurching as if he were drunk, he stood up from the table and climbed up onto the windowsill.

Evening was drawing near, a warm, spring evening; a square of dark blue, predusk sky hung over the interior courtyard of the university, and doves were slowly whirling through it, as if showing off. Suffused with oblique rays of the setting sun, the white birds seemed rose colored, like candied fruit. Egert wanted to weep and shout at the top of his lungs: he felt as if the weight of the curse had already been lifted and the shameful scar had already been scoured from his face, like a crust of sticky mud. Not daring to sing, he restricted himself to grinning expansively and joyfully at the homeless mutt on the grass.

"Hey, Egert!" He heard the astonishment behind him.

Still smiling, Egert turned toward the door. On the threshold stood Fox, his eyes round, amazed, and then he too grinned from ear to ear.

"This gold locket is known as the Amulet of the Prophet. It possesses tremendous magical power; this is none other than the door between the worlds. . . ."

A white hand with clean nails and a tattoo on the wrist turned the page over. On the yellow sheet there was a rough sketch of the locket on the chain. The hand of the artist must have been shaking when it was drawn— the amulet resembled a deformed flower or an exotic fruit.

"It may well be that the Doors of Creation are just a shadow of this amulet. . . . No one knows. For the inexperienced person it is mortally dangerous. . . ."

Fagirra sighed. Magicians always surrounded their craft with dark secrets. Secrets and fear: people must fear magicians and must feel inferior to them. The Order of Lash used the same methods. Why, why did the old mage refuse to collaborate? Everything would be simpler.

He sighed again and looked up—the sunlight was glowing from the only window.

> It is known that our world is an island of life among the black spaces of death. It is known that there is a monster, called the Third Power, outside. It comes and stops on the threshold, and it cannot enter, until someone unlocks the door for it. . . . Then the end will come to our world: it will burn, it will rot, it will be turned inside out . . . inside out. Only the Doorkeeper—the one who admits the Third Power to us—will acquire authority, might, and the delicious happiness of vengeance. . . . It is known that when the Third Power is on the threshold, the amulet rusts.

These words, rewritten in rough handwriting, gave him a strange feeling. The university was a strange place: even the most thoroughly kept secret sooner or later ended up in someone's notes. . . .

Fagirra reclined in the armchair and smiled.

---

It was not possible to conceal the special attention that Dean Luayan paid to Egert Soll from the son of the apothecary. It declared itself in the generous permission to avail himself of one of the dean's private books. Fox had already been dying of curiosity for several days, but he was accustomed to regarding the dean with respect and caution, so he refrained from peeking inside the book without permission or from asking Egert a direct question about it. Watching as Egert spent night and day over the yellowed pages, surely replete with magic, Fox was pierced by a certain respect for Egert; therefore, and moreover because he was simply a nice boy, Gaetan rejoiced at the change in Egert's mood and his consent, finally, to go out into the city.

Fox paused at the grand entrance to the university, unable to deny himself the pleasure of patting the wooden monkey on its rump. Buffed smooth by hundreds of hands, the monkey's bottom gleamed as though it were varnished. Egert plucked up his courage and followed Gaetan's example.

This unceremonious gesture gave Egert a bit more self-assurance. The night was warm, soft, and full of smells and sounds: not sharp, like during the day, but muted, diffused in the velvety-smooth haze of the approaching darkness. The sky had faded, but the arrival of night was still far away. Egert walked with his head thrown back, feeling the wind in his hair and the unfamiliar, almost completely forgotten sensation of joyful calm running through his entire body.

Meeting a loud group of students, Egert saw some familiar faces; Fox wasted nearly half an hour shaking their hands. They went on together. Egert tried to keep close to Fox while carefully observing his protective rituals. He squeezed his right hand into a fist, and in his left he clutched a button.

For starters they went to a tavern: a tiny place with a single, high table in the center, and with a cage hung from the ceiling that housed a fleshy, phlegmatic rabbit. For some reason the establishment was called At the Rabbit Hole, and the merry students drained their glasses of wine: a sour wine, in the opinion of the former gourmand Lord Soll, but the swill brought Egert greater pleasure than all the elegant wines he had previously drunk.

They streamed out into the street in a cheerful group. Slightly the worse for drink, Egert relaxed so much that he forgot about his defensive rituals. Fox paraded in front as leader and guide. Two nimble wenches were fished out of some alley, and the group continued on its way, accompanied by their constant yelps and rowdy giggles.

The next tavern on their journey was simply called Quench, and they stayed there even longer than at the last. Egert's wine slopped out of his glass, dripping all over his collar, and the two girls, unerringly homing in on the tallest and most handsome lad in the crowd of students, swam around Egert like a pair of nimble fingerlings around a worm skewered on a hook.

Irrepressible, the mass of students set out for another establishment. Noticing a light in the first-story window of a house, Fox grabbed the nearest girl with unexpected strength for his puny body and dexterously lifted her up; piling her full skirt onto her back, he pressed her exposed backside to the glass of the window. The wild scream that was immediately emitted from the other side of the window caused the students to laugh so hard that their eyes were watering and they were clutching their stomachs. Gathering the girl up under his arm, Fox led his company onward, not waiting for the enraged inhabitant of the insulted house to leap out into the street.

They were all pleased with the joke. Seizing in turns first one girl then the other, Fox repeated it again and again with the help of his comrades. One time they had to flee for safety because the owner took it into his head to set his dogs loose. Those minutes of running were especially unpleasant for Egert: the usual terror called forth a coldness in his belly and a weakness in his legs, but the pursuit soon fell off, and Fox so hilariously mimicked the impotent rage of the townsman that Egert ceased being afraid.

The tavern Sweet Fancy was not honored with a visit: it seemed to Egert that the gray figures that were sitting in a corner, wallowing in their hooded robes, disconcerted the happy company. In all there were only two or three of the acolytes of Lash, but the students, without discussing it amongst themselves, left the tavern as soon as they saw them. Egert hurried after everyone, a bit regretful, but he had no real cause for regret because the next tavern, the One-Eyed Fly, proved to be above all praise.

This establishment served as a meeting place for all four generations of students. As if in imitation of the Grand Auditorium, benches and long tables covered the entire room, and in a corner there was a stand that bore a certain resemblance to the rostrum. Squeezing in, as usual, at the end of a bench,

Egert listened attentively to the endless stanzas of indecent songs: Fox, and all the others, knew many of them. First blushing like a girl and then roaring with laughter, Egert finally managed to sing along with the chorus, "Oh, oh, oh! Do not speak, my dear, don't say a word! Oh, my soul is fire, but the door is squeaking: it hasn't been oiled!"

They returned home in deep darkness. Egert held Fox's sleeve so as not to lose his way. They were both respectably drunk; stumbling into their room, first of all Fox demanded that the flame be lit; then he let the clasp of his cloak fall to the floor, sat on his bed, and wearily announced that his life was as dry and rough as a dog's tongue. Sympathizing with his friend and desiring to do him a service, Egert went down on all fours to search for the missing clasp. Clenching a candle in his teeth and peering under his own bed, he noticed a dusty object looming right by the wall.

"Hey," Fox asked drunkenly, "did you decide to sleep under the bed?"

Egert straightened up, holding a book in his hands.

"Well, that's good," Fox acceded weakly, untying his shoe. "That's probably the lad's, the one who lived here before. Did you find the clasp?"

Egert placed the candle on the table, put his discovery next to it, wiped a coat of dust off it with his palm, and opened it, trying to spread out the pages, some of which were stuck together.

The book was a history of battles and the commanders who fought them. Turning a few pages, Egert came across a firm paper square. One side of it was empty, with only a single ink spot in the corner, but the other side . . .

Egert stared at the drawing for a few seconds, suddenly feeling sober, as if he had been tossed into an ice-cold lake. Toria gazed up at him from the drawing.

It was a striking likeness; the artist, slightly awkward and inexperienced, but certainly talented, had captured the most important thing: He had managed to impart the expression of her eyes, that tranquil, slightly detached amiability with which Toria had looked at Egert the first time they met. The beauty marks on her neck were drawn with impeccable accuracy, as was the daring curve of her eyelashes. Her soft lips seemed just about to break into a smile.

Fox hiccuped and dropped his other shoe on the floor. "What's that?"

Tearing his gaze away with effort, Egert turned the drawing over, covering it with his palm so that it would be his secret, so that Fox would not know. A disturbing thought came to him, and he turned back to the book. He opened the first page, searching for a sign of the owner.

There were only two letters: *D.D.*

Egert felt suddenly feverish. "Gaetan," he asked in a whisper, trying to speak calmly, "who lived here before me, Gaetan?"

Fox was silent for a second. He leisurely stretched himself out on his bed. "As far as I know, only one boy lived here before you. He was a good lad; Dinar was his name. In truth, though, I never really got the chance to know him: he went away somewhere and was killed."

"Who killed him?" asked Egert in spite of himself.

"How would I know?" snorted Fox. "Some asshole killed him, but I don't know where or how. Listen; don't stand there like a pillar, put out the light, yeah?"

Egert blew out the candle and stood motionless in the dark for a few moments.

"I tell you," sleepily muttered Fox, "he must have been a really solid fellow, otherwise Toria—you know, Toria, the dean's daughter—she wouldn't have decided to marry him, if he wasn't. They say she was about to; the wedding was even set. But then—"

"He lived here?" whispered Egert through unruly lips. "Here, in this room? And he slept in this bed?"

Fox shifted, trying to make himself more comfortable. "Oh, don't get all scared. His spirit isn't going to appear. He wasn't the kind of man who would terrorize his fellow students at night. I tell you, he was a good guy. Go to sleep." Fox mumbled something else, but the words were indecipherable, and soon his muttering gave way to measured breathing.

Egert had to force himself to get undressed and climb into bed, where, as usual, he pulled the blanket up over his head. Thus he spent the whole night, clenching his eyes shut against the dark, and stopping his ears against the utter silence.

Every morning upon waking up, Dinar Darran had looked up and seen this arched ceiling with the two cracks that met in the corner. The pattern made by the cracks looked like a wide-open eye, and every morning this comparison occurred to Egert. But perhaps Dinar saw something else?

Every morning, Dinar had taken his cloak from the hook that was nailed into the wall over his bed, and perhaps he had glanced out the window. His gaze would have taken in the same exact scene that had diverted Egert so many times: the interior courtyard with the verdant flower bed in the center, the blank wall to the right, a row of narrow windows to the left, and the majestic stone back of the main building with its two circular balconies across the way. Right now on one of these balconies, a self-important servant was shaking the dust out of a geographical chart made of velvet and embroidered with silk; the dust spun around the entire courtyard.

The man who had been killed by Egert had lived in this small room, he had gone to lectures every day, he had read books about the history of battles and commanders, but he himself had not carried weapons and had not felt it was necessary. Toria, then still calm and happy, and not morose and alienated like now, had seen him every day. Carried away by discussions, for which they must have had a multitude of topics, they spent their free hours in the library, or the hall, or in one of spare teaching rooms; sometimes, Dinar would invite Toria to his room and then she, as was her wont, would perch on the edge of the table, and swing her feet, clad in narrow-toed slippers.

And then they had planned their wedding. Dinar had probably trembled when he presented himself to the dean to ask for Toria's hand. The dean had probably been well disposed toward Dinar, and then, happy, the future bride and groom had set out on a journey: on a betrothal trip? On a research expedition? What had they been searching for, some kind of manuscript, was it not? Whatever the cause, the goal of the travelers was Kavarren, where Egert Soll was sitting in a tavern with a group of his acquaintances.

Dean Luayan's purpose was inscrutable, but it was definitely not an accident that Dinar's killer now rested in his deserted cot. But what about that book with the portrait? How many days had it been lying there in the dark corner under the bed, waiting for Egert to take it in his hands?

In the morning, when Fox's departing footsteps had faded into the vigorous stomping of the other students' hurrying to the lecture hall, Egert finally threw the blanket from his head and stood up.

His bones ached from the sleepless night. The book rested there, under his pillow, and in the light of day Egert once again ventured to look at the portrait.

Never had the flesh-and-blood Toria looked at Egert the way she now looked out of the drawing. Perhaps she looked only at Dinar this way, and he, generous like all lovers, had decided to capture this look on paper, to share his joy with the world. But then again, perhaps not. Perhaps the drawing was not meant for others' eyes at all, and Egert was committing a grave offense, scrutinizing it minute after minute.

Scarcely able to avert his eyes, he turned them to look at the dented edge of the table. The painful feeling that had been born in him last night was gaining strength; soon it would develop into a full-blown melancholy.

He could hardly even remember Dinar's face, but then again, he had never really looked him in the face. All that remained in his memory was the simple, dark clothing, the challenging voice, and the feckless swordplay of an inexperienced man using someone else's sword. If someone were to ask Egert what color Dinar's eyes were, or his hair, he would not be able to say. He could not remember.

What had this unknown youth been thinking of when he touched the tip of his pencil to this paper? Did he draw from memory, or had Toria sat in front of him, teasing him and then laughing at the sudden onset of a certain tension? Why had these two needed to come to Kavarren? What evil fate directed their path, and why had that evil fate fallen on Egert's hand? He really had not meant to . . .

I did not mean to do it, said Egert to himself, but the oppressive feeling did not leave him; it felt as if iron claws, corroded with age, were ripping through his soul. Flogging his memory for the face of Dinar, he suddenly, and far too clearly, envisioned him sitting at the table in this very room, and he became afraid to turn around, lest he have to meet his eyes.

I did not mean to! said Egert to the imaginary Dinar. I did not intend to kill you; you impaled yourself on my sword. I can't really be a murderer, can I?

Dinar was silent. The rusty claws clutched at Egert.

He shuddered. He turned a page of the book, hiding the portrait of Toria beneath it, and his gaze fell on a black band of lines. Mechanically running his eyes over the same fragment a few times, he suddenly became aware of its meaning.

*It is believed that the protector of warriors, Khars, was once a real person, and furthermore that in the depths of unrecorded time he distinguished himself by his ferocity and brutality. It is said that he killed the wounded, those whose case was hopeless as well as those who might be healed, and that he did this, of course, not out of charity, but for purely practical reasons: the wounded were useless, a burden to all, and it was easier to bury them than . . .*

Dinar was buried beneath a smooth slab with no ornamentation. The sword had run through him, and the last thing he had seen in life was the face of his murderer. Did he have enough time to think of Toria? How long had the seconds of dying dragged out for him?

The cemetery by the city walls of Kavarren. The weary birds on the headstones. And that inscription on someone's grave:

I shall take wing once more.

The rusty claws clenched into a fist, and the realization that what he had done to Dinar was beyond recall descended upon Egert with an unbearable heaviness. Never before had he been so keenly aware that he lived in a world that was filled with death, a world that was divided by the boundary between all that could be amended and all that was irreversible: no matter how much grief it caused, there was no turning back.

Recovering his senses with difficulty, Egert saw that he was clutching the portrait in his hands: the slip of paper with the drawing was crushed. Egert spent a long time smoothing it out against the table, biting his lips and trying to think of what he should do now. Did Toria know about the drawing? Maybe she had searched for it and grieved at its loss; maybe she had forgotten about it, oppressed by the misfortune that had befallen her. Or perhaps she had never even seen the portrait: maybe Dinar had drawn it in a burst of inspiration and then lost it.

He put the drawing back inside the book; then he gave way once more and took it out again to have another look: for the last time because, whether he wanted to or not, he had to give the book to the dean. It is possible that this was a trap, and it would be best to put his discovery back where he found it, but might it not be important to Toria? The drawing should belong to her. Egert would hand it over to the dean, and he could decide when and how to show it to Toria.

He made the decision and immediately felt better. Holding the book in his hands, he walked toward the door, intending to go to the dean's study right away, but then he turned back. He sat at the table for a minute, then buried the dark book under his arm, clenched his teeth, and went out into the corridor.

His journey turned out to be long and arduous. As soon as he set out, Egert perceived the complete madness of his plan. He would show up at the dean's study, give him the book, and in so doing, he would confess that he had seen the drawing. And whose was it? Oh, just the deceased fiancé of Toria, the victim of his own cruelty.

He turned back two times, meeting shocked students along the way who looked askance at him. Clutching the book in numbed fingers, Egert finally stood at the doors to the dean's study, but he felt that he could not continue; he felt that if he carried out his plan it would be tantamount to an acknowledgment of his own infamy.

With his whole heart, he wished that the dean would be anywhere at that moment except in his study, and his heart fell when the familiar voice called out to him in greeting. "Egert? Please, come in."

The steel wing gleamed dimly. The cabinets and shelves beheld the guest in severe silence. The dean put his work aside and stood to greet Egert.

Egert could not hold his gaze and lowered his eyes. "I came to . . . give you . . ."

"You already finished it?" the dean marveled.

Egert took a faltering breath before speaking again. "This is . . . not that book. This is one I . . . I found . . ." And, unable to squeeze out another word, he held out the ill-fated volume to the dean.

Either Egert's hand was shaking or Luayan hesitated while taking the book, but, quaking as if it were alive, its pages flew open, and it almost fell to the floor. Breaking free as if by its own will, a single white slip of paper described a spiral in the air and then settled at Egert's feet; as before, the drawing of Toria seemed just about to smile.

A second passed. The dean did not move. Slowly, like a wind-up toy, Egert bent over and picked up the portrait; without looking up, he held it out to the dean, but another hand pulled at it with such force that the paper tore into two pieces.

Egert raised his eyes: right in front of him, pale, shaking with fury, stood Toria. Egert recoiled, burned to ashes by the hatred filling her narrowed eyes.

Perhaps she wished to say that Egert had committed a sacrilege, that Dinar's drawing was now defiled by the hands of his murderer, that in touching an object that had once belonged to her fiancé, Egert had transgressed all possible bounds of shamelessness: it is possible that she wanted to say these things, but the instantaneous flush of rage had robbed her of the ability to speak. All her pain and all her indignation, which had been restrained until this moment, now rushed forth; this man, tainted with Dinar's blood, desecrated not only the hallowed halls of her university, but also the very memory of her deceased beloved.

Without taking her annihilating glare from Egert, Toria extended her hand and took—no, snatched—Dinar's book from her father. She took a breath into her lungs, as if she was about to say something, but instead she suddenly walloped Egert in the face with the book.

Egert's head rang.

Having expressed her strangled fury in the blow, Toria regained the ability to speak, and the words were accompanied by another blow. "Scum! Don't you dare!"

It is scarcely possible that Toria herself knew at that moment just what it was that Egert should not dare to do. Having fully lost the power to control herself, she lashed out at the scarred face in a frenzy.

"Don't you dare! Scoundrel! Wretch! Get out of my sight!" Desperate, spiteful tears flew from her eyes in all directions.

"Toria!" Dean Luayan seized his daughter by the hand. She struggled with him briefly; then she convulsed into hysterical weeping, and falling on her knees to the floor, she gasped through fitful sobs, "I detest him. I . . . de . . . test . . . him. . . ."

Egert stood still, unable to take even a step. Blood flowed down his lips and chin from his broken nose.


He sat at the edge of the canal, where he could watch the arched bridge from below: the mossy stones flecked with water; the solid brickwork; the underside of the railing; the clattering wheels; the tromping feet; the boots, shoes, and bare soles, gray from dust; and again wheels, hooves, shoes. . . .

From time to time he lowered a bedraggled handkerchief into the water and applied it to his nose. The flow of blood had calmed, but at times it began to flow once more. The sight of it caused Egert to shudder involuntarily.

He watched the smooth surface of the stagnant water and remembered Toria crying.

He had never seen her tears before. Not even when Dinar died; not even at the burial. Though, truth be told, Egert had not actually been at the burial; he knew about it solely through the words of others.

She was not one to cry in front of witnesses. It was evident that her pain was quite unbearable, and it was equally evident that this pain had been inflicted by Egert, who was born into this world only to cause Toria suffering. Heaven, he would happily rid the world of his presence; he just did not know how. The Wanderer had left him no way out.

Egert flung the handkerchief, by this time only a filthy rag, into the canal.

He had to return to the university. He absolutely had to find the onetime lodger of the Noble Sword. He must convince the strange and dreadful man; he must implore him: he would beg on his knees, if need be. Just, dear Heaven, let him remove the curse; otherwise Egert would go out of his mind.

Struggling to stand up, he elbowed his way onto the bridge. He started back from a passing cart; then he slowly went along a street that was already long familiar, trying not to walk out into the middle of it and constantly peering about to see if there was any danger. The marks of Toria's blows still blazed on his face.

Passing through the square where the stone Spirit of Lash gleamed on a pedestal, Egert diligently avoided a small group of silent people attired in the same kind of robes as the Spirit wore. Intent gazes from under those brooding hoods seemed to alight upon him for a second, but in the same instant the gray figures turned and walked away.

A massive cloth rose, the emblem of a guild, swayed over the entrance to a perfume shop; the bloom of this noble flower, which was actually more reminiscent of a head of cabbage, hung listlessly from a thorny, copper stem. Jars and phials were frozen in the wide windows like soldiers lined up by rank. Egert's head spun from the thick, sweet smell that wafted from the wide-open doors. He hurried past the shop, and suddenly froze. A strange, unfamiliar sensation imperiously commanded him to stop.

In the shop, somewhere in its fragrant depths, a heavy object fell with a crash, breaking into pieces; directly after this a child's voice cried out thinly and the sound of swearing could be heard. Then a lanky gentleman with a fastidious expression on his face paraded out the door, wiping off his soiled sleeve: apparently an irate customer. Then the owner of the shop—Egert recognized him by that compulsory rose, tattooed on the back of his hand—pulled a boy out the exit by his ear. The boy was about twelve years old and obviously an apprentice.

Such scenes were hardly a curiosity in businesses, but especially so in artisans' quarters. Easily ten times a day, a person was thrashed here, and the passersby did not pay any special attention to the bawls of those who were being disciplined: they were content to allow the educational process to take its own course. The young apprentice had committed an offense, apparently a serious one, and the owner was moved to anger in earnest. Frozen in place five steps away, Egert saw how the hand that held the whip clenched nervously, and the rose petals on the tattoo stirred slightly from this barely perceptible movement.

The boy was firmly wedged between the powerful knees of the owner. Egert saw a small purple ear beneath a tuft of flaxen hair, round, frightened eyes, and the pink expanse between his lowered trousers and his lifted shirt. The boy submissively awaited his punishment, but Egert suddenly felt low, melancholy, and queasy.

The owner struck, and Egert was immersed in a wave of pain.

He stood five steps away, yet in some mysterious fashion the pain of an unknown boy descended upon him with such force, it was as if he were suddenly without skin, peeled like a carcass under a butcher's knife. Another feeling was added to the sensation of pain, a feeling that was not a whit better than the pain: Egert suddenly realized that the owner took pleasure in whipping his apprentice, that he was venting all his accumulated frustration on the boy, that it did not matter at all to him now who he was beating, just so long as it was strenuous, just so long as it went on for a long time, just so long as it could soothe his ravenous soul. Egert had no time to ponder how this agonizing new sense had appeared in him, nor did he have time to wonder at it: he vomited all over the pavement. Someone nearby swore, the blows continued to rain down, and Egert realized that he was about to faint.

He fled in whatever direction his feet would go, then he walked, and then he plodded along, barely able to shuffle his feet. From every window, from every entrance to a courtyard, from every side street he felt pain; it ran high, like water from an overflowing well.

These were only echoes: intense or weak, keen or sluggish. Someone was crying, someone was accepting blows, someone was inflicting them, and someone was suffering from the desire to hit someone without knowing who. A stench fell from one of the windows onto Egert: a man, skulking in a darkened room, was thinking about rape, and his desire was so avid that Egert, however hard it may have been to drag his feet, ran away. In another window, despair had taken up residence: impenetrable despair, which would soon lead to a noose. Egert groaned and quickened his pace. In a tavern people were brawling; a chill tugged at Egert's skin from the alien vehemence, the obscure, insensate passion of heavy fists.

The city loomed over Egert like a fetid chunk of porous cheese, mottled with the pits of windows and alleys. Violence emanated from all sides in waves. Egert could sense it with his skin, and it sometimes seemed to him that he could see ragged clots of it quivering like aspic. The violence was entwined with pain, and pain required violence; at times Egert's blighted senses blurred and refused to serve any longer.

Some intuition or miracle finally led Egert to the university. Someone hailed him as he neared the entrance, but Egert could not answer. Fox caught up to him, looking stunned.

"Hey, Egert! What in Heaven happened to your face? It looks like it's been crushed!"

Mischievous eyes the color of honey twinkled sympathetically: Fox had also received such injuries more than once. Gazing at his round, childlike face, Egert suddenly realized that Fox really was sympathizing with him, and that in this sympathy there was not the slightest hint of pretense.

"Don't worry about it, brother." Gaetan grinned widely. "Your face isn't some expensive piece of pottery. Smashing it up now and then can only make it stronger!"

The university building seemed like an island of inviolable tranquillity in a sea of wickedness. Egert leaned against its wall and smiled wanly.


Porcelain beads, which had slipped off the thread of a broken necklace, bounced across the dean's desk. The bulk of them were lost amongst the papers, but a few of the colored beads fell off the edge of the desk and came to rest in the cracks of the stone floor. Slowly, unreflectively, yet with a precision worthy of a better cause, the dean gathered them up and placed them one by one in his palm. A second after each bead hit his palm, a June bug awkwardly buzzed up out of his hand.

The heavy bugs crawled on the ceiling, flew out the open window, and returned. Toria had been sitting in a corner for a long time, her disheveled hair hiding her face.

"Contrition is beneficial," noted the dean with a sigh, letting the next insect up onto the ceiling, "but only to a certain degree. Even the deepest lake must have a bottom. Otherwise, where would the crabs go to mate?"

Toria remained silent.

"When you were ten years old"—the dean scratched the tip of his nose—"you got into a fight with the village boys. The mother of one of them then came to me to complain: You had knocked out two of his teeth. Or was it three? Do you recall?"

Toria did not even lift up her head.

"And then"—the dean raised an instructive finger—"he ran to our house every day, asking you to go first on a fishing trip, then to the forest, then wherever. Do you remember?"

His daughter whispered through the curtain of her hair, "It is very easy for you to talk, but Dinar . . ." She fell silent to keep herself from crying again. The old book and the forgotten drawing had aroused her dulled grief, and now Toria was once again revisiting her loss.

A massive June bug crashed into a shelf, fell to the floor, lay there senseless for a second, and then took the air once more with a methodical buzz.

"You know very well, my dear, how much regard I had for Dinar," said the dean quietly. "I had become accustomed to considering him my son, and in many ways he was. I bitterly regret the life you will not have with him, the books he will not write, the children you two will not have. He was a wonderful boy, kind and talented, and his death was an absurd injustice. But now imagine Soll, if you will. I know that even the name is unpleasant to you, but just think: Soll could have concealed that book. He could have thrown it out or given it to the scullery maid for kindling. He could have sold it, after all. But he decided to return it to me, and through me, to you. Do you understand what kind of courage this decision of his required?"

"Courage?" Toria's voice was no longer shaking from tears, but from contempt. "That is ridiculous, like . . ."

"Like the dancing of a jellyfish on a drum," coldly completed the dean.

Toria fell silent, perplexed.

The dean pensively followed the reeling of the insects along the ceiling with his eyes, muttering the words to an old children's song under his breath.

"Jellyfish dances for us on a drum, but Mole gets shellfish for dinner. . . ." His hand came down sharply on the desktop, as if he were swatting a fly. "Yes, you are correct; it is absurd. But we are now remembering Dinar, and I for one do not think that he would revel in his hatred so, were he in a similar situation. I just can't imagine it. Can you?"

Toria nearly leapt at him. "That's a dirty trick, Father!"

The dean sighed again and shook his head, as if wishing to say to his daughter: And how else can I convince you? Toria sprang up, tossed her hair behind her back, and met the tranquil eyes of the dean with her own tearstained eyes.

"A dirty trick! Dinar is dead, laid out in the ground. And no one, except for me, has the right to judge if he would have behaved one way or another.

Dinar is mine, and the memory of him is also mine. And this . . . Soll . . . he dared . . . He is a murderer. How you can allow him to . . . I cannot see him. I cannot think about him. I do not wish to know anything about him. How could he dare to touch Dinar's things? How dare he even look at them? But you . . ." Toria sobbed and fell silent.

The June bugs circled the ceiling in a strict order; the dean sighed and wearily raised himself from behind the desk.

Toria seemed too small in his arms, trembling and soaked like a lost kitten. He hugged her hesitantly, wary of offending her: after all, she had not been a child for a long time. Toria froze for a second and then burst into tears, shedding her tears directly into the dean's black chlamys.

A few minutes passed by; having cried herself out, Toria quieted and began to feel a bit ashamed. Backing away, she spoke to the floor. "You are a good man, Father, and it is obvious to me that you pity Soll, and that you are interested in his situation. But he was a courageous villain, and now he is a cowardly villain. That is in no way better: it is worse, Father. He does not belong here. He'd be far better off among the acolytes of Lash!"

The dean winced. Just yesterday the rector expelled some unlucky boy, the son of a copyist, who'd spied on the university and had even fallen to theft. They said he went right to Lash's tower. The dean pitied the boy, but he could not forgive him.

He tenderly traced his finger along the book spines, scratching at one that was covered in fur. He asked in a low voice, not turning around, "All the same, I think . . . Why did the Wanderer treat him so? What for? Why should he care if there is one more vagrant and one less bully?"

Toria drew a faltering breath. "You know very well that there is no way for us to determine why the Wanderer behaved one way and not another, but I think he acted justly. If I were to meet him, I would clasp his hand and bow to him."

"By all means"—the dean nodded—"you can clasp his hand for whatever reason. Just don't argue with him."

Toria smiled sourly.

"Yes, well," continued the dean without much pause. "At one point I greatly desired to meet the Wanderer, but I am now happy that meeting never occurred. Who knows what might have happened, had he decided to receive me."

Slumping her shoulders, Toria walked wearily to the door. At the threshold she turned slightly, as if she wanted to say something, but she remained silent.

Luayan raised his eyes in pensive thought. The June bugs collapsed from the ceiling as beads and bounced across the stone floor.

Several days passed, and Egert could not for a minute free his mind from strained, complicated thoughts. Fox had gone home to visit his parents for a little while, and Egert became the sole proprietor of the room. At times he delighted in his solitude, and at others he suffered from it.

The new sense that had opened up within him, the agonizing ability to feel violence with his skin, had dulled for the time being; it had gone into hiding like a stinger retracts into a bee's abdomen. Egert was thankful for the respite, but he was quite sure that the onerous ability had not left him and would show itself once more.

The hours devoted to thoughts of Toria were especially painful. Egert tried to chase them away, but the thoughts returned, as sticky as wet clay, and just as shapeless. Wearied by the struggle, he took the book of curses in his hand and sat by the window.

> . . . and that well was cursed, and the water in it became rank. It is said that a brave man can distinguish groans and laments in the screech of its pulley. . . .
>
> . . . and a curse fell on the castle, and from that time forward the steps of its precipitous stairways opened onto an abyss, and a monster settled on its towers. And should a man look out from its walls, all he will see, for miles around, is stinking swamp. And should a man walk its halls, nevermore will he find his way out into the world of men. . . .

One day Egert's solitude was so unbearable that it overwhelmed his terror. Not having the strength to see the dean and not wishing to keep company with his fellow students, bedeviled by his thoughts and persecuted by grief, Egert decided to walk around the city.

He shuffled along, his head retracted into his shoulders, warily hearkening to his senses. Minute after minute passed, and the city leisurely traded, worked, and played, but the waves of its passions rarely wafted to Egert, and when they did they were vague. It is possible that these distant echoes were the fruit of Egert's imagination; whether or not that was the case, he calmed down slightly, bought himself a cream pastry on a stick, and ate it with voracious appetite.

Mechanically licking the long empty stick, Egert stood on the curved bridge, leaning against the railing. From his earliest childhood he had loved looking at water; now, following the progress of a slowly sinking rag with his eyes, he remembered the bridge beyond the city gates of Kavarren, the turbulent vernal Kava, and the stranger with light, perfectly clear eyes who had undoubtedly already resolved upon Egert's doom well before they ever fought.

He tossed his head, trying to get rid of the recollection. Reluctantly, he stepped away from the railing and started off back toward the university.

A beggar sat in a small, deserted alley. The ground around him was obscured by the folds of his ample yet almost completely decayed cloak, and his extended palm, dry and black as a dead tree limb, motionlessly grew out of his wide, tattered sleeve. The beggar sat without moving, like a deformed statue, and only the wind tousled the gray hair that entirely covered his face.

It was not quite clear from whom or when the beggar thought he would receive alms: there was not a soul about, the blank walls were devoid of windows, and the upturned palm was extended toward nothing but a pair of homeless dogs, shamelessly abandoning themselves to coition in the very middle of the alley. The beggar's efforts were no doubt in vain from the very start, but he sat there all the same, without moving, as if he were hewn from stone.

Egert had passed by beggars a thousand times without looking or delaying in the slightest; however, the old man, forgotten in the empty street with his hand stretched out into space, somehow touched his heart: perhaps because of his humble patience or perhaps because of Egert's own weary resignation. Egert's hands reached into his purse. All he had to his name were two gold pieces, ten silvers, and ten coppers. Egert took out a coin and, overcoming his timidity, stepped toward the old man, intending to lower the money into his blackened, wizened palm.

The beggar shifted. His eyes flared up in the thicket of his silver gray hair, and the unexpectedly loud, piercing cry that burst from his mouth spread along the street. "Many thanks!" In that instant, the withered hand seized Egert by the wrist with such strength that he involuntarily shrieked.

A beefy young ruffian emerged from one of the recessed alleys like a phantom: a young man with the red, businesslike face of a butcher. The beggar ran his free hand through Egert's clothing with uncommon dexterity, caught hold of his purse, and ripped it from his belt. It seemed the old man was not that old after all. The purse flew through the air to his accomplice and fell with a clink, and only then did Egert, struck dumb from fear, try to escape.

"Shhh . . ." A broad, rusty knife appeared in the hand of the young rogue. "Quiet, now. Shhh . . ."

Egert could not even scream. His throat dried up instantly, and his chest, compressed by a spasm, could not take in air. The ruffian adroitly flung a lariat around his neck, almost simultaneously tying his hands behind him: obviously, it was far better in this city to choke the robbed, rather than risk the chance that they might identify their robber. Egert struggled, but feebly, far too feebly, for he was paralyzed by fear.

The rope around his neck gave a jerk. From somewhere beyond came the tramp of feet and a sharp "Stop!" Egert's head was bent toward the ground, but then all at once he sensed his freedom: he lunged away, straightening himself up as he escaped his captor. The beggar, his frayed cloak whipping out behind him, and his collaborator fled down the alleyway, and the stomp of their steel boots echoed against the blank walls. They disappeared around a corner, and the stomp became fainter until it finally quieted altogether.

The rope and Egert's paltry purse had tumbled two steps away onto the pavement. Egert stood, unable to take even a step.

A hand picked up the purse from the stones and held it out to its owner. "This is yours, is it not?"

A fairly young man of medium height, wearing a gray hooded cloak, stood in front of Egert, who flinched involuntarily, immediately recognizing the habit of the Brotherhood of Lash. Smiling slightly, the acolyte of the Sacred Spirit flicked the hood back off his forehead.

Now that the face of the stranger was completely revealed, nothing ominous or frightening remained in his appearance. He was simply a passerby, and his eyes, gray blue like Egert's, beheld him compassionately.

"That was very dangerous. You should not wander into deserted alleyways with a full purse. You young people are so incautious."

The stranger said "you young people," even though he himself was older than Egert by no more than a few years.

"They . . . Did they leave?" asked Egert, as if he could not trust his own eyes.

The stranger grinned. "I frightened them off. The city's robbers are a cunning and cowardly lot, and I, as you can see—" He touched his hood. "—possess a certain amount of authority."

Having lived in the city for a few months, Egert knew quite well that the sight of a gray habit really was capable of routing a pair of robbers, if not an entire gang. He nodded hastily, unable to find the words to express his thanks. With an encouraging smile, the acolyte of Lash again held out his clanking purse.

"That really is all I have. Thank you," mumbled Egert, as if trying to excuse himself.

The stranger nodded, accepting the gratitude. "Money is not the most important thing. You could have been killed."

"Thank you," Egert repeated fervently, not knowing what he should do or say beyond this. "You saved me. I truly don't know how to thank you."

The acolyte of Lash broke into infectious laughter. "Please don't mention it again. Honest people should help each other, or else the swindlers and villains will wipe us from the face of earth. My name is Fagirra, Brother Fagirra. And you, are you a townsman?"

Following the customs of politeness, Egert introduced himself.

Hearing mention of the university, Fagirra gave voice to his satisfaction. "Oh yes, a worthy place for honorable young men. Which subjects do you prefer?"

Egert felt ashamed that he was not a better student, but he finally spat out that he was most interested in history.

Fagirra nodded in understanding. "History is, I suppose, the most interesting of all subjects. Ancient tales, books full of wars, heroes, rulers, mages . . . Speaking of mages, the thought occurs to me that it was the venerable Dean Luayan who inculcated you with a love for his own subject matter, yes?"

Egert brightened: what, did Master Fagirra know the dean?

The acolyte of Lash gently corrected Egert: First of all, he should be called Brother Fagirra, and secondly, he himself did not have the honor of being acquainted with the dean. However, whispers of Master Luayan's wisdom had long ago passed beyond the walls of the university.

They had been conversing amiably for some time now, strolling through the side streets. It seemed strange to Egert that he was talking with a man in a gray robe so informally. Up until now the Host of Lash had seemed like a horrifyingly mysterious assemblage beyond the comprehension of lesser mortals; hesitating at first, he finally confessed this perception to his new friend, which aroused yet another assault of Fagirra's mirth.

Chortling, the acolyte of Lash clapped Egert on the shoulder. "Egert, Egert.

I won't deny it: The name and deeds of our brotherhood are enshrouded in a secret, to which not all people can dedicate themselves. A secret and a sacrament are similar words, and we are the acolytes of Lash, the acolytes of the Sacrament."

"I asked," Egert mumbled timidly, "I asked many people and no one could explain to me what exactly the Brotherhood of Lash is."

Fagirra became more serious. "Much that is gossiped about us is superfluous and untrue. There are always many wild conjectures surrounding the Brotherhood of Lash, as there are around anything unknown. But you, Egert, would you really like to learn more?"

Egert was not entirely sure he wanted to know more, but he did not dare confess his own indecision. "Yes. Of course."

Fagirra nodded thoughtfully. "The thing is, Egert, the Host of Lash does not place its confidence in just anyone, but your face seemed to me, from the very first glance, the face of a worthy man. Tomorrow, friend Egert, you will have a rare chance to visit the Tower of the Host of Lash. Would you really like to come?"

Egert inwardly cringed away from the steady gaze coming from beneath the hood, and tormented by fear, he did not have the courage to refuse. "Oh yes."

Fagirra nodded encouragingly. "You're a bit scared; I understand. But, believe me, only carefully selected people are favored with such an honor. I will await you at seven o'clock in the evening on the corner of Violet Street. Do you know where that is?"

Then, having already taken his leave, Fagirra suddenly turned back.

"Oh yes, that reminds me: I must ask you to keep this in the strictest confidence. Lash is a secret, a sacrament. Are we agreed? Now if you'll excuse me."

Egert nodded and then watched for a long time as the man in the spacious gray robe walked away.

Fox was still visiting his relatives, so there was no one to ask Egert why he was so irritable. Egert mastered the desire to go to the dean for advice; both his sleepless night and his long, lingering day were full of hesitations.

Friendly students, meeting Egert at the exit, wished him a good night out and a successful rendezvous. Egert answered them vaguely, not understanding their meaning.

On the way to the place where he would meet Fagirra, he managed to convince himself that a visit to the Tower of Lash was an entirely ordinary, even trivial occurrence for a townsman, then he comforted himself with the thought that this inconceivable event offered the prospect of a beneficial change in his fortune, and he finally assured himself that the visit to the Tower would not take place at all, because Fagirra would fail to appear at the designated place.

Fagirra, however, was waiting; Egert flinched when the silent figure, his face hidden by the hood, appeared out of the shadows as if from nowhere.

The route they took through winding alleyways was so tortuous that there was no way Egert could have remembered it, even if he had wished to. The hem of Fagirra's gray habit slid along the pavement before him, and two uniformly strong emotions battled in his soul: fear of going to the Tower and fear of refusing the invitation. Contrary to Egert's expectations, Fagirra did not lead him through the main gates. The alley gave way to a small courtyard, which was so dark that Egert could hardly make out the man who appeared from out of the gloom with a bunch of rattling keys and a blindfold.

Bewildered, blind, led and nudged along the way, languishing from the fear that was as familiar as a chronic toothache, Egert was finally ordered to stop. The blindfold was whipped away from his eyes, and Egert saw that he was standing in front of a wall of heavy black velvet, which exuded a faint, bitter aroma unknown to him.

"You have been permitted to be present." Fagirra's robe rustled next to Egert's, and the rough edge of his hood touched Egert's cheek. "To be present and to keep silent. You are not to move from this spot. You are not to turn your head."

Egert swallowed the sticky saliva that suddenly overwhelmed his mouth; Fagirra was obviously awaiting his answer, so Egert forced himself to nod.

A delicate, sweetish, slightly smoky fragrance was soon added to the bitter smell of the velvet. As he gazed at the black partition in front of him, Egert's hearing became unusually acute. He heard a variety of sounds: far and near, subdued and susurrant, as if a horde of dragonflies were creeping about the inside of a glass jar, brushing their wings against the transparent walls.

The multitude of whispers was suddenly replaced by a desolate, muffled hush, which lasted long enough for Egert to slowly count to five. Then the black velvet partition shivered and the long, drawn-out sound, like nothing else on earth, instantly caused Egert to break out into a sweat: it was the dreary bellow of the ancient monster. That distant echo, which was heard by people out in the square and which had for so long disturbed the imagination of Egert, was nothing but a feeble shadow in comparison to this.

The velvet shifted again and then suddenly crashed down to the floor, dissolving in Egert's vision from a blank wall into a black expanse, for there before his astounded eyes was revealed a hall of unimaginably large proportions.

It was inconceivable how such a colossal room could fit inside the Tower; for the first minute, Egert could make no sense of it, but upon closer inspection he saw that a line of tall mirrors encircled the hall. A long-nosed dwarf in a habit so fiery red that it scorched the eyes entered the velvety black space, encased in remote folds of fabric. His image was repeated many times in the mirrors' luminous depths. He hoisted a vast trumpet to his mouth, using both hands to steady it, and with that instrument he produced that very same lingering sound that so boggled the imagination. Clouds of dense, dark blue smoke wafted from the mouth of the trumpet, which was turned upward while he blew on it.

There was an echoing rustle as many hundreds of hoods were lowered. The fiery red stain of the dwarf's habit disappeared in the sea of gray robes, and a rustling whisper struck Egert in both ears, "Lash . . . ash . . . ashsha . . ." At first it seemed very far away, regardless of how keenly it penetrated Egert's ears, but as it gathered strength, it became a piercing chant, echoing off the walls of the chamber. The chant entranced Egert, ushering a peculiar torpor into his body, and once again the long note of the vast trumpet resounded, filling the space above the lowered gray hoods with a shadowy figure, molded from swirls of smoke.

Egert's heart thudded in his chest. The smoke had an unusually strong, pleasant, yet at the same time repulsive smell. "Lashhh . . . asha . . . shash . . ." The chant now came close, now receded, and Egert seemed to see surf rhythmically breaking against the shore of a gray sea composed of hoods.

The figures, shrouded in robes, were moving, some smoothly and regularly, some suddenly shuddering in sync as if from an unexpected convulsion. The space in the center of the hall gradually cleared, and an old man appeared, stretched out on the black, velvet floor. His silver mane spread out around his small, wizened face, which seemed to be framed by whiteness, like the moon is framed by shafts of light. The gray robes once again converged, and Egert saw the resplendently silver gray head rise up like a wisp of foam above the sea of gray hoods.

The ceremony, fascinating yet incomprehensible, beautiful yet monotonous, continued perhaps for a minute or perhaps for a full hour: Egert had lost all sense of time. When finally a wave of fresh evening air hit him in the face, he realized that he was standing by a grilled window, clutching the thick bars and staring at the main square, which was very familiar to him even though he was seeing it from this vantage point for the first time.

Then the ever-present Fagirra, laying his hand on Egert's shoulder, whispered right in his ear. "I know a good dozen of the wealthiest and most eminent people of this city who would give their right arm for the singular good fortune of being present in the Tower during the sacramental."

Turning toward the square, Fagirra exposed his face to the wind. The wide sleeves of his robe slipped up, revealing his wrists. Egert caught a glimpse of a green tattoo, the official mark of a licensed guild: the guild of swordmasters.

Fagirra smiled, having noticed Egert's glance. "The paths that lead people into the shade of Lash are intricate and often inscrutable. Let's go, Egert. The honor that has been conferred upon you is boundless. The Magister awaits you."

The Magister's hair seemed even whiter up close: like snow sparkling in the sun, like bright clouds at noon, like the finest quality linen. Inhaling a new scent—the smoke of various harsh fragrances wafted densely through the Magister's study—Egert, feeling more dead than alive, answered questions. Yes, he was an auditor at the university. Yes, Dean Luayan was, without a doubt, an archmage and a man of immense worth. No, Egert was not yet succeeding at his studies but he hoped that, with time . . .

Egert's blundering recital of these hopes was smoothly interrupted by the soft voice of the Magister. "You are unhappy, aren't you, Egert?"

Egert stopped short and fell silent. He could not tear his eyes away from the shaggy crimson carpet that covered the floor of the study from wall to wall.

"Do not hide your head. Any man with even the slightest bit of perception can see this at first glance. You have survived some misfortune, haven't you?"

Meeting the wise, all-knowing gaze of the decrepit Magister, Egert experienced an overwhelming desire to recount everything he knew about the curse and the Wanderer. He had already gathered breath in his lungs, but in the end he said nothing, for no other reason than the very first word pronounced by him turned out to be quite discordant and pitiful.

"I . . . a . . ." Ashamed at his weakness, Egert wilted.

After waiting a minute, the Magister smiled gently. "A man, unfortunately, quite often finds himself unhappy. At times he may also find that he is weak, irresolute, and vulnerable. Isn't that so, Egert?"

It seemed to Egert that hope itself was watching him from the eyes of the silver-haired elder. He leaned forward and nodded emphatically. "It is so."

"A man is vulnerable only when he is isolated," the Magister continued pensively. "Cowardice is the lot of the solitary man. Do you think that's true, Egert?"

Egert swallowed. He did not quite understand where the Magister was going with this line of questioning, but to be on the safe side he agreed once again. "Yes."

The Magister stood up. His silver mane swayed majestically. "Egert, you have a difficult path in front of you, but at the end of it you will find power. It is not customary to tell neophytes of the more profound mysteries of Lash, but know this: The Sacred Spirit attends to every word I say. So, while I cannot immediately reveal to you the secrets toward which your soul undoubtedly strives, I invite you to enter our order under the authority of Brother Fagirra. You will become a soldier of Lash, and there is no more honorable service on this earth. Many mysteries will be revealed to you as the years go by, but even now the Sacred Spirit and legions of his acolytes stand behind you. Any insult that is heaped upon you will become an insult to the order: even a wry glance cast at your back will be swiftly and inescapably punished. All your actions will be righteous, even if they are seen by others as bloody crimes. We will gather you unto ourselves, for anything you do for the will of Lash is just. You have seen how lesser mortals fear and respect the brothers of the Order of Lash: a single glimpse of a man in a gray robe summons forth solemn awe in ordinary men, and soon—" The Magister raised his hand. "—soon that awe will grow into veneration. Power and might instead of solitude and eternal terror. Do you understand, Egert?"

Egert stood as if thunderstruck. The Magister's offer had caught him unawares and now, terrified, he tried to gather the fragments of his scattered thoughts.

The Magister held his peace; his eyes, his wise, tired eyes, seemed to look straight into Egert's soul.

Egert coughed and forced himself to speak through his confusion and fear. "And what would you require of me?"

The Magister took a step toward him. "I have faith. I have faith in you, Egert, just as Brother Fagirra immediately, from the very first glance, had faith in you. For the time being, all you have to do is stay silent: that is the first trial, the trial of secrecy. Remain silent about the fact that you met Brother Fagirra, that you were in the Tower, and that you were present at one of the Sacraments. Also, tell no one of this conversation; when we are sure that you are able to keep silent, as silent as a stone, then you will be told of our other requirements, Egert. You can rest assured that they will be within your power. As we part today, I offer you the promise of another interview. The gray hood will give you faith and security; it will raise you up above the crowd. Good-bye for now, Egert."

In utter silence, Fagirra led Egert from the premises of the Tower by a secret path, but a different one from that by which Egert first found his way into the tabernacle of Lash.

# 6

Egert did not tell anyone about his visit to the Tower. Several weeks went by, but the Brotherhood of Lash did not exhibit any more signs of interest in the auditor Soll, so his nerves began to settle: it seemed that he could put off making any decision for an indefinite period of time.

More than once he donned the gray robe in his mind's eye. Hearing the long, melancholy sound that occasionally resounded from the Tower, he recalled the bitter smell of the thick velvet, the slow dance of shadowy faces, concealed by hoods, and the face of the Magister, white as the moon. The pledge of security and, in time, power was a great temptation for Egert, but every time he thought about the hooded mantles of the acolytes, he experienced a strange spiritual unease. Something hindered him; something disturbed him and clawed at his soul. He put it down to his usual diffidence, but he soon learned to shun both thoughts of the Order of Lash and chance encounters with his acolytes on the street.

In the meanwhile, a heat wave had descended on the city, a true summer heat wave. At noon the rutted back streets were drenched in sun from wall to wall, and the flecks of sunlight dancing on the canals were painful to look at. The shore of the river just outside the city served as a meeting place for the endless stream of picnickers who came and went; the townsmen, bathed in sweat, plunged into the water using ferns as screens, and the townswomen perched in close-knit groups to bathe in the reeds, where they often fell prey to Fox, who had taken to swimming underwater with a reed in his mouth. He never let the chance slip to sneak up on some hapless female bather and pinch her on whatever part of her body was most conspicuous at the time he passed.

Egert was one of the dense group of students who oversaw Fox's adventures and who each in their own turn had to contrive diversions appropriate to studious young men. The shore was full of splashing, shrieks, and giggles. Having found a set fishing line under the water, divers would treat their comrades to greasy fish soup. For the most part Egert sat on the shore and would go into the water only up to his waist; his timidity was noticed, but beyond a few good-hearted jests, the matter was left to rest.

Soon, however, the exams, which would elevate the students to the next level, approached: the Inquirers wished to become Reasoners, the Reasoners desired to become Aspirants, and these, in their turn, wanted to become Dedicated. The university seemed as if it were burning with fever: bloodshot eyes, red rimmed and salty from sitting behind books night and day, peered out of every corner. Egert watched as the learned youths entered the headmaster's study one by one, some with deliberate buoyancy, some with overt terror. Many of them, it turned out, believed in omens: in their various devices and tricks—spitting, prayers, and complicated signs formed with their fingers—Egert was shocked to recognize some of his own protective rituals.

Egert never had the chance to see what went on beyond the austere doors of the headmaster's study. The other students told him that the headmaster, Dean Luayan, and all the teachers who had ascended the rostrum in the course of the year sat behind the long table in the headmaster's study, facing the examinee. They said that all the examiners were extremely strict, but Dean Luayan was especially so. Not every student succeeded in passing the exam; moreover, a full half of the unfortunates who fell short owed their failure to the severe mage.

On the eve of the exams, Fox fell into a panic. He excoriated himself in every way possible: the blandest of the oaths that he heaped upon his own person were "idiotic, half-witted fool" and "brainless chicken shit." Gaetan stared at the book he was studying, then threw his gaze at the ceiling in despair, then flopped down on his bed and declared to Egert that he, of course, would fail, that it was impossible to remain a Reasoner forever, that his father would not give him any more money and that he would force his son to be the clerk of a stinking apothecary in perpetuity, where even the flies withered and died from the smell of castor oil. When Egert timidly suggested that perhaps it might be a good idea to turn to the dean for help, Fox started brandishing his arms at him and drubbing his feet on the floor; he called Egert a lunatic, an idiotic joker, and explained that there was only one thing left for him to do: he had to leave the university once and for all.

On the day of the exam, Fox was not at all himself. Egert could not drag a single word out of him all morning. At the door to the headmaster's study the young men, stuffed full of knowledge, gathered in a tense, excited knot, hissing and cursing at each other. Many of the faces had frozen into the intense expression of a tightrope walker, inching his way along a rope with a lit candle clenched in his teeth. As each exited the study, they immediately poured out their souls to their comrades, some joyful, some despairing. Egert, who as an auditor was not subject to compulsory examination, shuddered at the very thought of being required, like Fox, to appear before the eyes of the strict, academic judiciary.

Regardless of his paranoid expectations, Gaetan passed the exam; immeasurably happy, he immediately invited Egert to come visit the house of his father in a nearby town. Egert was stunned yet grateful, but in the end he had to say no.

The students, who received two months of vacation, enthusiastically discussed their plans for the summer. A large portion of them decided to spend their break in their family homes, whether those were grand estates or tiny hovels; a smaller portion of the students, mainly the poorest, decided to find work on a farm somewhere: they too invited Egert to join them. He recalled his unpleasant experience with rural labor under the guidance of the hermit and refused them as well.

Upon the departure of Fox, Egert again found himself alone.

The corridors of the university emptied, as did the annex; in the evenings, light gleamed out of only the occasional window. An old servant, equipped with a torch and a cudgel, made nightly tours of the university buildings and grounds. An old washwoman, having tidied the annex, brought dinner to the dean and his daughter, and to the few employees and servants who remained for the summer. Egert would also have been relegated to this group, but he unexpectedly received another missive from home and was able to make a new payment for his keep.

This time a note accompanied the money. Egert's heart crashed against his rib cage when he recognized the handwriting of his father. The elder Soll did not ask a single question; he only coolly informed his son that he had been deprived of his lieutenancy and expelled from the regiment, and that the epaulets had been publicly shorn from his disgraced and mud-splattered uniform. The vacant lieutenancy had been filled by a young man by the name of Karver Ott; by the way, he had inquired as to Egert's current location.

Reading and rereading this letter, Egert at first relived his shame; then that feeling was exchanged for nostalgia for Kavarren.

He imagined his home with the militant emblem on the gates an infinite number of times, and the most desperate, inconceivable plans crept into his head. In his dreams he saw himself secretly arriving in town and climbing up his own front steps, also secretly because no one had forgiven his desertion. But then witnesses of his former degradation appeared who tracked him down specifically so that they could spit in his scarred face. And would he really have to talk to his father? And how could he look his mother in the eyes? No, while the curse remained upon him, he could not return to Kavarren.

Then his thoughts turned in a different direction: Time was passing and every long day brought him closer to his meeting with the Wanderer. This meeting became a constant thought for Egert, a fixed, obsessive idea; the Wanderer began to appear in his dreams. The curse would be broken and Egert would return to Kavarren with every right to do so. He would not hide from anyone: he would walk through the main street with his head held high, and when the people shrank back at the appearance of the guards, then, in front of them all, he would challenge Karver to a duel.

Sitting in the damp, half-lit room, Egert trembled with fervor and agitation. It would be a beautiful, gallant challenge. The crowd would hush, Karver would blanch and try to squirm his way out of it, Egert would deride him for his cowardice in front of everyone, he would draw his sword and cross blades with the contemptible coward, and he would kill him: he would kill his former friend, who had become a mortal enemy, because villainy deserves to be punished, because . . .

Egert winced and shivered. His dream broke off like the chirruping of a grasshopper when a hand is cupped over it.

He had killed three men. The first was called Tolber: he was a guard, a rooster who was guileless to the point of idiocy. Egert did not even properly remember what caused the argument; perhaps it was over a woman, but it may have merely been the result of drunken boldness. The duel was brief yet ferocious. Tolber charged at Egert like a rabid boar, but Egert met his attack with a brilliant, unrelenting counterattack. Then Egert Soll's sword struck his opponent in the stomach and Egert, whose veins were boiling at that moment not with blood, but with hot, violently burning oil, understood only that he was victorious.

Egert could not even remember the name of the second man who died by his hand. He was not a guard, but simply an arrogant landowner who came to town with the intention of having a proper binge. He went on that binge, and, drunk as a swine, he cuffed Egert on the ear and called him a snot-nosed brat; and indeed, the man was about twenty years older than Egert. He left behind a wife and three daughters. Egert was told about them after the burial.

Glorious Heaven, what else could he have done! He could not really bear all insults alike and not punish the offenders, could he? True, he increased the number of widows and orphans in the world, but the landowner got what he deserved, and so did that first one. It was really only Dinar who had suffered innocently.

Three girls, the oldest about twelve. A bewildered, mourning woman. Who informed her of her husband's death? Heaven, if only I could remember the name of that man . . . But memory resolutely refused to extract from the distant past a word that had long ago been forgotten because it no longer mattered.

Far in the distance, somewhere in the recesses of the darkened corridors, a cricket chirped softly. It was very late in the night. Shuddering against his will, Egert immediately lit five candles. It was an inconceivable waste, but the room was lit up as though it were day, and in the muddled depths of the iron looking glass that hung on the wall by the door, Egert saw his scarred face.

And at that very second, the ability to feel pain and violence as it crawled across his skin returned to him with such force that he staggered.

Glorious Heaven! The city beyond the thick walls of the university felt like a solid, aching wound. The university itself was almost empty, and the annex was completely empty except for Egert, but Egert sensed suffering not that far away: a habitual suffering, like a permanent migraine.

His knees buckled slightly at the thought that he would have to walk through the darkened corridors and stairs. Clutching candles in his sweaty palms—three in his right and two in his left—Egert nudged open the door with his shoulder.

Niches yawned blackly; columns threw out malformed, creeping shadows. The faces of great scholars, which adorned the walls in bas-relief, loomed over Egert with contemptuous grimaces. In order to bolster his confidence, Egert proceeded to sing in a trembling voice: "Oh, oh, oh! Do not speak, my dear, don't say a word! Oh, my soul is fire, but the door is squeaking: it hasn't been oiled!"

Hot wax dripped on his hands, but he did not feel it. The source of the pain was in front of him, located in the library.

A light shone up from under the massive doors. Egert wanted to knock, but both his hands were occupied so he softly scraped the toe of his boot against the door. The sound of the dean's surprised "Yes?" carried from beyond.

Egert tried to grab the brass handle without letting go of his burning candles. It is possible that his efforts might have been crowned with success, but then the door opened in front of him, and in its opening stood Dean Luayan. He was not the source of the pain: it was coming from someone in the twilight of the book-filled hall.

"It is I," said Egert, although the dean surely recognized him and would not confuse him with anyone else. "It is I . . ." He faltered, not knowing what else to say.

The dean stepped back slowly, inviting Egert to enter.

Toria, as usual, was sitting on the edge of a table, and her empty book cart was leaning against her knee like a frightened dog. Egert had not seen Toria since the day he brought the dean Dinar's book and was smacked by the heavy tome in the face. Now her eyes were shadowed in darkness. Egert could not see if her gaze was fastened on him, but the sensation emanating from the girl, the sensation of blunt suffering, became stronger, as if the very sight of Egert aroused in her a new episode of pain.

"Yes, Soll?" asked the dean dryly.

Egert suddenly realized that they had been talking about him, though he did not know where such certainty came from. "I came to ask," he said dully, "about broken curses, about curses that have been lifted. Does it depend . . . does the possibility of deliverance depend on . . . does it depend on the extent to which the person is guilty?"

Toria slowly turned toward her father, but she did not get up from the table and she did not say a word.

Having exchanged glances with his daughter, the dean frowned. "What is it you don't understand?"

Toria—her left temple began to ache even more, so much so that Egert wanted to press his hand to his own head—said blandly and levelly into the darkness, "Undoubtedly, Master Soll wishes to find out if he, as an innocent sufferer, has any advantage."

Egert's heart collapsed like a baited dog. Barely moving his lips he whispered, also into space, "No, I . . ."

There were no words; Toria sat as still as a statue, not betraying her aching pain the slightest bit.

"I'll leave now," said Egert softly, "and you'll get better. I only . . . Forgive me."

He turned and walked toward the door. Behind him, Toria let out a faltering breath and at that moment a spasm of pain seized her, such a spasm that Egert stumbled.

The dean also felt that something was wrong. Quickly glancing at his daughter, he shifted his glance, cool and distrustful, to Egert. "What is wrong with you, Egert?"

Egert leaned his shoulder against the doorpost. "Nothing's wrong with me. Can't you see? She's in pain. How can you not feel it? How can you tolerate it, that she——" He took a breath. Father and daughter were staring at him without blinking; the jaws of the spasm unclenched incrementally, and Egert felt a wave of relief flow over Toria.

"You should put, I mean, it might help if you put a cold cloth on your forehead," he whispered. "I'm already leaving. I know that I am guilty; I know that I am a murderer. What was done to me, it was only what I deserve. Perhaps——" He shivered. "——perhaps the Wanderer will not take pity on me, will not remove the scar. Would that . . . would that make it easier on you?"

Even in the half dark of the gloomy library it was apparent how large and dark her eyes had become.

"Soll?" asked the dean briskly.

Toria finally did what Egert had long wanted to do: she pressed her palm to her temple.

"I am leaving the university," Egert said, barely audibly. "I am useless here and seeing me hurts her. I do understand." He stepped through the door and walked away down the corridor. Only then did he notice that the candles, convulsively clutched in his fists, had dripped wax all over his clothes and shoes, and had burned the palms of his hands.

"Soll!" the dean called out behind him.

He did not want to turn around, but the dean grabbed him by the shoulder and twisted it back, peering into Egert's exhausted face. There was such intensity and aggression in his gaze that Egert became terrified.

"Oh, just let him go," Toria requested softly. She was standing in the doorway and her soul seemed somewhat easier: perhaps because her headache had abated.

Gripping Egert by his elbow, the dean marched him back to the library and forcefully sat him down in a creaking chair. Only then did he turn to Toria. "Why didn't you take a cure immediately?"

"I thought I could manage," she answered distantly.

"And now?"

"Now, it's better."

The dean looked searchingly at Egert. "Well, Soll? Is it better? Is it true?"

"It's true," he answered, barely moving his lips. His candles had extinguished; prying his fingers apart with difficulty, he let the stubs fall to the floor. Velvety moths pivoted around the ceiling lamps with soft rustles, and the far-off cry of the night watch echoed through the dark window facing the square.

"How long has this been going on?" asked the dean casually, as if he did not care about the answer.

"It's not constant," explained Egert, gazing at the moths. "It happened once before, and today . . . today was the second time. I have no control over it. Can I go now?"

"Toria," asked the dean with a sigh. "Do you have any questions for Master Soll?"

She remained silent. As he left, Egert twisted his head around to look at her and caught her gaze, filled with blank astonishment, following him.


Summer in the city choked on hot dust, and in the course of one long, hot day, the lemonade hawkers earned more than they usually did in a week. People on the streets sizzled in the heat, and even the Tower of Lash emitted its ritual howl less frequently than usual. Hawkers erected flaxen awnings with long silk tassels over their heads: it seemed like enormous, many-colored jellyfish were oozing across the square. In the university's great building dust whirled, content to settle everywhere without the constant disturbance of clopping feet; it gleamed in shafts of sunlight and covered the rostrum in a thin layer; it enveloped the benches, the windowsills, the statues of scholars, and the mosaic floors. Life glimmered only in servants' quarters; in the dean's study, where he was working hard on the biographies of archmages; in the room of his daughter; and in the annex, where the auditor Egert Soll lived in complete solitude.

The old washerwoman, who had abandoned her cleaning for the time being, now prepared only dinner; Toria took it upon herself to cook breakfast and supper for herself and her father. Knowing full well that the dean, absorbed in his work, might eat nothing more in the course of a day than a few sunflower seeds, Toria went out into the city every day to purchase food. She brought the food to his study and paid close attention so that every last crumb was, in the end, eaten.

Egert almost never left his room. Sitting by the window, he often saw Toria crossing the university courtyard with a basket on her arm. After thunderstorms, which then once again gave way to severe heat, a broad puddle lingered for a while on the path through the courtyard. One day, as she made her way home from the bazaar, Toria came across a sparrow that was bathing in this puddle.

But perhaps it was not a sparrow: its sodden wings were puffed up and Egert could have easily taken the gray, insolent fellow for some far more noble bird. Apparently, the bather was receiving indescribable pleasure from its warm bath, and it did not notice Toria as she approached.

Toria slowed her pace and then stopped. Her proud, chiseled profile, like the mint of an empress on a coin, was turned toward Egert. He expected that she would step over the puddle and go on her way, but she did not move forward. The bird splashed in its bath with abandon while the girl, holding a heavy basket in her hands, waited patiently.

Finally the sparrow—or whatever kind of bird it was—finished his bath and, without paying any attention to the considerate Toria, flitted up to one of the exterior rafters to dry off. Toria shifted the basket from one hand to the other, calmly and amiably nodded to the wet bird, and continued on her way.

Returning from the market the next day, Toria only just avoided running straight into Egert by the grand entrance.

The basket was in considerable danger and would surely have suffered harm, had Egert not swept it up with both hands. They were both startled by the unexpected meeting and simply stared at each other for a time.

Toria would not admit to herself that Egert had surprised her yet again. Apparently, some alteration had occurred within him: his scarred face was still as exhausted and mirthless as before, but that hunted expression had disappeared from his eyes. It was the expression of a dog cowering before his master's stick; Toria had become accustomed to seeing it in his eyes and had learned to despise it. Now they were simply tired, human eyes.

Recently, Toria caught herself thinking about Egert Soll far too often. She believed that thinking about him was unseemly, but avoiding the thoughts turned out to be impossible: he had greatly confounded her that night in the library. He had stunned her not so much by his ability to sense pain as by his admission of his own guilt, an admission that was inconceivable, in her estimation, from the mouth of a murderer. Without being completely aware of it, she now wanted to see him again and examine him more attentively: Did he really grasp his own baseness? Or was it nothing more than a trick, a pathetic attempt to arouse sympathy and obtain a reduction of his sentence?

"Return the basket, please," she said coolly. There were no other words that would come to her tongue at that moment.

Egert obediently handed her goods back to her. The green tips of a magnificent bunch of scallions swayed, hanging over the edge of the basket; the neck of a wine bottle and a hard, round piece of golden yellow cheese peeked out from under the thicket of scallions.

Grasping the basket by its rounded handle, Toria walked farther along the corridor. The load pulled down her shoulder, and in order to keep her balance she had to compensate by throwing her free arm out to the side.

She had just made it to the corner when behind her she heard a hoarse, uncertain voice. "May I . . . help?"

She slowed to a stop. Over her shoulder, without turning, she said, "What?"

Egert repeated himself dispiritedly, already anticipating her refusal. "May I help? That's got to be heavy."

Toria stood for a second in confusion; her usual asperity sprang to the tip of her tongue, but she did not let it loose. She suddenly recalled that heavy book, smashing away at the pale, drawn face, at the scarred cheek, at the bloodstained lips. Then her heart, as well as her arm, began to ache, as if she had kicked a homeless dog for no reason at all.

"You may help me," she said with ostentatious indifference.

Egert did not immediately understand, and understanding, he did not immediately approach her: it was as if he was afraid that she would strike him again. Toria frowned peevishly and looked away.

The basket again changed hands. In silent procession they both walked on, Toria in front and Egert behind. Without a single word they traveled through the courtyard to the household annex. In the deserted kitchen Toria took the basket with a regal gesture and set it on the table.

It was high time for Egert to turn around and leave, but he tarried. Was he waiting, perhaps, for her to thank him?

"Thank you." Toria let the words tumble out of her mouth. Egert sighed and she, without planning it, suddenly asked, "Before, you didn't ever feel others' pain, did you?"

Egert said nothing.

"And it is true," Toria explained to herself, "that if you had felt it, then you could not have thrust your sword into another living man, yes?"

She immediately regretted her words, but Egert only nodded wearily. He affirmed impassively, "I could not have."

An onion, a bunch of carrots, and a bunch of parsley were extracted from the basket. Egert watched as though spellbound while a poppy seed muffin; sweet, yellow butter; and a pot of cream followed these items into the light of the world.

"And now," Toria continued relentlessly, "right now, this very second, are you able to feel it?"

"No," Egert responded dully. "If it happened constantly, I would go out of my mind, and I wouldn't have to wait for my meeting with the Wanderer."

"Only a crazy person could want to meet the Wanderer," snapped Toria, and once again she regretted what she said because Egert suddenly blanched.

"Why?"

Toria was not happy with such a turn in the conversation, and so the fresh cheese, folded in a napkin, was thrown onto the table with a certain amount of temper. "Why? Don't you know anything about him at all?"

Egert slowly traced his finger along his scar. "This is all I know. Will this knowledge suffice?"

Toria paused, unable to find an answer. Egert looked at her for the first time since encountering her by the entrance: he looked at her without averting his eyes, sorrowfully and a little guiltily, and his gaze bewildered Toria. To hide her confusion, she bit off a piece of the muffin without thinking.

Egert swallowed and averted his gaze. Then, cheered that she could smother her own discomfort, she plucked a white crumb from her lip and asked, "Do you want something to eat?"

She had suddenly remembered that, because he lived in the annex, he was fed only once a day when the good woman, hired to carry dinner, delivered his meal to him. Somewhat disconcerted by this revelation, she hesitated slightly and then handed him a piece of the poppy seed muffin.

"Take it. Eat."

He shook his head. Looking to the side, he asked, "But you, what do you know about the Wanderer?"

"Take the muffin," she said adamantly.

For a few seconds he just looked at the rich morsel, dripping heavy crumbs, then he stretched out his hand to take it, and, very briefly, he brushed Toria's fingers.

They both experienced a momentary awkwardness. With deliberate efficiency, Toria continued to unpack her purchases, and Egert thrust his white teeth into the muffin as soon as he came to his senses.

Toria watched as he ate; demolishing in a second both the inside and the poppy seed-strewn top, he nodded gratefully.

"Thank you. You are . . . very kind."

She twitched her lip mockingly: My, what a polite young man.

Egert again looked her right in the eyes. "So you really don't know anything about the Wanderer?"

Drawing a long kitchen knife from a drawer, she focused on testing it with her finger to see if the edge had dulled. Casually, she asked, "Didn't you already talk about this with my father? If anyone in the world knows something about your acquaintance, it would be my father, true?"

Egert shrugged his shoulders drearily. "Yes. It's just that I understand very little of what Dean Luayan says."

Toria marveled at his candor. She ran the blade of the knife across an ancient, worn grindstone a few times; then, galled at her own complacency, she said, "That's hardly surprising. You probably wasted all your time in swordplay. I doubt you've ever even read a book in its entirety besides a primer."

She expected him to go pale again or lower his eyes or even run away, but he only nodded wearily, agreeing with her. "That's true, but what's to be done about it? Anyway, there is no book that can tell me how to find the Wanderer, how to talk to him . . . so that he understands."

Toria pondered this for a bit and then said carelessly, playing with the knife, "And are you really sure that you need to find him? Are you convinced that without the scar you will become better?"

Only now did Egert lower his head; instead of his face, she saw a pile of disordered blond hair. For a long time there was no answer. When he did speak, he directed his words at the floor. "Believe me, I very much need to find him.

There is no getting around it: I must either be freed from the curse or I must die. Do you understand?"

Quiet set in and lasted for so long that the fresh bunch of parsley, sitting in a patch of sun on the table, began to wither. Toria shifted her gaze from Egert's lowered face to the sunny day beyond the window, and it was clear to her, as clear as the day, that the man standing in front of her was not lying, not being overly dramatic, not acting: he really would prefer to die if the curse of the scar were not broken.

"The Wanderer," she began softly, "appears on the Day of Jubilation. No one knows his paths or his roads; it is said that he can cover inconceivable distances in the space of a day. But on the Day of Jubilation he comes here. As to why, well, fifteen years ago on the same day in the square—from this window you can't see it—but there, in the square, in front of the courthouse, a scaffold was erected. The town magistrate had decided that, as a prelude to the merrymaking, an execution would be performed and that it would forever be associated with the beginning of the festival. They sentenced some stranger, a vagrant, for the unlawful misappropriation of the rank and title of mage."

"What?" asked Egert reluctantly.

"He claimed to be a mage, but he was not a mage. The law forbidding that is ancient and obscure. He was sentenced to be beheaded. People gathered, thick on the ground, excited by the prospect of fireworks, carnival, a man sentenced to the block. . . . The executioner lifted his ax, but the condemned man surged up and disappeared right in front of the whole city. It was as if he never even existed. No one knows precisely how this happened. Perhaps he was a mage after all. It was not the Spirit Lash that saved him, as some people say."

Egert winced at the mention of Lash, but Toria did not notice.

"From that time until now the Day of Jubilation has begun with an execution, but one of the condemned men is pardoned by lottery. They draw lots right there on the scaffold, and one is released while the others, well, they get the usual fate of the condemned. Then, Egert, there is a citywide celebration, and everyone rejoices."

She realized that, carried away by her tale, she had called him by his first name. She frowned.

"What can you do? Heathen customs die hard. You would probably be interested in seeing an execution, yes?"

Egert averted his eyes. With barely noticeable reproof he said, "Hardly. Especially if my ability returned, as I imagine it would. So, I think not."

Toria lowered her eyes, a bit disconcerted. She muttered through her teeth, "I don't know why I am telling you all this. Father is of the opinion that the Wanderer has a connection to the man who so abruptly disappeared right out from under the ax. He believes that both before this and after, the man experienced considerable ordeals, and a change came over him. All this is, of course, extremely vague, but in my opinion my father thinks that he and the Wanderer are one and the same man."

Again a long pause followed. Toria pensively scored the surface of the table with the tip of the knife.

"So every year," slowly continued Egert, "he comes here. On that very same day?"

Toria shrugged her shoulders. "No one knows what interests the Wanderer, Soll." She cast a glance at her companion and suddenly added with uncanny boldness, "But I think that you would interest him very little."

With a habitual gesture, Egert touched his scar. "Well, that just means that I have to find a way to interest him."

On the evening of that same day, Dean Luayan dropped in on Egert.

Twilight reigned in the small room. Egert was sitting by the window, the book on curses lay open beside him on the windowsill, but Egert was not reading. Staring at the courtyard with unresponsive, wide-open eyes, he saw in his mind's eye first the square, where a scaffold was swelling upward like an island in the midst of a sea of humanity; then the thoughtful eyes of Toria; then the kitchen knife, cleaving through a stalk of parsley; then finally the ax, cleaving through a man's neck. A recollection of the dean's ambiguous story about the mage deprived of his magical gift came to his mind; then his thoughts turned to the Order of Lash, and the Sacred Spirit broke in upon his thoughts, resembling its own sculpted image the way two drops of water resemble each other: shrouded in its robe, it descended onto the scaffold and saved the doomed man from the block.

At that moment a knock came at the door. Egert shivered and tried to convince himself that in fact there had been no knock, but the rusty hinges screeched and the dean was standing on the threshold.

In the gathering darkness Egert could not have traced the pattern of lines on his own palm, but the face of the dean, which was several steps away, was plainly visible: that face, as usual, was a paragon of passionless detachment.

Egert leapt up as if the mouth of a volcano were under him instead of just a rickety chair. The appearance of the dean here, in this wretched little room, which Egert had grown accustomed to thinking of as his home, seemed an occurrence equally as unthinkable as a visit from the moon to the nest of a wagtail.

The dean looked at Egert inquiringly, as if Egert had come to see him and was about to tell him something. Egert was silent, having been deprived of the gift of speech as soon as the dean entered.

"I beg your pardon," the dean said somewhat sarcastically, and Egert thought in passing that Toria was strikingly similar to her father, not so much in appearance as in habits. "I beg your pardon for barging in on you, Soll. At our last meeting you said that you were ready to quit the university and that you were motivated to do so in part because of your, hmm, uselessness . . . that is, your ignorance. Did you say this seriously or was it just a pretty turn of phrase?"

The darkened, arched ceiling came down and crushed Egert's shoulders. He was being turned out, and they had every right to turn him out. "Yes," he said dully. "I am ready to leave. I understand."

For a short time they were both silent, the dean dispassionately, Egert anxiously; finally, unable to endure the silence any longer, Egert muttered, "I truly am useless, Dean Luayan. Studying for me is like an ant taking on the heavens. Maybe it would be best to give my place to another?"

He suddenly broke into a sweat. He was horrified at his own words: his place already belonged to another. It was Dinar's place.

The dean rubbed his temple, and his wide sleeve swayed. "Well, Soll. There is nothing wrong with your reason: you usually speak sensibly. Your academic work does, however, leave something to be desired. Even though you are an auditor, you should not neglect your studies. And so, I've brought you this." Luayan took a medium-sized tome in a leather binding and a smallish pamphlet bound in pasteboard from the folds of his dark garment.

"I asked Toria to select something relatively straightforward for the beginning. Fortunately, you do know how to read. When you have got through this one, turn to the other. And don't be shy about speaking up if something is too difficult for you. Perhaps Toria might take a shot at tutoring you . . . though perhaps not. Sometimes it seems to me that she has no patience at all."

The dean nodded, bade him farewell, and when he was already in the corridor, suddenly said in a dreamy tone, "You know who had a native gift for teaching? Dinar. He had a distinctive gift: he never imposed ideas; rather, he compelled his students to think. Beyond that, for him it was a game, a passion, a pleasure. . . . No, Soll, there is no need to go pale: I am not saying this to rebuke you. But I have, you understand, neither the time nor the inclination to teach you myself, and so I was just thinking aloud: it would have done you good to study with Dinar. . . . However, there's nothing to be done about that: you'll have to venture it alone."

With that the dean left. Only then did Egert fully realize that all around him there was a darkness so deep that it should have been impossible to distinguish a human face or clothing or books. Covered in goose bumps, Egert thrust his arm out toward the table. The books were there, but the leather binding felt cold, and the pasteboard felt as rough as sackcloth.

The books were titled *The Structure of Creation* and *Conversations with Young People*. The author of the first book was a boring, stern old man who set forth his thoughts concisely and clearly, but required constant effort on the part of the reader. The writer of the second book adored long digressions, which continued on in the notes. He addressed the reader as "my dear child," and Egert envisioned him as an amiable, somewhat sentimental, rosy-cheeked, and corpulent fellow.

The pages of the pasteboard-bound book bored Egert, and he scrambled through the chapters of the leather-bound tome as if they were prickly thickets. His eyes finally became accustomed to daily reading and no longer teared up. In order to stretch his tired back Egert got into the habit of walking into the city every morning. He issued forth leisurely, with ambling steps and the look of a man who had not yet decided where he should direct his feet; nevertheless, every day his feet brought him by diverse paths to the bazaar that was situated not far from the university. There he wandered among the stalls, successively tasting bacon and cream, fruit and smoked fish, while amongst the flickering hats and headscarves he searched for the black-haired head of Toria.

She noticed Egert immediately, but she pretended that she was fully engrossed in her shopping and that she had no wish to turn her eyes to the side, not for any reason. Passing from stall to stall, pointing and bargaining, she gradually filled her basket with food, while Egert strolled nearby, never losing sight of Toria, but also never appearing directly in her line of sight.

Having finished her shopping, Toria would set out on the return trip. Every time, Egert had to overcome his awkwardness when, having run in an arc to get ahead of her, he happened upon her path home as if by chance.

Toria always received him coolly and without surprise; taking the curved handle of the basket from her arm, Egert was always covered in goose bumps.

They always returned to the university in silence. Casually glancing to the side, Toria would see next to her a round shoulder and an arm with a rolled-up sleeve. On this arm the basket seemed as light as a feather, and the muscles under the white skin, untouched by sunburn, played only slightly under its weight. Toria would avert her eyes and they would pass through the courtyard to the household annex, and just as silently, they would part ways in the kitchen, after Egert had received in reward for his labor sometimes a roll with butter, sometimes a dripping fragment of honeycomb, sometimes a glass of milk. Carrying away his loot, Egert would return to his room and, with a light heart, sink into a book with the hard-earned delicacy sitting ready at hand in anticipation of the moment when it would finally be eaten.

At the dean's request, Toria did try to tutor Egert two or three times. These attempts, unfortunately, were a decided failure: both tutor and student went their separate ways annoyed and exhausted. The joint lessons were discontinued after one memorable episode when Toria, beginning to enjoy the philosophical discussions about creation and mortality, exclaimed, leafing through the pages, "But that isn't so, Dinar, it's—"

Stopping short, she met Egert's terrified gaze and immediately said her good-byes. That evening the two of them, in different parts of the massive, dark building, abandoned themselves to the same oppressive thoughts.

In all other respects, a tepid neutrality now held sway between Egert and Toria. Toria taught herself to nod when she ran into him, and Egert learned not to blanch when he heard the light tapping of her heels at the end of the corridor.

In the meantime, melons, pumpkins, gourds, and squash appeared in the stalls in the city, the heat of the day gave way to the chill of the night, and the studious youths, sunburned and plump from home cooking, gradually began to return to the university.

The annex was revivified. The dust was chased from the corridors, halls, and auditoriums. The cook returned and commenced her work, so there was no longer any reason for Toria to walk to the bazaar every day. A cleaning woman fluffed pillows and feather mattresses, and down flew about in clouds, as if a horde of geese and ducks had gathered in the university courtyard for a fateful battle. In the mornings two or three youths with bundles over their shoulders usually gathered in front of the grand staircase: these were prospective students who had traveled to the university from far-off cities and town-ships.

Mouths agape, the newcomers gazed upon the iron snake and the wooden monkey, became embarrassed whenever someone asked them a question, and hesitantly followed Dean Luayan, who invited them to join him in his study for an interview. After the interviews, a portion of the prospective students, despondent, set out on the return trip home; Egert suffered and felt despicable as he watched those who were turned away: any one of them was far more worthy of the standing of a student than Egert.

It must be said, however, that the summer days spent behind books had yielded their own modest fruits; in the domain of academia, Egert felt himself to be somewhat more confident, although he was certainly not going to set the heavens aflame with his brilliance. In exchange for *Conversations with Young People,* he received from the dean a book of monumental proportions and ex-travagant title: *The Philosophy of Stars, Stones, Herbs, Fire, and Water, as Well as Their Incontrovertible Relationship to the Features of the Human Body,* and in addi-tion to this weighty tome, he received *Anatomy,* which was full of graphic and colorful illustrations.

These illustrations shocked and horrified him, and at the same time they aroused an unprecedented interest in him. Egert marveled at the intricate net-work of veins, the extraordinary arrangement of bones, and how the liver, seemingly enormous and quite brown, resembled those he had seen at mar-ket. In his innocent simplicity, Egert had always thought that the human heart looked exactly like those little hearts that were drawn in the corners of love letters, and he was shocked when he saw on the page that complicated knot, resembling bagpipes, with all its chambers and blood vessels. The dreadful skeleton, which only lacked a scythe in its hand to be truly terrifying, lost all its horror as soon as Egert delved into the study of the minute explanatory inscriptions that accompanied it: detailed and meticulous, these commentar-ies completely dispelled all thoughts of death, evoking instead reasonable and practical questions.

While Egert was studying *Anatomy,* Fox returned to the university.

Their reunion was heartfelt and boisterous; Fox's copper hair had grown down to his shoulders, his nose was burned by the sun and peeling like a boiled potato, but neither solemnity nor gravity had been added to his hab-its. From his knapsack appeared an entire smoked goose with dried plums, a string of black blood sausages, home-baked scones, and a variety of vegetables, prepared in diverse ways. At the very bottom of Fox's sack was nestled an enormous bottle of wine, thick as blood. The food, which Gaetan's loving mother had collected for her son, intending them to last at least a week, was demolished within a few hours. Fox was, without a doubt, a slacker and a trickster, but in no way was he a miser.

The very first sip of wine turned Egert's head. Grinning inanely, he watched as the room filled with familiar students. Soon there was no room left, not on the beds, or at the table, or on the windowsill. They were all laughing, clamoring, and recounting tales, licking greasy fingers and proclaiming toasts, gulping wine straight from the bottle. Having laid waste to Fox's knapsack, the students, as ravenous as young locusts, decided to go out into the city; Egert no longer had any money, but all the same he decided to go out with the rest of them.

They visited At the Rabbit Hole and then dropped by Quench; at the latter tavern a dashing company of guards was drinking, apparently just off duty. Egert was rattled by their close proximity, but the city guards hailed the students complacently and without any distaste whatsoever, and the intoxication that had earlier spun Egert's head around accepted their company and even dulled his habitual fear.

The two groups swapped bottles, toasts, and amiable taunts; then the troop of guards took up that ancient pastime of all armed men: they started throwing daggers at a target that was painted on the wall. The students quieted down, watching; the most skilled with a knife of all the guards was a broad-shouldered young man with a predatory look, whose hair was tied back with a leather cord. A short sword hung on his belt. Egert examined the sword with interest. No one bore such a weapon in Kavarren.

Knives and daggers whacked into the wooden wall, some closer than others to the center of the target, painted by some dabbler in the shape of a crooked apple. The guards became excited and began to play for money. The broad-shouldered young man, the owner of the short sword, was well on his way toward lightening the purses of his comrades, when one of the guards voiced the thought that it would be a good idea to challenge the tipsy students to a competition.

After a bit of embarrassment on the part of the students, some of them decided to stand up and defend the honor of the university. Fox scurried about, handing out advice and trying to nudge the next knife thrower as close as possible to the target, at which the guards were rightly outraged and pushed him

back to his former position, which was marked out by a chalk line. Unfortunately, the knives thrown by the students' arms resolutely refused to stick into
the wall: slamming into the target sideways, they disgracefully flopped to the
floor accompanied by the laughs and jests of the guards. However, the taunts
fell short of offense and a full-blown quarrel.

The students lost three bottles of wine, a pile of silver coins, and Fox's
dress hat: being a gambler by nature, so little did he want to admit the defeat
of his group that in the end he was throwing knives himself. Every toss was
preceded by a hot-tempered bet and soon Fox was deprived of all his money
and his well-made leather belt.

Not the slightest bit disconcerted, Fox would probably have bet his father's
apothecary, had not his eyes at that very moment fallen upon the languid
form of Egert, who was blissfully enjoying the general merriment and sitting
complacently on the edge of a bench.

"Hey, Egert!" Instead of his belt, Fox had tied up his trousers with a cord.
"Is there some reason you aren't playing for your own people? Perhaps you'd
like to give it a toss, or is their money too good for you?"

Smiling self-consciously, Egert stood up. At that moment the despondent
students, whose defeat was apparently shattering and complete, really did
seem to be his own people, almost his family; furthermore, he suddenly be-
grudged the loss of Gaetan's belt.

The broad-shouldered guard with the cord in his hair smirked, handing
Egert a dagger. Egert measured the distance to the target with his eyes,
squinting, and at that moment it was as if he switched on a long-forgotten but
still faultless ability.

His hand weighed the dagger, determining its center of gravity; the blade
came alive, twisting in Egert's palm like a small, nimble animal. The tip flashed
in a searing arc and with a crunch embedded itself in the very center of the
painted apple.

The tavern hushed from astonishment; a stunned cook peered out of the
kitchen.

Egert smiled as if apologizing; the guards exchanged wondering glances,
as if they did not believe their eyes and had to check if their companions had
seen the same thing: maybe they'd all gotten really drunk? The students were
simply frozen, their faces stretched long in shock; Fox broke through the general bewilderment.

"But how did you do that?" he asked in a deliberately drunken voice.

The broad-shouldered guard stepped forward resolutely, shaking a purse. "I'll put up the money. Best of five, what do you say?"

Egert again smiled guiltily.

After that, everything happened quickly. In a silence that was broken only by the subdued gasps of the audience and the dull thuds of blades hitting wood, Egert won back Fox's belt and hat, all the money lost by the students, and even the money that the broad-shouldered youth had won off his comrades. Egert's eyes and hands acted almost independently, executing a long-familiar and pleasant task; daggers danced in Egert's hands, spun round into a glinting fans, flew up into the air and then fell into his palm as if they were glued there. He threw them almost without looking, like clockwork, and they all rushed toward the exact same point: soon a hole, studded with wooden splinters, appeared in the center of the lopsided apple.

The broad-shouldered guard with the cord wound in his hair turned respectfully to Egert. "I swear to Khars, this lad has not spent his whole life wiping books on his trousers, oh no!"

Finally, Egert's excitement ran dry: unintentionally glancing at the dagger in his hand, he suddenly saw it as a murder weapon and winced at the thought of lacerated flesh. However, no one noticed his distress, because the company of students had long ago recovered from their shock and exchanged it for exuberant high spirits.

They surrounded Egert, shaking his hand and patting him on the back; one by one the guards approached and gravely attested to their heartfelt esteem. To drink away their newly earned money, the triumphant students headed off to the One-Eyed Fly. A pair of girls trailed along after them, apparently lured by the beauty and prowess of the "fair-haired Egert."

They continued to celebrate Egert's skill almost until midnight. They stopped by the students' pub, where Egert finally met Fox's longtime girlfriend: a good-looking, perpetually laughing woman by the name of Farri. She had missed her sweetheart over the summer, and so at first she pouted her lips aggrievedly, then she threw her arms around Gaetan's neck, and then she proceeded to flirt recklessly with one and all, trying to call forth Fox's jealousy. The situation ended when, begging leave of Egert and the whole company, Fox expertly scooped Farri up under his arm and hauled her away. From that moment on, Egert lost interest in the party; scarcely able to escape from the two girls who were besieging him, he wormed his way out onto the dark street. Just as he was about to turn the corner, he ran into a man in a spacious robe. The face of the robed man was hidden by a hood.

"Good evening, Egert," said a voice out of the darkness.

The voice was affable: without a doubt, it belonged to Fagirra. Egert stepped back. In the months that had passed since his visit to the Tower, Egert had managed to convince himself that the brotherhood had lost all interest in him and no longer wanted him in their ranks. The appearance of Fagirra was like thunder in a clear sky.

"Are you surprised to see me, Egert?" Fagirra smiled under his hood. "I'm happy to inform you that you've successfully endured the first trial, the trial of secrecy. We should talk. Wouldn't it be better if we moved away from that noisy tavern?"

Laughter and shouts alternating with drunken songs were wafting from the One-Eyed Fly. At that moment the raucous sounds of the students' revelry seemed dear to Egert, like a lullaby remembered from childhood.

"Yes," he muttered indistinctly, "of course."

Taking Egert by the hand, Fagirra dragged him into an alley. Egert was afraid that they would find a secret passageway that led into the Tower of Lash.

Fagirra stopped. His white teeth flashed in the dark. "Egert, I'm glad to see that you are in good health. We have little time. Soon, by the will of Lash, we will become comrades-in-arms, brothers, but in the meantime you must know that the world is changing, that the world has already changed. People have drifted too far away from Lash: woe unto them. Have you not noticed, Egert? Fools, all fools. The city magistrate heeds the advice of the Magister, but the magistrate is ill and who knows how his successor will conduct himself? Even now voices can be heard that contravene the will of Lash. Woe unto them, Egert, woe unto them all!"

Egert listened, not understanding or even trying to understand, only feverishly wondering what Fagirra would demand of him.

"Great ordeals are approaching, ordeals that all living things must endure, but what those ordeals are, you will learn only once you have passed through the rites of initiation. You must hurry, Egert. You must find the time to cleave to Lash before that which must happen, happens. You will meet it with us, and you will find salvation, whereas others will cry out in horror."

The acolyte talked ever more rapidly and ardently, his eyes glinting in the darkness. With each word, Egert became more terrified, as if he suddenly saw wings of shadow stretched out over his ordinary, familiar life.

"Soon, Egert. But there is still time. You must pass through the second trial. By the will of Lash it will be the last, and then the Tower will shelter you, consecrated against that . . . against what will happen here, below the sun. Are you ready to listen?"

Egert's tongue answered of its own accord. "Yes."

Fagirra brought his cowl close to Egert's face. "Then listen. These are the conditions of the final trial: First, keep silent as before; second, and this is the most important, Egert, you must watch and listen. It is for this that you have been given eyes and ears, Egert: to watch and listen. The Magister himself will receive your reports. In the university you will encounter both those who are our friends and those who are our enemies. We must determine who is who. The Magister is especially interested in the venerable dean and his lovely young daughter. Watch and listen. You are no doubt privy to the plans of the dean concerning the book he is writing, yes?"

Egert stood there, feeling as though he had been doused in boiling water. He immediately forgot his fear of the impending ordeals. His cheeks and ears were burning; luckily, Fagirra could not see this in the darkness. Heaven, the former Soll, that long-forgotten Kavarrenian bully: he would put an end to such a conversation with one good punch to the face! But the former Soll was dead, and this latter-day Egert, marked by the scar, only whispered in a wavering voice, "Unfortunately, you exaggerate my acquaintance with Dean Luayan. I don't know anything about his plans."

Fagirra amiably placed his hand on Egert's shoulder. "Egert, this trial, it is not an easy one. I won't lie. It is possible that finding out about this will be difficult, but after all, it is possible, Egert, isn't it?"

"I don't know," whispered Egert. "I really . . . I'm not sure."

"Egert," drawled Fagirra reproachfully, "my friend. You've already taken the first step: You were present at the secret ceremony. You were shown great trust, weren't you? Do you really think it is unnecessary to justify that trust? Right now you find yourself under the influence of a momentary hesitation, but the penalty for such hesitation may be too onerous: it may be nothing short of inhuman. Don't let cowardice get the better of you. It will only be worse. Believe me, I am telling you this as your future brother. Would it be easier for you to submit reports directly to the Magister or to me?"

Egert could hardly keep himself from shaking violently. Fagirra's hands, as before, were resting on his shoulders: the acolyte would be able to feel it quite well. "To you," whispered Egert, wishing only to finish all this as soon as possible.

Fagirra was silent for a moment, and then he said softly, "Splendid. I will find you. Your business is to watch and listen. And to question, to question as inquisitively as possible but without intrusiveness: the dean is quite clever."

Fagirra started to walk away, but then he suddenly turned around again.

"You needn't feel so ill about all this, Egert. You'll understand soon. You've been offered a helping hand; you've been granted a unique chance. You will realize this later, but for now you just need to believe. All right?"

Egert could not find the strength to answer.


The anecdote about the daggers went the rounds of the university, and even completely unfamiliar students walked up to Egert in the corridors so that they could shake hands with him and ask him something insignificant. The academic year began, and Egert did not miss a single lecture, even though his soul was heavy.

After his encounter with Fagirra he vowed to himself that he would no longer show his face in town, but who knew whether or not even the university walls could protect from the Order of Lash? Egert knew full well that base fear would betray him at the very first opportunity, and his interrogator, whoever he might be, would be able to extract from him anything he desired to hear. The Order of Lash either knew or had guessed at his cowardice, and that meant that he was a prisoner of the Order, a spy and an inquisitor, and no pride or honor would be able to save Egert when his legs began to shake from fear and his parched tongue clove to the back of his throat, unable to prevent him from pronouncing words of betrayal.

The lengthy howl sounding from the Tower now rendered him horror-stricken.

One day, plucking up his courage, he took himself to the dean's study to confess everything, but on the way to the study Fagirra's face rose up before his eyes and his fitful voice whispered in his ears, warning of impending disasters. He had scarcely crossed the threshold when he blurted out an unintelligible question: What will happen . . . or will nothing happen . . . in the near future?

The dean showed surprise, but with touching gravity he supposed that in the near future something surely would happen, and in the recent past some-thing, alas, had already happened. Egert panicked, asked the dean's pardon, and fled, leaving the dean somewhat bewildered.

Sometimes Egert calmed himself with the thought that Fagirra and the hoary Magister seemed like men who were worthy of trust. Possibly he really did know too little; possibly the mission that had been entrusted to him was not a betrayal, but really a service to the university. After all, Fagirra had said, "You will realize this later, but for now you just need to believe. All right?"

All right, whispered Egert to himself, and he felt better; he even began to consider in earnest how he could best accomplish the task that had been im-posed on him, but then the abrupt realization of his own baseness drove him to despair. Cringing on the windowsill, he would not answer Fox's worried questions or look into those honest honey-colored eyes.

Fox now regarded Egert with greater respect, not only for Egert's rare ability in tossing knives, but also for the books he was reading, *Anatomy* and *The Philosophy,* which had been borrowed, according to Egert, from the dean himself. Gaetan trained himself to leave Egert in peace when he saw that his roommate desired solitude, but one evening, having blown out the candle, Fox ventured to ask his odd roommate a question.

"Listen, Egert. Who are you, actually?"

Egert, who had been drowsily recollecting his home and his parents, woke up fully. "What are you talking about?"

Fox's bed creaked. "Well . . . You're all quiet and shy, only I think I need to hide any knives from you or else who knows what might happen."

"Have no fear," Egert sneered bitterly.

Fox continued sullenly, "Of course. But if I had such a handsome face as you do, all the girls in the city would be spoiled. They run after you like they're on a leash, but you never so much as glance at them. You know you could, with them, I mean . . . Never mind."

Egert sneered again.

Fox came up with a new question. "Who was it that slashed your face?"

Egert sighed. He asked in a whisper, "Listen, the Day of Jubilation, is that soon?"

Fox wondered at this question in the darkness. After a pause, he answered, "Another month. Why?"

———

A month. A month remained until the designated time. Egert firmly believed that he would not become a scoundrel and informer if he could just hold out until the meeting with the Wanderer. Now he was a slave to the curse, but the real, free Egert would not be horrified either by direct threats or by promises of impending doom. The Order of Lash would lose all power over him, and it would be so pleasant to say to Fagirra's face: Get lost, look for your spies elsewhere! And Karver. And returning to Kavarren, seeing his father. And then—Egert was almost decided on this—then he would come back to the university and ask the dean to admit him . . . possibly . . . But that would be later. First, the Wanderer, and the meeting that would take place in a month.

Egert simply barred from his mind the thought of what would happen if the meeting did not take place or if the Wanderer refused to deliver him from the curse.

For several nights in a row, Toria dreamed unusually vivid, wondrous dreams.

Once she dreamed that she was standing on the deck of a galleon. She had often seen such ships in engravings but never once in real life. All around lay the clean, blue surface of the sea, the spherical vault of the sky curved over her head, her father stood next to her, and in his hand, for some reason, was a birdcage. A small bird, smaller than a sparrow, hovered in the cage. Toria's soul felt strangely light and she laughed in her sleep. But a mass of clouds, black as an ashtray, was gathering on the distant horizon, and the captain, for there was a captain on the ship, said with a grin, "There will be a storm, but we need not fear it."

And Toria was not afraid. Nevertheless, the clouds drew near far faster than they should, and the captain sensed that something was wrong only when it was too late: in the sky over the ship hung an owl of vast proportions, and it was simultaneously a bird and a cloud, only such a cloud as has never existed. Its eyes, two round saucers, glowed with a white, turbulent fire, and its wings, when extended, shut out the sky. The captain and the crew cried out in horror, and then Toria's father, Dean Luayan, flung open the door of the birdcage he held in his hand.

The bird, light, smaller than a sparrow, flitted free from the cage; it soared up impetuously and began to grow and grow and turn black and roll around within the cloud. When it equaled the owl hovering in the sky, there was a battle not for life, but for death—only, who won this battle, Toria was not allowed to learn, for she awoke.

Speculating on what it might mean, Toria walked into the city: the evening before, her father had asked her to stop by the apothecary. Returning, she came upon two girls who were standing by the front entrance, wearing compelling bonnets adorned with rose-red and jade-green flowers. The girls, blushing and nudging each other, turned to her with a question: Does there live here . . . that is, study here . . . a very tall boy, blond, with a scar?

Toria was taken aback. The girls, becoming more agitated, explained: They met a little while ago at a certain place and agreed to meet again but, although the students came into the city fairly often—This boy, he's so blond. Do you know him?—he hasn't shown his face in town for a few weeks now. . . . Perhaps he's ill?

At first Toria wanted to laugh, then she changed her mind and decided to be livid; then, recollecting herself, she wondered why she should have such a reaction. What business did she have with Soll's intimate affections?

After dryly explaining to the girls that the "blond with the scar" was well and would certainly soon appear "at a certain place," Toria continued on her way; from behind her rushed the words: Perhaps she could tell this boy that Ora and Rosalind were looking for him?

Toria would have been quite shocked if, the evening before, someone had told her that she would recall this unlooked-for encounter often, but she did recall it, feeling annoyed and astonished at her own idiocy. Likely, she was irritated by Egert Soll's choice: such vulgar, trashy girls! However, the students always were somewhat indiscriminate. But, Soll! Glorious Heaven, why was Soll supposed to be any better or worse than the others?

Running into him the next day, Toria could not restrain herself from pricking him. "By the way, your lady friends were looking for you. It seems you completely forgot about them, Soll."

For a long moment he looked at her, uncomprehending; she had time to see that his eyelids were red and his eyes were tired, as happens after a long night of reading. "Who?" he finally asked.

Toria searched her memory. "Ora and Rosalind. What taste you have, Soll!"

"I don't know who they are," he said indifferently. "Are you sure that they asked for me specifically?"

Toria again could not restrain herself. "And who else do we have here who is 'tall, blond, with a scar'?"

Egert smiled bitterly, touching his cheek with his hand as was his wont; for some reason Toria became embarrassed. Muttering something indistinct, she rushed off.

A little while later she saw him in a group of students, led by the redheaded Gaetan; Egert Soll stood head and shoulders above all his companions. The group was, of course, heading out into the city; the students were making a joyful racket. Soll was silent, holding himself aloof, but the regard that the other students showed toward him was not concealed from Toria's eyes. Next to Soll they all seemed a bit gawky, a bit rustic, a bit simple, while Soll, in whose every movement danced an instinctual, martial grace, seemed like a pedigreed horse lost in a herd of pleasant, merrily stomping mules.

With displeasure, Toria caught herself feeling something akin to interest. Of course Ora and Rosalind were inspired by him, and indeed how many more young fillies were champing at the bit, desiring to get their hands on such a pretty man?

A few days later, Egert unexpectedly received a package from Kavarren. The wheezing messenger brought a voluminous parcel, covered in wax seals, and a small, crumpled letter addressed to Egert into the university chancellery. The messenger would not leave until he received a silver coin for his troubles. The sack was full of home-cooked food and the letter, written on yellowing stationery, smelled of heartfelt, bitter tears.

Egert did not recognize the handwriting. His mother wrote rarely and unwillingly, and never had a single one of her missives been intended for her son, but he recognized the smell immediately, and his agitation threw him into a fit of shakes.

The letter was strange: the lines curved downward and the thoughts broke off again and again. There was not a single word in it about Egert's flight or current life in Kavarren. The entire letter was dedicated to fragmentary recollections of Egert as a child and as an adolescent, except that he himself could remember almost nothing of them. His mother had held in her memory the color of the tablecloth in which her young son had tied up a bowl of hot soup for himself, and the beetle, whose severed leg he cheerfully and persistently tried to glue back on, and some impudence for which his father wanted to punish him, but she intervened, inventing an excuse for her son. Egert could hardly read to the end of the letter: he was overwhelmed by an incomprehensible, pinching, sickly sensation.

Hoping to stifle it, Egert bade Fox to invite anyone and everyone who could possibly fit into their tiny, arched room to a feast. The students, companionable and always ravenous, did not make him wait long; soon the beds were groaning under the weight of the feasters, and the windowsill was threatening to collapse, and the table, intended to serve as a base of academic inquiries and not as a throne for robust young backsides, was rattling indignantly. The parcel full of food, which would have been enough to last Egert an entire month, was demolished, as is proper, within a few hours. Everyone was heartily satisfied, including Egert, who in the noise and intoxication of the revelry was able to smother both bitterness and grief, as well as his fears for the future.

The Day of Jubilation was just around the corner. First Egert wanted it to arrive as quickly as possible, then to extend the time by any means he could. More and more frequently, Fox anxiously asked him if everything was all right: at times Egert lapsed into a causeless, overwrought mirth and at other times into a deep, depressed trance, sitting for hours by the window, senselessly leafing through the pages of the book on curses and eating almost nothing. At other times he was agitated and sleepless, and he kept getting up in the middle of the night to drink from the iron cistern in the corridor; the clamor of the iron chains on which this drinking fountain hung woke his neighbors and they complained.

A week remained until that fateful day, when Dean Luayan asked Egert to visit his study.

Egert expected to see Toria there, sitting as usual on the edge of the desk and swinging her feet, but it was only the strict, focused dean and his fidgety, nervous guest who met face-to-face in the heavily curtained study.

Having installed Egert in a tall armchair, the dean remained silent for a long time. A candle burned away inside the glass sphere with the outline of continents etched on it, and in its light the steel wing hovering over the table seemed alive and ready to take flight.

"In a day or two he'll be in the city," the dean said quietly.

Egert's palms, which were gripping the wooden armrests, instantly became as clammy as frogs' feet.

"Listen to me," said the dean just as quietly, but the sound of his voice caused goose bumps to creep along Egert's skin. "I know that you have lived for the sake of this encounter. Now I ask you a final time: Do you really want to speak with the Wanderer? Are you sure that this is the only path you can take?"

Egert thought of Fagirra and of the girl in the carriage who had been made into a plaything for a gang of robbers, and only then did he think of Karver. "I am sure," he responded dully.

For a long moment the dean pierced him with his eyes. Egert did not move a muscle and managed to outlast that gaze. "Good," rejoined Luayan finally. "Then I will tell you everything that I know. But what I know is, unfortunately, not very much."

He walked over to the window, pulled back the edge of the curtain and thus, with his back to Egert, he began.

"I already told you about the man who was deprived of the gift of magic and who had to travel the path of experience. I talked to you about the Doors, seen by me in the Mirror of Waters: I was then a youth, my teacher had died, and I was alone. . . . A man stood before the Doors in my vision, and the bolt was halfway removed. You did not understand then why I recalled all of this, but now you should understand: listen well. The Wanderer walks the earth. No one calls him by his name and no one knows exactly why the abyss cast him out; he bears a power that no one, whether a mage or not, can penetrate. Not once, no matter how hard I tried, have I been able to see him in the Mirror of Waters, and I am quite skilled, Egert: any man who possesses the gift of magic is reflected in my Mirror sooner or later, but the Wanderer is inaccessible to my gaze. Moreover, every time I have tried to find him, it was as if I ran up against a blank wall. The inexplicable frightens me, Egert. The Wanderer frightens me, and I am no little boy. I cannot be sure; he may be an embodiment of evil, he may not, but who on this earth truly knows what is good and what is evil?"

The dean fell silent and Egert, pressing his palm against his scarred cheek, surprised himself by saying, "The curse is evil."

"And murder?" The dean turned his head around in wonder.

"Murder is also evil," replied Egert dully.

"And what about killing a murderer?"

The candle inside the glass sphere guttered.

"Let's move on," sighed the dean. "I'll tell you more. Half a century ago the world stood on the brink of a precipice. The majority of the living did not realize this. Something tried to enter the world from the outside. Manuscripts call it the Third Power. It desired to come into the world and rule over it. In order to pass through the Doors of Creation, the Third Power needed a Doorkeeper. That very same man, deprived of his gift, abused by the people he knew, blinded by his pride, decided to become the Doorkeeper. He would have received unprecedented power for opening the Doors, but the bolt was not removed. For some reason he decided at the final moment to abandon his task. It is unknown what happened next, but the man who dared to refuse the Third Power returned to the world of the living. He had been seared by the Power, but from that trial he received not damnation, as one would expect, but an inheritance of sorts. . . . It is said that ever since, he has roamed the world he saved, known from that time forward as the Wanderer. Does this seem like truth?"

Egert was silent.

"I too do not know." The dean smiled slightly. "Perhaps it was an entirely different man, and the nature of the Wanderer's power is altogether stranger. . . . Before, I desired to meet him, but now . . . now I do not wish it. Who knows . . . He is alien, he flees from encounters, and only from time to time do I hear chance tales of him."

"And I'm a thread," said Egert.

The dean stared at him. "What?"

"A thread, connecting you to the Wanderer. That is why I interest you, isn't it?"

The dean frowned. "Yes . . . You have accurately calculated that there is a certain pragmatism in my treatment of you. You are a thread to the Wanderer, Soll, and you are also the murderer of my favorite student, the fiancé of my daughter. You are the victim of a grim curse. And you are a man who is on the path of experience. You are all these things." The dean once again turned back to the window.

The candle in the glass sphere burned down and extinguished. The room became darker.

"What should I say to him?" asked Egert.

The dean shrugged his shoulders. "Whatever you like. You've altered enough that you can decide for yourself. Don't try to move him to pity: it will do no good. Don't abase yourself with pleading, but don't even think of being rude. That could only make it worse. And the most important thing, Egert, and you should think well on this, is that you will be under his power yet again should you find him. He may decide to award your persistence with something else, with something that would make the previous curse seem like a joke."

The dean searchingly inclined his head to his shoulder. Barely audibly, Egert whispered, "I'm afraid, of course. But, after all, I've already met him once. Maybe I'll find the words. Maybe I'll find . . ."

Egert was listening to the headmaster's lecture while a note, flitting through the rows like a butterfly, passed along from hand to hand, making its way through the hall. Egert was not paying attention to this, and thus a hissing whisper caused him to spring up nearly out of his seat.

"Hey! Egert!"

The note was concealed within a tube, and the inscription on it left no doubt that this missive was addressed specifically to Egert. Unfolding the rough paper, Egert read the short sentence in the middle of the clean sheet: *He is in the city.*

The rasping voice of the headmaster burst into his ears like shattered glass; then it receded, muted, and melded with the buzzing of a fly that was toiling against the glass of the round window.

Three days remained until the holiday. Red-cheeked serving girls wore themselves out hauling overcrowded baskets of food here and there. Butchers gathered from the surrounding villages, and right on the street they sold bloody animal carcasses, the heads of both pigs and cows, rabbit haunches and braces of dead quail. Egert was troubled when his gaze accidentally fell on an insensate, eyeless head, skewered on a pole for sale.

The human sea bore him farther and farther through the streets. Feverishly peering at all the faces turned toward him, several times he flinched, broke out in a sweat, and flung himself forward, but every time he found he was mistaken, and so he halted to catch his breath and calm his wildly beating heart.

In the aristocratic quarters it was a bit calmer. Laughing and calling out to one another, chambermaids were stringing garlands from window to window, hanging ribbons and flags in the wind, displaying songbirds in cages on the windowsills, and scrubbing the pavement until it glistened. Catching sight of a gray hooded robe at the end of the street, Egert dived into an alley and pressed himself up against a wall.

In the middle of the day the fine weather broke; rain set in, autumn rain. Soaked to the bone, hungry and tired, Egert decided he was attacking the problem incorrectly: he would not find the Wanderer by simply roaming the streets. He needed to collect his thoughts and try to imagine where the man, who had appeared in the city the day before, would most likely be.

He hit upon the idea of visiting hotels and inns. At some he was merely looked at askance, and at others he was chased off immediately. Fearful, he took coins out of his pocket and forced himself to ask servants and lodgers about a tall middle-aged guest with intensely clear eyes and no eyelashes.

His purse was soon empty. In two or three hotels he was even shown the room in which, according to the parlor maids and servants, the tall old man he was looking for was staying. Each time feeling as though he was going to faint, Egert knocked on the hotels doors and received an invitation to enter and, entering, instantly apologized, admitted he had made a mistake and took his leave.

Hardly able to drag his feet, constantly running the risk of bumping into Fagirra or some other acolyte of Lash, Egert returned to the main square. There axes and saws were rattling away with all their might: opposite the city courthouse with its own executed manikin by the entrance, a vast scaffold was being raised.

Egert squirmed, recalling Toria's words about the compulsory executions that opened the Day of Jubilation. The gang of professional carpenters was surrounded by street urchins: they were insanely curious. Vying with each other, they rushed to the aid of the carpenters, and when one of them was entrusted with holding a hammer, the pride of the fortunate boy was boundless.

Clenching his teeth, Egert assured himself that by the time of the executions he would already be free from the curse and thus he would be brave and unflappable. Dusk was setting in, and the rain, which had lightened for a while, returned again, and Egert, whose strength suddenly and completely ran dry, dragged himself toward the university.

The next morning he went out onto the streets at the crack of dawn and almost immediately saw a tall elderly man in a jacket that had seen better times, wearing a sword at his waist. Having settled accounts with a merchant who sold him a buckle for his baldric, the tall man slowly walked down the street, and Egert, afraid of being mistaken, afraid of losing the old man from sight, afraid of delaying and being too late, dashed after him.

Despite the early hour, the streets were teeming with people. Egert was pushed, scolded, and shouldered aside but, trying not to lose the wide-brimmed hat of the tall man from his sight, he tore after him with the perseverance of a maniac.

The tall man swerved onto a side street where there were fewer people. Having almost caught up with him, with his last strength Egert gasped, "Sir!"

The stranger did not turn around; panting, Egert ran closer to him and wanted to grab the sleeve of his leather jacket, but he did not dare. Instead he wheezed beseechingly, "Sir . . ."

The stranger looked back in surprise and took a small step backwards, seeing at his side a strong young man with a pale, drawn face.

Egert also stepped back: the passerby only resembled the Wanderer from afar. This was an ordinary, decent townsman who certainly wore a sword only out of respect for generations of distinguished forefathers.

"Excuse me," whispered Egert, retreating. "I mistook you for someone else."

The stranger shrugged his shoulders.

Melancholy at his failure, Egert meandered through populated areas, peering into back streets and slums. Ravenous old crones darted toward him as if he were a tasty morsel, and Egert barely broke free from their grasping, pleading hands.

Egert visited taverns as well. Looking around the rooms from the doorway and ascertaining that the Wanderer was not there, he overcame the desire to sit down and have a meal—he did not have any money left—and instead hastened on his way. In a small tavern called the Steel Raven, he happened upon a group of the acolytes of Lash, drinking and conversing.

Egert did not know if it just seemed to him that their attentive gazes focused on him from under the three lowered hoods, but when he came to his senses he was already on the street, and he vowed to himself that from now on he would be more careful.

The second day of searching yielded no results. Despairing, Egert appealed to the dean, asking him if there was any way he could accurately determine the whereabouts of the Wanderer.

The dean sighed. "Soll, if this were any other man, I could arrange an interview with him. But I have absolutely no power over the Wanderer; I cannot find him unless he himself wants to be found. He is still in the city; this at least, I can say accurately, and he will be here for the entire day of the holiday, but probably not longer. Hurry, Soll, hurry. I cannot help you."

On the eve of the Day of Jubilation the city was buzzing like a beehive. Dragging his feet like a sick, old man, Egert plodded along from house to house, searching the faces of the passersby. Toward evening, the first drunks were already sprawled against the walls in blissful poses, and beggars draped in rags sidled up to them furtively, like jackals to carrion, wishing to extract from the pockets of the drunkards their last remaining money.

It had not yet grown dark. Egert stood, leaning against a wall, and dully watched a street urchin who was pensively winding a ribbon around the tail of a dead rat. The rat was obviously being decorated with the dark blue ribbon in honor of the holiday.

Someone walked by, almost brushed Egert's shoulder and stopped, looking back; no longer having the strength to be afraid, Egert turned his head.

The Wanderer stood on the footpath directly in front of him. Egert saw his face down to the tiniest detail: the vertical wrinkles that cut his cheeks in two; his prominent, too clear eyes, cold and inquisitive; his leathery eyelids, devoid of lashes; his narrow mouth with the corners drawn down. Standing thus for a fraction of a second, the Wanderer slowly turned and walked away.

Egert gasped for air. He wanted to scream, but he had no voice. Darting forward, he rushed in pursuit but, as in a dream, his wobbly legs buckled and would not move. The Wanderer walked away without hurrying, but somehow very quickly. Egert stumbled after him, and then a viselike grip seized him by the collar.

Egert tried to wriggle free. The Wanderer was getting farther away, but the hand that was restraining Egert would not come loose. He heard laughter next to his ear.

Only then did Egert turn round. Three men had beset him, but he did not immediately recognize the man who was grasping his collar.

"Hello, Egert!" he exclaimed merrily. "And just where do you think you're going?"

The voice was Karver's. His fresh uniform sparkled with cords and buttons, and it seemed like the braid of his lieutenancy occupied half his chest. His companions were also guards: one was Bonifor, but the other was unknown to Egert, a young man with a tiny mustache.

Egert gazed after the Wanderer. He turned around a corner. "Let go," he said quickly. "I need to . . ."

"You need to? A little or a lot?" Karver asked sympathetically.

"Let me go!" Egert tried to jerk away, but feebly, because Karver, sneering, had raised his heavy, gloved fist to Egert's face.

"There's no need to rush off. We've been looking for you for a long time in this festering hellhole of a city. We're not going to let you go just when we've found you."

All three were regarding Egert with overt curiosity, as if he were a monkey at a village fair. Bonifor drawled wonderingly, "Look at you. . . . You look just like a student! You don't even have a sword!"

"Oh, Egert, where is your blade?" inquired Karver with deliberate sorrow.

Bonifor drew his sword from its sheath. Egert grew faint. His fear crippled him; it paralyzed him down to his last nerve. Bonifor grinned and ran his finger along the edge of his sword, and then Karver clapped Egert on the shoulder.

"Don't be afraid. As you, my little friend, were deprived of both military rank and nobility, deprived publicly before the regiment no less, no one will use his sword against you. We might slap you in the face, or even beat you: that's still allowed. It's unpleasant, of course, but generally very educational, don't you think?"

"What do you want?" asked Egert, scarcely able to move his parched tongue.

Karver smiled. "I wish you well. You are, after all, my friend. So much has passed between us." He smirked, and Egert was more afraid of that smirk than of the naked sword.

Karver continued leisurely, "We're going home. You have here the Day of Jubilation, but you will have no occasion to rejoice. . . . You are a deserter, Egert Soll: you shamefully ran away from your duty; you brought disgrace to the uniform. We've been ordered to find you, catch you, and present you before the regiment, and then who knows what will happen."

He released Egert's collar, and his two assistants firmly gripped Egert by his elbows, though in truth there was no need for this because fear had bound Egert more tightly than steel chains.

The Wanderer had long ago disappeared. He had dissolved into the busy streets, and with every second, the likelihood of meeting him again diminished, dissolved like sugar candy in water.

"Listen, Karver," said Egert, trying to keep his voice from shaking. "Let's come to an agreement, huh? You tell me where I need to go later, and I will go there, upon my honor. . . . But right now I really need to . . ." Egert was disgusted at how plaintive and beseeching these words sounded.

Karver bloomed like a bouquet under the window of a man's intended. "Well, if you really need to . . . Perhaps we'll let you go, eh?"

The young man with the tiny mustache gaped; Bonifor had to wink at him twice before he understood that Karver's words were no more than a lark.

"I need to find someone," Egert repeated fecklessly.

"Beg," Karver suggested gravely. "Beg well. Get on your knees. Do you know how?"

Egert looked at Karver's boots. They retained traces of recent polishing and less recent grime from puddles; several pieces of rotten straw were stuck to the sole of the right boot.

"What are you thinking about?" wondered Karver. "A rendezvous is serious business. Is she beautiful, Egert? Or simply a slut?"

"What did I do to you?" Egert had to wrench the words out.

The evening street came alive, filling up with laughing, dancing, kissing groups of revelers.

Karver brought his face close to Egert's eyes. He delighted in the tears that were welling up out of them and shook his head. "You are a coward, Egert. You are such a coward. . . ." Then he added, smiling sweetly, "Gentlemen, you don't need to hold him. He won't run away."

Bonifor and the other guard reluctantly released Egert's elbows.

Karver's smile widened. "Don't cry. You get on your knees and we'll let you go to your tryst, that's all. Well?"

Half an old rusty horseshoe lay on the pavement near their feet. Perhaps this is the final degradation, thought Egert. It couldn't really get worse, could it?

"He won't do it," said the young guard. "The pavement is filthy; it'll soil his trousers."

"He'll do it." Bonifor guffawed. "And he's already soiled his trousers: he's no stranger to that."

This is the last time, Egert told himself. The very last time . . . The Wanderer could not have managed to go far. . . . One last indignity . . .

"Well?" Karver sounded impatient. "You want to wait longer?"

The doors of a nearby tavern burst open, and a dashing, drunken, irrepressible group poured out onto the street like champagne from an uncorked bottle. Someone seized Egert by the ears, intending to kiss him passionately. Out of the corner of his eye he saw that a young girl was hanging on to both Karver and Bonifor at the same time, and then a frantic circle dance erupted, wrenching Egert aside, sweeping him away. The disappointed face of the young guard flashed by him in the crowd, but Egert was already running, as if on air, weaving in and out of drunken revelers with impossible agility, obsessed by a single thought, The Wanderer! Maybe he is still here. . . .

It was late in the night when Egert returned to the annex. Fox became fearful when he saw his friend's face, disfigured by despair. The encounter had not happened, and Egert now had only one day left: the Day of Jubilation.

The scaffold in front of the courthouse was ready at the very last minute. The carpenters were finishing the final touches, and the block had been lovingly sheathed in black cloth, which was draped with countless garlands of fresh flowers. It was a holiday, after all; when the cloth was swept back, the wooden block was revealed to be varnished and painted to look like a drum.

Egert had roamed the streets since early morning, and the unrelenting, strained searching of faces had caused his senses to dull, so he did not immediately recognize where the festive crowd was bringing him. Not wanting to go into the square, he managed to swerve down a side street, where he was once again swept up in a human flood, excited, smelling of sweat, wine, and leather, a flood that was straining to reach the courthouse, the scaffold.

He had never swum against a strong current in a tumultuous river, or else he would certainly have recognized the terror and hopelessness of a swimmer being mercilessly carried toward a waterfall. The crowd carried him away like a flood carries away trees, and the movement only slackened when the people, anticipating a spectacle, streamed out into the wide square with the monstrous structure in its center. People glanced at Egert enviously: such a beanpole would not need to stand on tiptoes!

He looked around helplessly: heads, heads, heads, an entire sea of advancing heads; they reminded him of chickens, stuffed into a coop. All faces were turned toward the scaffold; all conversations revolved around the forthcoming execution: the gossip was that the convicts numbered just two, both forest highwaymen and both guilty in equal measure, but one, as tradition demanded, would be pardoned. Fate would decide which man would be that fortunate soul; fate would decide: it would decide right now in view of all, ah, look, look, they're already coming!

Drums started pounding. A procession headed by the city magistrate climbed up to the platform. Not yet old, but thin and sickly, he was obviously being slowly eviscerated by some illness, and his lackluster eyes were almost lost amidst the folds of numerous wrinkles, but his gait and bearing remained majestic and full of pride.

The magistrate was accompanied by a scribe and the executioner, who looked like twins, only the scribe was wearing a plain, colorless robe, while the executioner delighted the eye with his cape, as crimson as a summer sunset. The former was armed with a scroll covered in seals, and the latter held an ax in his lowered hand; he held it humbly, innocently, and rustically, just as peasants who have gathered together in the morning to chop firewood hold their tools.

Surrounded by guards, the convicts ascended the scaffold, and there really were just two. Egert looked at them, and could barely keep to his feet. The uncanny ability, which had appeared twice before this, returned to him suddenly and mercilessly.

The convicted men were holding on with their last strength: in the soul of each hope fought with despair; each wished life for himself and death for the other. The crowd was a congealed mass of indecipherable feelings, among which were rapture and pity, but curiosity predominated, the avid curiosity of a child who wishes to see what is inside a bug.

Egert tried to elbow his way out of the crowd, but his efforts were similar to those of a fly trapped in honey. The sentence echoed across the square.

"On behalf of the city . . . For revolting . . . impudent . . . robberies . . . assaults . . . murders . . . retribution and punishment . . . through decapitation and commitment to oblivion . . ."

These highwaymen were just like those scoundrels who had stopped the coach in the forest. Rapists and murderers, insisted Egert to himself, but he felt even worse.

Unwillingly, he again glanced at the scaffold: the magistrate held two wooden balls, exactly the same size, in his hands. The white ball signified life, while the black ball would bring certain death by decapitation to one of the two. The scribe spread open an ordinary linen pouch, the balls were tossed into it one after the other, and the scribe carefully shook this instrument of the lottery for a long moment. Inside the linen sack, death knocked against life with dull, wooden rattles. The hopes of both convicts reached their peak, their horror of death achieved maximum intensity, and the crowd hushed, tormented by curiosity; at a sign from the magistrate, both the condemned men simultaneously thrust their hands into the pouch.

A silent battle ensued. The faces of the contestants were sweating, and their hands compulsively ferreted about in the linen darkness, each trying to possess the ball that was already gripped by his rival. The strain of their hope and despair snatched a groan from Egert; those standing next to him in the crowd began looking askance at him.

Finally, both the condemned selected their fate and, breathing heavily, exchanged long glances.

"Withdraw!" ordered the magistrate. The crowd froze in anticipation.

They delayed for a second longer then simultaneously jerked their hands from the pouch. Each eyed the ball that was gripped in the hand of the other.

The public in the square exploded into a roar: in front of the numerous spectators, the possessor of the white ball collapsed onto his knees, stretching his hand toward the sky and soundlessly opening and closing his wide, round mouth; the man who squeezed the black ball stood motionless and, as if he could not believe his eyes, shifted his gaze from the empty pouch to his own doom, clutched in his fist.

The magistrate gave a sign: the one who was dazed with happiness was led away from the scaffold, while at the same time his comrade's hands were jerked behind his back. The black ball crashed to the boards, and a piercing scream rattled around Egert's head: No!

The unfortunate wretch had not made a sound, but his entire essence shrieked shrilly at the mistake, the injustice, the dreadful misunderstanding: How! Why? Why him of all people! Is this really conceivable; is this really possible?

The soundless scream that arose from the block forced Egert to double over in pain. The crowd oppressed him with two incongruous emotions, powerful as organ chords: passionate joy for the pardoned and intemperate desire to witness the execution of the other, the one who was now doomed.

Cast upon the block, the entire man exuded supplication, terror, and despair. Egert pressed his hands to his ears and squeezed his eyes shut, but the keen No! penetrated his awareness without the assistance of sight or hearing. The ax soared up into the sky—Egert felt goose bumps thrilling over the skin of hundreds of onlookers at that moment—and on a high, sobbing note the soundless plea broke off; it broke off in a convulsion and died, but was immediately followed by a whirling, troubled wave of loathsome excitement, of satisfaction at the rare spectacle, of pleasure at thrilled nerves. . . .

Egert howled.

Unable to restrain the horror and pain, he screamed, tearing at his throat.

People in the crowd cringed away from him, but no longer seeing or hearing anything, he raved and yowled as he rushed through the gelatinous human wall, until the moment finally came when his consciousness mercifully left him in peace.

The rumble of the crowd outside hardly reached into the room filled with incense. Two men sat at a table made of polished wood, listening to a distant drum roar.

"We cannot wait anymore," said an old man with a mane of silver hair.

"I will obtain it sooner or later."

"*Later* does not suit us!" burst out the old man. "*Later* will not satisfy Lash! We will do it the way I wanted in the first place. And Lash will help us."

Fagirra lowered his head. His hood covered half his face, and the Magister did not notice the contempt in his cold squinted eyes.

Toria could feel herself fretting over the appearance of the Wanderer in the city.

"Does Soll have a chance?" she inquired breezily that first day, following Egert with her eyes as he set out into the city to search.

The dean, to whom this question was addressed, merely shrugged his shoulders.

Pre-holiday concerns distracted her attention, but on the next day she was still interested. "He hasn't found him yet?"

The dean shook his head. "Who knows? The Wanderer could be a needle in a haystack, or he could be a burning coal in a pocket. Who knows?"

On the morning of the third day Toria did not ask about the search, but the dean morosely said to her in a low voice, "I doubt there is a way out for him. The Wanderer is not one to reconsider a judgment. You might not believe me, but I feel pity for Soll, simple, human pity."

Toria raised her eyebrows but did not reply.

Least of all did she desire to witness the execution that was in preparation in the square. Even though she fastened her window tightly, she could still hear both the roar of the agitated crowd and the booming of the drums, as if through cotton padding. She greatly desired to know where Egert Soll was at this moment and tried hard to suppress the urge to visit the annex.

Several minutes passed. Toria, tormented by a presentiment, paced around her room; then, biting her lip, she flung the windows open.

The square was covered with people, like a living, moving carpet, and Toria no longer doubted that Soll had disappeared somewhere in that swarm. Cringing, she looked at the scaffold at the very moment when the glinting blade crashed down.

The crowd gasped with one voice, and then drew breath in its vast chest, about to break out into a cheer, but the crowd was anticipated by a single, solitary human voice, a heartrending voice full of pain. This voice was distorted beyond recognition, but Toria recognized it. She recognized it and flinched.

How long has this been going on?

I have no control over it.


The steps of the spiral staircase were already streaking past her eyes. Not knowing why, she ran to the exit, and the weary words repeated over and over again in her ears: I have no control over it . . . no control . . . no control . . .

Fireworks shot up over the square. The official celebration of the Day of Jubilation had begun.

Daylight was fading, but the streets were lit as if it were day. Torches burned in every hand, and clusters of lanterns and lamps transformed the city into one large, rejoicing tavern. Fireworks raged over the square, and under their short bursts traveling jugglers and acrobats performed tirelessly: the largest and most prosperous troop had laid claim to the empty scaffold, and their competitors could only sigh enviously as the fool's cap that continuously circled the crowd grew ever plumper and clanked more resonantly with each pass.

Barrels of wine stood at each crossroads, and drunken dogs, who lapped at the rose-colored streams that trickled along the pavement, crept, lurching, into courtyard entrances. Dissonant, shrill, yet lively music flooded over the city: people in the crowd played on whatever came to hand; herds of reed pipes, wine bottles, wooden rasps, and children's rattles squawked and clamored shrilly, and the haunting sound of a stray violin from time to time rose up over this tuneless noise. Strings of people, joined by the hands, skipping and laughing, weaved in chains from alley to alley, and there were times when the heads of these impossibly long human chains swerved into a street from which the tail was just disappearing.

Toria understood the folly of her plan right away: to search for a single man in this dancing city, however distinctive he might be, was a pointless exercise worthy of an imbecile. Soll had either been trampled right there in the square or he had long been drinking and dancing together with the rest. But if something bad had really happened to him and he needed help, why did she not immediately turn to her father? What was the good of flinging herself headlong into this drunken, festive cauldron?

Having thoroughly berated herself, Toria reluctantly turned back, but at that very moment a dancing chain leapt out onto the street in front of her. Toria halted and watched as all the faces turned into one laughing face in the light of the torches and lanterns, a laughing face that flew by her from alley to alley, grasping the hands of strangers and dragging them into the rabid dance. Last in line was a young, happy boy in a white shirt, and his clinging hand seized Toria by the wrist.

"With us, little sister! Let's dance, hey!"

The street rushed up to meet her.

Barely managing to run, stumbling and trying to break free, Toria flew at the tail of the dancing chain. Someone latched on behind, squeezing her palm with sweaty fingers; afraid of falling and being trampled, Toria matched the movements of her partners, skipping through sharp turns and trying not to fly into walls. At one point the chain snapped, and those dancing behind almost fell on Toria, but she adroitly wrenched herself free and, abandoning the laughing, human press, darted away.

Her heart was beating furiously, her breast was rising rapidly, but all the same she could not catch her breath; her hair had fallen down and her slim-toed slippers were as drenched in filth as the pavement. Supporting herself against a wall with her hand, Toria shivered, catching sight of a man lying motionless beneath that same wall. Overcoming her fear, she walked up and peered into his face. The drunkard was sleeping peacefully; he was a brunet with a magnificent mustache, and the black, luxuriant hairs now retracted inward, now puffed outward to the beat of his valiant snoring.

Toria staggered back and ran away. Some youngling tried to slip a caramel, held in his teeth, into her mouth: Toria gave him such a look that the poor fellow felt compelled to swallow the candy himself. Horsemen were rushing back and forth across the wide street, and with weary indignation

Toria speculated on murderous horse hooves and drunken pedestrians who had lost all sense of caution.

One of them had collapsed right in the middle of the street. Toria's blood ran cold as the boisterous riders came back.

"Get out of the way!" someone cried commandingly as hooves struck the stones right near the head of the man passed out in the road, but the noble animals, clearly surpassing in wisdom the people who had saddled them, did not tread on the drunkard, and the cavalcade galloped on.

The man on the pavement did not move. Toria overcame her fear and revulsion and walked up to him.

The prone man was unusually tall and wide of shoulder. His fair hair was matted at the back of his head with dried, black brown blood: it was obvious that this fall had not been his first.

Feeling how hard her heart was beating, Toria crouched down next to him on her haunches and peered into the face that pressed against the pavement. "Egert . . ."

He did not answer. His face was a gray, dusty mask, notched by the furrows of tears.

"Egert," she said, dismayed, "you can't stay here! You'll be trampled, do you hear me?"

Another dancing chain dashed by. A foot, shod in a heavy boot, stumbled and kicked the recumbent Egert on the back. He did not flinch.

Toria seized him by the shoulders. "Egert! Wake up! Come on, wake up! Quickly!"

Hooves were beating at the end of the street. It would be impossible to drag Egert: he was too heavy and tall. Gritting her teeth, she turned him over onto his back, then onto his stomach, and again onto his back. She rolled him like a woodcutter rolls a log; his head with the fair, clotted hair flopped limply.

The riders galloped through the place where Egert had just been, and the hooves struck bright sparks from the stones. Toria felt a gust of wind, smelling of wine and smoke. She pushed Egert up against a wall; his eyes were open, but his vacant gaze went right through the girl who was bending over him. It frightened Toria: never before had she seen such a strange gaze on a person.

"Egert," she said in despair. "Please, can you hear me?"

Not even a shadow of a thought glimmered in his cloudy, motionless eyes.

Grappling with her fear, Toria tried to get angry. "Oh, you! Tell me, why should I have to bother with such a drunken brute?"

She leaned over his face, trying and wishing to catch the thick smell of wine. But the smell was not there, and Toria was not so naïve as to not understand that Egert was indeed sober.

Then she lost courage. It seemed most natural to run to her father for help, and she had already taken a few steps away to do so, but then she returned. Somehow she knew without a doubt that leaving Egert now would mean his death. Her father would not make it here before the turmoil of the holiday devoured the lifeless Egert, and the city guards would haul his mutilated body to the university in the morning.

Gritting her teeth with a vengeance, she pressed her fingers to Egert's temples. The skin was hot and his veins twitched in time with the beating of his heart: at least he was alive. Toria took a deep breath and methodically, just as her father had taught her, began to knead and massage Egert's neck and the back of his head.

"Egert, come back. Wake up, please. . . . What am I going to do if you don't wake up?"

Her fingers grew numb and refused to keep working, but Egert's eyes remained as lifeless as before. Her ever-increasing certainty that Egert was lost in his mind caused Toria to be covered in chills.

"No," she muttered, "this is too . . . Don't do this, Egert, don't you do this!"

Dozens of tramping, staggering feet were whirling all around, and someone was bawling out an indecent song that rose up even louder than the universal din.

Toria was ready to start crying when the wide gray eyes finally flickered. The eyelids fell down on them and instantly flew up again. Now Egert was looking, dense and dazed, at Toria.

"Egert," she said promptly, "we need to go home. Do you understand me?"

His lips moved soundlessly; then they moved again. The words barely carried to the girl. "Who are you?"

She broke out into a sweat: could he really have lost his mind from the shock he experienced on the square? "I'm Toria," she whispered in dismay. "Don't you recognize me?"

Egert's swollen eyelids fell once more, screening his eyes. "There are such stars in the sky," he said quietly.

"No," she took him by the shoulders again. "That's wrong. . . . No sky, no stars. I'm Toria, and my father is the dean. Remember, Egert!"

The last word turned, broke into a sob, and Egert raised his eyes. His gaze turned strangely warm. "I . . . I'm not crazy. You . . . don't be afraid, Toria. Stars . . . constellations, like the beauty marks . . . on your neck."

Toria involuntarily put her hand to her neck.

Egert moved his lips again. "They're singing. . . ."

A discordant, drunken song rang out somewhere nearby. A squeaking could be heard from the nearest roof: a reveler, who had somehow managed to get up there, was resolutely unscrewing a weathervane.

"Is it night?" asked Egert.

Toria took a breath. "Yes. Today was the Day of Jubilation."

Egert's eyes dimmed. "I did not find . . . didn't find . . . Now I won't find . . . Never . . ."

"The Wanderer?" Toria asked in a whisper.

Egert moved with difficulty and sat up, supporting himself against the wall. He nodded slowly.

"But he'll come again next year," she said as casually as possible.

Egert shook his head. "A whole year. I won't live through it." In his words there was not a drop of theatrics, only a calm conviction.

Toria suddenly came to her senses. "Egert, we need to leave. Get up! Let's go."

Without moving from his spot, he gravely shook his head. "I can't . . . I'll stay here. . . . You . . . go."

"You mustn't," she tried to speak as convincingly and gently as possible. "You mustn't, Egert. You'll be trampled underfoot here, let's go."

"But I really can't," he explained, amazed, and he continued without transition, as if pondering the problem. "A beetle without wings. He was without wings. . . . Going back . . . impossible. Stay inside, Mama. . . . Why did it go wrong? The dead . . . probably . . . don't walk. Impossible to go back . . ."

His eyes once again clouded over. Panicking, Toria began to shake his limp shoulders with all her strength. "You are alive! Alive! Egert! Get up, now!"

"Toria," he whispered distantly, "Tor-i-a . . . What a name! I'm alive. No, not that. Toria . . ." He stretched out his palms, folded together. "This could be a butterfly. . . . It settled on my hand . . . like a gift . . . once in my life . . . And I killed it, Toria . . . then, in Kavarren. I killed . . . him. And I killed myself because . . ." He separated his fingers, as if letting unseen sand flow through them. ". . . because I lost . . . Toria." He slumped backwards weakly.

She stared at him, not knowing what to say.

"Is it really you?" he asked in a whisper. "Or is all just . . . Will they meet me there?"

Frightened, Toria said, "No. It's me."

He tentatively stretched out his hand and carefully touched her cheek. "I never had anything so . . . Poor Egert. The sky is empty, not a single star . . . Nothing . . . real . . . only Toria alone . . . nothing else. The road is hot, sun . . . I am alone . . . I don't need to live. I'm . . . there. Thank you . . . that I saw you," His hand fell. "Thank you, sweet Toria. . . ."

"Egert," she whispered in fear.

"So bitter," he said, lowering his eyelids. "A necklace of stars . . . I wronged you so. Never in my life . . . Forgive . . ."

He flinched. He opened his eyes.

"Toria. A square of murderers. Murderers on the block, murderers in the square, and I'm a murderer . . . Heads, eyes, teeth, mouths . . . Why does no one want to finish me!" He suddenly jerked, almost stood up, and then once again fell down, subsided, went limp.

"Egert," she said desolately, "you must not think about that right now. If you don't get up right this second I don't know what I'll do." And, in truth, she did not know.

"Leave," he replied, without opening his eyes. "All kinds of people . . . on the streets. Holiday . . . night. They will want . . . If they want to hurt you, I won't be able to save you, Toria. I will stand by and watch . . . And I won't be able to help . . . Leave." He raised his eyelids and Toria met his hopeless, gentle, pain-filled gaze.

"Oh, don't you worry about me!" she rapped out, trying to speak past the strange feeling that suddenly squeezed her by the throat. "I'll take care of myself. Now, get up!"

Whether her voice had gained an especially imperative intensity or whether Egert had somehow finally recovered his senses, he tried to do as she commanded, but only with their combined efforts could they stand Egert's heavy, clumsy body on his feet. Toria offered her neck. Egert's arm now lay across her shoulders, and even through the coarse fabric of her dress, the girl could feel how his arm stiffened, wary of causing her pain.

"Yes, be brave," she whispered, trying to stand more steadily. "Hold on, Egert. It's nothing. Let's go."

Walking turned out to be more difficult that she had thought. Egert's legs did not work very well. Despairing, she finally gasped, "No, this will not do! I am going to run to the university. I'll get help."

Egert immediately sagged down onto the pavement, and Toria could hardly keep her balance. Experiencing a strange unease, she repeated as confidently as she could, "I'll be quick. It's really not all that far. You'll wait for me, yes?"

He lifted up his head.

Toria caught sight of his eyes and sank down next to him. "Egert, I'm not abandoning you. I'll get people, my father will help. Egert, I am not abandoning you, I swear."

Egert was silent, lowering his head. The words dropped from his mouth quietly, "Of course. Go."

She sat next to him for a while then said briskly, "No. We'll get home ourselves. We'll rest for a while, and it will be easier. Okay?"

Without looking at her, Egert took her hand. She flinched but did not pull away.

For a long time he smoothed her palm with his fingers. Then he squeezed it, not painfully, but Toria could feel the beating of his pulse in his hand. "Thank you . . . Surely I . . . don't deserve it."

They walked for the rest of the night, stopping now and then to rest as they made their way through the intoxicated revelers. A foggy dawn rose up. The city, worn-out and enfolded in silence, seemed like a vast, disarrayed feast table, welcoming the morning after a cheerful and bounteous wedding. The smoke of torches, fireworks, and crackers dispersed. The morning wind played in piles of discarded rubbish; chased bottle corks, tattered ribbons, and curls of streamers along the pavement flooded with wine; tore the damp fog crouching in the breezeways to pieces; and chilled the two haggard wayfarers to the bone.

Toria and Egert walked toward the arched bridge over the canal. A paper cap with a tassel, lost by someone, was floating on the surface of the water, which was as rough as a rasp. The empty streets and blind windows seemed abandoned, uninhabited; there was not a single soul around except for a tall man who stood motionless in the very center of the bridge, gazing at the water.

"We're close," wheezed Toria, arranging Egert's arm around her shoulders more comfortably. "We're almost there."

With his free hand, Egert caught hold of the railing. He suddenly stood stock-still, as if he had sunk up to his knees in the stone.

The man on the bridge turned his head. Toria caught sight of an elderly face, cut through with vertical wrinkles, with large, clear eyes. The face seemed familiar to her; only after several seconds did she remember that the man standing before her had once stayed in the tragically memorable Kavarrenian inn, the Noble Sword.

The Wanderer stood motionless, not taking his eyes off Egert and Toria. His gaze expressed nothing, or at least it seemed so to her.

"Egert," she said through suddenly parched lips. "It's fate."

Egert took a step forward, clawing along the railing with his hand, and then he stopped, unable to make a single sound.

The Wanderer turned his face away. He held a bunch of tiny sparklers in his right hand: one of them dropped into the canal, leaving a wide, spreading ring on the water.

Egert remained silent. Minute dragged after minute and one after the other the sparklers fell into the water.

"Egert," whispered Toria, "Come on! Take a shot. Try! Now."

Having depleted his entire stock of sparklers, the Wanderer cast a farewell glance at the two stricken travelers and, the bottom of his cape fluttering in the wind, began to walk off the bridge away from them.

A dry hissing sound became audible: Egert was forcing air into his parched mouth, which was as wide open as a black pit.

Flinging away his arm, Toria darted forward so quickly that the hem of her dark dress blew out in the wind like a sail. "Sir! Stop a moment. . . . Sir!"

The Wanderer slowly came to a stop. He turned his head round, curious. "Yes?"

Toria ended up so close to him that if she had wished it, she could have stretched out her hand and touched the intricate hilt of the sword at his waist. Hardly able to withstand his unwavering stare, she blurted out right into his wrinkled face, "Here is a man. He wants . . . He needs to talk to you. It is a matter of life and death; I implore you, hear him out!"

The long, thin mouth twitched slightly. "Is he mute?"

Toria was at a loss. "What?"

The Wanderer sighed loudly. He was smiling now, he was definitely smiling, but this smile did not comfort Toria at all. "Perhaps your man is mute? Why are you speaking for him?"

Toria helplessly looked back at Egert. He was standing on the bridge, his hand gripping the railing, as silent as if he had forever more lost the gift of speech. The wind tousled his matted blond hair.

"Egert!" Toria yelled at him. "Pull yourself together! Speak! You wanted to speak, so speak!"

Egert watched just as a fox cub caught in a trap watches the hunter, and he remained silent.

The Wanderer bowed slightly to Toria and stalked off.

Struck by the absurdity and improbability of what had happened, she rushed after him like a vulgar panhandler chases after the prospect of change. "Sir! Please . . ."

It seems that she had even grabbed him by the sleeve; she was just about ready to fall to her knees when the Wanderer turned again, now surprised. "What?"

"Don't leave," she whispered, gasping. "He'll speak now. . . . He will speak."

The Wanderer measured her with an intent, scrutinizing gaze; she began to tremble, feeling like she was transparent, that he could see right through her. The thin lips yet again twitched in a slight smile. "Well . . . Perhaps you are right. Perhaps." The Wanderer unhurriedly returned to the bridge.

Egert was standing in exactly the same place.

The Wanderer walked up close to him, almost touching, and his eyes were on a level with the eyes of the tall Egert. "Well?"

Egert swallowed the lump in his throat. He stuttered under his breath, "Kavarren . . ."

"I remember." The Wanderer smiled patiently. "A fine town . . ." Then he suddenly asked, apropos of nothing, "What do you think? That lottery before the execution, was it a mercy or a cruelty?"

Egert flinched. He forced himself to whisper, "Both the one and the other. There is hope in the night before the execution, but there are also doubts, torments, a passage from despair to faith and back again. . . . Afterwards, the betrayal of hope, and the man is not ready . . . to die with dignity. . . ."

"Not everyone manages to die with dignity," remarked the Wanderer. "Still, how do you know? There has never been a night before an execution for you, so how would you know of such despair and such hope?"

"It seems to me," breathed Egert, "that I do know a little, just a little. I have . . . learned. But to you, of course, it is clear: you know, what the night before an execution is like. . . ."

Toria, standing nearby, went cold.

The Wanderer, it seemed, was surprised. "Indeed? Well, that much is familiar to me, that is true. My, but you are a diligent student, aren't you, Egert Soll?"

Egert shuddered at the sound of his own name. He pressed his hand to his cheek. "Can you remove this?"

"I cannot," uttered the Wanderer, gazing into the water. "One can't reattach a decapitated head. Only a complete child would torture a fly by trying to glue back the wing that he himself had ripped off. And some curses also possess an inverse power. You'll have to come to resign yourself to it."

It became quiet. The paper hat, which had all this time been roaming from shore to shore, finally became soaked through, became unglued, and gradually began to sink.

"I thought as much," said Egert desolately. There was something in his voice that made the hairs on the back of Toria's neck stand up.

"Egert." She stepped toward him and caught hold of his hand. "Egert, everything will be . . . everything will be all right. Things will work out. Don't . . . Let's go home. Everything will . . . You'll see, Egert—" But at that moment her will betrayed her, and she burst into bitter tears.

Egert, frozen in place from shock, steadily offered her his arm, and she took hold of his elbow. Slowly and silently they walked away. From behind they suddenly heard, "Wait a minute."

Flinching, they both turned around.

The Wanderer stood, leaning against the railing, and pensively examined the toe of his own boot. He raised his head and squinted against the rising sun. "The curse does not have inverse power, and it may be cast off . . . in exceptional circumstances. This moment will occur just once in your life, and if you let it slip away, all hope will be forever lost. The circumstances of this moment are these."

Lightly casting his cloak behind his back, he descended toward them, and it seemed to Egert in that instant that the Wanderer was the same age as he.

"Hear me and remember, Egert:

"When that which is foremost in your soul becomes last.

"When the path has reached its bitter end.

"When five questions are asked and you answer yes."

The Wanderer fell silent for a moment. He added softly, "The curse will fall away of its own accord. Do not falter. It is quite easy to err, and a mistake will cost you much. Farewell, to the both of you. Don't repeat your mistakes. . . ."

———

With narrowed eyes the acolyte watched in astonishment as the auditor Egert and the daughter of the dean, Toria, walked up the front steps of the university. Both were as pale as the dead, and they looked ready to collapse, but each was using the other's arm for support.

# PART THREE

*Luayan*

# 7

On summer days the stone courtyard, which served as both a playground and a main square, glowed with heat like the floor of an iron forge, and the air over it shimmered and wavered. The streets of the village that clung to the cliff flickered, disappeared from sight, then reappeared, changing their contours. His teacher Orlan smiled mysteriously, "Appearance. The unfamiliar is concealed within the familiar; the unknown abides in the known. No matter how you tried, you could not dig to the bottom of this well. . . . However, what good is the bottom to you? Drink up, and be grateful. . . ."

Young Luayan did not immediately understand what kind of well his teacher was speaking of. In the courtyard on the cliff there was no well: water had to be hauled up from below, and it was quite difficult.

On the other hand, it was cool in the mage's home, even on the most scorching days, and the steel wing fastened over the entrance was an appeal for the preservation of the inhabitants from adversity, illness, and enemies. Luayan knew all too well that as long as his teacher lived, so it would be.

As long as his teacher lived . . .

The dean tore his gaze away from the yellow flames dancing in the fireplace: after the Day of Jubilation, true autumn days, damp and chilly, had set in. His teacher had been in the habit of lighting a fire even in the middle of summer; Orlan maintained that a fire in the fireplace promoted reflection. It is possible that he was right, but Luayan had not adopted this practice, and so in the summer his fireplace stood cold and empty.

Who knows how his destiny might have unwound if Orlan had lived even a few more years?

So many mistakes. His whole life was a repository of mistakes, and always on the eve of disaster he felt a drawing cold in his chest. Just like today.

He turned around. Toria, his daughter, was sitting on the very edge of his desk, and her face, lit by the firelight, looked severe, even harsh. From out of this face another woman gazed reproachfully at the dean: her equally young and beautiful mother. The dean rubbed his temple pensively, but the hazy foreboding did not desist; behind Toria, the bloodshot eyes of Egert Soll gleamed in the half dark.

The dean turned a log in the fireplace, and the flames flared brighter. The dean recalled how the fire in the hut by the cliff had burned just as brightly, and how two armchairs with high backs had stood facing each other, an old man sitting in one, and in the other a young boy entranced by his elder's words. I'm getting old, he thought sarcastically. The past comes to my mind far too clearly, but where does this aching, vague presentiment of evil come from?

"Five yesses," Egert yet again muttered from the gloom. "Someone questions me five times? And I just need to answer?"

Toria was looking at her father with demand in her eyes.

He averted his face. How could Luayan solve this riddle; where would he find the answer? He needed help now, but the only man who could help him had been lying in a stone tomb, carved into the cliff, for the past several decades.

Toria flinched and Egert whipped his head around: someone was knocking erratically on the heavy door.

The dean lifted his eyebrows in shock. "Yes?"

Gaetan's angular face peeked warily through the crack of the partially open door; other students stood behind him, whispering tensely and then shushing each other.

"Dean Luayan," gasped Fox, "there . . . in the square. Lash."

Egert felt a wave of sepulchral cold flood his chest.

The square was, as usual, filled with people, but it was unusually silent. The Tower of Lash had flung open its perpetually shut gates, and a thick wall of heavy smoke poured out of those gates, emitting a bitter odor. Gray robes flickered in the shroud of smoke, but none of the townsfolk, dazed by this unprecedented event, could make out what was happening in the compact, umber clouds.

A group of students sliced through the crowd like a knife; Dean Luayan served as the tip of this knife. Egert held back, and Fagirra's insinuating voice resounded in his ears: Great ordeals are approaching, ordeals that all living things must endure. You must hurry, Egert . . . before that which must happen, happens. You will meet it with us, and you will find salvation, whereas others will cry out in horror.

The heavy brown smoke slowed and began to flow upward toward the sky. On the spot where it had just been eddying, a motionless human ring became apparent: the acolytes of Lash stood shoulder to shoulder, close together like the sharp, pointed stakes of a wooden fence. Their hoods were pulled low and their faces, turned toward the inhabitants of the town, were concealed by the coarse cloth. Egert sheltered behind someone's back: it seemed to him that vigilant, focused gazes were searching for him from underneath the hoods.

"What's all this for—?" Toria began derisively, but at that very moment a drawn-out note that pulled at the soul instantly stopped the mouths of everyone who had assembled in the square.

The fiery red robe of the dwarf flashed through the gray circle of hoods; another sheaf of smoke puffed up behind backs that were still as stone, and then, as if elevated on these clouds, the Magister rose up over the square. It is possible that Egert alone knew that this was the Magister: everyone else saw only a white sphere of disheveled silver hair, which rose like the moon over a battlement of hoods.

The square was suddenly full of whispers, rustles, and exchanged glances; the peeling sound repeated, and again a dead silence, unnatural for a crowded place, fell. The heavy smoke grudgingly drifted up into the sky, as if against its will.

Once again red flashed through the circle of hooded men, and the dwarf, carrying his instrument, also seemed to be rising up over the crowd. His thin lips moved—or did it just seem so to Egert?—and words tumbled out of the trumpet, accompanied by more heavy smoke.

"It approaches!"

Egert's blood ran cold. Great ordeals are approaching. . . .

"Prepare yourself. Prepare your home. Prepare your life."

You must hurry, Egert. . . .

"The Ages have flowed by. The Ages have run out. The river is not eternal.

The Age has passed. It is close. Prepare yourself. The End of Time approaches!"

The square remained silent, uncomprehending.

"The End of Time . . ." The hollow words were punctuated by plumes of smoke, weaving over the trumpet. "The End. Lash beholds the End of all things. He is there before you. Stretch out your hand. . . . He is there. A week, maybe two or three . . . Maybe just a day, or an hour . . . That is all that remains until the End. Lash beholds all. Lash beholds all. The End of the World. The End of Life. The End of Time. Lash beholds . . ."

The dwarf took the trumpet away from his crooked lips and spit slowly, with relish.

"The words have been spoken!" the Magister yelled in a penetrating voice. "The sand is flowing out of your hourglasses. The End!"

As if obeying an unspoken command, the gray figures slowly raised their arms; wide sleeves fell back, and a cold wind blew over the assemblage. It seemed to many that the wind reeked of the grave.

"The End," The murmured chant rose up from beneath many hoods. "The End . . . The End . . ."

And smoke again began to pour out of the Tower, but this time it was black, as if the entire world were burning. The smoke obscured the Magister, the red-robed dwarf, and the wall of motionless, faceless men from the eyes of the people in the square: this spectacle was so majestic and yet sinister that a woman who stood near Egert in the crowd started rambling hysterically.

"Oh! Oh, dear people, oh! Oh, how can this be? No, no, no! It can't be! I refuse . . ."

Egert turned his head toward her: the woman was pregnant and as she wailed she pressed her palms first to her wet cheeks, then to her enormous round belly.

The formation of robed men mutely disappeared through the gates of the Tower. The gates closed just as silently, and the smoke was shut off: only trickles crept out from underneath the iron doors. These black trickles writhed like harassed vipers.

Egert rushed to the dean's side. The dean, catching sight of Toria's inquiring glance, smile wanly. The smile was pensive and reassuring, but Toria only frowned more deeply.

The dean dropped his hand onto her shoulder. "We should go."

The crowd dispersed. Dispirited people hid their eyes. Somewhere a frightened child sobbed, and the lips of many a woman trembled traitorously. An old man, apparently deaf, snatched at all and sundry by the sleeves, trying to find out what "these folk in capes" had said; people brushed the old man aside, some sullenly, some crossly.

A strained, unnatural laugh suddenly broke out over the crowd. "Here now, they made it up, didn't they? It's their little joke, right?" The man who was laughing received no support, and his laughter faded pitifully.

A crowd of students stood by the entrance to the university, right between the snake and the monkey. All eyes followed the dean, but he passed by without saying a word, walking through a path that had formed in the crowd, and the unvoiced questions of the youths were left unanswered. Egert and Toria followed after Luayan.

In the university courtyard they ran into Fox. He had installed himself on the shoulders of a sturdy youth, and, blowing out his cheeks so far they seemed about to explode, Gaetan assiduously blew into a tin trumpet and cried out dismally from time to time, "It approooooaches . . . Aaaaaaa . . ."


There came a day when another man sat down in the armchair of his teacher.

The boy had heard of Lart Legiar from Orlan many times, but his first encounter with the archmage, who appeared one day at the hut by the cliff, could have cost Luayan dearly because, immature and overconfident, he tried to test his skill against the unwelcome guest.

The vanity and pride of Luayan received a palpable blow on that day: he was forced to throw himself on the mercy of his opponent who was not only far stronger than a fourteen-year-old boy but also than many of the wisest, gray-haired mages. It was not in Lart's nature to spare an opponent, however young he might be, but the boy capitulated and his reward was a long, initially oppressive, but subsequently fascinating conversation.

Toward the morning of a long night, the archmage Lart Legiar summoned the boy to him: it was a chance to change his fate, a chance to find a new teacher. Luayan did not miss this chance: he simply refused it. He refused it calmly and deliberately. He was not one of those who could easily exchange teachers even if being the pupil of Legiar would be an incredible honor.

Many times after he had grown up, Luayan had asked himself if it was worth it. Such fidelity to the grave of Orlan: did it cost him too dear? Abandoned at the age of fourteen in the company of wise but indifferent books, he had transformed himself into a mage, but he would never become an arch-mage.

The bitter taste lived within him for many years. Both to his face and behind his back, people called him "master mage," "great magician," and "arch-mage," but not a one guessed that the already middle-aged Luayan had not progressed much in his magic from the time of his adolescence.

However, he had not wasted a single drop of the knowledge and power that he obtained under the steel wing of Orlan. He was entirely competent in the magical arts, even if he was far from the heights. He immersed himself in academia and became an unparalleled expert on history. However, two mor-bidly painful flames always smoldered in his soul. The first was Toria's un-happy mother; the second was the vexing awareness of his own frustrated greatness.

Never before had he so greatly regretted those unachieved heights. Hav-ing closed the door of his study, he stood idle under the extended steel wing, trying to gather his thoughts. His reason calmly assured him that there was nothing to worry about: the wearers of the gray robes had always been fond of effects designed for spectators, and the end of time was nothing more than their most recent subterfuge, invoked to rivet the diminishing attentions of the city's inhabitants on the Tower. Thus insisted his reason, but the presenti-ment of disaster strengthened, and the dean knew from experience that he should have faith in his presentiments.

He knew this feeling. It had come on especially keenly that night when he had let his dearly beloved and despised, bedeviling wife leave the house: he had let her go, insulted and piqued at her disdain, and she had met her death.

The wing stretched out over his head, commanding him to shun forbidden thoughts. He stood for a time in front of a tall cabinet. The cabinet was barred with both a lock and an enchantment, just to be on the safe side. Luayan breathed a sigh and removed both the lock and the enchantment.

A jasper casket rested on a black satin pillow; it was small, about the size of a snuffbox. The dean placed it on his palm then touched the lid, which sur-rendered without effort.

A medallion lay on the velvet bottom of the small chest: a delicate disk of pure gold on a gold chain. The dean was unaware that he held his breath as he put the faintly gleaming disk, covered with intricate, ornately carved re-cesses, on his palm. Nothing could be simpler, one would think, than to peer deep into these recesses, into rays of sunlight, but Luayan was pierced by trepidation at the mere thought of doing so. He was the guardian of this medallion, not its master. . . .

. . . When he met Lart Legiar for the second time, Luayan was a respected mage and the dean of the university.

At that time Luayan was already aware that the Third Power had vainly tried to force its way through the Doors of Creation, and that the Doorkeeper had refused to lift the bar and let it through. Whatever role Lart Legiar had played in this affair was hidden from the eyes of men, but the dean had flinched the first time he looked at his guest's face. The great Legiar had aged, and his face was seamed with scars that had not been there before; one eye was blind and stared blankly past his host, but the other, which had escaped whatever disaster stole the first, was observant and slightly mocking.

"The world remains the same," Legiar declared in lieu of a greeting.

"But it is we who change," responded Luayan, trying to divine the intentions of his visitor.

They looked at each other for a long moment. A multitude of questions tormented Luayan: about the strange Third Power that wished to invade the world, about the fate of the Doorkeeper, and about Legiar's own fate, but he remained silent because he knew that he did not have the right to ask.

"No," Legiar sighed finally. "You have not changed. You've hardly changed at all."

Luayan understood what his guest meant, but he smiled pleasantly, wishing to hide from the other's pity.

"Well, the fewer archmages there are in this world and the less frequently they encounter one another, the easier it is for us ordinary mages to live."

Legiar cast up his eyebrows in astonishment. "You've checked your arrogance? The last time we met, I was sure that would be impossible. Or are you acting against your soul's inclination?"

"It is not given to all to be great," Luayan observed dispassionately.

"But it was given to you," objected Legiar.

They both fell silent.

Luayan frowned as he gazed steadily, with barely perceptible reproach, right into Legiar's undamaged eye. "I remained Orlan's student. I think he would have understood."

The one-eyed man sneered. " 'He would have understood. . . .' From that I take it that you think I don't understand?"

It became quiet again. Legiar perused the densely packed shelves, studying the titles with interest. Luayan did not rush him; he waited patiently for the continuation of their conversation.

"You have done well." Legiar turned back, blowing book dust from his fingers. "You have done well in your studies. But I have come to you, not as a scholar, not as a dean, and not even as a mage: I have come to you as the student of Orlan."

Luayan gazed, without breaking away, at the intent, narrow pupil that was fixed on him. His guest's dead eye was like a round piece of ice.

"As the student of Orlan, look." On Legiar's palm lay a gold disk with elaborate indentations in the center; a gold chain hung down between his fingers, and a bright yellow arc of light ran across the darkened ceiling.

"This is the Amulet of the Prophet," Legiar resumed hollowly. "The strength of the Amulet is well known, but no one knows all its properties. Ever since its master, the Prophet Orwin, perished, it has been dormant. It must now search for a new master, a new prophet. The person who puts it on gains the ability to look into the future, but this can happen only if the medallion itself has chosen him. The medallion will simply kill the vainglorious or foolish man who tries to make use of it without the right to do so: gold knows no mercy. I cannot keep it with me; I am not its master. I cannot deliver it into the hands of any of the archmages, for then doubt, suspicion, and envy would gnaw at me until finally . . . The medallion does not belong in the hands of anyone who is not a mage, however, so what am I to do?"

Legiar narrowed his eyes: the sighted eye collapsed into a slit, but the dead one acquired a strange, almost crafty expression.

"I have brought the medallion to you, Luayan. You are the student of Orlan. Vanity and pride were alien to him. He was wise, far wiser than all who live today. He was only your mentor for a short while, but he is in you; he is, I see it. I would have brought the medallion to him, but he is dead, so you must take it. Treasure and preserve it."

Luayan took the gold disk in the palm of his hand. The medallion seemed warm, like a living creature. "What should I do with it?"

Legiar smiled slightly. "Nothing. Hide it. Keep it safe. It selects its own master; don't try to assist it. Glance at it every once in a while to see whether there is any rust on it. Yes, I know, it is gold, not iron. Rust on the Amulet augurs peril for the living world: thus did the First Prophet proclaim, and as Heaven has witnessed, the elder was right." The corner of Legiar's long mouth mournfully crooked down.

As he was leaving, he turned on the threshold.

"You see, I am old. . . . Many of us are now old and those who should have taken our places . . . did not. You are happy in your university. And somewhere yet another frustrated hope roams the earth: the former Doorkeeper; even I don't know who or where he is now. Guard the medallion . . . and farewell."

He left, and Luayan never saw him again, but his life's work sprang from this memorable meeting: a history of the deeds of the archmages.

The medallion lay comfortably in his hand. The dean raised it to his eyes, inspecting it as closely as he could: there was no rust. Not a dot, not a speck. However, the presentiment of misfortune ripened and matured like an apple, like an abscess.

Half a week had passed by after the Tower's declaration of the End of Time. Several times a day the Tower of Lash emitted its howl, which chilled the blood coursing through the veins of the city's inhabitants; thick smoke reluctantly drifted up into the sky from the grilled windows of the Tower, but not a single robed man appeared on the streets of the city. The townspeople were tormented with anxiety.

The consumption of spirits increased tenfold in the city: the idea that intoxication expels unwelcome thoughts and blunts fear was, apparently, well known to men other than Egert Soll. Wives waited for their husbands in anxiety and alarm, and when their husbands returned home on all fours or creeping on their bellies, their first, slurred words were assurances that time would not end. The neighborhoods of craftsmen and merchants gradually fell under the sway of too much drink, while in the aristocratic areas of the city decorum reigned for the time being. Even there, however, one might encounter a tipsy lackey or a coachman who had gotten so drunk that he toppled from his perch. The high windows of the wealthy houses were thickly curtained, so who knows what really went on behind the cover of those curtains, so dense that they did not even let air through. Many of the inhabitants who had relatives in the villages and outskirts considered it best to pay them a long visit; all day carts and wagons loaded with household goods wheeled out of the city gates one after another.

The taverns flourished: the proprietors of alehouses and pubs passed off swill that had long been stagnating in barrels as first-class wine. But even though people drank nervously in the majority of such establishments, only wishing to drown out their fear, in the student tavern, the One-Eyed Fly, genuine and unconstrained merrymaking prevailed.

Fox was a colossal success: ten times a night he imitated first the hooded acolytes, then the Magister, then the dwarf with the trumpet; in Fox's performance, the uncanny, prolonged sound that was emitted by this instrument was transformed into a noise of ridiculous lewdness. The students applauded, sprawled out on the benches. Only Egert did not take part in the general merriment.

Hunching, as usual, in a corner, barely able to squeeze his long legs underneath the bench, Egert scratched at the tabletop with the tip of a blunt knife. His lips moved soundlessly, repeating the word "yes" over and over, and the glass of wine that stood in front of him on the table remained almost untouched.

When the path has reached its bitter end. When that which is foremost in your soul becomes last. What, after all, was foremost in his soul? Could it be his perpetual terror? Then in order to dispose of the curse, he must first dispose of his fear, but this was a closed circle: so as not to be afraid, he just had to cease being afraid. But if there were something that stood before all else in his soul, and it was not fear, then what was it?

Egert sighed. He was going around in circles like a horse harnessed to a thresher; the key to his soul was either cowardice or his desire to get rid of it: no third option entered his head.

The long table teetered. Someone sat down next to him. Egert did not raise his head right away; it was probably one of his fellow students who had stepped away from the noisy crowd so that he could drink his wine or have a bite to eat in relative peace. Meanwhile, Fox renewed his prancing jokes. Laughter filled the tavern, but Egert distinguished a quiet snicker coming from the man next to him.

He turned his face and looked at his neighbor. At first glance this strong young man seemed completely unfamiliar to him, but already in the next second Egert, chilled, recognized Fagirra.

Fagirra was sitting in the student tavern. Never in all the times Egert had been there had a single one of the robed men come in. Fagirra was dressed modestly and simply, similarly to any of Egert's comrades. Freed from the ominous hood, he seemed even younger than his years, perhaps even the same age as Egert. No one was paying Fagirra any special attention. Resembling the others, he casually took a sip of something from a large tankard and amiably glanced at the stupefied Egert. Egert could just see his tattoo peeking out from under his sleeve; that tattoo marked him as a professional blade master.

Egert could think of nothing better to do than to pick up his own glass and also take a sip. Fagirra smiled. "Good health, my friend. On the eve of great trials, I am especially pleased to see you in such good health."

Egert murmured an inaudible greeting. Fox, who had gathered the entire company of students around the platform, was being far too successful in his mockery: the jokes, each more wicked than the last, were all aimed at the Order of Lash. The students were roaring with laughter.

Fagirra listened attentively, and the somewhat absentminded, benevolent expression disappeared from his face: thus does an elderly teacher attend to the incoherent answer of an indolent student, already counting the number of whippings that he will administer to the schoolboy. Egert was horrified.

"I see that all those hours spent studying do not add to the youths' wisdom," breathed Fagirra. "Meanwhile, the time is nigh."

"Nigh?" The word burst out of Egert, and he panicked immediately. "I mean to say . . . when . . ."

Once again, Fagirra smiled softly. "We know when. But this knowledge is intended for those who are with us. Are you with us, Egert?"

He felt a sudden, inexpressible desire to say yes. Not just to appease Fagirra, though he did desire that as well, but because a wild thought flashed through his head. What if this answer proves to be the first in a series of five? What if the Wanderer's puzzle was connected with the Order of Lash?

"Well, Egert?" Fagirra sighed reproachfully. "Are you hesitating? On the eve of the End of Time, are you wavering?"

Fox had wrapped himself up in a tablecloth. He had fashioned a hood from its edge and was now pacing about the tavern, dismally nodding his head and occasionally mournfully raising his eyes to the soot-stained ceiling. Egert remained silent.

Fagirra shrugged his shoulders as if to say "what a pity." With a blindingly quick movement, imperceptible to any onlookers, he placed his hand against Egert's ribs. "Keep your seat, Egert. Hold still, for Heaven's sake. Be calm."

Egert tilted his eyes to the side. A slender, elegant stiletto with a tiny, dark drop of some unknown substance glistening on its very tip pressed gently into his side.

Egert could not remember the last time he had been seized by such utter, instinctual terror. The only reason he did not leap up with a howl was that his legs and arms quickly refused to serve him.

"This is not an instantaneous death," said Fagirra in the same soft, calming tone. "It is lingering, Egert, lingering and hmm . . . unpleasant, yes? A single prick is sufficient, and the wound will not be large. Do I make myself clear?"

Egert sat still; he was as pale as sun-bleached bone. His blood pumped loudly in his ears.

"Now, pay attention, Egert. Were you with the dean when he heard of the End of Time?"

Egert's throat had dried up; he could only nod.

"Good. What did Master Luayan say; what did he do?"

Horrified at himself, Egert squeezed out, "He left. He went to his study."

"And what did he do in his study?"

Egert's heart suddenly felt lighter: he realized that he did not know anything about this.

"What did he do in his study, Egert?"

Students were dancing around the room; Fox was twirling the pretty Farri, and in the midst of this lighthearted carousal both the murmuring voice of Fagirra and the drop of poison at the end of his elegant stiletto seemed utterly improbable.

"I don't know," whispered Egert. "I did not see."

"You were asked to watch and listen, don't you remember?" The tip of the stiletto was touching his shirt.

"No one saw. It would have been impossible. He locked the door."

Fagirra sighed dejectedly. "That's bad, very bad. But it reminds me: Did Master Luayan ever open his safe in front of you? Is it secured with a lock or with an enchantment?"

Egert's memory traitorously presented him with a picture of the dean approaching one of the locked cabinets.

"With a lock," he moaned, in order to have something to say.

"What's inside? Did you see?"

None of the frolicking youths noticed either the stiletto or Egert's pallor. Fox announced loud enough for all to hear that the time was approaching, the time when he would have to answer the call of nature. He left.

"No," Egert gasped. "I don't know."

Fagirra suddenly stopped smiling: his face transformed from affectionate to rigid and cruel, like the executioner's block. "Don't you dare lie. Be very

careful how you answer me: Is the dean planning to take any action in anticipation of the End?"

The heavy outer door flew against the wall with a crash. The scholarly
youths all turned toward it in surprise.

First a foot in a jackboot stained with filth barged into the tavern, followed
by an enormous gilded sword hilt, and then the rest of Lord Karver Ott entered; behind him tramped in two swords of ominous size, attached to two
guards: Bonifor and the nameless one with the tiny mustache.

The One-Eyed Fly had not seen such visitors in quite a long time. All the
drinkers eyed them silently, as if trying to determine what they were. Even
Fagirra interrupted his interrogation and frowned at them.

Karver examined the students with round, slightly cloudy eyes: the newly
minted lieutenant was drunk; however, neither Egert, hunched over in the dark
corner, nor Fagirra, sitting very close to him, escaped the notice of his gaze.

"Ah!" exclaimed Karver loudly and joyfully. "Is this your lady friend?"

Everyone was silent; stomping his boots and dragging his heels with each
step, Karver walked through the tavern and stopped opposite Egert and Fagirra, whose stiletto was concealed from the others' eyes behind the massive
table.

"There's something I don't quite understand," drawled Karver thoughtfully,
switching his gaze from Egert to Fagirra and back again. "Just who is whose
girlfriend, eh? Bonifor"—he glanced back at his associate—"take a look at
this: They're sitting here like doves, snuggling up against each other." He hiccuped and then continued, turning to his second companion, who in this way
finally gained a name, "Dirk, make sure to keep an eye on that one. We wouldn't
want to make a widow out of Egert's girlfriend, now, would we?"

Egert felt the poisoned blade reluctantly move away, and he breathed more
freely.

"Hey, swordsmen!" The students had gathered in a dense mass, and the
looks they were directing at the newcomers were far from affectionate. "Have
you lost something? Do you need help finding it?"

Karver nodded to the unarmed youths and casually spit on the well-used
wooden floor. The spittle unfortunately landed on the boot of the mustachioed
Dirk; he hurriedly wiped off his offended boot with the side of the other. His
spur clanked.

"Get up, Egert," suggested Bonifor cordially. "Say good night to your sweetheart. It's time to go."

Glancing to the side, Egert saw that the venomous barb of the stiletto was concealed in a tiny iron sheath attached to Fagirra's bootleg. He could have passionately kissed all of them: Karver, Bonifor, and the mustachioed Dirk.

Karver, in the meantime, had stepped forward, and his hand adamantly seized Egert by the collar; some confusion followed because both Dirk and Bonifor simultaneously tried to carry out the exact same action. Fagirra stood up leisurely and retreated to the side.

"Hey! Hey! Hey!" several voices yelled in admonishment. The compact group of students surged forward, and the learned youths surrounded the guards and Egert.

"Egert, what's this about?"

"Oh, their buttons are so shiny! Let's pluck them off, yeah?"

"Would you look at that, three on one, and they're still baring their teeth!"

"Give Egert a pair of knives, let him throw them. Their buttons will fall off all on their own."

Karver smirked scornfully and put his hand on his sword hilt; the wall of students moved slightly, but the scholarly youths did not disperse.

Just then Fox, having answered the call of nature, returned to the tavern in high spirits. Pushing his way through the crowd of his comrades and sweeping his eyes over the three armed newcomers who were looming over a very pallid Egert, Gaetan instantly assessed the situation.

"Papa!" he yelped, flinging himself on Karver's neck.

Confusion reigned again. Dirk and Bonifor spun away from Egert and gaped in shock at the redheaded lad who was blubbering on the chest of their lieutenant.

"Daddy, why did you forsake Mama!"

Giggles could be heard in the mass of students. Karver was furiously trying to tear Fox's hands away from his ribbons and epaulets.

"You . . . You . . . ," he snorted, unable to add anything further.

Fox wrapped his arms and legs around Karver, who was barely able to keep his feet under him. Gaetan gently clasped his ear and said in a theatrical whisper, "Do you remember how you dragged my mama to a hayloft?"

"Get him off me!" Karver snapped at his companions.

Fox emitted a distressed howl. "What! Are you denying it?" Leaping off the lieutenant, he fixed him with round, shocked, honey-colored eyes. "You're renouncing your own son? Well, look at me: I might as well be a copy of you! We have the same disgusting snouts!"

The students were falling over themselves with laughter, and even Egert smiled wanly. Dirk was looking around nervously, and Bonifor's bloodshot eyes darted around the room ever more rapidly.

Suddenly, as if stricken with a thought, Fox screwed up his face suspiciously. "But maybe . . . Maybe you don't know how to make babies, after all!"

Finally getting his bearings, Karver drew his sword. The students sprang back, all except for Fox who, with a mournful expression, took a pepper pot from the table and, with a quick toss, emptied it into the lieutenant's face.

The owner, the cook, and the servants all jumped out of their skins at the wild howl; gasping and coughing, Karver fell down onto the floor, trying to scratch out his own eyes. Dirk and Bonifor both seized their weapons, but their heads were bombarded from all sides by stools, beer mugs, and any cutlery that fell into the furious hands of the students. Showered with taunts and insults, climbing over a mountain of capsized furniture, futilely swinging their blades and promising to return, the gentlemen of the guards disgracefully retired from the field of battle.

On the following day, Toria climbed up her stepladder, peered into the lecture hall through the small round window, and did not see Egert Soll among the students.

Having run her eyes over the rows of students more than once, Toria frowned. The absence of Egert piqued her: after all, her father was on the rostrum! Climbing down, she thought for some time while observing the free and easy games of the library's mouser; then, feeling querulous, she set off for the annex.

She perfectly remembered the way to this room even though Dinar had not been fond of her visiting there: undoubtedly he was ashamed of the small room. She visited just the same and perched on the edge of his desk while the poor fellow scurried about, gathering up stray items and wiping the dust off the windowsill with his palm. . . .

Calling Dinar to mind, Toria sighed. She walked up to the familiar door, suddenly unsure of herself. All was quiet beyond the door, and it seemed likely to her that there was no one in the room. How stupid I look, thought Toria, and knocking once, she entered.

Egert was sitting at the desk, his head gravely lowered; Toria noted in passing the sheet of paper lying in front of him and the quill stained with ink.

Turning his head around to greet his guest, Egert flinched; the inkpot, grazed by his hand, teetered and overturned.

For a minute or two they were distracted by silently and intently wiping up puddles of ink from the tabletop and floor. Toria's gaze involuntarily fell on the pages, full of writing, much of it crossed out, and without even realizing what she was doing, she read in Egert's bloated, clumsy handwriting: *and then we shall manage to remember all, and all that was* . . . She hastened to avert her gaze; noticing this, Egert smiled wearily.

"I've never been one for writing letters."

"There is a lecture now," she remarked dryly.

"Yes," Egert sighed, "but I really need, especially today, to write a letter to . . . to a certain woman."

The autumn wind gathered strength beyond the windows; it howled and slammed into the loose shutters. Toria suddenly realized that it was damp in the room and chilly, and almost completely dark.

Egert turned away from her "Yes. I finally decided to write to my mother."

The wind tossed a fallen maple leaf—yellow as the sun—against the window; sticking there for a second, the yellow leaf tore away and flew farther on, dancing playfully in the wind.

"I didn't know that you had a mother," said Toria quietly and almost immediately became confused. "That is, I didn't know she was alive."

Egert cast his eyes to the ground. "Yes."

"That's good," mumbled Toria, unable to think of anything better to say.

Egert smiled, but the smile came out bitter. "Yes. The thing is, I am not a very good son. That's for sure."

Beyond the window the wind gusted particularly strenuously. A draft swirled through the room, proprietarily rustling through the papers on the desk.

"Somehow it seems to me . . ." Toria unexpectedly found herself speaking. "It seems to me that a son, even one who has gotten into trouble, would be loved regardless. Perhaps even more intensely . . ."

Egert glanced up at her quickly, and his face brightened. "Really?"

For some unknown reason Toria recalled a young boy, a stranger to her, weeping over a dead sparrow: she was fourteen years old, and she went up to him and explained in all seriousness that the bird needed to be left alone, for only then would the Sparrow King appear and bring his loyal subject back to life. Widening his tear-filled eyes, the little boy had asked her then with that same abrupt, sincere hope, "Really?"

Toria smiled at her recollection. "Really."

Rain started drumming against the hazy window.

Whenever Toria returned home with yet another hole in her stockings, her mother, silently shaking her head, took her wooden needlework box down from a shelf. Toria peered covetously into its mysterious depths: there among a tangle of wool and silk thread, brilliantly lustrous pearl buttons gleamed at her like eyes. Her mother extracted a needle from the box and set to work, occasionally biting off a thread with her sharp, white teeth. Soon in the place where the misshapen little hole had been, a red bug with black spots appeared; after several weeks had passed, Toria's new stockings were always embroidered with an entire swarm of red bugs, both small and large. She liked to imagine that they would come alive and crawl over her knees, tickling her with their little feelers.

And if her mother were still alive? What if her father had not let her go, what if he had locked her up, locked the door and fastened it with an enchantment?

Father and daughter had lived together for many years, and in all that time she could not remember a single other woman with him. Not one.

The Tower of Lash launched into its mournful howl. Toria winced peevishly and in the same breath frowned, seeing how Egert's face changed. It must be difficult to live in constant fear.

"It's nothing," she said briskly. "Don't listen to it. Don't listen. Only undertakers believe in this nonsense about the end of time: they're hoping to make some money." She smiled at her awkward joke, but Egert did not stop frowning. A painful-looking fold loomed between his eyebrows.

The sound came again, even more plaintive, with a hysterical sob at the end. Toria saw that Egert's lips were starting to quiver; flinching, he hastily turned his back to her. Egert silently tried to compose himself, and Toria, who was also uncomfortable, had to witness this mute struggle.

For a long moment she considered if she should tactfully retire or if, on the contrary, it would be best to pretend that nothing was happening. The Tower finally fell silent, but Egert was overcome with the shakes and had to hold his twitching jaw with his hand to still it. Without saying a word, Toria went out into the corridor, filled an iron mug from the water fountain, and brought it to Egert.

He gulped it down and started choking. His pale face became engorged with blood; tears welled up in his eyes. Desiring to help, Toria clapped him on the back one or two times. His shirt was as damp as if it had just been pulled out of a laundry basin.

"Everything will be all right," she mumbled, suddenly overcome with shyness. "Listen to me: There won't be an 'end of time.' Don't be afraid."

Then he drew a deep breath and suddenly told her everything: he told her about Fagirra, about the Magister, about the ceremony in the Tower, about their promises and threats and about his secret errand. Toria heard him out without interjecting a single word, but when he got to the last encounter with the disguised acolyte, Egert fell silent.

"That's all?" Toria looked him in the eyes.

"That's all." He averted his eyes.

A few moments passed in silence.

"You don't trust me?" Toria asked softly.

He laughed: it was a strange question after all that had been said!

"Tell me, right to the end." Toria drew her eyebrows down.

So he told her about the poisoned stiletto.

The ensuing silence lasted for about ten minutes.

Finally, Toria raised her head. "So, you didn't tell him anything?"

"I don't know anything," Egert explained wearily. "But if I had known, I would have reported it all to that dear soul."

"No!" said Toria as though she was shocked at the very possibility of such an idea. "No, you wouldn't have told him. . . ." But at the end her voice lost its confidence.

"You yourself have seen what I've become," uttered Egert peevishly. "I am no longer myself. I'm a wretched, cowardly animal."

"But can't you . . . try to overcome it?" asked Toria cautiously. "Try to keep yourself from being afraid?"

"Try to keep yourself from blinking," Egert suggested, shrugging.

Toria tried. For some time she heartily looked out the window with wide-open eyes as if she were engaged in a staring contest, but then her eyelids twitched and, ignoring the command of her reason, fluttered.

"There you have it." Egert's gaze was fixed on the floor. "I am a slave. I'm a total slave to the curse. All I think about is what is first in my soul, and what is last, and who will question me five times, so that I might answer 'yes' five times."

Toria rubbed her temple, exactly like her father. "I cannot believe it. What if you were forced to do something completely impossible? Wouldn't you be able to resist?"

Egert smiled crookedly. "If I had a knife at my throat . . ."

"But really you . . . you're not a bad man . . . ," she muttered without confidence.

He was silent. An enormous, impudent raven was strutting ceremoniously through the wet university courtyard like a judge.

Egert exhaled deeply, seeing a scaffold in his mind's eye. Stuttering, he told her about the girl in the carriage and the highwaymen who had intercepted that carriage on the road.

Another long silence followed. Egert expected Toria to simply get to her feet and leave, but she did not.

"And if," she asked finally, her voice unsteady, "if it had been . . . there . . . if that had been me?"

Egert buried his face in his hands.

For a long time Toria looked at the unkempt, disordered waves of his blond hair, at his shoulders, impressively wide but hunched and shaking like a child's; then she rested her narrow palm on one of them.

Egert froze.

As persuasively as she could, Toria said, "You are not responsible for the deeds of others. You are simply ill and you need to find a cure. And we will find it."

She spoke reluctantly, like a doctor assuring a patient who is near death and covered in sores of his imminent recovery. The tense shoulder shuddered under her hand as if it was relaxing slightly; the change was barely perceptible, but in the next moment she sensed all the confusion of Egert's feelings: hope, gratitude, and the desire to believe. Then, still holding her hand against his warm shoulder, she wished with suddenly awakened compassion that her belabored words would prove to be true.

The door swung open with a crash. Holding a pair of dilapidated notebooks at his side, Fox, grinning widely, burst into the room.

His honey-colored eyes dwelled on Egert who sat, hanging his head, on the edge of the bed and on Toria whose hand was resting on his shoulder. For several moments nothing happened, and then in an instant Gaetan's angular face was pierced with surprise: his eyes became as round as plums, his mouth swept open in a round hole, and muttering an indistinct apology, Fox leapt away without even trying to pick up his books, which had crashed to the floor.

Toria did not remove her hand. Waiting until the Gaetan's clatter faded in

the corridor, she said earnestly, "This is what I think. The curse will be broken if you fall into a hopeless situation and yet somehow overcome it. When
the path has been reached its bitter end: don't you think the Wanderer was
speaking of this?"

Egert did not answer.

After a few days the rain changed into clear, fair weather. Squinting in the
cool autumn sunlight, the townspeople were somewhat cheered. "Time is not
even thinking of ending," said neighbors to each other, stepping out onto
their little porches in the morning, "On the contrary, time is on the loose. . . ."

The Tower of Lash loomed over the square like an admonitory finger: it
even seemed that it had recently shriveled and dried up just like a geriatric
digit. It was as if a bald spot had appeared in the square around the Tower:
everyone tried to travel around the sinister building, all the more so since smoke
rose from the windows ever thicker, the dismal sound rang out ever more
often, and passersby who happened to be in the square late at night assured
their acquaintances that they heard a dull, subterranean rumble rising up
from its depths.

The city authorities were silent and apparently had no plans regarding the
Order of Lash. Among the students it was considered good form to address
witty remarks and taunts to the Order of Lash: Fox recalled for this purpose
his old, foolish nanny, who had frightened four of the apothecary's sons in
sequence with one and the same bogeyman, and yet none of them were ever
devoured by him. Lessons continued as if nothing had happened, and only a
few bewildered youths, using various excuses, left the university for home.

"Father is worried," Toria said one day.

They were sitting in the library late one evening. A single candle was guttering on the book cart.

"He tries not to give that impression, but I know him. Lash alarms him."

The candle was dissolving into droplets of wax.

"Lash," Egert repeated, barely audibly. "That time, in Kavarren . . . You
were searching for manuscripts. Didn't you say that the Order of Lash was
founded by some lunatic mage?"

"The Sacred Spirit," whispered Toria. "It is said that that mage became the
Sacred Spirit after his death. But it is an absolute mystery. Father asked Dinar
to research him, but we found nothing, absolutely nothing. An abyss of time

has passed since he died. All the manuscripts that concern the history of Lash have either been lost or ruined, as if someone intentionally destroyed them."

"They speak of a secret." Egert smiled bleakly. "They are quite capable of keeping it."

Toria was silent for a moment. Then she confided reluctantly, "They importuned my father. They offered . . . I don't know what they offered. Cooperation? Money? Power? But he was always dismissive of them. And now he is worried. He is expecting . . . Even he doesn't know what he is expecting."

Egert was amazed. "Really? But mages can comprehend, I mean, they should be able to access any secret, even the future, shouldn't they?"

It seemed to Toria that there was doubt of her father's magical ability in these words. Nettled, she jerked up her head. "What do you know! Yes, my father sees many things that we would not be able to understand, but he is not a prophet!"

Egert thought it might be best to hold his peace. He did not want to get into an argument and besides, he did not like to display his ignorance. Toria regretted her outburst and apologetically muttered, "You see, the future is open to Prophets. They are mages who have a special gift, and they are also the masters of the Amulet. The Amulet came into the world at the hands of the very first Prophet, and ever since it has passed from master to disciple." Toria had become agitated and could not find the proper words.

"From father to son?" asked Egert avidly.

"No. The Prophets are not connected by ties of blood. There can be only one Prophet in the world at a time. When he dies, the Amulet itself searches for his successor. Objects also have the ability to search, and the Amulet is much more than a mere object. It is unimaginably ancient. Truthfully speaking, I don't even know what sort of object it is." Toria drew a breath.

Egert raised his head; books gazed at him from the shelves, and it seemed to him that a wind from this lurking depository of magic touched his face. He had wanted desperately to speak with Toria about the world of magicians for so long now, and it suddenly seemed all the more risky to scare off this usually forbidden yet terribly interesting topic. He asked cautiously, "So, where is the Prophet right now? The man who carries the Amulet, where is he right now, this second?"

Toria frowned. "There is no Prophet right now. The last one died about fifty years ago, and since then . . ." She sighed. "That's how it is. The new Prophet probably hasn't even been born yet."

Egert was silent for a moment, not knowing if he had the right to question her further; curiosity, however, proved to be stronger than apprehension and so, just as cautiously, he asked, "And what then does this Amulet do in the meantime? Is it traveling or waiting or hiding from people?"

"It is lying in my father's safe," Toria blurted out and in the same breath bit her tongue.

A minute or two passed by. Egert stared at the girl with round, deeply horrified eyes. "Why did you tell me that?"

Toria understood quite well that she had made a mistake, but she attempted to bring the conversation back to idle chatter. "And what of it, really?" she asked, nervously smoothing the folds of her skirt against her knees. "It's not like you're planning to announce it to one and all, now, is it?"

Egert turned away. Toria understood full well what he meant, and he knew that she understood.

Adjusting the blazing logs in the fireplace with a poker, Dean Luayan examined them both from the corner of his eye.

Toria's resemblance to her deceased mother frightened him at times: he was afraid that along with her beauty, the exquisite beauty of a marble statue, Toria might also have inherited the tragic instability and cruel luck of her mother. When he consented to the marriage of his daughter to Dinar, he had sincerely hoped that everything would be different for Toria, but the disaster that followed dispelled his hopes. Toria was far too like her mother to be happy. The dean's heart contracted whenever he saw that proud, perpetually solitary figure, dressed eternally in black, haunting the twilight of the library.

Now Toria was sitting on a low stool, her knees gathered up under her chin, bristling like a wet sparrow, vexed at her own foolishness: She had said too much, and she was no talker! Her face, even with a grimace of annoyance, was delicate and feminine, and the dean suddenly realized that the changes he had been noticing in his daughter recently were gaining strength.

Egert stood next to her, almost touching her shoulder with his hand, but not quite; Toria had not allowed even Dinar, who had been her fiancé, to stand so close to her. After his death everything had become worse: perpetually shrouded in the transparent shell of her own grief, of her own mysterious internal life, the severe daughter of Luayan had scared off other young people, even from afar. They scattered like a pile of autumn leaves in her wake, taking her detachment and alienation for contempt and pride. Now the murderer of Dinar was standing next to her, and Luayan, peeking over his shoulder at the two of them, was astonished to observe in his daughter an abundance of small, previously inconceivable changes.

She had become more feminine. She had certainly become more feminine, and the lines of her beautiful lips were softer, even now when she was scowling. She seemed profoundly aware that Egert was standing next to her, a man she would have gladly destroyed not all that long ago!

Having caught fire, the dry logs crackled. The dean forced himself to reenter the conversation.

"It's all my fault," said Toria in a penitential voice. "Curse my tongue!"

The dean cast a sidelong, censorious glance at her. "Be wary of curses." Then, having contemplated his next action for a moment, he walked up to one of the tall cabinets and unlocked the door.

"Father . . ." Toria's voice faltered.

The dean extracted the jade casket from the safe, flicked open the lid, and took from the black satin pillow an object that quietly jingled on a yellow chain. "Here it is, Egert. Take a look; it's all right."

A gold disk with ornate fissures in the center lay on his palm: a medallion on a chain.

"This is the Amulet of the Prophet, an inconceivably valuable object, hidden in secret."

"You can't let me leave this room," said Egert in horror. "I could tell them everything."

The dean caught the compassionate glance that Toria directed at Egert, thought for a moment, and then shook his head. "It is within my power to make you forget what you have seen. Just as your friend Gaetan forgot about a certain event, to which he was a chance witness. It's possible, but I will not do it, Egert. You must walk your path until the bitter end. Fight for your liberty." The dean leaned toward the medallion with these last words, as if invoking it.

"But what if the Order finds out about it?" Toria's voice was high.

"I do not fear Lash," replied the dean vaguely.

The flames in the fireplace blazed up even more vigorously, and the medallion in Luayan's palm cast spots of light onto the ceiling.

"It is completely faultless," said the dean in an undertone. Both Egert and Toria looked at him in wonder.

"What?"

"It's clean," explained the dean. "The gold does not have a spot of rust. Not a speck. If we really were on the eve of great ordeal, then . . . It senses danger threatening the world, and it rusts as an indicator. So it was half a century ago when the Third Power stood at the Doors. I was a young boy then, but I remember that forebodings tormented me, and the medallion, so they say, was completely covered in rust. Now it is clean, as though there were no threat. But somehow I know that this is not so!" Swallowing a bitter taste that burst forth in his mouth, the dean returned the medallion to the safe in utter silence.

"Do you think Lash is the threat?" Toria asked in a whisper.

The dean tossed another log into the fireplace. Egert jumped back to avoid the scattering sparks.

"I don't know," the dean confessed unwillingly. "The Order of Lash undoubtedly has some sort of connection to it, but the thing that threatens us the most, that is something else entirely. Or someone else entirely."


Winter arrived in the space of a single night.

Upon awaking in the early morning, Egert saw that the gray, damp ceiling of the cramped room had turned as white and frosted as the hem of a wedding gown. Neither the wind, nor footsteps, nor the clamor of wheels could be heard from the square: snow was drifting down to earth in solemn silence.

According to tradition, all lectures were canceled on the day of the first snow. When he learned of this custom, Egert rejoiced far more than he would have otherwise.

Merriment was soon in full swing in the university courtyard. Under the leadership of Fox, the peaceful student body suddenly transformed into a horde of soldiers. A dazzlingly white snow fort was hastily constructed and soon snow battles were raging. Egert entered into the melee with pleasure.

Before long, however, the battle somehow devolved into a fight of the one against the many, with Egert taking the role of lone defender against the horde of students, like some hero of antiquity; it seemed he did not have two hands, but ten, and every snowball he threw hit its mark, dusting an opponent's flushed face with crumbs of snow. Attacked from all sides, he dived under hostile missiles and they collided over his head, sprinkling his fair hair with snow. Despairing of striking a moving target, especially one that moved the way Egert did, his opponents were about to engage in hand-to-hand combat, planning to tumble their invincible adversary into a snowbank, when Egert suddenly noticed that Toria was observing the skirmish.

Fox and his comrades immediately faded into the background; Toria leisurely bent down, scooped up some snow, and rolled it into a ball. Then, swinging her arm back, she threw it and hit Egert in the forehead.

He walked over to her, wiping slush from his face. Toria looked at his wet face seriously, without the slightest shadow of a smile.

"Today is the first snow. I want to show you something." Without saying another word, she turned around and walked away. Egert moved off after her, as if he were tethered to her with a leash.

Snow lay everywhere. It covered the university steps, and it had settled on the heads of the iron snake and wooden monkey, creating two large, wintery snowcaps.

"Is it in the city?" Egert asked worriedly. "I wouldn't want to run into Fagirra."

"Do you really think he'd come anywhere near you when I'm around?" Toria smiled.

The city was submerged in silence; instead of the thunder of carts, sleighs crept noiselessly through the streets, and the wide tracks left by their runners seemed as brittle as porcelain. Snow tumbled and fell, covering the shoulders of pedestrians, speckling astonished black dogs with white, concealing all refuse and dirt from the eyes.

"The first snow," said Egert. "It's a pity that it will melt."

"Not at all," replied Toria. "Every thaw is like a short spring. It'd best thaw, or else . . ."

She wanted to say that the smooth surface of the snow reminded her of the pure, white shrouds used to cover the dead, but she did not. She did not want Egert to think that she was always so gloomy. Winter really was beautiful: it was not to blame for the fact that it was possible to freeze to death in a snowbank, just like her mother.

Red-breasted robins with white snowflakes on their backs were sitting on girders attached to walls, looking like the guards in their bright uniforms; and presently the guards themselves strolled by, with their tall pikes and their red-and-white uniforms, shivering just like the robins.

"Are you cold?" asked Egert.

She tucked her hands deeper into her old muff. "No. Are you?"

He was not wearing a hat. The snow fell right on his hair and did not melt.

"I never get cold. My father raised me as a soldier, and soldiers must be able to endure anything, not least of all cold." Egert grinned.

They passed through the city gates; the wet snow formed grinning jaws on the serpents and dragons that were welded there. Sleds were sweeping along the road. Toria turned confidently and led Egert to the very shore of the river.

Just like frosted glass, the surface of the water was covered in a skin of ice, thick and dull by the shores, thin and latticed toward the center. A narrow stream remained free in the middle; it ran dark and smooth, and on the very edge of the ice stood an unkindness of black ravens, strutting about and displaying their magnificence.

"We'll walk along the riverbank," said Toria. "Look around; there should be a footpath."

The footpath was buried under the snow. Egert walked in front and Toria tried to place her light shoes in the deep tracks of his boots. Thus they walked for quite a long time. The snow finally stopped falling, and the sun began to peek through jagged holes in the clouds.

Toria squinted, blinded: how white, how sparkling the world suddenly seemed! Egert turned his face back to her. Snowflakes gleamed brightly in his hair.

"Is it much farther?"

She smiled, almost not understanding the question. At that moment words seemed to her like an unnecessary addition to the snowy, sun-drenched splendor of this extraordinary day.

Egert understood, and hesitantly, as if asking for permission, he smiled in answer.

They walked on side by side: the footpath had emerged onto a hill where the snow was no longer so deep. Toria held one hand in the warm depths of her muff, and the other leaned on the arm of her companion. Egert pressed his elbow firmly to his side so that her hand, sheltered in the folds of his sleeve, would not freeze.

They paused for a short while, looking back at the river and the city. Wisps of smoke stood over the city walls in dove-colored columns.

"I've never been here," admitted Egert in wonder. "It's so beautiful."

Toria smiled briefly. "It is a memorable place. There is an old graveyard here. After the Black Plague, they buried everyone who had died here, in one pit. It is said that the hill became three times taller from all the dead bodies. Since then this place has been considered special: some say it is blessed; some say it is cursed. Children sometimes leave a lock of their hair on the summit so that a wish will come true. Sorcerers from the villages come here in pilgrimage. But in general . . ." Toria faltered. "Father does not like this place. He says . . . But what have we to be afraid of? It's such beautiful white day."

They stood on the summit of the hill for almost an hour and Toria, pointing with her frozen hand first at the river, then at a snow-covered ribbon of road, then at the close gray horizon, spoke of the centuries that had passed over the earth; of the belligerent hordes that had descended on the city all at once from three sides; of the deep moat, of which now only a small furrow, invisible under the snow, remained; of the unassailable defenses, erected at the cost of many lives. The hill, upon which Egert and Toria were now standing, was a remainder of a fortification that had been worn away by time. Egert, listening attentively, suggested that the enemy hordes were all cavalry, and furthermore that they were extremely numerous.

"How do you know that?" wondered Toria. "Did you read it?"

Egert, ducking his head, confessed his complete and utter ignorance: no, he had not read it, but from the placement of the defenses, as Toria had described them, it should be clear to anyone that they were not built to defend against foot soldiers, but against a vast quantity of mounted enemies.

For some time Toria was silent, wondering. Egert stood next to her, also silent, and their long blue shadows merged on the lustrous mantle of snow.

"If you watch the horizon for a while," Toria suddenly said quietly, "if you do not take your eyes from it for a very long time, then you begin to imagine that the sea is beneath us. The blue sea surges beneath us, and we are standing on the shore, on a cliff. . . ."

Egert started. "Have you seen the sea?"

Toria began to laugh merrily. "Oh, yes. I was quite young, but I remember it well. I was—" She suddenly became sad and lowered her eyes. "—I was eight years old. My father and I traveled all over the world so as not to grieve too hard over Mama."

The wind swept over the snow, picked up a handful of scintillating white powder, and played with it, strewing it about before letting it drop and moving on to pick up another handful. Egert did not know if his distressing ability to sense others' pain had returned or not, but the instantaneous desire to protect and comfort Toria deprived him of both his reason and his reticence: Toria's shoulders drooped, and then for the first time his hands dared to sink down onto them.

She was a head shorter than him. Next to him she seemed like an adolescent, almost a child; through her warm shawl and thin coat he felt how her narrow shoulders flinched under his touch and then froze. Then, desiring for all he was worth to console her and yet mortally afraid of offending her, he cautiously drew Toria toward himself.

Their blue shadows paused on the snow, merged into one; both were afraid to move, lest they startle the other. The city beyond the walls remained impassive, and the frozen river gleamed coldly. Only the wind showed any sign of impatience; it hovered like a dog around their legs, foundered in the hem of Toria's skirt, and sprinkled Egert's boots with sprays of snow.

"You will see the sea," said Toria in a whisper.

Egert was silent. He had known scores of different women in his brief life so far, but he suddenly felt himself inexperienced, a clueless boy, a silly puppy: thus does the apprentice of a jeweler tout his own skill while polishing glass, and thus does he sweat from fear the first time he receives in his hand a precious stone of unheard-of rarity.

"On the shore of the southern sea there is never any snow. There is warm sand there, and white surf. . . ." Toria spoke as if in a dream.

Glorious Heaven, he was afraid to let go of her; he was afraid that all this was an illusion; he was so afraid to lose her. And truly, he had no right to her. Can you really lose that which does not belong to you? And did not the shadow of Dinar stand between them?

Toria shivered, as if sensing his thought, but she did not move away.

Over their heads the cloud patterns changed, twisted, their sides burned by the sun like loaves in an oven. Hearing how Egert's distraught heart beat under his jacket, Toria, with almost superstitious horror, suddenly realized that she was happy. She very rarely managed to catch herself in this feeling; her nostrils flared, breathing in the smell of the snow, the fresh wind, and Egert's skin, and they wanted to raise her up on her toes so that they could reach Egert's face.

She had never caught the scent of Dinar. It was unthinkable, but she had no memory of how his heart beat. Embracing him, she had experienced a companionable tenderness, but what was that childish fondness compared to this delightful stupor, when the very thought of moving was terrible, when she hardly dared to breathe?

What is this? she thought, panicking. Betrayal? Betrayal of the memory of Dinar?

Their dark blue shadow slowly crawled across the snow like the hand of an enormous clock. A snowflake, round and flat as a grindstone, settled on Egert's shoulder right in front of Toria's nose. The sun hid behind a cloud, and the shadow on the snow faded.

"We should go," whispered Toria. "We need to—I promised to show you."

They descended the slope in silence. The river here was twisting, skirting around a small spit of land that resembled a peninsula. The earth here apparently found tall pine trees entirely to its liking: they grew in great, massed circles, and their boughs, weighed down with snow, looked like old, sagging mustaches.

They walked, wending their way through tree trunks, now and again brushing the snow from a branch: then the magnificent boughs, liberated, would rush upward, violating the consistency of the winter landscape. Finally Toria stopped and glanced back at Egert as if inviting him to look.

Right in front of them towered a stone structure, like the remnant of an ancient foundation, covered with snow. Yellow, porous stone intertwined with gray, smooth stone: Egert had never before seen anything like it. Most extraordinary was the stunted, thin-trunked tree, which was clinging to the stonework by its roots as if growing right out of the stone. Even though it was the middle of winter, the tree remained green; not a single snowflake fell on the narrow leaves, and here and there between them, round petals glowed a pale red, seeming unreal, as if they had been cut from cloth. But they were real: Egert assured himself of this when he touched one and it left a small amount of black pollen on the tip of his finger.

"This is a tomb," said Toria, trying to conceal the storm raging in her soul behind a businesslike tone. "It's several thousand years old. An ancient mage rests here, perhaps the First Prophet himself. But then again, perhaps not. This tree blossoms year-round, but never bears even a single fruit. It is rumored that it too is several millennia old. It's miraculous, isn't it?"

The magical tree was not more miraculous than the strange connection that was now invisibly growing between Toria and Egert. He wanted to ask her about it, but he did not. They both stood, gazing at the ancient sepulcher, which in turn was a witness to their silence. The snow-covered pine trees also remained silent: austerely, but without condemnation.

Dusk was falling as they returned home. The cold had intensified and near the city gates they found it necessary to stop for a while to warm their hands over a fire. The guard, with a face that was copper from the flames and shining with sweat, threw more firewood and kindling, collected that day from peasants entering the city, onto the blaze: in winter it was the custom to collect the toll in kind.

Watching the flames dance in Toria's motionless pupils, Egert found within himself the courage to bend toward her ear. "I will break the curse. I will recover my courage. I will do it for the sake of . . . you know. I swear."

She slowly lowered her eyelids, cloaking the sparks that danced in her eyes.

The first snow melted, covering the streets, porches, and intersections with shining filth; a cold wind howled through the days, and worry crawled back into the hearts of the townsfolk who had been slightly calmed by the snow. The Tower of Lash ominously elevated its fragrant smoke up to the sky: "Soon!" A few more students disappeared from the university, and the rowdy evenings at the One-Eyed Fly ended of their own accord. Dean Luayan became the focal point of a universal gravitation, as it were: people sidled up to him, hoping to gain some measure of composure. Complete strangers from the city came to see him. They stood for hours on the grand porch of the university, hoping to see the archmage, seeking his help and reassurance. Luayan avoided long conversations, but he never rewarded the petitioners with anger or annoyance. His conscience would not allow him to appease them, and his reason would not let him frighten them, so he regaled his visitors with monotonous, philosophical parables that did not relate in any way to the reason they had come.

The frightened people still came and went, regardless of the dean's efforts to put them off. Egert was not the least bit surprised to see a worn-out old man with an extremely straight back and spurs on his boots standing one morning on the steps between the serpent and the monkey. Nodding his head in welcome, he was about to walk by, but the old man smiled painfully and stepped forward to intercept him.

Egert recognized his father only after several seconds. The elder Soll had miraculously begun to resemble the portrait that hung in his study in Kavarren: a portrait of Egert's grandfather, painted when he was already quite advanced in years, gray haired, with a drooping mustache and rugged wrinkles on his face. Recalling the portrait, Egert recognized his father, and he was astounded at how quickly old age had descended upon him.

Silently, accompanied only by the dull jingling of spurs, father and son walked to the small hotel where the elder Soll was staying. The old man hammered with his flint and stone for a long time before lighting the candles in the candelabrum. A servant brought in wine and glasses. Sitting in a creaking armchair, Egert watched with pain in his heart as his father tried to gather his thoughts. But he could not gather them; he wanted to start a conversation but could not find the words. Egert would have happily helped him, but his own tongue was also helpless and mute.

"I . . . I brought money," said the elder Soll finally.

"Thank you," mumbled Egert and finally put the question that had tormented him the entire walk here into words. "How is Mother?"

His father smoothed out the threadbare velvet tablecloth on the small round table.

"She is ill, extremely ill." He lifted his haggard, watery eyes to his son. "Egert, they are saying here that time is coming to an end. If time is at an end then to hell with them, with the regiment; to hell with them and their uniform. What a regiment they are, when they . . . Egert, my son . . . My father had five sons. We only have you. You are the only one that lived. It's already difficult for me to get up into the saddle. Getting up on the roof is also difficult. Why did you leave us? There are no grandchildren. . . ."

Feeling how his throat had dried up, Egert muttered into a dark corner, "I know."

The old man sighed loudly. He bit his upper lip, chewing on his mustache. "Egert, your mother begs you. Pay your last respects, that's all. Your mother entreats you. Let's go home. To hell with them, with all of them. Let's go to Kavarren. I even brought you a horse. A mare, she's a marvel." His father's gaze brightened somewhat. "Raven black, very high spirited. She's the daughter of our Tika. You loved Tika, remember?"

Egert silently passed his fingers through the flame of a candle.

"Son, let's go today. The horses are frisky and well rested. I, of course, will get tired, but not before . . . Well, we could try it anyway. We could be home within a week. What do you say, Egert?"

"I can't." Egert would have rather damned the whole earth than to speak those words. "I cannot. How can I return like this?" His hand touched the scar.

"You think about it," sighed his father gravely. "You think about it. You can't ignore your mother, Egert. What kind of a son are you?"

It seemed to him that there would now be no rendezvous with Toria, and that something would fracture, would give way, would tear apart his innards. Happily, she met him on the steps as if she had been waiting for him there.

"Egert?"

He told her how his father's hands shook when, as they said their good-byes, Egert had shifted his eyes to the side and mumbled an assurance that he would come home soon.

Mud squelched under their feet. The city had quieted; it felt as if it were abandoned. Without picking any particular route, they roamed through the streets and alleyways, and Egert talked without ceasing.

His mother was very ill. His mother was waiting for him, but how could he return bearing this curse? How could he crawl back to his father's house bearing this cowardly brute in his soul, a brute that at any minute could turn him into the basest scoundrel? He had made a promise to himself; he had made a promise to Toria. Perhaps he was wrong? Perhaps for the sake of his mother's serenity he should swallow yet another humiliation and return defeated, a coward? Should he fetch his shadow to her feet and burden her with another woe?

He had tried, as far as he could, to explain this to his father. He had foundered in the words, had sunk into them like an amateur fisherman in his own net, but the old man could not understand him, and Egert, exhausted, had finally said to him, "I am ill. I have to find the cure, and then . . ." His father was silent, and for the first time in his son's memory, his eternally straight back slumped wearily.

Now Toria listened to all of this. Dusk was thickening; here and there the streetlamps smoked, and every shutter was shut tight. It seemed as though the houses had obstinately closed their eyes against the night, against the filth, against the foul weather. At one point it seemed to Toria that dim shadows were following them at a distance, but Egert noticed nothing. He talked and talked, and appealed to Toria as a witness: Was it possible that he really was wrong?

Trying to escape the wind, they turned into some gates and found themselves in a deserted courtyard, full of refuse. A cook stalked through the yard from a storehouse and cast them a look that was somewhat unfriendly, but more indifferent than anything else. The door slammed shut, ruthlessly grinding down clouds of steam that were breaking loose from inside. A streetlight dimly illuminated a small sign by the door: THE GOAT'S MILK. The scruffy goats stood listlessly in a narrow enclosure beneath an awning.

The streetlamp weaved in the wind, and Toria shivered, only now feeling both the wind and the damp.

"Come on, let's go. Why are we here?"

Egert opened his mouth to repeat all his reasoning from the beginning, but he found he could say nothing. In the wan light of the streetlamp, Lieutenant Karver Ott towered before him like a dripping wet ghost.

The lieutenant looked unimpressive: during his time spent in the city his uniform had been worn constantly, and since his purse had been depleted by all the taverns he had visited, it had not been cleaned. It showed. The appearance of Bonifor and Dirk, who were standing behind him, was also not very decent. Instead of gentlemen of the guards, they now resembled bandits or highwaymen, an impression that was heightened by the fact that both rested their palms on the hilts of their swords.

Toria did not understand what was happening. She did not recognize Karver, so she thought that she and Egert had been tracked down by common thieves. She had no intention of waiting for them to demand their purses. She smiled scornfully and was about to say something scathing, but Karver forestalled her.

He recognized her, even in the muddy light of the swinging street lantern, and he could hardly keep his eyes in their sockets. "Lady! We are acquainted!" he drawled with an expression of sheer amazement. "For shame!"

Bonifor and Dirk leaned forward to see Toria a little better.

"Oh yes, Egert," continued Karver. "You seem to have attained your goal. But what is the meaning of this, my lady?" He turned to Toria with a perfectly polite demeanor. "Have you so easily forgiven him for the base murder of your studious fiancé?"

"Who are you?" asked Toria in an icy tone. The iron undertones in her voice caused Dirk and Bonifor to wince slightly, but Karver was not the slightest bit put off.

"Allow me to introduce myself. I am Karver Ott, Lieutenant of the Guards of the city of Kavarren, sent here with a special commission: to bring the deserter Egert Soll back to the regiment. These are my fellow guardsmen, remarkably worthy young men. That, my lady, is who we are, definitely not the thieves of the night you seem to think us! And now allow me to ask you, just who do you think that man is, the one who is now hiding behind your back?"

Egert was not at all hiding behind Toria's back, but he had instinctively retreated, horrified as a tenacious wave of his eternal companion, animal fear, arose in his chest. Karver's words lashed him like a whip.

"This man," responded Toria, undaunted, "is under the protection of the university and of my father, Dean Luayan. And Master Luayan is a mage, as you should have heard by now. And now, be so kind as to clear the way. We are leaving."

"But, lady!" cried Karver in bewilderment, either real or feigned. "I cannot believe this. You are such a distinguished individual, how could you be involved with this, this . . ." The lieutenant's lips involuntarily curled in a grimace of aversion when he glanced at Egert. "I repeat, he murdered your fiancé. I think that even then in the depths of his soul he was already the thing he became just a bit later. Do you know what he became!"

"Allow us to pass." Toria stepped forward, and Karver slowly stepped to the side.

"Please. We have no desire to bring even the slightest shadow of insult to the beautiful daughter of the dean, the gentleman mage. But this man, lady . . . Wouldn't you be interested to find out what Egert Soll really is?"

Egert was silent. Gradually, he began to understand that what was happening now was, if anything, more terrible than Fagirra's poisoned stiletto. There was nothing he could do to stop this dreadful game from playing out; Egert would have to drink this cup to its dregs.

As if responding to his thought, Karver pulled his sword out of its sheath with a subtle movement. In the light of the lantern, Egert saw the silver ribbon of the blade and his knees began buckle.

"You'll answer for this," spat Toria.

Karver raised his eyebrows. "For what! Am I doing something improper to the lady? My lady may stay or she may go. In the second instance she will finally see the true face of her, hmm, friend." The tip of the impossibly long Kavarrenian sword touched Egert under the chin.

Egert felt faint. Karver's voice continued to reach him, but it was as if it came through the roaring of a waterfall; the sound of his own blood in his ears deafened him. Vainly trying to overcome his horror, he suddenly recalled the words Toria had once spoken. The curse will be broken if you fall into a hopeless situation and yet somehow overcome it. When the path has reached its bitter end: don't you think the Wanderer was speaking of this?

"I feel pity for you, lady," said Karver in the meantime. "Cruel fate brought you into contact with a man who is, to put it mildly, entirely unworthy. On your knees, Egert!"

Egert reeled, and Toria caught his gaze. The curse will be broken if you fall into a hopeless situation and yet somehow overcome it. Heaven, how

could he be victorious over a rock, a landslide, an avalanche that was careen-
ing down a mountainside? Egert's soul was wailing and thrashing about. The
pitiful coward died a thousand deaths, and Egert knew that within a second
the vile beast would completely subdue him.

"Did you hear me, Egert?" repeated Karver calmly. "On your knees."

Toria is here. Toria will see, then she'll really think . . .

Without following the thought to its conclusion, he sank down into the
slimy muck below. His knees buckled against his will, and now Karver's frayed
belt and sleek riding breeches were right in front of his eyes.

"Do you see, lady?" Karver's reproachful voice rang out above Egert's
head. "Demand something of him now; demand anything you like. He will
answer."

Egert could not see Toria, but he felt her next to him. He sensed her pain
and her striving and her rage and her confusion, and her hope.

She hopes. She does not understand that it is impossible. Impossible to
overcome the strength of the curse laid on me by the Wanderer. Never.

The sword jerked in Karver's impatient hand. "Say 'I am the nastiest
wretch in creation.'"

"Egert," sighed Toria, and his name seemed to echo from the distance,
from the bright winter day when he stood with her by the eternally blooming
tree on the tomb of the First Prophet.

"I am the nastiest wretch in creation," he gasped through parched lips.

Karver chuckled contentedly. "Do you hear that! Repeat after me, 'I am a
lady's cowardly lapdog.'"

"Egert," repeated Toria under her breath.

"I am a lady's cowardly lapdog," his lips murmured of their own accord.

Dirk and Bonifor, who had been silent until now, burst out into merry
laughter.

"Repeat, Egert, 'I am a creeping piece of shit and a sodomite.'"

"Leave him alone!" shrieked Toria, beside herself.

Karver was amazed. "Why are you so bothered? Is it because he's a lover
of men? He is definitely a bugger, we found him with his boyfriend in some
tavern. But you did not know, of course?"

Her silent entreaty reached Egert. Stop this, Egert. Stop it. Break the curse.

A door slammed open wildly. The morose cook walked to the storehouse,
casting a glance, as oppressively indifferent as before, at the people by the
fence.

Fiddling with his blade, Karver waited until she hobbled back and slammed the heavy door; then he spun his sword right in front of the face of his victim. "Answer, scum. Are you Egert Soll?"

"Yes," wheezed Egert.

"Are you a deserter?"

"Yes." And then he broke out into a sweat, but no longer from fear. All he had to do to break the curse was say yes five times.

"Did you, scoundrel, murder the fiancé of this beautiful lady?"

"Yes."

Toria was shaking. She also understood. Through his slumped back, Egert felt her feverish, frustrated anticipation.

Karver smiled expansively. "You love this lady, don't you, Egert?"

"Yes," he screamed out for the fourth time, feeling how hard his maddened heart was beating.

It seemed to him that he could hear Toria breathing. Glorious Heaven, help me! But the chance would come only once, and that which was foremost in his soul must become last. Did that mean that he must cast off his fear?

He jerked up his head, awaiting the fifth question; meeting his eyes, Karver involuntarily flinched, as if seeing a phantom of the former, domineering Egert Soll. Falling back a step, he searchingly examined his victim. An enormous shiver struck Egert.

Karver smiled contentedly. "Are you shivering?"

"Yes!"

He rose from his knees in a single, fluid motion. He noticed the confusion in Karver's eyes; he felt Toria moving behind his back; he took a step forward, intending to grab the lieutenant by his skinny throat; Karver hastily raised his sword out in front of him; Egert extended his arm to turn the sharp tip aside; and in that moment an attack of nauseating, detestable terror turned his heart into a pathetic, fluttering lump.

His legs gave out, and he once again sagged to the ground. He touched his cheek with a shaking hand. The scar was still there; the rough, hardened seam was still on his cheek. The scar was in its place, as was the fear that harried his soul.

The streetlamp swayed, shrieking in its bracket. Egert felt like his knees were frozen in icy slush. From somewhere on the roof, water was dripping, *drip, drip*. Toria whispered something helplessly.

Karver, recovering himself, hostilely peered at him through slit eyes. "So then, that's how it is. You will now display your love for the lady." He abruptly turned toward his companions, "Bonifor. There is a nice little she-goat in that enclosure over there, do you see her? Her owner won't mind if we borrow her for a little while."

Still hoping, Egert moved his lips, repeating "yes" over and over, but Bonifor was already opening the enclosure, and Toria, not yet believing in their defeat, stared at Bonifor, Karver, and the mustachioed Dirk without understanding. The black surface of a greasy puddle gleamed like slate.

Hope twitched in his soul for the last time, and then it faded, leaving in its place a desolate, hopeless melancholy. Toria realized this and instantly lost her strength to fight back. Their eyes met.

"Leave," he whispered. "Please leave."

Toria remained where she was. Either she had not heard him or she had not understood or she no longer had the strength to move from the spot. Karver chuckled.

The goat, skinny and filthy, was accustomed to brutal treatment. She did not even begin to bleat when Bonifor, cursing under his breath, flipped her from his back to the ground at Karver's feet. He proprietarily fastened a rope on the neck of the miserable animal then glanced ruefully at the bewildered Toria.

"So, he loves you, you heard?"

Egert looked at the gray, twitching tail of the goat. There would be no miracle. There would be no miracle. Fear had already conquered both his will and his reason, he had lost himself, and he would lose Toria. The Wanderer had left no way out.

Karver seized the goat by the muzzle and turned it toward Egert. "Well, here is a partner worthy of you; here is your love. Kiss her, go on then!"

Why doesn't Toria understand that she must leave? Everything is over; does she need to be tormented by this abhorrent scene?

The swords of Bonifor and Dirk threatened him from either side.

"Look how nice she is! A lovely creature. So kiss her!"

The stench of unwashed animal assaulted Egert's nostrils.

"You heard him. He loves you?" Karver's low voice reached him from a distance. "And you believed him? Look at him; he's ready to exchange you for the first goat that comes along!"

"What do you mean for the first one that comes along?" Bonifor flared up theatrically. "She's a charming goat, best in the pen, right, Egert?"

"You should be ashamed." Egert hardly recognized Toria's voice.

"We should be ashamed!" Karver, unlike Bonifor, flared up in truth. "We, and not him?"

"Leave," implored Egert. Toria stood still. Heaven, could her legs have grown numb? The cold edge of a blade once again touched his neck.

"Come on now, Egert! I declare you man and wife, you and your darling goat. Let's skip straight to the wedding night!"

Dirk and Bonifor, stunned by Karver's inventiveness, turned the goat around so that her tail faced Egert.

"Get to it! It will take all of five minutes. Have at it and all will be well; you can escort your lady home. Yes, lady, are you really still reluctant to return alone?"

It started raining. The water was rippled through the matted hair of the goat. His knees were frozen solid, and Egert suddenly imagined that he was a boy, standing up to his knees in the Kava river in spring, and on the near bank unbearably yellow flowers were blooming. He stretched out, trying to pluck one. . . .

He winced from pain. Karver had put his blade to Egert's ear. "What are you thinking about? A sharp sword can cut off an ear, a finger, whatever is desired. Or has it happened already! It is true that students are castrated, isn't it, lady?"

Fear had taken away from Egert the ability to think or feel. From Karver's words he understood only that Toria was still here, and reproachfully, with almost childish hurt, he thought, Why?

The shrieking, black streetlamp swung in the wind. The night seemed to Toria like a viscous wad of tar. The sticky air blocked her larynx and it was impossible to draw in the breath for words or a shout. Undoubtedly, she should call for help, drub her fists on doors and shutters, run to her father in the end, but shock deprived her of the ability to struggle; it turned her into a mute, impotent witness.

The goat moved hesitantly. Bonifor cut short her attempt to escape, squeezing her head between his knees.

Karver brought his sword up under the chin of his victim. "Well, Egert? Unfasten your belt!"

Then the darkness thickened, compressed Egert from all sides, squeezed his head and chest, filled his ears like a cork and plugged his throat, not letting the tiniest bubble of air into his lungs. For a second it seemed to him that he was buried alive, that there was neither top nor bottom, that the earth was pressing, pressing . . .

Then everything became lighter, and with his last glimmer of consciousness, Egert understood that he was dying. Thank Heaven. He was simply dying, gently and without torments. The damned Wanderer had overlooked something; there was something he had not taken into account! Egert could not conquer his fear, but he also could not transgress this boundary. He could not, and so here was death. Thank Heaven.

He smoothly keeled over. His face crashed into the dirt, which turned out to be as warm and soft as a feather bed. How easy. The black lantern keeled over, the black sky keeled over, and Karver yelled and waved his little sword. Let him: Egert was not here, he was no longer here. Finally.

The three guards leaned over the prostrate man. The miserable goat, bounding away, began to bleat keenly and mournfully.

"Egert! Hey, Egert! Quit pretending. Hey!"

Toria darted forward, hurling first Dirk to one side and then Bonifor to the other with a glance. Egert was lying on his side. His face, detached and stiff, now fell into shadow, now again was snatched from the darkness by the light of the swaying streetlamp.

"And now you will answer for this," Toria said with surprising calmness. "You will answer for everything. You have murdered him, you scum!"

"But lady," mumbled Bonifor in confusion. Dirk moved backwards, and Karver thrust his sword into its sheath.

"We didn't even lay a finger on him. What is it that you think we are guilty of!"

"You will answer," promised Toria through her teeth. "My father will hunt you down and put you in the ground far from your wretched Kavarren, at the world's edge."

Dirk kept stepping back farther and farther. Bonifor, looking sideways first at the lifeless Egert, then at Toria, followed his example. Karver, it seemed, had lost his courage.

"You have never seen a real mage before," continued Toria in a voice that was not her own, but somehow strange and metallic. "But you will instantly recognize my father when he appears before you!"

Karver raised his face to her, and in the dim light she saw in his eyes common fear, aroused not by the curse of the Wanderer, but by an innate cowardice, concealed in vain.

Unable to restrain herself, she spit at the ground near his feet. Within a minute the courtyard was empty except for the body lying prostrate on the ground and the petrified woman wringing her hands.

Once already she had wept over the lifeless body of a man lying on the ground. Now it seemed to her that this terrible nightmare was fated to repeat itself. Once again she had been left alone, completely alone. The rain drizzled, and drops rolled down the severe, frozen face of Egert. She had so hoped that the curse would not hold, that it would fail in the struggle with his nobility, but the curse proved stronger than its bearer. Egert fell first.

She sat in the cold dirt, and a lingering convulsion shackled her arms, her tongue, and her head. She did not try to bring Egert back to life; she did not feel for his pulse; she did not chafe his temples: unable to squeeze out any more tears, she sat helplessly, slumping her shoulders, dropping her numb hands to the ground.

They could bring him to his knees, but it was not within their power to turn him into an animal. Cowards in their souls, they elevated themselves in their own eyes by debasing a man they considered weaker. The Wanderer did not have enough curses for all scoundrels, but Egert lay there with his scar in the dirt, and no amount of yes could abolish the horror he had already lived through.

Finally, she began to cry.

A homeless dog appeared from out of the darkness. It sniffed sympathetically at the man lying on the ground and peered into Toria's eyes. Toria cried, lifting her face to the sky. The rain on her cheeks mixed with her tears. The dog sighed; its gaunt, ribbed sides rose and fell, and then, having scratched itself, it trotted back into the darkness.

Many years had passed since they buried her mother, and the grass had twice grown up and withered on the grave of Dinar. The rain, it seemed, would fall forever, and the eternally blooming tree on the tomb of the First Prophet would fade, and Egert would be cursed forever. Why? Why had she, Toria, forgiven him for the death of Dinar, but the Wanderer had not? Why did the curse not have inverse force; why did anyone besides herself have the right to judge Egert?

It seemed to her that his eyelashes moved slightly, or perhaps it was just the swaying of the false lamplight. She leaned forward, and Egert responded to her cautious touch; he shifted and raised his eyelashes with difficulty.

"Are you here?"

She winced. How dull and unfamiliar his voice sounded! He looked at her, and she suddenly realized that his eyes were the eyes of a hundred-year-old wise man.

"Are you crying? Don't. Everything will be all right. I now know how to die. It's not frightening. Everything will be all right now. Please." He attempted to get up, and with the third attempt he sat, and she nestled close to his chest without restraining herself.

"I'm such a," he said drearily, "such a . . . Why didn't you leave? Why did you stay with me? Why do I deserve that?"

"You swore," she whispered, "that you would cast it off."

"Yes," he muttered, stroking her hair. "Yes, I will cast it off. Without fail. Only, I may not be able to do it in this life, Tor. If I don't succeed, you'll kill me, won't you? Death wouldn't be terrible then. It's awkward for me to ask this of you, but who else can I ask? Never mind, forget what I said. I'll think of something, you'll see. Everything will be all right now, don't cry."

The stray dog with the thin sides compassionately watched them from a gateway as they stumbled away.

Several hours later Toria came down with a fever.

Her bed seemed hot to her, like a tin roof glowing red from the sun. Egert was allowed in her small room for the first time. He sat on the edge of the bed and held her hand in his. Without saying a single word, the dean brought in a flask of smoking, sharp-smelling potion and placed it on the side table.

Toria was lying on her back. The white pillow disappeared beneath piles of her disheveled locks, and the haggard face of his daughter, blemished by a sickly flush, again struck Luayan with the similarity it shared with a long-dead woman.

Back when he was traveling about the world, he had stopped once for a night's lodging in a small snow-covered village. The goodwife who gave him shelter did not know any more than that he was a mage. She informed him of a misfortune: Next door the daughter of the town elder, an unearthly beauty, was dying of an unknown ailment. Then he saw his future wife for the first time. Her head wallowed in the pillow in just the same way, her black hair snaked out over the white linens, and her face, haggard and feverish, already held the seal of her approaching death.

He cured her and left the house. Sudden happiness followed like a whirlpool in a calm and sleepy river, then the fear of losing everything, then happiness again: the birth of his daughter. Then there were five painful years, years that tossed Luayan from fever to chill, that taught him to forgive despite his pride: terrible years; his best years. He remembered them with a shudder, and would have given anything in the world to go back and live them again.

It is unlikely that she was meant to have a long life. One day, already saved by Luayan once, she passionately went out in search of her own death and found it, leaving him as mementos an unceasing sense of his own guilt and the young Toria.

Toria turned her heavy head, and her father looked into her eyes. Instantly, the dean shifted his gaze to Egert; Egert winced and thought the dean wanted him to release Toria's hand, but he kept it pressed between his own.

Glorious Heaven, she resembles her mother too much. She is too like her mother to be happy. When he had given his blessing to her marriage with Dinar, he at least had known what it would entail: solace and security; friendly affection and shared labor in the ancient walls of the university would have firmly united his daughter and his favorite pupil. Egert had put an end to these hopes, and here Egert sat, on the edge of her bed, tormented by the gaze of the dean, realizing that he should leave, but unable to release her hand. Luayan could clearly see how well Toria's palm nestled in his.

In his life there was nothing more precious than his daughter.

Two years ago her engagement had seemed to him a natural, inevitable part of a tranquil, measured life, but today a vague shadow hovered over the city, over the university, over these two who now held each other by the hand. Even though he was a mage, he could not determine what this threat was, but its presence could be felt more distinctly with each passing day. How should a person act today, if he did not know what might happen to him tomorrow?

Egert sighed brokenly. From the corner of his eye, Luayan saw how he tried to count her pulse, how he worried over her, how he was annoyed at him, Luayan, for his apparent inaction: If he truly were a mage, why didn't he use his magic to cure her?

Egert was marked. He would bring misfortune to all who had the imprudence to be near him. So the Wanderer judged. But who knows what the Wanderer is or what would happen if his curse were reversed?

Toria stirred. The dean once again looked into her eyes, and it seemed to him that her eyelids lowered by a hair, as if Toria wished to nod to him.

The dean hesitated then nodded to her in answer. He delayed for a second, once more sweeping his gaze over Egert, who was enshrouded in silence, and then he stepped out of the room, firmly closing the door behind him.

The two who remained were silent for a long time. An expiring log crackled, softly and delicately, in the fireplace.

Finally, Toria smiled with obvious effort. "Your shirt is too small."

Egert had borrowed the shirt from Fox because his own clothing was in need of washing. Gaetan's shirt threatened to rip with every movement Egert made. His hair, freshly washed and not yet fully dry, seemed darker than usual. The light from the fireplace gleamed directly behind his back, and Toria's burning fever created the illusion that Egert had bronzed shoulders.

Bending over her, he repeated the same questions several times; concentrating, she finally understood. "How can I help you? What do you need me to do?"

Even after they returned from the dank, raw night, she could not stop crying for a long time. She had radiated tears; she had drowned in their salty water like a dying sailor in the bosom of the sea. Egert, who had experienced a far greater shock that evening, held up better. He carried the shivering Toria for the last block before the university: her legs failed her and no longer desired to work. In her whole life only her father had ever carried her, and only in her remote childhood. She quieted and went limp, not helping Egert support her weight, but he stepped lightly as if he really were carrying a child or a small animal, as light as a feather, that had come to grief.

As he carried her, he felt each strained nerve, each quivering muscle, the beating of her heart, her fatigue and her distress. Then he pressed her more firmly to himself; he wanted to enfold her, to swath her in his own tenderness, to shelter, to warm, to protect.

The encounter with the dean, of which he was so afraid, passed without a single word. Submitting to Luayan, Egert helped Toria get into bed; a wailing old serving woman already waited nearby. The dean intently examined the guilt-ridden, tense Egert, but he never opened his mouth.

An ember prowled about the coals in the fireplace. Toria smiled faintly. The worst was far, far behind her; her present health, feverish and weakened, did not oppress her. On the contrary, she wished to dwell forever in this burning cloud, relishing her own frailty, serenity, and security.

"Tor. What can I do to help?"

Egert's concern and anxiety pleased her. But her father . . . her father was always aware of everything.

The potion prepared by the dean steamed on the bedside table.

"It's not all that serious," whispered Toria, softly squeezing Egert's hand. "There's nothing to worry about. The medicine will help."

He withdrew for a second to stoke the fireplace. The light flared up more brightly, and it seemed to Toria that Egert was now surrounded by copper tongues.

Laboriously, she sat up in her bed, holding the coverlet to her chest. "Give me the flask."

Scooping the potion from his hands, she kneaded it into her temples for quite a long time. Soon she no longer had the strength to continue, but she did not think to summon the elderly nurse. Seeing that she was wearied, Egert offered yet again to help. Cautiously, overcoming his clumsiness, he proceeded to rub the ointment into the skin of her face and neck. The medicine smelled even more strong and bitter than wormwood warmed by the sun.

Her fever fell almost instantaneously, but instead of relief she again felt grief, and covered in sweat, she at first gave a short sob, then losing control over herself, she commenced to shake violently as tears streamed down her face.

Egert was at a loss. He considered running for the dean, but he could not release her quaking, moist hands. Egert leaned over the invalid, and his dry lips found first one tear-filled eye and then the other. Savoring the bitter taste in his mouth, he smoothed her disheveled, dark hair and drew his cheek against her cheek, scraping his scar along her skin. "Tor, look at me. Don't cry."

The fireplace burned evenly, and the warm potion smoked, having not yet cooled off completely. Murmuring something vague, tender, and soothing, Egert fondly stroked her neck, tracing the pattern of beauty marks with his finger, that memorable constellation that decorated the heavens of his disastrous dreams. Then he began to rub the ointment into her shoulders and slender arms, freed one after the other from beneath the coverlet. The room was warm, even sultry. Toria's shaking gradually subsided, and she sobbed less frequently. Her breast, damp from sweat, still heaved under her thin chemise, forcing air in her lungs.

"Thank Heaven," he whispered, feeling the sickly trembling leave her. "Thank Heaven. Everything will be all right. You really are better, aren't you?"

Toria's eyes seemed impenetrably black; her pupils were wide, like an animal's at night. She stared at Egert, and her hands convulsively clenched the ends of the pulled-down coverlet. The fire burned down. It needed to be stoked again, but Egert did not have the will to leave her, not even for a second. It became dusky in the little room. Shadows danced, scattering ruddy light along the walls. Toria let out a lengthy sob and drew Egert to herself.

They curled into each other. Egert inhaled the bitter, unexpectedly pleasant odor of the medicine and held her lightly, fearing to squeeze her shoulders too intensely and thus inflict pain. Toria, blithely closing her eyes, nestled her nose into his shoulder. The fireplace died out and the darkness deepened.

Then his hand, tormented by its own audacity, reached under her chemise to her feverish breast, quaking from the beating of her heart.

It seemed to Toria that she was lying at the bottom of a reddish black, incandescent sea, and that tongues of flame were dancing over her head. She lost herself in the flames, refusing to think about anything else, and she ceased struggling against her mounting dizziness. Egert's hand was transformed into a distinct living creature, which roamed along her body, and Toria experienced an ardent gratitude toward this affectionate creature, completely her own.

They dissolved into each other in a dreamy delirium. As they lay in the darkness, Egert realized suddenly that, even though he was a highly experienced lover, not once in his riotous youth had he experienced any feelings that even vaguely resembled this urgent desire to touch, to give warmth, to envelop.

The coverlet slipped off toward the wall. The gossamer fabric of her chemise became superfluous; Egert sheltered Toria from the outside world with his own body.

She abruptly awoke from her fantastic euphoria. Her physical relations with Dinar had gone no further than a few prudent kisses. Recognizing what was happening, she became frightened and froze under Egert's caresses.

Instantly perceiving this, Egert pressed his lips to her ear. "What?"

She did not know how to explain. Distressed at her awkwardness, she artlessly ran her hand over his face. "I . . ."

He waited, gently placing her head on his shoulder. Fearing to insult him or surprise him, she could not find the words. She felt bashful and out of place.

Then, guessing what troubled her, he embraced her as firmly and as tenderly as he had never before embraced her or anyone else. Still full of fear and apprehension, she sobbed, grateful that there was no need to explain.

"Tor," he whispered soothingly. "You're afraid, aren't you?"

She was indeed afraid. The night floated through the room, warmth radiated from the just-extinguished fireplace, and from Toria's soul radiated a fondness and an almost childlike gratitude toward the man who understood everything without words.

He drew her to himself tenderly. "Don't worry. Everything will be just as you wish, just as you say. Tor, what is it, why are you crying again?"

She suddenly recalled a dragonfly that had flown into her room when she was a child. Heavy and green, with dark eyes like round teardrops, it had rustled in the corner, chafing against the wall with its lacy wings. It flew up to the ceiling and fell almost to the very floor. "Beyond stupid," her mother said with a laugh. "Catch it and let it loose outside."

Where does this memory come from, and why?

Toria caught the dragonfly. Carefully, afraid to clench her hand too tight, she carried the poor thing out into the yard and let it go, following its flight with her gaze. For a long time afterwards she still felt the light tickling of the dragonfly's wings and tiny feet on her palm.

She breathed nervously. This is happening today; this is happening right now. So many fears and hopes, so many dreams . . . This stood before her, waiting, and she would change; she would become a different person; she was afraid, but how could she be otherwise: this was inevitable, like the rising of the sun.

Egert again understood her without words. His joy communicated itself to her, drowning out her fear. From out of the darkness she heard her own happy laughter, which was immediately followed by a confused thought: Was it appropriate to laugh? Images of the dragonfly's wings, lights beyond the river, snow sparkling in the sun all flashed before her eyes, and just as she lost herself in a new delirium, she had time to think, Now.

# 8

On a black, winter evening, Dean Luayan interrupted his usual work.

Ink was drying on an unfinished page, and a quill was poised in the dean's motionless hand, but he sat, frozen behind his desk, unable to tear his gaze from a candle that was guttering in a candelabrum.

Beyond the window, the wet wind of a protracted thaw raged; in the fireplace, the fire burned in an even, hospitable manner. The dean sat, widening his eyes that were watery from strain. An impenetrable, nocturnal horror watched him from the flame, and the same horror rose to meet the dean from the depths of his soul.

The presentiment of a mage, even one who has not achieved the level of archmage, does not occur without reason. Now disaster was approaching so near that the dean's hair stirred from its breath. Right now, already now perhaps, it was too late to salvage anything.

The Amulet!

He jumped up. The incantation that secured the safe released immediately, but the lock resisted for a long time, disobeying his shaking hands. Finally opening the jasper casket, Luayan, who had never been shortsighted, squinted his eyes.

The medallion was uncorrupted. Not a single spot of rust disfigured the gold disk. The medallion was clean, but the dean still gasped from the stench of impending doom.

Not trusting himself, he once again examined the medallion. Then he hid it, and lurching, he rushed to the door.

"Toria! Tor!"

He knew that she was nearby in her room because he had called upon her earlier for help, but now she appeared almost instantly, and she was almost as pale as he was himself: evidently, something in his voice had terrified her. "Father?"

Behind her he could distinguish the silhouette of Egert Soll. In the last few days the two of them had become inseparable. Heaven help them.

"Toria, and you, Egert, get me water from five sources. I will tell you which, and where they are. Take my lantern; it will not go out even under the strongest wind. You, Toria, put on your cloak. Quickly."

If they wanted to ask him what was going on, they either could not or decided not to. The dean did not seem himself; Toria flinched upon meeting his gaze. Without saying a word, she took the five vials, which were attached to a belt. Egert swept her cloak over her shoulders, and as he did so she felt the affectionate, encouraging touch of his palm. A rotten winter without frost howled beyond the walls. Egert raised the burning lantern up high, Toria took hold of his arm, and they set out into the winter night.

As in a ritual, they crept from source to source: in all there were five. Thrice they had to gather the water from a pipe walled in stone, once from a small well in a courtyard, and once from the iron muzzle of a snake in an abandoned fountain. The five vials were full, the belt they were in weighed down Egert's shoulder, and Toria's cloak was soaked through when, staggering from exhaustion, they stepped back over the threshold of the dean's study. Usually gloomy, on this night it was full of light. Rows of candles crowded on the desk, on the floor, were molded to the walls; the tongues of flame jumped and waved when the door opened, as if greeting the two who entered.

In the middle of the room stood a strangely shaped object with birdlike claws at the bottom; on top, three more claws supported a round, silver basin.

Obeying the impatient gesture of the dean, Egert retreated into the farthest corner and sat there, right on the floor. Toria arranged herself nearby on a low taboret.

The tongues of flame elongated more and more; their length was unnatural, strange to the eyes. The dean stood over the silver basin and poured each of the vials into it. His hands moved slowly upward; his lips, firmly set, did not move, but to Egert it seemed—though perhaps it was his fear that made it so—that in the stillness of the study, in the howling of the wind beyond the windows he heard sharp words that clawed at his hearing. The ceiling, on which patterns of shadows fused and then decayed, seemed choked with swarms of insects.

Something knocked against the window from outside. Egert, taut as a bowstring, shook convulsively. Toria rested her hand on his shoulder without looking at him.

The dean's lips twisted, as if from strain. The flames of the candles stretched painfully and then diminished, regaining their usual shape. Standing motionless for a second longer, the dean whispered under his breath, "Draw near."

It was as if the waters in the basin had never existed. There, where their surface should have been, rested a mirror, as silver and vivid as mercury. The Mirror of Waters, thought Egert as he stood transfixed.

"Why can't we see anything?" Toria asked in a whisper.

Egert was almost resentful. For him, the mirror itself seemed miracle enough. However, at that very moment the silver haze shimmered, darkened, and then it was no longer a haze, but night, and a wind, the same wind that blew beyond the windows, whipped the branches of naked trees, and drew sparks torches, first one, then two, then three. Without trying to decipher the image, Egert marveled only that here in this small circular mirror something strange and secret was being reflected, something that was taking place who knows where. Entranced by the magic and by his own participation in the secret, he came to his senses only when he heard Toria cry out in a resonant voice, "Lash!"

That single, short word sobered Egert like a slap in the face. Obscure figures prowled in the mirror, and even in the meager light of the few torches, it was possible to distinguish hoods, some pulled low over the eyes and some flung down onto the shoulders. An entire troop of soldiers of Lash was for some reason swarming about in the night, permitting the wind to torment and harass the hems of their long robes.

"Where is that?" Toria asked, fearful.

"Silence!" Luayan gasped through clenched teeth. "It will be lost!"

The image faded, crusted over by a dirty, milky-white film, then turned back into the silver, waxen haze, and only in the extreme depths of that haze did a muted spark continue to gleam.

"What an evil day," muttered Luayan, as if marveling to himself. "What a wicked night."

Stretching out his hands, he spread his palms over the mirror and Egert, unable to move, saw how the web of his veins, his tendons and his blood vessels protruded through his skin.

The mirror wavered and darkened again. The dean withdrew his hands as if they were burned, and Egert was once again able to make out the night, the men, and the torches. The flames had become larger, and they all moved in a strange procession; the hooded men stood in a circle, rhythmically and regularly bending their backs as though bowing. Were they counting off the bows?

"Egert," asked Toria in a low voice, "are they performing some kind of ritual? Do you know which?"

Egert silently shook his head; this allusion to his old complicity with Lash, however unwitting, however invalid, felt like a severe rebuke. Toria realized she had hurt him and guiltily squeezed his hand. The dean cast a swift sidelong glance at them both and again bent over the basin.

At times the figures disappeared into the darkness, at times they loomed close, but the image was never completely clear; it comprised fragments, wisps, separate details: a boot in wet clay, the soggy hem of a robe. Once Egert flinched, recognizing the disheveled silver mane of the Magister. Now and then the silver, waxen mist rose up, and then the dean gritted his teeth and extended his palms over the mirror, but the haze never dissipated immediately: it was as if it was reluctant to depart, as though it was in collusion with the hooded men.

"Where are they, Father?" Toria kept asking. "Where is that? What are they doing?"

The dean only gnawed at his lips, time after time recovering the elusive, faithless image.

Toward dawn all three were exhausted, then the mirror, exhausted as well, finally submitted entirely, bowing to the will of the dean, and the silver fog receded. The night that was concealed in the silver basin also receded; the image grayed, the flames of the reflected torches faded, and all three of them, bending over the mirror, simultaneously unraveled the riddle of the seemingly ceremonial bows.

Drawn up around a tall hill—Egert recognized it as the place from which he and Toria had admired the river and the city—the hooded men, armed with spades, were tirelessly digging into the ground. Black piles of earth towered here and there, as though marking the path of an enormous mole, and in places yellow objects showed through the dirt. Egert leaned forward, unconsciously widening his eyes: the objects were yellowed bones and skulls, undoubtedly human, undoubtedly old, and the earth was creeping out of their vacant sockets.

"That's," Toria exclaimed panicked voice, "that's that hill! That's—"

The mirror shattered. Water surged up in all directions. Dean Luayan, always imperturbable and unemotional, beat at the water with his palm, churning it up into splashes with all his might.

"Ah! I overlooked it! Damn it! I let it pass by! I ignored it!"

The candles, which had burned all night without guttering even once, were extinguished as if by a gust of wind. Blinking his half-blinded eyes, Egert could not immediately discern the grief-twisted face of Luayan in the dawn's pale light.

"I overlooked it. It's my fault. They are lunatics, scum; they are not waiting for the end of time: they are summoning it! They have already summoned it."

"That hill," Toria repeated in horror. The dean grabbed his head with his hands, which were still dripping water.

"That hill, Egert . . . That is where the victims of that monstrosity, the Black Plague, were buried; there is its lair, smothered by dirt, kept concealed from the people. The Black Plague once ravaged the city and provinces, and it will devastate the earth, if it is not stopped. Lart Legiar stopped the Black Plague before. Lart Legiar did it, but that was many decades ago. Now there is no one. Now . . ."

The dean groaned through clenched teeth. He gasped, turned his back on them, and walked to the window.

"But, Dean Luayan," whispered Egert, barely coping with his trembling. "Dean Luayan, you are an archmage. You will protect the city and . . ."

The dean turned around. His expression caused Egert to bite his tongue.

"I am a historian," said the dean desolately. "I am a scholar. But I have never been an archmage and I never will become one. I've remained a pupil, an apprentice. I'm not an archmage! Don't be shocked, Toria. And don't look so mournful, Egert. I have made do with what I have: intellect and knowledge have made me worthy of the title of mage, but I am no archmage!"

For some time quiet enveloped the study; then, nearer and farther, quieter and louder, one after the other, catching fear from one another, dogs began to howl around the city.


Who could have guessed that so many rats huddled underneath the city?

The streets teemed with their grayish brown backs; the dogs fled upon hearing the drumming patter of their tiny paws and the rustle of hundreds of leathery tails. The rats rushed about; they squeaked and ground their sharp teeth; they crowded in doorways until heavy stones crashed into the walls next to them, thrown by hands made inaccurate by trembling. Especially brave men armed with heavy canes went out into the streets and beat them, pummeled them, whaling away at their pink, whiskered snouts that bristled with yellow teeth.

On that day the shops did not open and the factories did not produce. A universal terror hung over the city like an oppressive curtain, and the rats ruled the streets. Cowering in their homes with the shutters tightly fastened, the people feared to speak aloud: many that day had the feeling that an intent, glacial, scrutinizing gaze prowled through the streets of the city, peering under the cracks of doors.

The Plague watched the city for two more days, and on the third day it showed itself.

The calm of the vacant streets ceased. Within a few hours the exhalation of the Plague tore open useless shutters and doors, releasing lamentations to Heaven, moans and wailing. The first to fall sick that morning were the first to die that night, and those who had brought them water soon took to their beds, suffering from thirst and lacerated by boils, without any hope of salvation.

The quarantine cordon that was set up at the city gates did not last long. People, seeing hope only in escape, knocked it down, throwing themselves on pikes and swords, sobbing, pleading, hectoring; a portion of the guards drew back in the wake of the fugitives, and before long the Plague descended upon the outskirts, the surrounding towns, the villages, the lonely farmsteads. Astonished wolves found easy meat lying amid the fields and then died in agony because the Plague would not spare even wolves.

Complying with the disordered commands of the mayor, the guards patrolled the streets, remaining loyal to their duty. Bundled up in layers of sackcloth garments, armed with curved pitchforks that resembled malformed bird claws, they moved steadily from house to house, and high wagons sided with wooden slats rattled through the streets behind them, weighed down by the multitude of bodies. The next day they no longer gathered the corpses, and entire homes were transformed into charnel houses, waiting for a merciful hand to throw a lit torch into an open window.

The Tower of Lash shut itself off from the Plague in a thick cloud of fragrant smoke. A horde of people, awaiting salvation, besieged the tabernacle of the Sacred Spirit day and night, but the windows and doors were secured from within and the thinnest cracks, where even the blade of a knife could not enter, were meticulously sealed up and closed. But the strange smoke still rose inexplicably, and people inhaled it in the hope that the sharp, harsh odor of it would defend them against death.

"Idiots," the dean said bitterly. "Imbeciles. They think to hide themselves and thereby save themselves; they hope the smoke will keep it at bay! They are obstinate, spiteful children, setting fire to their home, sure in their faith that the blaze they play with will not harm them. The end of time for the world, but not for Lash . . . They are fools. Wicked fools."

The first wave of the Plague ebbed after three days. Many of those who survived imagined that they were marked by a special good fortune and, possibly, that they abided under the protection of Lash. The deserted streets were subjected to the efficient incursion of looters. Ravaging the wine cellars and household stores of their neighbors, the enterprising family men boasted of their loot to their wives and children, and young lads gave their surviving girlfriends bracelets plucked from dead wrists. They all intended to live for a long time, but the Black Plague began its second feast, starting with them and with their kinsmen.

The dean forbade the students to leave the university, but the power of his prohibition proved insufficient to hold within the thick walls young men, each of whom had family or fiancées somewhere in the city, the outskirts, or some distant town. At the beginning the students rushed to Luayan for help and salvation, but he locked himself in his study and did not wish to see anyone. The hopes of the youths gave way to bewilderment, then to resentment, then to despair: they left the university one after another, complaining bitterly about mages who shirked mere mortals at the very time when their help was most needed. Egert gritted his teeth when he overheard curses addressed toward the dean who had left the students to the mercy of fate. It was difficult for him to wrap his mind around the thought that Luayan was not all-powerful, but it was even more difficult to perceive that the dean's behavior looked like betrayal.

It was no easier for Toria. For the first time in her life her father was not by her side as they faced hard times, but by himself, in solitude, and her awareness of this was for her far more onerous than all the troubles of the epidemic. Egert kept close to her at all times; fear, obtrusive as a toothache, his chronic fear for his own hide paled now before the thought of what fate might bring to

Toria, recently discovered by him as if by a miracle, and what it might bring to her father, the university, the city—and to the city of Kavarren.

Kavarren was far away. Kavarren, hopefully, would remain unharmed. Kavarren would have time to set up cordons, to institute a strict quarantine. Kavarren would defend itself. But in a dream that recurred every night, Egert saw the same thing: howling dogs in front of the Noble Sword, smoke ranging along the deserted streets, mountains of corpses on the embankment, the barred gates with their emblem grown dim from soot . . .

The dean had said that the Black Plague would lay waste to the world if it were not stopped. There were many hundreds of Kavarrens on the earth. What was some small, albeit ancient and proud, provincial town to the Plague?

The remaining students at the university kept close together, like sheep in a harassed herd. Neither hide nor hair was seen of the headmaster, the servants ran away, the teachers failed to appear, and the youths, who had until recently considered themselves to be solid, respectable, learned men, turned out to be feckless boys. One day the walls of the Grand Auditorium resounded with the most sincere weeping. One of the Inquirers was sobbing on his rough bench like a small boy; he was just a village lad, for whom the first year of his studies had turned into a nightmare. The others averted their eyes, not wanting to look at the pale faces and quivering lips of their comrades, and then Fox suddenly grew savage, boiling up into a white-hot fury.

No one had ever heard such scathing speech from him before. He proffered a thimble to each and every one of them so that they could gather up their snot; he suggested that the wide skirts of their mothers might be very warm to hide under and called for a chamber pot to be brought into the hall in the event of sudden need. He strode up to the rostrum and rained insults down on his classmates: they were slack-mouthed, snot-nosed, scruffy little shits, receptacles for spit and piss, and limp-dicked mama's boys. The weeping lad sobbed one last time then opened his mouth wide and blushed a deep red color, as if his cheeks had been brushed by a lady's cosmetics.

The incident ended in a boozer. Fox appointed himself supply officer, broke into the university's wine cellar, and uncorked many ancient bottles of wine. They drank right there in the lecture hall; they drank and sang and reminisced about the Old-Eyed Fly. Fox roared with laughter as if he were rabid then started a game: Everyone without exception must relate their first sexual experience, and those who did not have one would be obliged to make up for their neglect the very next day. Already drunk voices heckled each other, interweaving hysterical laughter with outbursts. Egert watched this carousal from the round window that adjoined the lecture hall to the library, and the discordant sounds of a song wafted to his ears. "Oh, oh, oh! Do not speak, my dear, don't say a word! Oh, my soul is fire, but the door is squeaking: it hasn't been oiled."

He turned back to Toria and entertained her for a while with anecdotes about Fox's previous pranks, some of which he had seen, some of which he had only heard of, and several of which he thought up while he was telling her the stories. Listening to his deliberately cheerful chatter, Toria at first smiled palely and then to please him she even burst out laughing, though with obvious effort.

After midnight the cries and shouts in the Grand Auditorium ceased and Toria fell asleep. Sitting next to her for a while then carefully smoothing back her hair, Egert departed below.

The students were sleeping side by side, some on the benches, some on the tables, and some simply on the chilly stone floor. Fox was nowhere to be found; Egert realized this from the very first glance, and for some unknown reason his heart shrank into his chest.

Gaetan was not in their room, and his worn cloak was not hanging from the iron hook. Egert stood on the university steps for a long time, peering out into the murky night. Windows gleamed faintly in the courthouse, the executed doll on its circular pedestal weaved in the rain, and the Tower of Lash soared overhead, mute, sealed like a crypt, indifferent to the city dying at its feet.

Fox did not return in the morning. The fog that had thickened in the night did not disperse with the sun, but instead it congealed like jelly; even the wind got stuck in its clinging, damp wisps. The door of the dean's study remained firmly shut, and Toria began roaming the stacks of the library as if she were lost, muttering responses to her own thoughts as she compulsively rubbed a velvety-smooth rag over the spines, slipcovers, and gilded edges of the books.

Egert did not tell her where he was going. He did not want to worry her.

The chill dampness and his own terror caused him to tremble as, his teeth clenched, he stepped out onto the deserted square. There were no merchants; there were no shoppers: there was only the deaf, muffled silence, the gray silhouettes of the houses, and the merciful fog that covered the city like a shroud covers the face of the deceased.

Egert soon realized that he would not find Fox. He encountered dead bodies along his path. Egert averted his eyes, but just the same his gaze found first a woman's hand, stretched out convulsively, clinging onto a jewel; then hair spread out over the cobblestones; then the rakish boot of a guard, wet from the sagging droplets of fog and therefore gleaming as if it had just been polished for a parade. The smell of smoke mixed with the scent of decay. Egert walked on, but then he stopped, flinching, scenting the familiar aroma of a bitterish perfume in the still, dead air.

The Tower of Lash, having accomplished its dreadful business, continued to smoke slightly. Egert approached it, strangely impassive; by the entrance to the Tower a completely gray man in a laborer's coveralls was flailing his fists against the stone masonry.

"Open up! Open up! Open up!"

Several apathetic people were crouched nearby on the pavement. A pretty woman in a nightcap that had slipped off her hair was absentmindedly stroking a dead boy lying in her lap.

"Open up!" spat the gray man. His knuckles were completely devoid of skin from punching at the stone. Beads of blood dropped down onto the pavement. Nearby a broken pickax wallowed in the dirt.

"We must pray," someone whispered. "We must pray. Oh, Spirit of Lash . . ."

The gray man in the overalls pounded at the sealed door with a renewed frenzy. "Open up! Ah! Scum! Undertakers! Open up! You can't hide! Open up!"

Egert turned and stumbled away.

Fox would not be found. He had gone missing; he had disappeared somewhere in this pestilent cauldron; no one could help; nothing would make it better; and Egert would die as well. At this thought the animal fear raged in his soul, but with his heart and his mind he understood clearly that the most important thing left to him in his shortened life was Toria. Her final days must not be darkened with horror and grief. Egert would not allow himself the luxury of dying first: only once he had made sure that nothing could ever threaten Toria again would he close his own eyes.

Egert saw a collapsed boy on the pavement in front of him, and he was about to make his way around it, keeping it as far away as possible, when the man moved, and Egert heard the faint scratching of iron against stone. A sword rested in the hand of the dying man; Egert could see beads of moisture on the costly sheath, on the heavy monogrammed hilt, on the baldric decorated with semiprecious stones. Then he shifted his gaze to the face of the man lying in the pavement.

Karver said nothing. His chest was rising rapidly, trying to suck in the wet air; his lips were parched and his eyelids were swollen. One hand, clad in a thin glove, clawed at the stones of the pavement, while the other squeezed the handle of his sword as if the weapon could defend its master even from the Plague. Karver stared at Egert, unwilling to move his eyes away.

The plaintive whickering of a horse, muted by the fog, could be heard in the distance.

Karver gasped fitfully. His lips jerked and Egert heard, as quietly as the rustle of falling sand, "Egert . . ."

Egert said nothing because there was nothing to say.

"Egert . . . Kavarren . . . What is happening in Kavarren right now?"

Such a keen, imploring note slithered through Karver's voice that Egert momentarily remembered that shy, thin-lipped boy who had been the friend of his childhood.

"This . . . this death . . . will it reach Kavarren?"

"Of course not," Egert said with certainty. "It's too far. And they will have set up a quarantine, and patrols. . . ."

Karver breathed deeply; it seemed he was relieved. He threw back his head and shaded his eyes with his hand. He whispered with a half smile, "Sand . . . Den, tracks . . . Cold . . . water . . . They laughed. . . ."

Egert was silent, taking these incoherent words for raving.

Karver did not tear his gaze away; it was an oddly vacant gaze that seeped out from under his heavy eyelids. "Sand . . . The Kava river . . . You remember?"

For a second Egert saw a sun-drenched bank, white on yellow like sponge cake covered with icing, green isles of grass, a group of boys, raising fountains of spray up to the heavens. . . .

"You always . . . threw sand in my eyes . . . remember?"

He tried as hard as he could to summon such a recollection, but there was only the wet, shiny pavement before his eyes. Could it have been so? Yes, it could. Karver had never complained; he had submissively washed all the sand from his inflamed eyes.

"I didn't mean to," Egert said for some reason.

"Yes, you did," Karver objected quietly.

They were silent for a while. The fog did not wish to disperse, and smoke and decay and death approached from every side.

"Kavarren," whispered Karver almost inaudibly.

"Nothing will happen to it," Egert replied.

Searchingly gazing at Egert, Karver tried to raise himself up onto his elbow. "Are you sure?"

The smooth surface of the Kava river gleamed in Egert's mind's eye; sunlight flared up and died out on the water, where the quivering copper green of
Kavarren's roofs, turrets, and weathervanes was reflected.

Knowing that he lied, he smiled widely and tranquilly. "Of course I'm
sure. Kavarren is safe."

Karver sighed deeply and lowered himself back onto the pavement. His
eyes closed halfway. "Thank . . . Heaven . . ."

No one would ever hear him say another word.

The fog dispersed, and the square appeared before Egert's gaze. It looked
like a field of battle. Here would be enough food for a thousand ravens, but
there was not a single bird in the city; nothing disturbed the dead, as though
the scavengers of the world were obeying a taboo.

However, that was not entirely true. Egert looked around; a boy ran from
corpse to corpse with his back bent low. He was about eighteen years old,
medium height, scrawny, with a canvas sack over his shoulder. Beggars gathered their alms in such sacks, and Egert guessed what the youngster was
gathering in his. Stooping over a corpse, he dexterously fished out a purse or
a snuffbox or whatever finery caught his eye from the dead person; rings were a
bother: they did not wish to slip off the swollen fingers. The lad sniffed the
air, keeping a wary eye on Egert, but he continued his business, scrubbing at
dead hands with a piece of soap he had saved specially for this occasion.

Egert wanted to scream, but his fear proved stronger than his fury and
disgust. Spitting on his soap, the looter skirted around Egert in a wide arc and
then took to his heels at the sound of a shrill whistle.

Egert, struck dumb, watched as the lad fled. On the very edge of the
square he was overtaken by two broad-shouldered figures, one in the white-
and-red uniform of the guards, the other in a slovenly black smock. The lad
screamed like a rabbit, tried to dart away, cowered in their arms, then thrust
the sack away from himself as if trying to pay them off. Egert did not want to
watch, but watch he did as the man in guard's uniform beat the lad over the
head with his sack. He heard the next words, painfully strained, carry
throughout the entire square.

"No! I'm not! They don't need it! They don't need it! The dead don't
need—ah!"

Passing into an inarticulate shriek, the screaming died out. The scrawny body crumpled to the ground in the glow of the streetlamps with the canvas sack on its chest.

Fox returned late that evening. Egert, whose intuition that day had become as sharp as a spear, found him before anyone else.

Gaetan stood by the entrance, on the stone porch of the university; he stood embracing the wooden monkey by the shoulders. His tricornered hat, crumpled out of shape, slid down his forehead. He was, of course, blindly, staggeringly drunk. Egert, who experienced colossal relief at the sight of his friend, wanted to lead him in out of the cold and put him to bed. Hearing Egert's footsteps behind him, Fox shivered and turned around. The light of the lantern in the doorway fell on his face. Gaetan was sober, as sober as the day of the exam, but his honey-colored eyes now seemed dark, almost black.

"Egert?"

Egert did not understand what had frightened his friend so. He took another step forward, extending his hand. "Let's go."

Gaetan recoiled. His gaze compelled Egert to come to a dead halt; not once in their long acquaintance had he seen in the eyes of his friend such a strange expression. What was it? Loathing? Scorn?

"Fox?" he muttered uneasily.

"Don't come near me," Fox replied desolately. "Don't come near me, Egert. Don't you come near me, I beg you. Go away. Go back." He staggered, and Egert suddenly realized that the sober Gaetan could barely stand on his own two legs: he was being dragged to the ground. He was being dragged into the ground.

He understood now what that expression was that had frozen in Fox's eyes. It was fear of approaching death and fear of carrying away with him another person, his friend, Egert.

"Gaetan!" groaned Egert through his teeth.

Fox hugged the monkey tighter. "Don't . . . You know, Farri died yesterday. Do you remember Farri?"

"Gaetan . . ."

"Go back. I'll just take a little . . . stroll. Maybe I'll make my way to the One-Eyed Fly. If the innkeep is still alive, he'll give me a drink. On credit." Fox laughed, arduously stretched out his hand and, barely reaching it, patted the monkey on his shiny wooden bottom.

Egert stood on the steps and watched him walk away. Fox staggered as he walked, sometimes falling, just as he had so many times when returning from a night out; his cap with the silver fringe lay like a parting gift at the feet of the wooden monkey. The sightless sky, full of dark clouds, brooded over the city, and the Tower of Lash, mute, sealed shut, mantled in smoke, brooded over the square.

For a whole long day and night they thrashed about like two fish at the bottom of Toria's reddish black incandescent ocean.

Coming to her senses, Toria felt echoes of shame: never in her life would she have imagined that within herself she carried this covetous, insatiable, inexhaustible beast, ready to tear off not just clothing, but skin. Panicking, she tried not to look at Egert, who was lying next to her; she did not dare touch his skin, not even with her breath, but the ardent beast quickened and upended all her notions of dignity and decency, and afflicted by passion, she responded to the similarly grasping, indefatigable passion of Egert.

Heaven, it can't really be like this for everyone, can it? Toria thought, because then life was completely foreign, completely different than she had ever thought it was, because there seemed to be powers that controlled her, forces that overrode all her preconceptions, and she could finally understand dark, shadowy forces that had beguiled her mother. Mother? But why dark and shadowy? Why beguiling? This is happiness; this is joy. Egert! Egert, I could have died a remote old crone, never knowing the world of truth! But could I be wrong? What if this is not truth, but obsession, delirium, deceit!

Swallowing, her throat husky from groans, her cheeks stained with tears that she did not bother to wipe away, she relaxed, abated, melted into Egert's embracing arms as if burrowing into a warm, secure den. Closing her eyes, she lazily sorted through the fragmentary images that rushed through her brain, and from time to time plucked from the stream one that seemed to contain unmistakable truths.

It was a truth that if had she become the wife of Dinar, she would never have known of any other love besides friendly, brotherly love. It was a truth that the loss of Dinar had blessed her. Heaven, this is monstrous, this is impossible. Dinar, forgive me! Toria began to weep silently, without tears, and in his sleep Egert embraced her more tightly. She dozed off, and she saw Dinar nearby, sitting on the couch opposite the bed as he usually had when he came to her room. Serene and earnest, he looked at Toria without reproach, but also without indulgence, as though desiring to say that he was done, that he would never come back, but don't cry, he loves you so . . .

Then the vision of Dinar faded away, disappeared in succession of others. Toria dreamed of her mother, frozen in a cold bank of snow, and of her father, forever weighed down by a sense of guilt. But where is the guilt of a woman, whose passions overwhelm her own identity, like a wave washing over the deck of a fragile ship? And if it was true that in her face she duplicated her mother, then did she not also inherit her passions?

However, right now it no longer mattered. Now they were all standing on the threshold of death, on the threshold beyond which Dinar had already stepped. She and Egert were a couple, even if they did not live to see their wedding, but her father was alone, alone in his study. If she feared, it was only for her father. Have I forsaken him for the sake of my own happiness? Could it be true that I have abandoned him? Could it be true?

Toria began to cry again. Egert kissed her glistening eyes and mumbled something tender; she could not make out a single word of what he said, and that was good: words were unnecessary.

Then she fell into a deep sleep and dreamed of a green mountain.

The mountain was covered with short, smooth grass. She hovered over it, occupying half the sky, and the second half was a deep blue. Toria recalled that the windows of their home were painted with this blue. The mountain was an emerald on blue. Toria inhaled, ascending even higher, and it was a good thing she did because there, on the summit of the mountain, stood her mother, wearing a dazzlingly white head scarf, laughing and stretching out her palms, which held a scarlet handful of strawberries, the first strawberries, and how long will it be until this winter is ended? There is still half a year until the next strawberries, there is still half a year, there is still time . . .

She awoke because Egert, groaning in his sleep, had firmly squeezed her shoulder.


They slept in the predawn hour; they both slept peacefully, deeply, without dreams, and therefore could not hear how, scraping softly, the door of the dean's study opened, the door that had for many days been locked from the inside. In the recesses of the dark room the last flames of the candles were dying down, and the unbearably stuffy, smoky, thick air rushed to freedom.

Books lay on the desk, on the floor, on all the shelves: laid bare, spread out, helpless as jellyfish driven to shore. The taxidermied rat shackled to its chain grinned evilly, the glass globe with the candle inside was covered with dust, but the steel wing spread out just as confidently and potently, and underneath it on the dean's desk gleamed the faultless gold of the Amulet of the Prophet.

The dean stood for a long time in the doorway, leaning against the door-jamb. Then he straightened up and firmly closed the door behind himself.

The corridors of the university were familiar to him down to the last crack in the arched ceilings. He walked and listened to the sound of his own foot-steps, rushing through the empty passageways. He stopped in front of his daughter's room, pressing his cheek to the heavy door.

For the time being they were happy. The dean did not need to open the door to see the hazy morning light pouring over two heads on one pillow; the entwined arms, hair, knees, and thighs; the entwined breath, dreams, and fate. It seemed that there, in that room, a single blissful, calm, weary creature, who knew nothing of death, slept sweetly.

The dean absentmindedly stroked the door. The ancient wood seemed warm, like the skin of a living organism. He stood there for a bit longer, not wanting to intrude on their bliss, and then Luayan walked on.

He could not count the number of times he had walked out onto the uni-versity steps and paused between the iron snake, the incarnation of wisdom, and the wooden monkey that symbolized the thirst for knowledge. Ravaged corpses now met the dawn on the formerly busy square, above them the abode of Lash towered, like a curse, grimy with smoke, and the university behind the dean held its peace, strangely defenseless before the gaze of the Tower.

The Plague would devastate the earth if it was not stopped. Luayan had been fourteen years old when Lart Legiar appeared in his deserted home. Lart was at the peak of his power; Luayan knew much about him, but there was only one thing he wanted to ask: Is it true that you stopped the pestilence?

Decades ago the Black Plague had devoured entire cities far from the coast, but the sea had overflowed its shores from all the corpses that con-gested it. Luayan had an indistinct memory of spurts of flame scurrying across the faces of motionless people; a palm covering his eyes; the weight of sackcloth, flung over his head and shoulders; and a distant howl, not of a wolf, but of a woman. The Plague had deprived Luayan of his home, of his parents, of his memories of the past. That Plague had spared him; breaking suddenly like rotten rope, it had spared him and, an orphan, he had set out on the road with a crowd of other orphans, and had wandered until either a merciful chance or cruel fate led him to the house of Orlan.

Later, he found out that the Plague never departs on its own. That time it had been stopped by an archmage called Lart Legiar.

Luayan raised his face to the gray, impenetrable sky. For his entire long life he had fallen short of greatness.

He looked back over his shoulder at the university, then at the Tower. He rubbed the bridge of his nose with his habitual gesture. Heaven, how strong he had seemed to himself at the age of fourteen, and how weak he had been in actual fact. His world had been so hot then, in the foothills, the sun had beat down so brightly, the stones had been so incandescent, and the weather-beaten face of Orlan had been so obscure.

Wet snow, fine as milled grain, started to fall.

The city had gone dumb with horror. It had been stunned. Those who were still living cowered in deep shelters, and only the dead no longer feared anything. Luayan walked by them without averting his eyes. A looted shop slammed its door, which was hanging from one hinge; its owner, long dead and therefore indifferent to the ruin, lay huddled in the doorway. He squinted up at the mage with a single, withered eye: a mass of maggots swarmed in place of the other. Luayan kept walking. In a wide entryway an urchin was swinging on a swing; two sections of thick rope were attached to an overhead gantry. The boy held on to them with his hands, pumping his legs with abandon, accompanying himself with indistinct muttering, first flying into the darkness of the deserted house then flying out, passing over a dead woman in a black dress who was staring up at the sky. A rabbit hutch stood nearby and a rabbit, alive and starving, followed Luayan with its gaze. The boy did not even so much as glance at Luayan as he walked by.

The closer he came to the city gates, the more often he came across burnt-out and half-burnt-out houses. Black as if they were dressed in mourning, they gazed at Luayan with the rectangles of their windows, and on one sill he saw a sooty flowerpot with dead twigs hunkered over.

The stench of smoke and decay pulled at him from every side. He walked, stepping over bodies, swerving around capsized carriages, bundles of collected belongings, piles of purses, and the corpses of animals. The water of a narrow canal had acquired a thin film of ice overnight, and through the ice a yellow, lipless face stared up at Luayan from the bottom.

Sometimes darting, living eyes peered out of dark recesses at the sound of his footsteps and then immediately disappeared. Luayan never managed to meet these gazes. But the dead did not shield their eyes, and he honorably looked back at them, not once averting his eyes, as if he knew neither fear nor revulsion.

Lart Legiar was an archmage. Orlan was an archmage. But he, Luayan, was nothing more than a scholar; he was weak, heavens, how weak he was.

He took the wrong road, got lost on familiar streets, and twice he returned to the same place. On a tin beard—the sign of a barber's shop—swayed a lynched looter. A weathervane that had wrenched free of its socket screeched like a hacking cough.

Lart had invited him to study under his tutelage. The boy should have leapt toward that fate, but now he was gray, and he was old, irredeemably old.

A wing of the gate was swaying back and forth, shrieking stridently. Someone moved near the gates. Luayan stopped, looked, approached.

A man was dying on his back in a cold puddle; once he had been young and strong, but now he was frightful, like a half-rotten corpse. Twisting, he tried to drink some of the icy water; he sipped at it, coughed, squinted at Luayan, and tried again. His parched lips sought after every muddy drop that cost him such backbreaking labor.

Not knowing why, Luayan bent over him, but he recoiled immediately; for the first time in his present journey, he recoiled.

The Plague showed itself to him, opening its eyes, gaining a face and a form. The dying man was being smothered, ensnared, fondled by loathsome fingers; they petted, rubbed, and stroked, and they moved in that same elaborate pattern with which the numerous legs of a spider trap a fly.

The dean stumbled backwards, retreating. The yards and streets, every house was filled with the Plague, with black clots and twitching growths; pale eyes watched from every crevice, full of heaving, pus-filled hatred, indifferent yet at the same time ravenous, gluttonous. Black fingers caressed the dead, palpating distorted faces, slipping into half-open mouths, shamelessly examining the prone bodies of men and women. It seemed to Luayan that he could hear the rustle of parting clothing and slit skin, that the air around him coagulated, filled with an overwhelming desire for death and the yearning to kill.

Staggering as if drunk, he made his way to the city gates. The dead here lay in a heap, and the fingers of the Plague waved over them like grass in a wind.

The gates, the heavy city gates, were smashed in, swept from their hinges. Beyond them he could see the road and a field, flat and bleak, where shapeless piles of rags stirred in the wind.

Luayan turned his face back to the city.

Glorious Heaven! Orlan, my teacher, help me. Lart Legiar, you were once successful, I preserved your medallion, help me. Wanderer, wherever you may be, whoever you may be, if you can, help me. You have seen for yourself how weak I am.

He closed his eyes. Then he jerked up his head, lifted up his hands, and stared at the city, at the new dwelling place of the Black Plague.

. . . Why is it so hot? Well, it is noon, the sun is at its zenith, and the stones are as white as sugar. Coolness rises from the well, and there in its humid, dusky depths yet another boy lives, a boy reflected in the round surface of the water. Oh, how his teeth ache from the first swallow, but the bucket is already splashing back into the water with all its tin flesh, and the sound intensifies the boy's thirst. . . .

By whatever power is given to me, I order and invoke, I draw from the living, I draw from the dead, from their gaping mouths, from the emptiness of their eyes, from their nostrils, from their veins, from their flesh and blood, from their bone and hair. I draw as roots are drawn from the earth with a hoe, as an arrow, nestled in flesh, is drawn. By whatever power is given me, I command . . .

. . . The bucket plunges down, sinking ever deeper. Its slightly corroded interior floods with water, and now it can be pulled up, but the pulley is stuck, it is so difficult, as never before. His hands grow numb, his teeth clench, but the bucket scarcely pries itself away from the water, and drops, shed from its edge, echoes down into the water. . . .

I command and exhort, I expel you from the streets, I expel you from the water, I expel you from the wind, from the hearths, from the holes and crevices. Let it be done. By whatever power is given me, I bind you.

. . . And now the bucket comes ever higher, but he does not know if he will have enough strength. The sun scorches and so wants to drink the well dry. The bucket swings heavily, and the echo of falling drops becomes ever more subtle. . . .

Pale eyes, glossy fingers caress the dead. Dark coils and clots stir. The hill, the disinterred hill.

. . . to drink, I want to drink. Heaven, do not allow my hands to let go of the pulley, do not let the bucket spill over, I am so tired . . .

I drive you back from whence you came; I drive you deep down into the earth, into the upended depths, where neither spade nor another's strange purpose may reach you. I drive you back, I exhort you, I seal you in. You have no place on the surface of the earth; you have no power over the living. I myself lock you away and will remain here, as a sentinel. Forever.

. . . What hot stones, what turbulent grass, and in my ears rings the sound of the cicada, but the water proves sweet, sweet and thick, like honey, and it flows down my chin, down my chest, down my legs, spilling onto the parched earth. And the sun is at its zenith . . . The sun.


That evening, when all those living in the city timidly began to move about, peering from their shelters and asking themselves if this indulgence would last; when the sick began to feel so much better that their loving attendants with haggard eyes finally let loose their tears; when dogs appeared from out of nowhere; when ravens beat their wings over the streets, belatedly gathering to their feast; then Egert and Toria found the dean.

Luayan lay on the summit of the unearthed burial mound, as if covering it with his body. Egert looked once at his face, and would not let Toria even glance at it.

# 9

But on the next day the cold returned, and it was necessary to hurry before the earth froze over.

Egert and Toria buried Luayan on a hill not far from the tomb of the First Prophet. Egert wanted to put the gold medallion in with him, but Toria, who had in the course of one day forgotten how to cry, stopped him: leaving the Amulet in his grave would afflict that grave. The two of them performed all the necessary rites over the body, and no one interfered with them, even though the mayor, who turned up out of the blue, had strictly ordered that all the victims of the Plague be buried in the same place, in the unearthed burial mound.

Toria, who did not have the strength to credit her loss, could not enter her father's study. Egert went in. Among the open books and burnt-out candles only the dean's manuscript appeared to be in full order: his heavy, voluminous, unfinished manuscript, to which had been appended a legible catalog of prepared sections, fragments, and drafts, and a detailed plan of the as-yet-unwritten chapters. There were no letters, no notes, only the manuscript, as if it was his last will and testament, and the Amulet of the Prophet, as if it was a bequest.

Hearing Egert enumerate the contents of his study, Toria tried to smile. "He did become an archmage, didn't he? In this manuscript, there should now be a chapter on him. Don't you think? We must finish it."

And immediately, without transition, she said, "Egert, promise me you'll never die."

———

The city did not believe its good fortune right away. Grave-digging teams hastily committed the dead to the earth, while the afflicted *started* to recover. The casualties were enormous, but it turned out that a great many had been spared as well. Still sheltering in their recesses, they anxiously repeated variations of a single question to one another: What about time, had it ended or not?

A day passed without any new victims, then another day, then another; people who were fatally ill began to get to their feet, and for an entire week not one person died in the city. Mountains of earth, brought to the disturbed hill, separated the living from the dead, and on that day it became taller, full of hundreds of bodies. The streets, freed from corpses, remained desolate and frightening, but the surviving townspeople already assumed that the Plague had finally passed.

Not yet had all of the deceased been transported from deserted houses and alleyways into the trench intended for them, when the city broke out into explosions of fireworks.

Not one of those who then spilled out onto the streets and squares had ever seen a festival like it. Strangers embraced and cried on each other's shoulders; they cried from the joy of suddenly granted life, such sweet life, to which many of them had already said their good-byes. Yesterday they were the dead, but today they were drunk on the awareness that tomorrow would bring a new day, and beyond that there would be another one, and spring would come, and children would be born. Laughing women in bedraggled clothing joyfully bestowed their favors on those whom they loved, and they loved everyone, even the cripples and the beggars and the tramps, and the guards, youths, and elders. Fourteen-year-old boys became men right on the street, but then lost their happy ladies as they disappeared into the crowd, shrieking with laughter. The frantic, insane festival of people driven mad with joy led to a few fatalities—someone drowned in a canal, someone was trampled by the crowd—but the deaths passed unheeded because on that day in the streets of the city, the people believed in eternal life.

The Tower of Lash indifferently beheld the frantic dancing of the survivors. As before, its doors and walls were sealed tight, and not a single wisp of smoke rose over the gabled roof. The hysterical merrymaking gradually abated, and then whispers began to crawl throughout the city.

The End of Time: Would it happen or had it already been prevented?

Where had the Plague come from? Why had it come? Why had it left? What did the sealed walls of the abode of Lash withhold? Why did the robe-wearers not partake in the common doom, skulking behind their walls, and what would happen now? People whispered to one another, looking at the Tower, some warily, some balefully; sometimes voices would rise up, asserting that it was the acolytes of Lash who had invited this disaster with all their talk of the End of Time. It was even whispered that they had loosed the Plague on the city and then sheltered behind strong walls; it was said that the archmage, the former dean of the university, had disappeared to parts unknown on the very day the Plague ended, and that now his daughter accused the robe-wearers of all the deaths. The townsfolk were agitated; they exchanged glances with one another, not wanting to believe. The Tower did not rush to contradict the rumors that were stirring up the city, and the glances that were cast toward it became ever more sullen. Contrary to the remonstrances of the mayor, an assault with crowbars and pickaxes was already planned when the stone works that barred the doors crashed down, broken through from the inside.

Egert, who at that moment was in the library, flinched, feeling a solid thud that shook the earth. From the window he could see quite clearly how the crowd besieging the Tower fell back as if repelled by a gust of wind.

In the black breach stood a hunched gray figure with disheveled hair as white as the moon.

Less than half the soldiers of Lash remained among the living. The bodies of the deceased robe-wearers lay in front of the Tower; they lay in long rows, and wide hoods concealed the dead faces to their chins. The living acolytes stood just as motionless as their dead comrades, and their hoods fell over their faces just as low, and the wind pulled at the clothing of both the living and the dead with the same sluggishness.

Egert did not hear the Magister's speech; fear kept him from approaching. The crowd listened in silence. In the flood of the Magister's voice, in the most passionate section of his speech, Egert did hear a brief "Lash!" The people shuddered, involuntarily lowering their heads. Then the Magister fell silent, and the crowd slowly dispersed, docile and hushed, as if lost in solving the riddle presented by the Magister.

Several weeks passed. The surviving students rejoiced when they met one another on the steps of the university, but after boisterous embraces and greetings an uneasy silence usually followed: inquiring about the fate of their friends, far too often they received the most grievous of all possible news. However that may be, the university soon came back to life. The news of the dean's death was transmitted in a whisper, and many shuddered at hearing it, but many also grieved, and therefore reached out to Toria, wishing to share her grief.

The headmaster expressed his condolences to Toria. She accepted them with reserved dignity. Her father's study became her own, and she spent many hours under the steel wing, reviewing Luayan's papers, especially his manuscript. The Amulet of the Prophet, at the request of Egert, was hidden in a place known only to her: Egert did not want to know the secret, and Toria, biting her lips, respected his wish.

Meeting Toria in the corridors, the students greeted her with almost the same respect with which they had previously greeted the dean. Egert always trailed behind her, and everyone already knew that immediately after the period of mourning he would become her husband. No one took it into his head to be astonished at her choice; they all silently recognized that Egert had the right to this distinction.

One day the heiress of Luayan gathered the students in the Grand Auditorium. After an hour, the university turned into a seething cauldron because Toria, ascending to the rostrum for the first time, calmly and simply informed them all of the truth about the crimes of the acolytes of Lash.

Tempers inflamed and boiled over; one suggested they take to the streets, one called for the destruction of Lash, and one brought Fox to mind: he was right, the poor fellow; he had no love for the robed men; he would have shown them! The headmaster, blanching to the top of his shiny bald head, was scarcely able to keep his pupils from revolt.

Toria was called to the headmaster's study, and the conversation went on for a long time. Egert saw how bewildered the headmaster seemed when, standing in the doorway to his office, he shook his bald head at Toria.

"I don't think . . . I don't think, my child, that what you said should become public knowledge. And then there really is no proof, and . . . I should hardly think . . . Desist, I beg you, from untimely accusations. It's not worth it. That is . . ."

The headmaster talked and talked, but Toria had already left, holding her head unusually low.

"He's afraid," she said with bitterness, closing the door of her father's study behind herself and Egert. "He doesn't want to believe. No, he doesn't believe, when all's said and done. He thinks I'm frantic with grief. And in the city people now think that the acolytes of Lash stopped the End of Time with their incessant ceremonies, rituals, and prayers to their Spirit. They are already gathering money for a new memorial to Lash. How can this be?"

"I don't understand," Egert said helplessly. "There were so many corpses among their soldiers. What did they hope to accomplish?"

Toria smiled dismally. "Do you remember what my father said? 'They are obstinate, spiteful children, setting fire to their home, sure in their faith that the blaze they play with will not harm them.'"

She abruptly stopped short, as if her throat were compressed by a grasping claw of a bird. Recollections about her father were beyond her strength. Turning her back on Egert, she was silent for a long time, and her trembling palm absently stroked the pages of the open manuscript.

Egert could hardly restrain himself from rushing to her with consolation, but right now that might be inopportune. He simply watched her silently, and together with compassion for Toria's grief and his habitual fear for his own hide, another, stronger feeling grew in his soul.

"Tor," he said as carefully as he could. "I know that you will not like what I am about to say, but I agree with the words of our headmaster: it is not worth it, and there is no point in getting mixed up with the acolytes of Lash. They are very dangerous. That's all there is to it, now you can berate me."

She turned around slowly. Her lips, squeezed tight, paled, and the look in her narrowed eyes forced Egert to step back.

He wanted to explain that he was motivated not only by his fear, that the memory of Luayan was as priceless to him as it was to Toria, that his murderers were no less abhorrent to him, but the Order of Lash was full of madmen who would stop at nothing, and in resolving to be in conflict with them, Toria was standing on the razor's edge, and for him, Egert, there was nothing more valuable in the world than her life. But as Toria seethed silently, her eyes conveyed a chilly reproach, and beneath that gaze Egert could not gather all his disordered thoughts into a coherent speech.

"I will not berate you," she said so distantly that Egert became frightened. "The curse is speaking for you. But since when has its cowardly voice become so similar to your own?"

A pause hung, long and painful, and Egert recalled that day when the heavy book in the hands of Toria beat at his face.

"I had so hoped for the support of the headmaster," Toria finally said, and her voice shook. "The support of only the students is too little. . . . But how can it be—" She considered something and did not continue right away. "—that although I find support, it is not from you!"

Egert wanted to get down on his knees before her, but instead he walked up to her and said directly into her unrelenting dry eyes, "Think of me what you will. Judge me how you wish, but the curse is not the cause here; no one cursed me to be afraid for you! But I . . ." And again he faltered, although he very much needed to tell her how frightful and monstrous the thought of losing her was, losing her now, when it was just the two of them amid a hostile world; and how painful it was to be aware that he was in no condition to protect the most precious, most beloved thing he had. He needed to clothe all this in words, but his pitiful efforts were futile.

She turned her back, not even waiting for him to continue. Looking at her unnaturally straight spine, he feared that a rift had opened up between them, that this conversation could never be forgotten, and that he needed to save Toria and save himself. He realized this last and as before remained silent because she was right, because he was a coward, not a man, and therefore not her equal.

Steps sounded in the corridor, not normal, measured steps, but strange and hasty. Egert heard the incoherent voice of the headmaster and raised his head in surprise. Toria turned around slowly; someone knocked on the door, at first hesitantly, as if frightened, then sharply and demandingly, even rudely. Egert was sure that never in the entire time of its existence had the door to the dean's study received such treatment.

Toria raised her eyebrows coolly. "What's this all about?"

"In the name of the law!" dryly carried from beyond the door.

And immediately the voice of the headmaster, nervous and muddled, rang out, "Gentlemen, there has been some kind of misunderstanding. This is a cathedral of academia! You cannot come in here with weapons, gentlemen!"

The door shook with new blows, and with each of them Egert's soul felt as if it were being hammered out on an anvil. He clenched his jaw, silently praying, Heaven help me conduct myself with dignity!

Toria sneered disdainfully. She threw up the hook that latched the door and rose to her full height in the doorway. Cursing himself, Egert retreated to a dark corner. Invisible from without, he spied from behind Toria's back the red-and-white uniforms, the bloodless pate of the headmaster, the crowd of nervous students, and the angular, composed face of an officer with a ceremo-

nial whip clutched in his fist: the sign that at the present moment he was fulfilling the will of the law.

"This is my father's study," Toria said coldly. "No one is allowed to break
down this door, and no one is allowed to enter here without my permission. Is
that acceptable to you, gentlemen?"

The officer raised his whip. "Then you acknowledge that you are the
daughter of Dean Luayan?"

"I will say it a thousand times, and a thousand times know that it is an honor."

The officer nodded, as if Toria's answer gave him pleasure. "In that case,
we invite the lady to come with us."

Egert felt streams of cold sweat running down his back. Why did the most
horrible, most incredible things, appropriate only in nightmares, always happen in his life?

Toria pulled her head up even higher, even though it seemed impossible that
it could go any higher. "You invite me? Why on earth should I go, and what if
I refuse?"

The officer again nodded, again contentedly, as if he had only been waiting
for a similar question. "We are acting on the behalf of the city magistrate." In
support of his words he shook his ornamental whip. "We are empowered to
compel the lady if she refuses to come with us of her own free will."

Egert wanted Toria to look to him, even though it was inconceivable.

What could be simpler than for her to look back in search of help, support,
protection? But from the very first he knew that she would not turn to him,
because there was no point in awaiting protection from Egert, and if she
looked into his suffering, guilt-ridden, haggard eyes, she would experience
neither comfort nor hope. He knew this and all the same he silently implored
her to turn to him, and it actually seemed that she was about to do so, but then
she froze, having turned only halfway.

"Gentlemen," interrupted the headmaster, and Egert saw now how his utterly ancient head wobbled on his thin neck. "Gentlemen, this is unbelievable.
Never before has anyone been arrested within these walls. This is a sanctuary! This is a refuge for the spirit. Gentlemen, you are committing a sacrilege!
I will go to the mayor!"

"Don't worry, headmaster," said Toria, as if pondering. "I am of the opinion that this misunderstanding will soon be worked out and—"

Breaking off, she turned to the officer.

"Well, I understand that you will not stop short of force, gentlemen, and I do not desire that these hallowed halls should be further desecrated by violence. I will go." She stepped forward and quickly shut the door to the study behind her, as if wishing by this last action to shield Egert from outside eyes.

The door was shut. Egert stood in his corner, clawing his fingernails into his palms, listening as the clatter of boots, the whispering of the distraught students, and the lamentations of the headmaster receded along the corridor.

The courthouse was a very grave, very ponderous, very awkward structure that stood on the square. Egert had accustomed himself to avoid the iron doors, carved with the inscription DREAD JUSTICE! He knew at least ten paths that bypassed them because the round black pedestal with the small gibbet, where a manikin dangled in a noose, seemed frightful and loathsome to him.

A wet snow was falling. It seemed dirty gray to Egert, like cotton packed in a wound. His overshoes stuck in the slush, and water trickled in streams past the lamppost that Egert was using as a refuge. Trembling from head to toe, shifting from foot to foot, he stared at the closed doors until his eyes hurt, initially deceiving himself with a foolish hope: that the iron maw would spring open and release Toria.

The flock of students, which had at first gathered around him in a crowd, gradually dispersed; downcast, subdued, they wandered off without looking at one another. Various people went in and out of the courthouse: bureaucrats, haughty and self-important or solicitous and preoccupied; guards with javelins; petitioners with their heads drawn down to their shoulders. Blowing on his cold fingers, he wondered, Had they accused Toria of anything? What might they accuse her of? Who could help them now if even a visit from the headmaster to the mayor came to naught?

He spent a long night full of fear on the square, illuminated by the barely gleaming light of the streetlamp and by the ominous reflections in the windows of the cheerless building. Dawn broke late, and in the pale morning Egert saw acolytes of Lash entering the iron doors.

There were four of them, and all of them looked like Fagirra. The doors closed behind them, and Egert hunkered down by his post, wearied from fear, anxiety, and despair.

The accusation, of course, originated with the acolytes. Fagirra's words spilled out of Egert's distant memory, "The city magistrate heeds the advice of the Magister." Yes, but the Order of Lash is not the court! Perhaps I'll be able to explain to the magistrate, to open his eyes. It is likely that the Black Plague has also robbed him of those close to him, for the Plague respected neither rank nor office.

A group of guards hurriedly exited the iron doors. Egert thought he recognized the officer who arrested Toria among them. Pitilessly tramping down the slushy snow with their boots, the guards rushed away, and Egert berated himself for his foolish suspicion: that they once again headed for the university.

If only the dean were alive. If only you were alive, Luayan. How can they dare? And now Toria has no one to turn to except for . . .

He pressed his cheek to the cold, wet lamppost, waiting for the whip of fear at the idea of going up to those iron doors, of passing by that executed manikin, of stepping over that threshold. But then, Toria had already stepped over it.

He spent a long time convincing himself that there was nothing frightening in what he planned to do. He simply had to enter the courthouse, and then he would leave right after he had seen the magistrate. He needed to convince him. The magistrate was not Lash. But Toria was already there, and Egert might get to see her.

This thought decided him. Immediately recalling his protective rituals, interweaving the fingers of one hand and clutching a button in the other, he moved toward the iron doors following an intricate, winding route.

He would never have summoned the courage to seize hold of the door handle, but fortunately or unfortunately the door opened in front of him, producing a scribe with a bland expression. There was nothing else for Egert to do but step forward into the unknown.

The unknown turned out to be a low semicircular room with many doors, empty desks in the middle, and a bored guard by the entryway. The guard did not so much as glance at Egert as he entered, but a flabby young clerk, who was absentmindedly tracing the point of his rusty penknife along the tabletop, nodded inquiringly but without any special interest.

"Shut the door behind you."

The door swung shut firmly without Egert's help, like the door of a cage. The chain attached to the dead bolt clanged.

"What's your business?" the clerk asked. His expression, sleepy and entirely ordinary, comforted Egert slightly. The first person he encountered in this formidable institution seemed no more sinister than a shopkeeper. Gathering up his courage, squeezing his button for all he was worth, Egert forced out, "The daughter of Dean Luayan, of the university, was arrested yester-day. I . . ." He faltered, not knowing what to say further.

The clerk, in the meantime, had brightened. "Name?"

"Whose?" Egert asked foolishly.

"Yours." The clerk, evidently, had long ago become accustomed to the obtuseness of petitioners.

"Egert Soll," said Egert after a pause.

The cloudy eyes of the clerk flashed. "Soll? The auditor?"

Unpleasantly startled by the clerk's knowledge of him, Egert nodded re-luctantly.

The clerk scratched his cheek with the tip of his knife. "I think . . . yes. Wait just a moment, Soll. I will announce you." And sliding out from behind his desk, the bureaucrat dived into one of the side corridors.

Instead of being glad, once again Egert became frightened, more intensely than before, so that his knees were shaking. His legs took a step toward the doors. The somnolent guard looked at him, and his hand settled absently onto his pikestaff. Egert froze. A second guard, who unhurriedly walked out of the very corridor down which the clerk had disappeared, examined Egert critically, like a cook examines a carcass that has just been brought back from market.

The clerk, peering out an entirely different door, beckoned to Egert with a crooked finger. "Come with me, Soll."

So, submissive as a lost boy, Egert followed the clerk toward his fate. He crossed the path of four of the robed men in the corridor. The familiar, harsh odor wafted toward Egert, and it repulsed him so much, he felt he might vomit; not one of the soldiers of Lash lifted his hood, but Egert felt their cold, intent gazes on his back.

Crooked folds hung over the face of the magistrate, submerging his small eyes, sunken in flesh. Egert glanced into them once and immediately lowered his eyes, examining the smooth floor with marble veins, onto which water flowed from his soaked shoes. The magistrate studied him. Without raising his head, Egert could feel the weighty gaze eating into his skin.

"We expected to see you sooner, Soll." The strained voice of the magistrate was scarcely audible; it seemed that every word cost him effort. "We expected you. After all, wasn't it the daughter of Dean Luayan, your wife, who was ar-rested?"

Egert flinched. The magistrate had to wait quite a long time for his answer.

"Well, we are going to get married. That is, we plan to." Having whispered this despicable phrase, Egert was pierced by an abhorrence of himself, as if, by informing the magistrate of this simple truth, he had somehow betrayed Toria.

"That's one and the same," sighed the magistrate. "Justice is counting on you, Soll. You will appear as the chief witness in court."

Egert raised his head. "A witness? Of what?"

Brisk voices and the stomping of boots could be heard from beyond the door; then a clerk emerged from behind a curtain and began whispering something quickly into the ear of the magistrate.

"Tell them that the command has been revoked." The magistrate's voice soughed like snakeskin on dry stone. "He's already here."

Egert's strained nerves unerringly ascertained that the magistrate was talking about him. He recalled the guards that set out for the university, and he licked parched lips that had lost all sensation.

"You have nothing to be afraid of." The magistrate smiled, observing him. "You are nothing more than a witness. A valuable witness, inasmuch as you were close to the family of the old necromancer. Isn't that so?"

Egert felt his ashen cheeks become hot and red. Referring to Dean Luayan as an old necromancer went beyond all bounds of disrespect, but then fear swallowed this spasm of indignation like a bog swallows a stone tossed into the mire.

The magistrate spoke dispassionately. "Just one virtue is required of a witness: to speak the truth. You know how grievously the Plague cost the city. You know that it did not appear on its own."

Egert's skin felt stretched.

"The Plague did not appear on its own," continued the magistrate in his rasping voice. "The old necromancer and his daughter used their magic to summon it from out of the earth, from the gloom where it should have stayed hidden for generations. The Sacred Spirit Lash foretold the End of Time, but his acolytes were able to stop the assault and overwhelm the necromancer with ceaseless prayers and ceremonies. The city has been saved, but there are so many victims, Soll, so many victims. You must agree that the perpetrators of this crime should answer before the law; the families of the slain require it, and justice itself requires it."

The magistrate's hoarse voice seemed deafening to Egert, like the bellowing of a herd being led to slaughter.

"That's not true," he whispered, for at that moment even the fear in his soul was stunned. "That's not true. The acolytes of Lash dug up the den of the Plague: it is they who summoned it, and the dean stopped it at the cost of his own life. I saw it, I . . ."

Fear recovered from its shock and called out. It swept over his mouth and snapped it shut; it poured streams of clammy sweat over his body and flung him into a merciless, fevered trembling.

"Slander against Lash," observed the magistrate, "is absolutely forbidden, and the first offense is punishable by a public whipping."

Silence fell and for several long minutes Egert's inflamed imagination presented him with a picture of the whip, the crowd, and the executioner. Stinging welts seemed to be already burning on his back.

The magistrate sighed. Something caught in his throat then burst forth, as if tearing through a pustule. "However, I understand your situation. You are not completely the master of yourself and are not responsible for your own words; therefore, I will pretend that I did not hear them. It is likely that the trial will take place as soon as the interrogation of the prisoner is finished. As for you, Soll, I do not have any basis for detaining you, but the prosecutor wants to ask you a few questions."

The magistrate stretched out his hand toward a small bell on the table. Without waiting for the ring, a squat guard appeared from behind a curtain that until this moment had been invisible to Egert. Rubbing at his sore thighs, Egert stepped beyond the concealed portiere.

Wood lice skittered along the damp walls. In the light of torches braced to the walls, the shadow of Egert's escort thrashed about like an enormous moth. Listening to the sound of his own footsteps, Egert agonized, thinking of Toria.

They interrogated her and will interrogate her again. About what? She . . . Heaven, would they really dare torture a woman!

Then in the echoing silence of the corridor a distant scream, muffled by stone walls, seemed to hover in the air around him. He could not restrain himself from groaning. The guard escorting him looked back in surprise.

A keyed turned in a concealed door. The guard forced Egert through the door, slightly nudging him in the back. The dark, narrow room looked exactly like a cell, and Egert was sure that he had been brought right into the prison. But then the torch being brought in by the guard illuminated a tall armchair in the corner and a man sitting in that chair. Without surprise and even without an increase in his fear, Egert recognized Fagirra.

Placing the torch in a bracket, the guard bowed low and left. The tramp of his boots receded down the corridor.

Fagirra did not move. His hood rested on his shoulders, and it seemed to Egert that decades had passed since they last met: so much horror had happened since that time. Fagirra had aged suddenly. He no longer possessed his previous youthful appearance. Egert was struck by the thought that the true age of Fagirra was revealed to him only now.

Several minutes passed before the robed man sighed noisily and stood up, ceding the only chair in the room to Egert. "Take a seat, Egert. I can see that you are hardly able to keep on your feet."

"I'll stand," replied Egert dully.

Fagirra shook his head seriously. "No, Egert, you will not stand. You yourself understand this. Your pride and your cowardice will tear you asunder, but something tells me that your cowardice will prove stronger. You can, of course, lament this fact without end, torment and castigate yourself, or you can simply sit down and listen to what a man who sympathizes with you has to say. Because I do sympathize with you, Egert, and I have from the very beginning."

"You are the prosecutor," Egert declared at the dark corner; he declared, not asking, but simply expressing his certainty. "The prosecutor in the trial against Toria. I should have expected it."

"Yes," Fagirra confirmed dolefully. "I am the prosecutor, and you will be the witness."

Egert leaned against the wall, feeling how each of his muscles came into contact with the cold stronghold; then he bent his knees and sat, pressing his back against the wall. "Fagirra," he said wearily, "did you see the Plague? I don't know what happened there, behind the walls of the Tower, but the city . . . If only you could have seen . . ."

Fagirra paced around the narrow room. Egert watched as his well-made boots, hidden down to their ankles by his robe, stepped across the floor.

"Egert." Fagirra stopped. "Did anyone you know die?"

"A friend of mine died," responded Egert desolately. "And my teacher perished."

"Yes." Fagirra resumed his pacing. "I understand. As for me, Egert, six members of my family died: my mother, my brother, my sisters, and my nieces. They lived in the outskirts and all died in the course of one day."

Egert was silent. He understood immediately that Fagirra was not lying; the robed man's voice had shifted in an unnatural and strange way.

"I didn't know that acolytes of Lash had families," he said hoarsely.

"According to you," Fagirra laughed bitterly, "the acolytes of Lash grow off trees, like pears?"

For some time the only sounds in the room were the crackling of the torch and the soft tread of Fagirra's boots along the stone floor.

"I apologize," Egert said finally.

Fagirra smirked without stopping his pacing. "You weren't there in the Tower when all the entrances were sealed, when the Plague began, and there was nowhere to put the corpses."

"You yourselves . . . ," Egert said in a whisper. "You yourselves willed it."

Fagirra broke into a rough grin. "It is not for you to judge our designs."

"But it was madness!"

"Yes, because the Magister is a madman!" Fagirra emitted a dry, sharp laugh. "He is a madman, but the Order, well, the Order is not composed of only the Magister. The Magister's time is passing, but the Order remains, the Secret remains." Here Fagirra's voice slid into overt sarcasm. "And the Power that is bound to it also remains." He became serious again. "You can't understand, Egert. You are not a lover of power."

"It is you who is a lover of power," clarified Egert under his breath.

Fagirra nodded. "Yes. Do you know who will be the next Magister?"

"I know," Egert replied dully, and it was quiet again for some time. Then somewhere in the dungeons below, iron rattled, and it seemed to Egert that once again he heard vague, distant screams. He felt chilled to the bone, but quiet reigned throughout the courthouse as before. It was possible that the terrible sounds were born from Egert's afflicted imagination.

"Listen to me," he said in despair. "Power is all well and good, but you know the truth no less than I do. You know where the Plague came from, and who defeated it. We owe our lives to Dean Luayan: you and I, the magistrate, the guards, the mayor, the townsfolk. The man gave us back our lives. Why do you wish to punish his innocent daughter?"

"Luayan was even stronger than I thought." Fagirra stopped, squinting in the light of the torch. "He truly was an archmage."

These words, spoken so simply and without reservation, compelled Egert to lean forward. "So you admit it?"

Fagirra shrugged his shoulders. "Only a madman, like the Magister, would wish to deny it."

Egert clasped his sweaty palms together in desperation. "For Heaven's sake, tell me what you want to accuse Toria of?"

Fagirra looked into Egert's beseeching face, sighed, and sat down next to him on the stone floor, leaning his back against the wall. Somewhere in the distance, in the bowels of the building, an iron door clanged.

"You'll return home," said Fagirra without any expression on his face. "You have a decrepit father and an ill mother in a little town called Kavarren."

"What do you want to accuse Toria of?" Egert repeated, almost soundlessly.

"Yes, she is beautiful. She is too beautiful, Egert. She will bring you misery. She was the reason, albeit indirectly, for the death of her first fiancé, that man you—"

"How do you—?"

"—that man you killed. She is not like other women; there is something in her. . . . A gift, I would call it a gift, Egert. An exceptional woman. I understand what you are feeling right now."

"She is innocent," Egert spoke into Fagirra's eyes, which were twinkling in the gloom. "What do you accuse her of?"

Fagirra averted his eyes. "Of necromantic acts that resulted in the Plague."

The walls did not collapse, and the earth did not tremble. The flame continued to wreath the resinous top of the torch, and the silver threads that adorned the empty armchair in the corner gleamed.

"I don't understand," Egert said helplessly. But he had understood, and immediately.

Fagirra sighed. "So try to understand. There are some things that are more valuable than mere life and simple, worldly justice. A sacrifice is always innocent, otherwise how is he or she a sacrifice? A sacrifice is always better than the crowd surrounding the altar."

"Fagirra," said Egert in a whisper. "Don't do this."

His companion shook his head dejectedly. "I understand. But I have no other alternative. Someone must carry the punishment for the Plague."

"The guilty should."

"Toria is guilty. She is a malevolent sorceress, the daughter of Dean Luayan," Fagirra responded levelly. "And think on this, Egert. It is within my power to make you an accomplice, but you are no more than a witness. Do you realize how close you've come to the abyss in these last few days?"

Egert clenched his teeth, waiting for a dreary wave of fear.

Fagirra touched his knee with his hand. "But you are just a witness, Egert. And your testimony will carry weight because you love the defendant, but for the sake of truth you must repudiate your love."

"For the sake of truth?"

Fagirra stood; a long, dark shadow grew on the wall. He walked over to the armchair and leaned his elbows on the backrest. In the torchlight he seemed like an old man.

"What awaits her?" Egert's unruly lips asked.

Fagirra raised his eyes. "Why do you want to know how she will die? Return to your Kavarren immediately after the judgment. I don't think you'll be all that happy, but time draws in even such wounds."

"I will not be a witness against Toria!" bellowed Egert before the fear had a chance to squeeze shut his jaw.

Fagirra shook his head. He shook his head, thinking about something, then nodded to Egert. "Get up. Come with me."

At first his numbed legs refused to work; Egert stood on the second attempt. Fagirra drew a jangling ring of keys from the depths of his robe. A narrow iron door stood in a dark corner, and beyond it a steep, winding staircase led below.

A short, broad-shouldered man in baggy clothes was picking his teeth with a lath. The appearance of Fagirra and Egert caught him unawares, and he almost swallowed his toothpick as he sprang forward to meet the robed man. Taking the torch from Fagirra's hand, he walked in front of them, cringing, while Egert tried to remember where he had seen him before. Egert's speculations came to an end when their escort obsequiously flung open a squat door with a meshed window.

Two or three torches burned here already, and in their light Egert could see ugly torture devices, which could only have been conceived by a fiend of hell, staring at him from their places on the stone walls.

He halted, instantly feeling weak. Fagirra supported him with an exact, efficient movement, firmly taking his arm just above the elbow. Instruments untouched by rust, kept in full readiness, hung on hooks and lay on shelves in heaps: pliers and drills, knee splitters and thumbscrews, boards studded with spikes, cat o' nine tails, and other abominable things, from which Egert quickly averted his eyes. Among the instruments of torture crouched a brazier, full of banked coals. Nearby stood a three-legged stool and an armchair with a high back, exactly the same as the one left behind in that small, empty cell. Egert's darting eyes discerned a worn wooden trundle with dangling loops of chain that rested on a short raised platform.

He now remembered where he had seen the broad-shouldered master of the torture devices. On the Day of Jubilation he had ascended the scaffold together with the magistrate and the convicted men. Then, an ax had been in his hand, and he had held it just as unpretentiously as he now routinely and expertly blew on the coals in the brazier.

"Egert," Fagirra asked quietly, still holding him by his arm, "where is that gold bauble located: the medallion that belongs to the dean?"

The coals changed from black to crimson; the executioner would have made an excellent fire-stoker. Egert began to wheeze, trying to utter even one word.

"You remember, I once asked you about his safe. Our people searched the dean's study and found nothing. Where is the medallion now, do you know?"

Egert said nothing, but on the edges of his consciousness, befuddled by terror, thoughts smoldered. Sacrilege. The study, the steel wing . . . they profaned it. Dean Luayan, where are you?

"Egert." Fagirra peered into his eyes. "I am very interested in the answer to this question. Believe me, the screams of the tortured afford me no pleasure. Where is it?"

"I don't know," said Egert soundlessly, but the robed man read his words from his lips.

He slowly and eloquently shifted his gaze from Egert to the executioner and from the executioner to the brazier. Then he sighed, rubbing the corner of his mouth. "You're not lying to me, Egert, are you? I would not believe any other man, but you, well . . . It's too bad, but if you really don't know." Fagirra lowered his hand. "Toria knows, doesn't she?"

Egert nearly fell. Not knowing what he was doing, he tried to sit down on the trundle with the chains and staggered back. Fagirra gently pushed him into the armchair, and Egert, unable to keep his feet, slammed the back of his head against its high wooden back. His hands clawed at the armrests with a deathlike grip.

The executioner looked inquiringly at Fagirra, who snapped at him wearily, "Wait a minute!"

He pulled the three-legged stool over in front of Egert and sat down, carpeting the floor with the folds of his robe.

"I repeat: I sympathize with you, Egert. I'll keep no secrets from you. The law describes a punishment for the refusal to testify or for false witness: Those who commit this crime are immediately chastened by having their lying tongues ripped out. Show him the pliers." He turned to the executioner.

Measuring Egert with the gaze of an experienced tailor, the executioner darted to a corner and pulled from a clattering pile an instrument that, in his opinion, would do the trick. Grease glistened on the curved blades of the pliers. The executioner was masterful and precise in his work, and he had even adapted the long handles of the pliers for a special use: they were as sharp as two enormous awls.

Egert squeezed his eyes and lips shut.

"That won't help," sighed Fagirra in the darkness that was closing in around Egert. "It will do you no good to be childish. This is life, Egert. All sorts of things happen, regardless of whether or not you shut your eyes. Fine, don't look. It isn't really necessary. The trial will convene, in all likelihood, the day after tomorrow. We will keep an eye on you, and make sure you come to it. I don't have to tell you that it is not a good idea to run away, do I? No, you understand. And after this is all over, if you need some money for the road to Kavarren, I will lend it to you. You can return it to me when you get there. Are we clear?"

Egert tried to remember Toria's laughing face, but he could not.


The city, crippled by the Plague, once again wanted to live.

Heirs appeared from both far and near, laying claim to the deserted and properly ransacked houses, factories, and shops. Quarrels and lawsuits sprang up like mushrooms. The guilds, substantially thinned out, retreated from their time-honored rules and admitted apprentices who had not yet completed their studies into their ranks. Both cheerful and spiteful provincials flooded the city gates from dawn till dusk. They were generally ambitious youths who desired to rise quickly above the crowd: that is, to get rich and marry an aristocrat. The aristocrats also returned; once again the clatter of hooves and wheels resounded along the cobblestones, sedans carried by liveried servants swayed through the streets, and children reappeared. Both rosy-cheeked babes in the arms of wet nurses and dirty gutter trash exulted in the clean, white snow that finally fell.

Liveliness reigned in the city during the day, but not one night passed by without the moans and tears of nightmares and sorrowful memories. Madmen, who had lost their reason in the days of the Plague, roamed around the burned houses. They were pitied and feared even by the homeless dogs. Families had been culled, and their losses were unbearable; therefore the city rioted when the voice of the town crier, hoarse from the cold, informed them of the upcoming trial.

After a single night not one window remained intact in the entire university. Those townspeople who did not believe in the heinous crime of the dean and his daughter scolded their neighbors and family members under their breath, alleging their innocence with a single damning argument: It could not be! The majority doubted the logic of this argument, twisted their lips, and shrugged their shoulders: Mages, who knows what they are capable of? Common folk could never understand these mages, and after all, the Plague had to have come from somewhere. Let all sorcerers be damned.

Fighting broke out in the square: a small group of students grappled tooth and nail with a mass of embittered craftsmen. Blood was shed, and only the rough intervention of the guards put an end to the brawl. The students, bloodied and baring their teeth, retreated behind the walls of the university, chased by flying stones.

"You said Lash would protect us!"

Once the clerk's son had had round and fat cheeks like a roll. Now his cheeks were deep, sunken, and circles lay around the eyes.

"You said Lash would protect us, but instead . . ."

"You are alive," said Fagirra tiredly.

"Yes, but all of them . . ."

"You are alive. But do not think that the tests have ended."

The clerk's son shrank into himself. His blue eyes were enlarged, but they did not look more bright.

"The Order is on the threshold of supreme power," Fagirra said. "But do not think that the tests are over."

"I . . ."

"Keep silent." Fagirra did not raise his voice, but the son of the clerk wanted to become a wood louse on the wall.

Fagirra looked around him. He smiled rigidly.

"The End of Times will come eventually. Possibly not tomorrow. But it will arrive. And think about whose side you are on. . . . Go!"

The former student, and now the servant of Lash, slipped from the room, happy that he had been permitted to leave.

Fagirra looked at the wall in front of him for several seconds. The Order might be on the threshold of power, but this was not enough. Sooner or later the monstrous Third Power would enter the Doors of Creation again, and the new Doorkeeper would meet it at the threshold. The Amulet of the Prophet would rust and this little toy was the key to the End of Time. . . .

But where is it? And why, until now, did the girl keep silent? She will talk. Before or after the trial she will start talking.

The evening before the trial, the first spectators appeared in front of the courthouse. At dawn the square was so congested with people that the guards had to set their whips in motion to clear a path to the building. People gave way without the benefit of whips, groaning and pressing against one another, before a procession of the acolytes of Lash that made its way to the court. The university gaped with broken windows, but a crowd of students, forcing a path through the shouts and insults, also came. Four sturdy guards with pikes held across their bodies conducted one of them into the courthouse: a tall fair-haired man with a scar on his cheek. A rumor that he was the chief witness went the rounds.

There was far from enough room in the court to let everyone in, but bearing in mind the importance of the trial, the magistrate graciously allowed the townspeople to occupy the space between the doors, as well as the corridor leading outside and the steps of the building, and in the end the spacious courtroom was connected to the square by a wide ribbon of humanity. People reported what they heard from ear to ear like water is delivered from hand to hand during a fire, and everything that was said in the court became the talk of the square within a matter of minutes. The beginning of the hearing kept being delayed; sitting on a long, rickety bench, Egert watched impassively as the acolytes of Lash talked behind the empty judgment seat, as a clerk sharpened his quills, as the bench opposite him was slowly filled with frightened shopkeepers: they were also witness, witnesses of the Plague. Everything must go according to the rules. What a pity that it was impossible to summon to court those unfortunates whose bodies reposed under the hill; what a pity that it was impossible to summon Dean Luayan. He could not rise to his feet from under the earth, not even to help his beloved daughter.

Turning his head toward the hall, Egert saw the fringed caps of the students and instantly averted his eyes.

Two scribes were fidgeting behind a long table. Egert overheard one of them ask the other in a low voice, "Do you have a nail file? My nail broke, damn it!"

The crowd fidgeted, jostled one another, whispered to one another, and examined with equal curiosity the somber decorations of the hall, the scribes, Egert, the guards, the judgment seat, and the toylike gibbet on the table in front of it. It was an exact copy of the one that overlooked the entrance. The prisoner's dock was empty, but right next to it, perched on a stool, was the short man of unprepossessing appearance dressed in a shapeless smock. A canvas bag rested on his knees, and by its contours Egert's eyes effortlessly divined the nature of the object concealed inside.

The long-handled pliers.

Ten minutes passed, then another ten. The spectators finally began to look around excitedly, and Egert saw the magistrate striding toward the dais. A man in a hood accompanied him; Egert knew who he was. Treading with difficulty, the magistrate climbed the velvet-pleated steps and sat down heavily in the judgment seat. Fagirra stood next to him without raising his hood, but Egert still felt his observant gaze rest on him. The magistrate sighed something in a strained voice, and the clerk took up his words like a resonant echo.

"Bring in the accused!"

Egert mired his head deep into his shoulders, riveting his eyes to the gray fissures in the stone floor. The noise in the hall dimmed, steel clanged, and then Egert's ability to feel others' suffering returned to him.

His head still lowered, Egert's skin sensed Toria entering the court. She was a solid lump of pain and fear, constricted by her obstinate will. He felt how with her very first glance, covetous, full of hope, she searched the hall for him and how that glance warmed as it settled on him. He realized that she already knew everything. She knew about the role that had been prepared for Egert, but all the same she rejoiced at the opportunity of seeing him; all the same she hoped as devoutly as a child. She placed her hope in this man, most precious to her.

Then he raised his head.

The days of interrogation had not been kind to her. Meeting Egert's eyes, she tried to smile: almost guiltily because her bitten lips had no desire to obey her. Her black hair was pulled back with unusual precision; it was smoother than usual. Her bloodshot eyes were dry. The guard sat Toria down in the prisoner's dock. With an obvious display of disgust, she moved away from the touch of his hand and once again looked at Egert. He tried to answer her look with a small smile of his own, but he could not bear it and turned his eyes away, right into the gaze of Fagirra.

The executioner sighed loudly, and his sigh echoed over the entire hall because just at that moment a breathless hush had settled over the crowd. The prosecutor stood up and flung off his hood with an abrupt movement.

Egert felt Toria's horror. She even flinched when Fagirra looked at her. At the thought that the man had tortured her with his own hand, Egert's jaw clenched with the desire to kill him, but fear soon overrode that desire and returned everything in his soul to its accustomed place.

Fagirra began to recite the prosecution's charges, and from the very first word Egert understood that it was hopeless, that Toria was doomed and that no mercy would be given.

Fagirra spoke simply and plainly. The people listened to him with bated breath, and only in the back rows was there any whispering: the words of the prosecutor were being transmitted along the chain to the square. From his words, as considered and precise as the work of a jeweler, it incontestably followed that the dean had long planned to blight the city and that his daughter, of course, helped him. Fagirra mentioned such details and produced such proofs that Egert's heart began to ache: either a spy of the Order had been hidden in the university for a long time or Toria, under torture, had told Fagirra about the most private, most secret details of her father's life. The crowd became indignant; Egert felt how their righteous anger spread along the chain beyond the walls of the court, how the human sea on the square was filled with wild rancor and the thirst for retribution.

Toria listened, cringing internally. Egert felt how she tried to gather together her scattered thoughts, how she flinched from the accusation as if from blows. Her hope, which had flared up at the sight of Egert, now gradually faded like a smoldering coal.

Glancing intently at Egert, Fagirra finished his speech, flipped his hood back over his head, and approached the judgment seat. One by one the witnesses were called to the stand at a sign from the magistrate.

The first, a fleshy merchant, had the most difficulty: he did not know what to say, and so he simply lamented his losses, somewhat inarticulately. He was listened to with sympathy, for every man in the crowd could say the exact same words in his place. Everyone who was called up to the witness stand after the merchant behaved similarly; the lamentations were repeated; women cried, enumerating their losses. The crowd hushed, borne away into grief.

Finally the flood of witnesses of the Plague dried up. Some lad from the crowd started yelling out his own experiences, but he was quickly admonished to keep quiet. As if it were a single entity, the gaze of the crowd, stern and sour, lunged at the accused. Egert felt a slap of hatred strike Toria. Groaning noiselessly, he jerked on his bench, wishing to shelter and defend her, but he remained seated while the magistrate coughed something and the clerk repeated that now the prosecutor would question the defendant.

Toria stood up, and that single movement cost her agonizing effort. Egert felt how every nerve, every sore muscle quaked. Taking the stand, she quickly glanced at Egert, who leaned forward, silently supporting, embracing, and reassuring her. Fagirra walked close to the stand. A convulsion passed over Toria's entire body, as if the intimate presence of the robed man was unbearable to her.

"Is it true that Dean Luayan was your father?" Fagirra asked loudly.

Toria—Egert knew what effort it cost her—turned her head and looked him straight in the eye. "Dean Luayan is my father," she replied brusquely, but loudly and steadily. "He is dead, but he still exists in the memory of the thousands who knew him."

The hall, which had been silent, broke out into whispers.

Fagirra's lips quivered slightly. It seemed to Egert that he was about to smile. "Well. Daughterly affections are commendable, but they do not justify the deaths of hundreds of people!"

Egert felt Toria flinch as she tried to overcome her pain and fear.

"Those people were killed by you. You hooded executioners! And now you weep over your victims?! On the night the Plague appeared"—Toria turned toward the hall—"on that very night—"

"Save your breath! Answer the questions without superfluous words," Fagirra interrupted her. "On that very night, you and your father performed certain magics in his locked study. Yes or no?"

Egert realized how terrified she was. Fagirra stood next to her, piercing her bloodshot eyes with his gaze.

Toria staggered under his aggression. "Yes. But . . ."

With a sweeping, eloquent gesture, Fagirra turned to the magistrate, then to the hall. "Hundreds of candles burned all night in the dean's study. Your loved ones were still alive. In the morning, dogs howled throughout the entire city, and your loved ones were still alive, but then the Plague descended, called forth by these conjurers."

"A lie!" Toria wanted to shout, but her voice broke. She glanced at Egert, pleading for help, and he saw how her hope died.

"A lie . . . ," echoed from the corner where the students lurked. The crowd grumbled so loudly that the clerk banged on his table and the guards held up their pikes.

Encouraged by this unexpected support, Toria regained control of her temper. Egert felt how a desire broke through the black pall that shrouded her mind: a furious desire to resist, to denounce.

"It's a lie that the Plague came through the will of my father. It was the Order of Lash that summoned death to us. They went to the hill where the victims of the plague were buried and dug it up! They let death go free!"

The crowd hummed loudly. Egert held his breath: he thought that the truth said loud enough was capable of changing the court's direction.

"Did you see this yourself?" asked Fagirra.

"Yes!"

"But where?"

"In the enchanted—" Toria stopped and then ended the sentence in a hoarse voice. "—in the enchanted mirror . . . in the water . . ."

"In the water," repeated Fagirra turning to the crowd, chuckling. "I'm sure that that's not the only thing the mage can show 'in the water.'"

There was an nervous laugh in the hall.

"Listen!" Toria gathered the last bits of her strength. "The Order of Lash is strong where everyone is afraid! Where people wait for the End of Time! The Order of Lash committed a crime to regain its former power! Has anyone ever seen the Lash facilitators bring people anything but fear? Who among you knows what the Order of Lash really is? Who among you knows what plans they nurture under their hoods? And who among you would not affirm that my father never brought evil to anyone in his whole life? Can even one of you ever recall him harming so much as a dog? With the help of magic or without it, he served at the university for decades. He worked for the good, and he is the one who saved all of you from the Plague. He sheltered us with his own body. He gave up his life, and now—"

Toria reeled from a sudden, resurgent pain; the tortures she had endured had left a multitude of agonizing marks on her body. Egert bit his hand, drawing blood. The crowd buzzed deafeningly. Astonished people repeated to each other the words of the accused, conveying them to the square, and it is possible that her words sowed doubt in some souls. The students stood strong, a fortress, a citadel of support for Toria. From the corner of his eye, Egert noticed the headmaster being buffeted toward the exit, holding on to his heart.

Fagirra was unfazed. With the corners of his pale mouth slightly raised, he uttered in a low voice, "You aggravate your guilt by slandering Lash."

It was agonizingly hard for Toria to start speaking again. "You have not brought one piece of hard evidence of the guilt of my father. Everything you've said means nothing. You have neither evidence, nor . . . witnesses."

She spoke ever softer and softer. Trying to make out her words, the crowd hushed, and only the scraping of soles along the floor and the breath of hundreds of people could be heard in the sultry air of the hall.

Fagirra smiled slightly. "There is a witness."

Toria wanted to say something. She jerked her head up, ready to vent all her wrath and disdain on Fagirra, but then she stopped short and said nothing. Egert felt how all her strength and all her will dissolved, receding like water through open fingers. Hope, which had lingered on until this moment and which had helped her to struggle, shimmered one last time and then died. In the growing silence Toria turned her head and met Egert's eyes.

He sat alone on an infinitely long bench, hunched over, doomed to betray. A wistful question stood in Toria's eyes, but Egert could not answer it. They looked at each other for several seconds, and he felt how pity, despair, and contempt for his weakness struggled in her soul, but then these feeling gave way to a deathly exhaustion. Toria's shoulders slowly slumped and, dragging her feet, she returned to the dock without a single word.

The silence in the hall lasted for a few more seconds; then a roaring quickly surged, flying up toward the ceiling. The clerk was about to pound on his table, but with a scarcely noticeable gesture Fagirra stopped him, and the hall, unrepressed, was free to express its astonishment, its indignation and its rage toward the sorceress who had capitulated in the face of overwhelming evidence.

Finally, Fagirra snapped his fingers, the clerk banged away at the tabletop, and the guards slammed the ends of their pikes on the floor. The crowd quieted, though not immediately. The magistrate said something Egert could not hear. The clerk loudly repeated his words, but these words did not reach

Egert, who had settled into a dreary stupor, until a guard standing behind him firmly seized him by the elbow and lifted him up off the bench.

He looked around like a frightened dog. Fagirra watched him from under his hood, and in his eyes stood a benevolent and at the same time imperious command.

Egert did not remember how he got to the stand.

There, beyond the walls, the sun was shining, and two of its rays fell in through the two tall grilled windows. In their corner the students, who had grown despondent, brightened. Egert heard his name repeated many times: it was repeated excitedly, loudly, and softly; it was repeated indifferently, with surprise, with joy and hope. Those who had shared room and board with Egert for many days, those who had sat next to him in lectures and had drunk wine with him in merry taverns, those who knew of the planned wedding were justified in expecting from him words appropriate to an honest man.

The executioner sighed again, trying to wipe a dark spot from his bag; the pliers clinked softly and Egert felt the first jolt of eternal, animal fear.

Toria was looking to the side, as before slumped over, harassed and passionless.

"Here is the prosecutor's main witness," said Fagirra pompously. "This man's name is Egert Soll. Lately he has been received in the dean's study and he has been close to the dean's daughter, which is why his testimony is so important to us. On that fateful night he was present during the accursed sorceries. We are listening to you, Soll."

A deadly, unnatural silence spread over the entire world. The two windows watched Egert, like two empty, perfectly clear eyes. He remained silent. Dust motes danced in the columns of light, and Toria, frozen on her own bench, suddenly raised her head.

It is likely that his pain and grief had been communicated to her, but in that very second he suddenly sensed how, perceiving the horror and despair of her beloved, she searched for his gaze.

He was silent, unable to force out a sound.

Fagirra sneered. "All right. I will ask the questions and you will answer. Is it true that your name is Egert Soll?"

"Yes," his lips spoke instinctively. A sigh passed through the crowd.

"Is it true that you came here from the town of Kavarren about a year ago?"

Egert saw the towers and weathervanes reflected in the water of the spring Kava; the pavement bathed by rain; a pony under an elegant, child's saddle;

shutters closing with a bang; and his laughing mother with her palm shading her eyes.

"Yes," he replied distantly.

"Good. Is it true that all this time you lived at the university, keeping close company with the dean and his daughter, and that she almost became your wife?"

He finally succumbed to the silent entreaty of Toria and decided to look at her.

She sat, leaning forward and not taking her eyes off him. Egert felt how she relaxed slightly as soon as she caught his gaze. Her face warmed and her gnawed lips tried to form a smile. She was happy to see him, even now, on the brink of betrayal, and she rushed to pour into him all her frantic, almost maternal tenderness, unextinguished by torture, for surely they were also torturing him, they would continue to torture him, perhaps more roughly and painfully, in front of the whole city, in front of the woman he loved; she understood how it was with him, what ailed him now and what would happen later: she understood everything.

It would have been easier for him to survive disdain than compassion. He turned his troubled gaze, full of hate, to Fagirra.

"Yes!"

At that moment something shivered in Toria's eyes. Egert returned her gaze, and his hair stood up on his head because he too understood.

His trembling hand lay on his scar. On one day only, and only one chance. Please do not let me err in answering.

"Is it true that on the eve of the Plague you were in the dean's study, and that you saw what happened there?"

The path must reach its bitter end.

"Yes," he said for the fourth time.

The executioner scratched his nose. He was bored.

Fagirra smiled victoriously. "Is it true that the magical acts of the dean and his daughter called forth the Plague upon the city?"

The steel blade had ripped through his cheek, and the curse had broken his life in two. He had been self-assured on that morning; the spring had broken out cold and lingering, and dewdrops had slithered down the tree trunks, as if weeping for someone. He had not shut his eyes when the Wanderer's sword sank into his face; there was pain, but there was no fear even then.

He felt the scar on his cheek come to life; it throbbed, full of fire. Still pressing his palm to his cheek, he looked down into the hall and met the gaze of perfectly clear eyes without eyelashes.

The Wanderer stood by a wall in the crowd, but seperate from all. Among the crowd of curious, overwrought, scowling, and tense faces, his long face, notched with vertical wrinkles, seemed as detached as a lock hanging off a door. When that which is foremost in your soul becomes last. When five questions are asked and you answer yes.

My fate steers me along a precisely designed line.

He shivered. At that very moment Toria also recognized the Wanderer. Without turning around, Egert saw how her swollen lips at first tentatively, then more boldly and joyfully, slipped into a smile.

Smiling, she would go to a horrible death. For it appeared that pardon for Egert sounded the death knell for Toria. She knew this and still smiled because in her life there had been the eternally green tree over the tomb of the First Prophet and those nights spent by the light of the fireplace and his promise to shed the curse for her sake.

The foremost in his soul must become the last. For her sake, for the sake of fulfilling his promise, he had to denounce and betray her; he had to let her be judged. Who had woven this web?

Heaven, he had paused for too long: already the hall was agitated and Fagirra was frowning, and the executioner was looking on with interest, casually lowering his sack to the floor.

He squeezed his eyes shut, but his imagination could spit on him for all it cared whether his eyes were open or not; his imagination obligingly pushed on him a vivid, meticulously detailed picture of the torture chamber. Chains dig into his flesh, holding him down, the executioner methodically bends over him; he is unassuming and repulsive in his shapeless sack, and in his hands he holds the pliers. Egert's clenched jaws are pried open with an enormous bar, the pliers come ever closer, the iron beak opens as if about to feast, Egert fitfully tries to turn his head away, somewhere in the darkness a placid voice utters the words "false witness," and Egert feels the icy pinch of steel at the root of his tongue. . . .

A man should not fear so. Thus do animals fear who have fallen into a trap, thus do cattle fear who are being driven to the gates of the slaughterhouse. By some miracle, Egert's legs did not fall out from under him.

Fagirra's gaze lay on him like a gravestone; Fagirra's gaze squeezed him, mastering his soul, disordering his thoughts. The fifth question had been asked.

He must answer now, while the pliers were still in the sack, while the Wanderer looked on, aware of everything in advance. He would answer, and the fear would cease tormenting him: for why else would the scar ache so? It throbbed and fretted as if it were a living creature, as if it were a leech that had sucked his blood for so many days and now, right now, it was fated to die.

"Egert." The sound of the word barely carried from the prisoner's dock. It is possible that Toria had not uttered it aloud, but he understood that she was giving her blessing to his fifth yes.

. . . Fire in the fireplace, dark hair on the pillow, childlike fear and faith, also childlike, trusting. The high window of the library, a wet bird on the path, and the sun, the sun beats at the window. A basket in his arms, green onions tickling his hand, a warm roll from her hand, and the sun again. The print of a heel in soft, warm earth, her palms over his eyes, and the sun shines in through her fingers. The scent of wet grass, snow melting on hair . . .

Toria quietly scraped her bench along the floor. "Egert."

How afraid she was for him. She wanted for this all to end as quickly as possible, for him to finally say the word.

His hesitation would gain him nothing. His fear would speak on its own, and his lips would be unable to form any word other than the magical fifth yes. His vocal cords would refuse to work, should he wish to step away from the designated path.

"Enough, Egert!" Fagirra glanced eloquently at the executioner. "I'll ask you one last time: Is it true that the magical acts of the dean and his daughter called forth the Plague?"

The Wanderer's lipless mouth quivered slightly. It is quite easy to err, and a mistake will cost you much. . . . This moment will occur just once in your life, and if you let it slip away, all hope will be forever lost.

So much pain in this hall! So much pain has settled into Toria's small body! Oh, how the scar aches.

Silence.

He raised his eyes. Two windows watched him from the indifferent eyes of the Wanderer.

"N . . ."

The fear bellowed at him. It roared and jerked about, lacerating his throat, paralyzing his tongue. All his vast, overwhelming, omnivorous fear, which had for so long been building its fetid lair in Egert's soul, howled and whirled like a raging monster.

". . . o."

The word broke free from his mouth and, nearly broken from exhaustion, he closed his eyes with a clear conscience, giving himself over to the lacerations of his fear.

The word boomed out in the silent hall like an explosion from a gun turret.

The students screamed victoriously, the crowd began to clamor, Fagirra snapped something sharply, and Toria, sitting stunned on her bench, exuded horror at the thought that the curse on Egert was now eternal and unbreakable. He perceived this and shuddered, his hands stretched out toward his mouth as if wishing to beat back the word that had just flown out, but he realized with relief that it was impossible to withdraw what had been said, however much the fear tried to turn him inside out. Reeling, he looked out into the hall, at the Wanderer, and his look contained something akin to a challenge.

And then the Wanderer, who alone had remained impassive in the excited crowd, permitted himself to smile.

The world lurched in front of Egert's eyes; it swam, it faded as if it were being burned away. He felt a pure, placid calm. He wanted to close his eyes and bask in the incredible tranquillity, but then the world returned; it collapsed in on him with the noise of the crowd and the shouts of the guards. Colors returned to it, and never in his life had Egert Soll seen such vivid colors.

. . . Who are all these people? Who is that man, hiding his face under a hood? How dare they restrain that woman . . . Toria!

The dais quivered. Egert realized that he was already running; someone in red and white flew off to the side in fear, sheltering behind a pike. The executioner's stool fell on its side awkwardly, like a dead rat, and the iron pliers tumbled out of the sack.

It seemed to Egert that he was moving slowly, like a fly bogged down in honey. Distorted faces flickered on the edge of his vision, shouts clamored on the edge of his hearing. Someone shouted, "Seize him!" Someone shouted, "Leave him be!" The students bellowed and the clerk hammered on his table, and the pale face of Toria moved ever closer. Ever closer were her eyes, flung open so wide that her curved eyelashes dented the skin of her eyelids and her enlarged pupils absorbed the light without sparkling; ever closer were her half-open, dry lips, her bitten, swollen lips. Egert ran for an eternity. The dais shuddered under his boots; someone stood in his path, but he flew off, swept away. Egert ran, and blood flowed over his cheek, over his lips, over his chin, dripping down onto his shirt: in the place of the scar now blazed an open wound.

And then his feet tripped over an outstretched sword sheath and he fell, losing sight of Toria's face, splaying out his elbows. The edge of the dais flashed before his eyes, then the high, dark ceiling, and from somewhere above him boomed the words, "Do you remember the punishment for false witness?"

He saw veins pounding in a temple; twitching, bloodless lips; and dark fissures in the corner of a mouth: it was the face of the man who had tortured Toria. In Fagirra's hands was a short sword, the weapon of the guards, and its tip was pointed directly at Egert's stomach.

Toria. He felt her weaken from intolerable terror; he felt the adamant arms of the executioner wrapped around her. A reddish black mist condensed in his eyes.

Dive. Flip. His body had not known battle for two years, and he waited for it to disobey him, but he felt only ecstatic joy from his muscles, like the joy of a dog freed from its chain.

Toria is struggling in someone's arms! Who would dare touch her?

He struck out, almost without looking, and the guard who had run up to him doubled over. His sword was about to fall out of his hands, but it did not fall, because Egert intercepted the heavy hilt. It was a short sword, an unfamiliar weapon, but his hand flew up, and to Egert's amazement he heard the clash of metal on metal and saw sparks fly. Fagirra's rabid, crazed eyes were right in front of him.

Toria jerked in her captor's hands. She was so close. Egert felt how the hands restraining her barbarically reopened the wounds left behind by torture, but she did not notice the pain. She emanated waves of fear for him, for Egert.

The swords crossed again. Fagirra opened his mouth halfway, his weapon again darted up, and then Egert, despising the barrier separating him from Toria, lunged into a counterattack.

It seems he yelled something. It seems someone in a gray robe dared to approach him from behind, Toria's fear surged, and in the next second a bloodied thing fell heavily onto the dais, a thing that looked like a hand clutching a dagger. The tiny gibbet was swept away from the table, and the manikin slid out of the noose for the first time in many years. Then Fagirra's sword flew out into the howling crowd, and Fagirra himself stumbled and fell; for a split second Egert looked down into his clouding eyes.

"Egert!"

Grubby hands were ruthlessly dragging her away. Egert bellowed indignantly and the short sword, won from an unknown guard, was already in flight.

The life of the city's executioner, his gray, dull life, ended in an instant. Clutching at the hilt that protruded from his back, the poor soul lay down on the dais at the feet of his recent victim. Toria stepped backwards and Egert met her eyes.

Why has this happened to her? Blood, terror: why this? Poor girl.

He ran again, and she darted forward to meet him. He was already stretching out his hand when he saw that she was staring at something behind his back. He turned just in time: Fagirra was already there, his teeth bared in his crooked mouth and his stiletto raised high.

No, Toria, don't be afraid. Never be afraid.

He managed to avoid the first attack, but the fencing master was strong and tenacious.

The stiletto almost grazed Egert's hand a second time.

A weapon! Heaven, send me a sword, even a kitchen knife!

He stumbled and barely managed to keep to his feet. He could not let the stiletto get near Toria. One scratch would be enough; one scratch from the sharp tip, gleaming with a dark drop of poison, would be sufficient to kill her.

The pliers clanked under his feet. He felt their weight in his hands as he flung them up in front of his body to defend himself and Toria. Just as he heaved them up, Fagirra launched into a violent, frantic attack.

Egert did not want Toria to see this. He took a step back and put his arm around her shoulders and his palm over her eyes.

Fagirra was still standing. The pliers protruded from his chest, and the wide-open iron beak snarled at Egert with impotent menace. Egert knew that the bloodstained handles peered out of Fagirra's back. The death agony of the robed man was terrible, and Egert pressed Toria into his arms, striving not to touch her painful welts.

Her face, half-hidden by his hand, seemed mysterious, as if it were under a mask. Her lips quivered like they were about to smile, her eyelashes fluttered against his palm, and for some reason he recalled the touch of a dragonfly's wings.

It felt like the passage of time altered; his hand tentatively raised itself to his face, and his fingers wonderingly explored his cheek. They did not find the scar.

Incredible things were happening in the hall. The students were fighting and denouncing the robed men, tearing off their hoods.

Egert did not notice. The roar of the crowd receded then disappeared completely, as if he had gone deaf. His vision split in some strange manner; casting his eyes over the pandemonium, he saw only the tall old man with his wrinkled face.

The Wanderer slowly turned and walked toward the exit, slicing through the crowd the way a knife slices through water. He turned slightly at the threshold, and Egert saw his crystal-clear eyes close slightly, as if saying farewell.

The world is dissected by the horizon, and all roads rush toward its edge. They scatter beneath your legs like mice, and it is difficult to know if you are setting off on your path or if you have already returned. . . .

The crowd roared.

Outside, people rushed into the courthouse from the square, desiring to see the witness with their own eyes and to understand what had happened. Inside the courtroom, tensions were very high.

"Silence!" shouted the judge, and suddenly he dived under the table. The man in the gray hooded robe roared in horror, forcing the bloodstained stump of a hand against his chest. The students, overwhelmed by their own courage, pressed on the barrier of guards.

"I am the witness!" Egert shouted, his voice ringing over the noise in the courtroom. "Did you hear that? I am the witness, and I am telling you: The servants of Lash caused the Plague! Toria is innocent, she told the truth! Dean Luayan saved us all! Do not dare to accuse his daughter!"

The ring of guards pressed on the platform. People in red-and-white uniforms watched what was happening: The witness just killed two people in front of the court and the public.

Meanwhile the fight continued out in the hall, but the hooded disciples of Lash, used to discipline, became an army within few seconds. Daggers and stilettos arose from under the sleeves of gray robes. The students still screamed out threats and curses—but they retreated, pressed by a powerful gray wall. They were unarmed—only the boldest managed to snatch a candlestick or a fragment of a bench.

"Here are the criminals!" Egert moved forward. "Hold the Servants of Lash!"

People crowded around the platform, and the guards were unable to push them away. The people saw what happened, just as the guards did, and if no one felt sorry about the city executor, the terrible loss of Lash's servant shocked and frightened everyone.

Egert tried to protect Toria: "She is innocent! Step back, everybody!"

An officer who survived the Plague and whose hair had become gray overnight moved forward, holding his naked sword: "Surrender, you murderer. The court will announce the verdict."

The students were encircled by exposed blades like cattle in a slaughterhouse. The citizens, who only yesterday threw stones at the university, did not hurry to help them.

"Surrender," the officer repeated grimly.

"You are not my enemy." Egert looked into his eyes. "The Servants of Lash are the murderers! Here they are, arrest them in the name of the city!"

The officer ignored Soll: "Arrest him."

The guards started to move in from three sides. For a second, Soll thought that he was observing the world with his ears, his skin, with the entire surface of his body; he saw Toria, frozen in horror, the corpse of Fagirra on the floor, the robed men with stilettos, students with broken noses, the judge on his knees crawling to the curtain. He saw the narrow door, behind which the sky turned blue and the crowd was roiling. He saw fear in the eyes of the guards approaching him . . . fear . . . but mixed with hope.

The guards moved toward him with ropes.

Egert smiled gently and took a step forward. He dived under their arms, tripping somebody's foot, gripping sombody's wrist wrapped in a leather glove, and pulled it over. He dropped this yielding body under the feet of his pursuers. Without looking, he struck the face of the guard who approached him from the rear with his elbow and managed to catch the sword of another guard after butting him with the top of his head. Someone in a red-and-white uniform tried to stop him—to his own dismay; Egert got hold of a second sword and jumped away.

The crowd in the courtroom made way for him in panic as he rushed toward the wall of gray robes.

The Servants of Lash backed up for a split second as death rushed upon them, death with a bloodred face and wild, fair hair. One of Lash's men moved too slowly and Egert stabbed him in the face. The others inched forward, short blades glimmering, their eyes swollen and insane.

Their enemy, enormous and bleeding, with two swords in his muscled hands, faced them unafraid.

"What did the Magister promise you? That you would remain alive, even after the city was destroyed by the Plague?"

And both his blades started to move like fish thrown out of the water onto the ground. The two swords looked like human creatures; they were extremely angry, they wanted fire and blood. But the Servants of Lash overcame their initial confusion. Two swords were confronted by two dozen blades, with many more behind those.

The whole scene was sparkling. Two acolytes leapt forward to attack and one of Egert's swords knocked away a dagger; with the other hand he repulsed the other's strike. And Egert, swift as a lion, swung his claws, one after the other, and there were two howling bodies on the floor.

"Did you hope to hide yourself behind your walls?"

The fighters in gray robes scattered in a semicircle. Soll was in the center of their ring and he was swinging as a reckless wasp with two stings. The air was howling, and the courtroom hadn't witnessed such a scene for centuries.

"When you were digging into the hill . . ."

Strikes, sparks, howls.

". . . did the Magister tell you that Lash would protect you?"

Strike. Gnashing. Ringing.

A dagger whizzed by his ear like a bullet. From the corner of his eye Egert noticed another one flying toward him—and at the last moment he bent down and let the death pass him. A follower of Lash behind him groaned— the knife deep into his shoulder.

Egert bellowed: "So let Lash protect you now!"

And he rushed into the attack, one man against dozens of skilled soldiers.

"For Luayan!" A heavy-built man in a gray robe fell, gripping his chest. "For Toria!" Another was skewered and fell down to the feet of his fellows. "Let's punish them!" A chopped-off hand flew in the air. "Let's punish them!"

"For Fox!" young voices chanted like a choir. The judge's heavy armchair, raised by three students, fell on the gray-robed heads.

"For the city! For the suburbs! For what you have done! You wanted power? You wanted worship? You shall have it!"

Encircled and forced to defend himself, Soll managed to force Lash's soldiers back. And then a strange thing happened: Lash's army, which had always seemed to be solid, unbreakable, and faceless, hesitated, their confidence broken. The hoods of many of them had been swept off their heads during the frantic battle . . . and now their faces appeared; the faceless robes of Lash turned into people.

Frightened. Embittered . . . even ashamed. For years they had inhaled the heavy incense of their rituals. They had admired Fagirra, thought him to be eternal . . . and now he was dead. They had idealized their Magister and now they were doubtful about him. Young, old, bald, mustachioed, squint-eyed, pale, it seemed they saw one another for the first time. It seemed they saw the people around them for the first time.

One of Lash's followers screamed, "We cannot abandon the Magister! We must do what Lash wills!"

"The will of Lash!" chanted the frenzied voices.

"The End of Times will come!" A plump fellow with sagging cheeks shouted at the top of his voice, and Egert suddenly recognized him: the clerk's shy son only recently was a student. "Lash will hide the believers!"

"His will . . ."

With renewed energy, they rushed into the attack again.

"Lash!"

"Lash!"

"This is the will of Lash!"

But their will and their confidence had been broken, and the students beat them down everywhere, with Egert Soll, once a coward, at the forefront of the fighting.

"Watch out, Soll!" someone shouted from the crowd.

Egert ducked, and a knife whistled above his head; he moved to the right, and another slashed down where he'd just been standing. Twirling around, as if in a dance, he repulsed two blades at a time—from the top and from the bottom, he struck the young servant's chest with his foot, forcing him to drop his weapon, he twisted around and saw his other adversary running away. It was the clerk's son running out of the courtroom—limping and trying to strip off his robe and hood.

"Hold him!"

Two or three students started to chase him. Soll realized that the ring of enemies around him was gone: someone motionlessly lay on the floor, someone turned moaning, someone stepped back, someone tried to hide. The battle was over.

Egert found Toria with his eyes. She remained standing where he'd left her—motionless, frozen, her face white. He nodded to her, encouraging and calming. He looked around; the room was still crowded, and strangely quiet. The city dwellers stood shoulder to shoulder—the ones who cursed Toria and her father, those who broke windows at the university. There were many strong men among them; Lash's servants were mixed in this crowd. The silence was more terrible than any roar: only puffing, moans, and rare curses, and shoe soles on the worn stones.

Students supported their wounded fellows. Almost all of them were covered in blood.

Suddenly a commotion started at the doors. All heads turned simultaneously. The guards were marching in, swords raised. There was a great number of them, all heavily armed; the crowd made room for them.

The gray-haired officer who had tried to arrest Egert stopped. Egert silently waited; would the guards dare to wound or even to kill random witnesses? His heart worked as a metronome, pacing the rhyme and time of the forthcoming fight.

Even the wounded ceased to moan. Egert looked into the eyes of the officer; strange, now there was no fear in the eyes of the guard. There was something new, what Egert did not understand. The officer straightened up and slowly raised his blade, saluting. The other guards repeated his motion like shadows. For several seconds none said a word.

Egert could hardly stand on his feet. He crossed the room, and the crowd respectfully made way for him; he went up to Toria, and took her tightly under her arm, letting his swords drop.

She leaned on him, pressing him but holding her back upright. People silently looked at them; the guards in red-and-white uniforms stood several steps away, as if expecting something.

"Arrest the servants of Lash," Egert said in a hoarse voice. "Don't let anyone in a hood leave. Gather them here for questioning. Do not use force: let them talk. Don't let anyone out, but the main thing is to find the Magister!"

The crowd stirred. The officer of the guards nodded to his people and he looked again into Soll's eyes: "Yes, Captain."


Spring came.

Climbing up the hill would have cost Toria too much effort; she was weakened from her lingering wounds. He carried her, treading firmly across the dampened loam, and not once did his legs slip.

On the summit of the hill was a grave, covered by the unfolded steel wing as by a hand. They stood, bowing their heads. Clouds shifted above, white on blue. Neither Egert nor Toria needed to speak about the man who now slept forever beneath the wing: even without that, he abided with them.

They stood, nestled against each other, just as they had on that distant winter day, except that their entwined shadow lay not on sparkling, clean snow, but on moist, black earth, overgrown with the first grass of spring. Egert flared his nostrils, catching the strong smell of green life, and he could not decide if it was the scent of Toria or the aroma of bulbs fighting their way to the surface.

A bright, gold disk on a chain hung from her hand as if Toria wanted to show her father that his bequest was intact.

Far, far away, in Kavarren, an old man read a letter to his wife, and the old woman listened to him, having sat up in bed for the first time in many days. The letter was signed by the burgomaster and the Guard's chief; in it Egert Soll was called a hero and a savior of the city. The elderly man cried, tears fell from his chin, and the woman understood that she wouldn't die soon.

Egert and Toria stood on a hill. Far below lay the black, swollen river, and from out the city gates wound the road, empty except for a single black speck slowly moving toward the horizon. They felt no need to talk about the man who was traveling away from them either; both held him in their memory, and so they simply gazed at the distance into which the Wanderer disappeared.

The world is preserved by the mother of all roads. She looks after the faithful traveler, relieving his solitude. The dust of the road covers the hem of a cloak, the dust of the constellations covers the curtain of the night sky, and the wind blows both the clouds toward first light and sheets hung up to dry with the same eagerness.

It is no misfortune if the soul is scorched by the sun; it is far more disastrous if a raging fire devastates the soul. It is no misfortune if you do not know where you are going; it is far worse when there is no longer anywhere to go. He who stands on the path of experience cannot step away from it, even when it has come to its end.

For the path is without end.